# BRILLIANT DIVORCES

# Also by June Flaum Singer

The Debutantes
Star Dreams
The Movie Set
The Markoff Women
The President's Women
Till the End of Time

# BRILLIANT DIVORCES

## JUNE FLAUM SINGER

WILLIAM MORROW AND COMPANY, INC.
New York

Library of Congress Cataloging-in-Publication Data

Singer, June Flaum.
    Brilliant divorces / by June Flaum Singer.
        p.        cm.
    ISBN 0-688-12001-6
    I. Title.
PS3569.I544B75 1993
813' .54 — dc20                                                                    93-6721
                                                                                              CIP

Printed in the United States of America

First Edition

1   2   3   4   5   6   7   8   9   10

BOOK DESIGN BY M M DESIGN 2000, INC.

For my brothers,
Gary and Marshall,
in affectionate remembrance
of a past well shared . . .

# ACKNOWLEDGMENTS

---

I wish to express my gratitude to Roslyn Targ for her good cheer and unflagging enthusiasm, to Liza Dawson for her unerring eye, faultless ear, and instinctive feel for the sense of the thing, and to Joe Singer for his warm support, his encyclopedic knowledge, and, as always, for the best of everything.

I would also like to thank Miriam Hope Bass, Ben Haller, and Kathleen Hughes for their delightful volume *Lifelog*, which proved to be a wonderful source of reference.

The clever and very rich Mrs. Vanderbilt always said that every woman should marry twice—the first time for money, the second time for love. But I always say that the first time should be for love and then after you have all that lovely romantic nonsense out of your system, the second time should be for convenience. Then the third time around should be—just once—for the fun of it. And then after that, one should certainly marry for money because that's what really lasts. But when you have all four in one package—the love, the convenience, the sex and the money, why then you've got it all—a brilliant marriage!

—NORA GRANT

# BRILLIANT DIVORCES

# BEFORE THE PARTY

## Los Angeles, June 1990

———•◦•———

Sitting at her dressing table, tilting her chignoned blond head this way then that, she studies her reflection in the mirror as she holds an elaborate ruby and diamond confection to a still creamy throat. No, she thinks. While the necklace goes beautifully with the hostess gown and matching coat the color of fine claret, it *is* a bit de trop. Not really appropriate for a buffet luncheon on the terrace in the noonday sun. And if anyone should ask—she *is* known to have a set of guidelines to cover practically every situation—she would be the first to advise that, while diamonds might be *forever*, or even a girl's best friend, they are definitely *not* for wearing before the sun goes down.

But then, sticking her tongue out at the face in the mirror, she fastens the necklace in place anyway. After all, she's almost as famous for breaking the rules as she is for her now practically notorious quote on marriage that appeared in the May issue of *People Today*.

Though she seemingly rattled it off from the top of her head when being interviewed, she knows every word of the quote, if not by heart then by way of honest experience. Well, *almost* honest, believing in the theory that sometimes a little white lie is better than a whopper of a devastating truth.

Now, in an attempt to distract herself from things she doesn't want to think about at the moment, she repeats the quote for the lady in the mirror almost word for word with self-deprecating inflections:

"The clever and rich Mrs. Vanderbilt said that a woman should marry twice—the first time for money, the second time

13

for love. But I always say the first time should be for love and *after* you've gotten all that romantic nonsense out of your system, the next time should be for convenience. Then the *third* time around should be—just once—for the fun of it, and then one should marry for money because that's what really lasts. But when you have all four in one package—the love, the convenience, the sex *and* the money, why then you've got it all—a brilliant marriage!"

Admirers considered the quote amusingly insightful, the height of insouciant sophistication, while her detractors (there *were* a few of those) judged it blatantly cynical and proof that she was, after all was said and done, a greedy woman who had the gall to want it *all*. And then there were those who regarded it as gospel: If anyone should know about the game of marriage it was she, who had been married all of *five* times.

Her expression turns somber. What she *really* knows is that for every marriage there's at least a tiny piece of a broken heart left behind, and that the flip side of a brilliant marriage is often the brilliant divorce.

"But in all fairness," she whispers, trying to make the morose lady in the mirror at least *smile*, "while I have been married five times—well, to be absolutely accurate, more like four and a half—the truth is I've been divorced only *twice*."

But this effort to cheer herself up proves futile too.

She sighs and reaches for the ruby and diamond chandelier earrings that match the necklace. *Why not?* As her mother, the village barmaid, always said, "In for a penny, in for a pound." Maybe the flash and glitter of the earrings will help her feel more festive, more in a party mood, since she's determined that today's affair will be as ebullient and sparkling as any of the hundreds of parties she's given over the years—in London, in Washington, or here in Los Angeles, where she arrived as a newlywed, already a bit older than springtime and hardly virginal, but still as starry-eyed and, in her own way, as naïve as any young bride.

Now she lowers lids powdered faintly violet over vivid blue eyes—her third husband had likened them to the splendor of sapphires—to check that she hasn't overdone the shadow. With makeup the general rule was, less is more, which was probably the case with husbands too. *Or was it?*

Now she rises to step back and get an overall view of the lady whom the writer of the *People Today* article described as ". . . a woman of 'a certain age' who's very much a woman of today, cheerfully indomitable, infinitely charming, dazzlingly ageless . . ."

Now she frowns. High-sounding words to be sure, but the writer missed out on an aptly descriptive phrase he might have added—that she's a woman standing at life's crossroads suddenly unsure in which direction to turn, and still with a way to go. . . .

She thinks of her mother's final words before she departed life for, hopefully, a smashing hereafter: "Remember, love, that all life is like coming to a fork in the road. If you take a right turn your life will turn out one way, if you turn left, it will turn out another. More often than not it's all a matter of chance."

*A matter of chance? Perhaps . . .*

But choices for the countrywoman who had loved a good time and a hearty laugh above all else had been fairly simple. There hadn't been that many forks in the road for her. But she herself has traveled a long and convoluted path, taking both the high road and the low to get to where she is now: the grand doyenne of one of Hollywood's most legendary studios and of a great country estate—a green oasis secluded in the heart of bustling L.A. that is much like she herself—an English transplant intertwined with the dazzling aura of luxe Hollywood accoutrements. . . .

*But where do I go from here? Which way do I turn?*

She goes to the window to look down at the terrace, where everything is ready and waiting for the celebrants, from the poppy-pink–clothed tables with their flowered umbrellas to the shell-pink napkins stiffly pleated into fans to the blush-pink roses that only appear to have been plucked from a country garden seconds before to fill the crystal and silver vases.

How pretty it all looks, she thinks, elegant enough for a tea party at Buckingham Palace or even a cinematic Hollywood wedding. Even the day is exactly right, golden and balmy—a

June day so rare a sunlit bride could dance barefoot in the grass
at her own wedding. . . .

She looks beyond the terrace now at the pool sparkling azure
in the sun, at the rolling emerald lawns, the bountiful gardens
and stately tropical plantings, with the California hills forming
a magnificent backdrop, and she is flooded with memories,
consumed by a bittersweet longing for the bittersweet past,
breaking another of her own rules about getting on with it and
not looking back.

Still, she lingers at the window. If she squeezes her eyes
nearly shut she can almost make out a young man so golden and
graceful moving across the clay tennis court; can almost *hear* the
three fourteen-year-old Hollywood princesses, all so dear to her,
plotting such glorious futures in the playhouse furnished with
fantasy-movie set castoffs—a playhouse where a fourteen-year-
old queen of France might have dallied before she lost her head.

Now the young man is no longer so young and he's been
away for ever so long and the three young girls are all grown up
and hurting, and she yearns to make things right for all of them.

And then, just for one agonizingly brief moment, she can
almost feel *him* in the room coming up from behind to wrap his
arms around her, to rub his body persuasively against hers, and
the yearning becomes a physical ache. . . .

The sensation is so real she whirls around, but the moment
is gone and she's not even sure who *he* was . . . a ghost from the
past or the sweet love of a man very much of the present.

*But do I take a chance on the future? Shall I? Can I? Dare I?* Even
she, who has never backed away from a challenge, must admit
that the odds against making that elusive brilliant marriage at
this stage of the game are scary. Perhaps the thing to do is to quit
while one is ostensibly ahead of the game.

Then again, while she's been married to all manner of
men for all manner of reasons, she's never been married *forever*. . . .

But now she sees that the guests are beginning to gather. Yes,
it's time to get on with it. She, who is almost as famous for the
parties she has thrown as she is for her five marriages, is giving
a very special kind of party today, celebrating not a marriage but

a divorce. And if things go as planned, and if luck is with her, it might well be the party to end all parties for a long time to come. Because if she knows anything, she knows that just as there are all kinds of marriages—and these hardly ever what they *appear* to be—there are also all kinds of divorces, and not all of them the sort that are finalized in court.

# PART ONE

# THE CLUB

---

## Los Angeles, June 1990

# ONE

————•••————

Honey Rose pulled the white Corniche convertible close to
the stanchion guarding the gilt-touched iron gates so that
she could push the buzzer and talk into the receiver without stretching. An anonymous voice responded and she gave her
name. At the same time she removed her big, dark sunglasses
and white wide-brimmed hat to reveal a mass of golden blond
hair and flashed a big ultrawhite smile so that she would be
easily recognized on the closed-circuit television, its recording
camera nestled in a royal palm overhead. These were automatic
reflexes based on an inherent modesty—there probably wasn't
a person over the age of five in the civilized world who wouldn't
recognize the image of the Honey Rose.

Now the gates swung slowly open to admit her to Grantwood Manor, the magical kingdom where all dreams could
ostensibly come true. At least that was how she'd thought of the
manor when she saw it for the first time years ago. That had
already been a day of firsts—her first day at the Beasley School
for Girls, the first time she met Sam and Babe, and the first time
she'd joined a club so exclusive its membership consisted of
only the three of them and so secret they'd vowed never to even
reveal its existence to anyone, either friend or foe. Then Sam,
eager for them to see what she called her ancestral castle, had
insisted they come home with her.

*Olaf, the Grants' chauffeur, opened the limousine door and they
tumbled out, three laughing teenagers delighted that they'd found
each other. When Babe cried, "Oh, it's like a castle in a fairy tale!"
and Honey whispered in awe, "It looks enchanted!" Sam, in spite of
her seeming sophistication, was childishly pleased with their reaction.*

*"It is and we three are its enchanted princesses and don't you ever forget it!"* Then Honey and Babe, too enthralled by now not to believe in enchanted castles and princesses, even if they were already too old for fairy tales, swore to remember it always.

But now it was twenty years later, Honey reflected, and almost everything was different, and the three princesses were *really* too grown up and far too world-worn to believe in fairy tales and enchanted castles anymore. *And she was getting a divorce from the man named Prince whom she had once loved desperately! That had to be the epitome of disenchantment.*

Besides, today she knew something that at fourteen she'd been incapable of understanding—that in spite of Grantwood Manor's lovely pedigree, it was, like the legendary T. S. Grant's movies, only a Hollywood fabrication, more cinematic wizardry than real. But it had taken some time before she realized that behind its sunny, idyllic façade lurked a few dark secrets that one would only associate with gloomy, mysterious Gothic castles.

In any case, she wasn't visiting today. She was picking up Sam so that they could go on to lunch with Babe, who was flying in for the day. Since Babe called Washington home more than L.A. these days, today's date was special—a chance for the three of them to catch up as well as celebrate her divorce.

She drove up the driveway lined with king palms to the bricked courtyard with its huge terra-cotta pots spilling over with masses of multicolored impatiens to find that there were at least twenty cars of all colors and denominations already parked—BMWs, Jags, Hondas, Land-Rovers—and she wondered to whom all the cars belonged. *Was this one of Nora's soirees?*

Just then, Sam, slender in emerald-green silk and dangerously high-heeled strapped sandals, her long red hair silkily swirling around her shoulders, threw the manor's massive oak doors open and cried, "Welcome to the club, Honey Rose!" Then her heart quickened and little goose bumps of recognition ran up her spine. After joining Sam's club so long ago, life had never again been the same.

"Do you mean there's a club meeting here today that includes *us?*'' she asked warily. "And we're *not* going to go to lunch with Babe? Okay, Sam, what club is it this time?"

"Come on, I'll show you." Laughing with anticipation, Sam pulled her into the house and down the long hall to the conservatory in the rear that overlooked the terrace and mosaic-tiled pool. Usually this room, filled with blooming orchids and airy ferns, and with its wall of windows that permitted the sun to filter in through prisms of age-faded stained glass, was an oasis of cool serenity. But today, drifting in from outside, was a loud buzz of female voices.

Then Sam drew her over to the windows so that she could see the scene on the terrace: pink-clothed tables with festive, flowered umbrellas, waiters carrying silver trays of tall champagne flutes and squat cocktail glasses, a pink-uniformed maid passing hors d'oeuvres, while thirty or so women dressed in everything from Valentinos and major jewelry to sweats and outrageous Melrose Avenue funk milled and trilled. "Take a look at this crowd!" Sam's green eyes gleamed. "What club would this be but the Hollywood Exes?"

"But I didn't know there *was* such a club," Honey wailed.

"Oh, Honey, I was only kidding. There *isn't!* But from that bunch out there I daresay it wouldn't be difficult to get it chartered today, and do you know who the president should be? The gal who scores the highest at marriage and divorce roulette, the clever exee who lands with both feet on Mr. Ex, digging her Ferragamo spikes into his bleeding guts . . . that rare female who comes out of her marriage holding not only all the loot but the bastard's gonads as well. And I have a feeling that that rare female is going to be *you!* That you're going to strip Joshua Prince of his last pair of Jockeys."

Honey fixed Sam with a withering look. "I'm not in the mood for this, Sam, and since the Hollywood Exes *doesn't* exist and is *not* the club meeting here today, would you please tell me what's going on? Is this one of Nora's fund-raisers?"

"Oh, all right, spoilsport, I'll tell you. It's *not* a club, and while it *is* a party, it's not one of Nora's usuals. It's a party in *your* honor, only it was *supposed* to be a surprise. You know, like the bridal shower Nora gave you? Well, since tomorrow's the big day when they're announcing your award, Nora's throwing you a *divorce shower!*"

Honey, stunned rather than pleased, corrected Sam automatically. "*Settlement,* not award."

"Settlement, award, half of the community property"—Sam shrugged—"does it matter what you call it?"

"It matters to me," Honey said stiffly. "As far as I'm concerned, award signifies something one is *given,* or a prize, and I want only that which I've earned, that which is *due* me."

"But how many of us get what's due us? And how many bitches get what's *not* due them, like Nora? Didn't she get everything that was *my* due? Anyway, everyone's talking about your settlement, waiting to see if you get everything you're asking for as well as that mausoleum you and Josh call home."

Honey grimaced. She was very much aware of the speculation her settlement had sparked in the Hollywood community. It would have been bad enough had it been only local, but, like it or not, she was a public figure like Liz or Madonna or Princess Di, and for months her divorce had been the stuff of national interest. One headline in a supermarket publication had read: THE BIG AWARD: HOW MUCH HONEY WILL TV'S QUEEN BEE SUCK FROM THE PRINCE OF PRIME TIME'S GARDEN OF GOODIES?

"Oh, I know how interested everyone is. It's as if it's their God-given right to know every last article in Crown House down to the solid-gold toilet seats they insist we own."

"Well, you can't blame people. Even I, when I think of what you're asking for—well!" She went into a mock faint and Honey had to laugh, though she didn't feel like going into a long discussion for the *nth* time explaining her position.

She didn't think that anyone, with the possible exception of Nora maybe, really understood that the settlement was not really about money but only about validation of herself as a real person, not just a revenue-producing Barbie doll who came complete with the last accessory—furs, jewels, purple workout suits, dreamy Rolls convertible, and big dream house.

One thing she knew for sure: no matter how large her settlement might be, it would never compensate for the pain, for the months of acrimonious in-fighting, for the decline and fall of what Nora Grant had once called a brilliant marriage.

She remembered how, as she walked down the aisle on her father's arm, he, ever the poetic romantic despite his own painful marital path, had softly recited Browning's sonnet to her about the depth and breadth of love. *"I shall but love thee better after death."* Poor Teddy. He hadn't known even then that that line was definitely passé. That the updated version would read: "I shall but love thee better until we split up the assets."

Well, no matter how much she ended up with, she was still going to feel totally devastated that the marriage that had started out with *"How much do I love thee?"* was going to end up with *"How much* money *can I squeeze out of this man?"*

To change the subject she teased, "You said this divorce shower was Nora's idea, but it sounds more like something *you'd* dream up, Samantha Grant."

"Well, I must admit that when Nora said she wanted to throw a party to cheer you up, I did kind of suggest a divorce shower would be fun. But what's the diff? Think how happy Nora is making this party for you. She's always been so fond of you. Remember how she called you that sweet little girl ever since the first day I brought you home? She used to chirp to Daddy, 'Isn't Honey the sweetest thing? It's really too bad that—' She never finished but Daddy and I both got the point. *You* were the sweet one and I was the little shit even though I was nearly six feet tall. Oh, forget it! But I want you to know that while it *was* I who suggested making this a divorce shower, I was only trying to help Nora out."

"Help her out?" Honey hooted. "How come? *Opposing* Nora usually makes your day. And just a second ago you—"

"Isn't it possible I had a change of heart?" Sam chuckled. "No, I can see that you don't buy it."

"You're right, I don't. Nor do I understand why, feeling about her the way you do, you moved back into the house."

"I confess I had an ulterior motive in moving back. You see, I'm getting these vibes that Nora's finally about to make a decision about the studio, that she's having an attack of conscience and is thinking about giving me back that which she stole from me. And I'm not just talking about the studio and the manor, I

mean my trust fund too. And no lectures about what a grand gal
Nora is and how wrong I've been about her all these years. Give
me a break. Anyway, I'm doing everything possible to get along
with her outside of calling her Mummy, even though just the
thought of making nice with her is enough to make me barf. Oh,
let's not talk about it, okay?"

Honey agreed, but if she hadn't been depressed before, she
certainly was now. She too suspected that Nora was about to
make a move with the studio—she'd heard a rumor. If it were
true, it would really break Sam's heart . . . perhaps beyond
repair. But of course it wasn't true, she reassured herself. Nora
would never undercut Sam like that. She gave Sam's hand a
squeeze. "Everything's going to work out if you give it half a
chance."

"Really? I just wish you sounded more sincere. But enough
of me and my travails. Today is *your* day and I only pray that
when you walk into that courtroom tomorrow you get the
record-breaking amount you're suing for! *One quarter of a bil!*
How clever of you to demand such a nice, round sum."

"Let's not talk about it. What about Babe? I don't see her
out there. She *is* coming to my divorce party, isn't she?"

"Yes, we're expecting her at any sec. Unless dear hubby
decided he couldn't make a speech or whatever without Babe's
adoring eyes fixed upon his manly senatorial figure."

"I'm sure not. So tell me, Sam, before I go out there, what
happens exactly at a divorce shower, so I'll be prepared? A
naked bodybuilder jumping out of the double-fudge cake?"

Sam snapped her fingers. "Oh, shit, I knew I'd forgotten
something! And personally I would have adored seeing you
violated by a muscular stud. I mean, men have to be good for
*something!* Oh, well, we'll do that one at your *next* divorce
shower. Anyway, you know how everyone brought gifts to your
bridal shower? Well, at a divorce shower the ladies bring stories
about marriages both legal and not, and divorces—their own or
maybe their best friend's—or just plain gossip, hopefully hot,
about some celebrated but sordid relationship. Actually, any
story about *any ex*—real or significant other—will do, or any
weepy tale of a romance gone sour with a man who was bad

news from the start, especially a bloodcurdling story of unusual marital abuse. And any report on a *really* kinky marriage is acceptable, but only if none of the juicy details are left out. And now, if you're ready— But wait, before we go out there, I want to make sure you look the part of a quarter-of-a-billion-dollar baby!"

Honey smiled wanly. "I thought I always did."

"Of course you did. What is it? Are you just feeling sensitive, or guilty about going for the big one? Didn't you learn anything from that woman you admire so much, Nora Grant? How do you think she got where she is without grabbing everything she could lay her greedy, oft-married little claws on?"

"Sam!" Honey warned. "Don't get started again."

"Okay, I'll stop! But I don't want you to think that I'm bitter just because my own two marriages netted me less than zero. Anyhow, we will now focus our attention on you. I don't want those hyenas out there to think that just because you've cut the first notch on the old divorce pistol, the dew is off the Rose. We have to show them that the Honey Rose still lives to bloom another day." She crouched down into a photographer's stance, pretending to look through a viewfinder. "Now, let's see that famous Honey Rose smile."

Honey obliged but Sam wasn't satisfied. She tried again but Sam shook her head. "If you can't do better than that, you know what I'll have to do. *Tickle* you into a big grin, and you know how you hated that in the good old days."

*The good old days . . . before we grew up to get married just so that we could get divorced. . . .*

"No, no tickling!" Honey begged. "I'll be good!" And she flashed an even wider smile, a smile as big as the Ritz.

*"Give it to me," he urged. "A smile as big as the Ritz."*

She had had no idea how big the Ritz was then, but he had said, "Give it to me," and what he asked for, he got. That was the way it had been with them whether it was a smile or anything else. He took and always demanded just a little bit more.

"Gorgeous!" Sam cried, leaping forward to whip at Honey's hair with her fingers as vigorously as if she were hand-tossing a Caesar salad. Then she stepped back to view her handiwork.

"Better! *That's* the famous Honey Rose Tousle!"

"*More hair! Bigger hair!*" he ordered the hairstylists. "*It has to be a definitive statement.*"

He'd stood over the hairstylists for hours, suggesting, in structing, correcting, and harassing in turn while she sat mute with her heart in her throat, frightened that he might never be satisfied, and then *what*? But finally . . . magically . . . he *was* pleased and she was able to breathe again.

"Now give us that notorious Honey Rose come-hither with the ol' topazes. You know, the 'Look'!" Sam cajoled.

*The Look! Think sex, he had instructed her.*

Every time she had looked at him she had thought sex. Thought of him poised above her as she looked into his deceptively soft eyes, felt him so beautifully inside her. Thought of how it felt when *she* was positioned above *him*, but of course that had never been *his* favorite position.

She obliged Sam now by thinking sex just as she had always obliged him, and Sam breathed, "*Yeah! That's it!* Now, do you think we might hike that hemline up an inch or two? We need a little more leg here." She went back into her crouch. "This is *really* good! You look almost as delectable as you did in that wet T-shirt poster that set world records for whacking off from Jackson Hole, Wyoming, to Peking, China."

Thinking about the poster, Honey sighed. All by itself it had generated millions, selling two hundred thousand copies in Tokyo alone. As a birthday present, he'd had the poster blown up to five times its size and framed in gold leaf to hang incongruously alongside the Picassos, the Renoirs, and the Warhol silkscreen rendering of a pistol-packing Honey in short shorts and thigh-high cowboy boots.

Who would get the art collection? Would it be a trade-off for Crown House? He loved the collection almost as much as he did the house, and he loved the house almost as much as he did Royal Productions. Where she had rated she still was not quite sure.

Then she heard Sam groan in mock gratification. "Okay, Honey Rose, we're ready. Let's go out there and kill 'em!"

# TWO

———————— •••• ————————

When the women cheered as she stepped out onto the terrace, Honey felt ridiculous. She hadn't saved the world from nuclear destruction—she'd merely demanded a shocking amount of money and an extravagant home as her share of the community property. Then, when Nora rushed up to hug her, murmuring, "Congratulations, love, on a brilliant divorce!" her eyes flowed over and Nora, seeing the tears, whispered, "You mustn't. It only hurts for a little while and that's where the money helps—it makes the pain go away. Besides, you look too beautiful to ruin the effect with tears. I always say it's more important to look beautiful when one's getting divorced than when one is getting married."

Despite her vow to make nice with Nora, Sam couldn't hold back and drawled tauntingly, "*Why* do you always say that?"

Ignoring her sardonic tone, Nora smiled. "Because a wedding is actually an ending—a culmination of two people meeting, courting, breaking up, then getting back together again. So loverly but still an ending, and endings are always sad. And the divorce! Ah, that's saying good-bye to the past and hello to the future, and one must begin anew looking lovely and feeling positive because it's good karma—it attracts the best of everything. Especially new and exciting men!"

"And *rich!* That's important, isn't it?" Sam persisted.

"To be sure, my dear," Nora said, refusing to be goaded.

"There you go, Honey!" Sam cried. "Another brilliant quote from the lady who has a brilliant saying to cover every topic, be it men, marriage, or divorce. And as *I* always say, no one's better qualified to do this than our Nora."

Nora laughed before turning away to tell the butler to bring out a few more bottles of the Cristal while Honey hissed at Sam, "I thought you said you were going to try to get along with her! Why are you being so snide and sarcastic?"

"You know the story of the frog and the scorpion? They come to a stream they have to cross and the scorpion says, 'I can't swim. Let me ride on your back,' and the frog says, 'But if I let you ride on my back you'll sting me and I'll drown.' Then the scorpion says, 'Don't be ridic! Of course I won't sting you! If you drown, so will I.' So the frog lets the scorpion get on his back, and sure enough, midstream the scorpion stings him, and as they're both drowning the frog croaks, 'But you knew this would happen. Why did you sting me?' and the scorpion says, 'Because I *am* a scorpion.' "

"Well, did it ever occur to you *not* to be a scorpion?"

"Of course, but that's the point. I *am* a scorpion."

*   *   *

"Honey, you're really *doing* it!" Lakey Owens, the star of a prime-time soap, pounded Honey on the back. "You're even putting Francie Lear to shame. *She* only got a hundred fifteen mil!"

"*Only?*" Chris Campbell, who was divorced from a rock star after a marriage of six months, screeched. "I'll take that *only!* I barely got enough to pay the rent on my one-bedroom."

"You were lucky to get that," Lakey said, snatching a glass of champagne from a passing waiter's tray. "Francie gave Norm her best years. How can you compare six months with Wild Bill Boynton to the kind of time she put in with Norman?"

"And you never understood the value of publicity," Pam Lee of Lee Real Estate, known for her multiple divorces as well as her multiple listings, added. "Look at Alana Stewart. *She* really dug its dynamics, marrying Rod with everybody looking and parting from him the same way, with shots of her and Rod's kids all over the place. Now she's living it up with fantastic support because who—even a rocker—wants to look like an

S.O.B. who doesn't give a shit for his own kids? If *you'd* been smart you would have stuck it out with Wild Bill for a couple of years, had a kid or two, and had it all documented with lots of togetherness photos."

"Had a couple of kids?" Chris fumed. "How was I supposed to do that? Once he married me he stopped pronging me. Then, when I was out shopping at Saks, he moved a groupie into my bed and my stuff out to the garage. And I didn't even have the garage remote with me!"

"Pathetic!" WeeGee Gosset, a gossip columnist wearing rhinestone-studded leather, slurped an oyster and sneered, "Don't you know that when you marry a rocker you need a clause written into the contract—no balling groupies?"

"Or at least you should have always carried the remote with you," Bambi Winters cracked, getting a big laugh. Everyone knew the story of how Bambi had won the family manse, which had only her husband's name on the grant deed, by simply refusing to move out even after the ex called the cops on her.

"Not funny," Dana Smith, the beauty queen from El Paso divorced from the CEO of a big studio, moaned, after which there was a tiny silence out of respect for her depression. Her ex had just announced his engagement to Mavis Madden, who'd been spotted only a month or so before holding hands with Warren Beatty at the China Club for nine nights running.

"Sooner or later they *all* stray," the middle-aged sitcom writer Rae Peters, in an orange running suit and lime Reeboks, lamented. "When you're hot, *they're* hot. But as soon as you give up what made you hot in the first place to rub their backs, run their baths, fix their drinks, and listen to their bull about how hard it is out there, they chill out so fast it makes the blood run cold. Then, instead of *banging* you they're letting you take their temperature while someone else is *raising* it, the moral being, if you sublimate your career to his, you're up shit creek without a paddle."

"*She* should talk," someone snorted in an undertone. "Whose temperature did she ever raise?"

"Some women are smart and hold on to their careers, give up zilch, and still come out on top. Look at Amy. She didn't give up her career, and now she not only has a hundred mil, Steve's kid as well as the current's, she kept Steve as a friend too. They're still having dinner together."

"Yeah, it's nice that the Spielbergs stayed friends."

"It's even nicer that Amy has enough cash now to call the shots on her own career. She can afford to pick and choose."

"Never mind Amy, how about our Honey? She's still going to have her career *and* Crown House *and* two hundred fifty million dollars!"

Honey looked at Sam: *Save me!* And Sam said, "Now we must go get Honey some nourishment—just thinking about two hundred fifty million dollars takes its toll, a *huge* expenditure of calories."

Before they moved away, the gravelly voiced Rae advised, "Take the money, Honey, and do something really *big* with it."

Lakey Owens quickly agreed: "Francie started *Lear's* with her millions, which really told Norm off in spades."

"How did Frances Lear starting up her own magazine tell Norman off in spades?" Honey asked Sam, who chortled, "*Lear's*, the magazine for the *older* woman, is also known as the 'Fuck you, Norman' publication because it's a feminist magazine and she used his male millions to launch it. She started a new life for herself, and at the same time thumbed her nose at Norm. And that's what *you* should do."

"*What* should I do?" Honey laughed. "Start a magazine or thumb my nose at Norm?"

"I'm serious. You should start a new career with your settlement money and at the same time stick it to Mr. Prince. Show him you can make it on your own in terms he understands."

"*New* career? And what do you mean by terms he understands?"

"What did you always want? A career as a *serious* actress and that *would* be a new career for you, all things considered. And what means the most to Josh? His company, Royal Productions, right? And if you took your money and bought a *real* studio that makes movies, not just grist for TV, and did the serious stuff Josh claimed you couldn't, wouldn't that be thumbing your nose at him, showing him you were *never* just a T-and-A bimbo? And if you made a success of it, wouldn't that be the ultimate in the fuck-you department?"

"But—"

"Not now. Here come some more of the girls. Smile and have some of this crab with black bean sauce. It's yummy."

But Honey was too preoccupied to eat. She wondered if there was a particular company Sam had in mind as her "fuck you" studio. It *was* a fascinating concept. In all the years they'd been married, she couldn't say that she had ever fucked Josh in the nonliteral sense. But, then, she hadn't fucked him too many times in the literal sense, either. It was he who had almost always *fucked her*, though sometimes she'd tried to assume the top position, enabling her to choose when to ease him into her or to savagely impale herself upon him—to set the tone, ride him as furiously as she desired or at a tantalizingly slow rhythm . . . to make *him* cry out in unbearable desire and plead with her to quicken her pace. No, he hadn't permitted that too often. Josh was a man who could relish life, love, and sex only if he called the shots.

*He was on top, his lips moving to her throat, then her breasts to mouth her nipples, those twin erections as hard as his own, which she invariably ended up pleading for. "Now! Oh, yes, please! I love you! Now, please! I love you!"*

She'd always ended up begging for that final thrust, though she always promised herself she wouldn't beg—not for his body or his love, not for all the best things in life he'd promised her and hadn't delivered. Oh, yes, she wanted to fuck him! Was it possible that she'd been lying to herself all along, that from the first that was what her divorce was all about—the need to have a "Fuck you, Joshua Prince" divorce?

She looked up to see Nora watching her, then, startled, she realized that Nora's expression was *sorrowful*. But then, as their eyes met, Nora shifted her gaze. What had Nora been thinking that made her look so sad? she wondered. Then she wondered as she had many times before: Of all Nora's marriages, which had been her most brilliant and which had been only for love?

If she knew the answer to that, maybe she would understand a lot of things, certainly why Nora was looking at her now with so melancholy an expression. . . .

\* \* \*

"My lawyer gave me four alternatives—capitulation, negotiation, litigation, or assassination, and I told him I was out for Jack's last drop of blood!" Tina Lally offered.

"And did you get it? That last drop?" someone demanded.

"Not even by half. We're not all as lucky as Honey."

Honey started to say that she'd never been out for *blood*, but decided not to bother. It hardly mattered at this point. Besides, they'd already covered every conceivable topic relating to divorce, from whether the big A stood for Adultery or Assets to how simple cheating compared to real "passionflower" mistresses. Plus, they had discussed prenups and celebrated settlements, from Johnny and Joanna to Joan and the Swede to Rambo and the Bimbette Brigette, to the point of exhaustion.

She'd had enough and Babe still hadn't arrived, and after all this morbid conversation, Babe with her healthy marriage would be like a ray of sunshine on a rainy afternoon. She turned to Sam. "Don't you think it's time to check on Babe?"

"We'll escape to the library," Sam agreed, and as they tiptoed down the hall, Honey whispered, "It's funny, but not one of them had a good word to say about *any* man."

"Did you think that they would?" Sam laughed. "Those women *are* the Hollywood Exes, after all."

"But you'd think that at least *one* woman would say, 'We didn't make it but he's a good guy and I wish him the best.' "

"What about you, Honey? Would you make that statement?"

"Well, let's just say I'm not *unwilling* to make it. And I *do* wish him the best."

*The very, very best. And who knows? It's quite possible that I'll always wish him love. . . .*

# THREE

———•••———

" **I** 'll call D.C., but if we don't get anywhere *you'll* have to call
Babe's mother, Honey. I'm not in the mood for Catherine.
You know—how she picks up with that queen-mother irritation in her voice as if you had just interrupted her as she was
having an orgasm on the crapper?" Sam went to the oak bar to
take down a bottle of Courvoisier. "It's always the same old shit
with her." She poured a little brandy into two snifters, then
judiciously poured a little more into each glass before handing
one to Honey.

"It's always 'Oh, it's *you*, Sa-*man*-tha. I suppose you want
Babette?' And I always feel like answering, 'No, actually I want
Babette's daddy, your husband, Judge Tracy. It's been a long
time since we've been together between the sheets and I wanted
to ask him over for a quickie.' Then, if Babe *isn't* there, Catherine loves to say she hasn't heard from her in *weeks* just so I'll be
sure to worry that something's wrong. Then she asks, 'Is there
anything *else* I can do for you?' and then I almost say, 'Yes, bend
over to touch your toes while I stick a hot poker up your ass!' "

"Okay," Honey said after she finished laughing, "you call
Washington and if you have no luck, I'll call Catherine, though
I don't know what I ever did to deserve this pleasure."

"Because you get along with her so well, as you get along
with Nora. You're the girl every mother loves to mother."

*No, I can think of one notable exception—my own.*

"That was Babe's secretary," Sam said, hanging up. "I didn't
even know she had one. Anyway, she said Babe left Washington
at eight on TWA—Senator Ryan's chauffeur took her to the
airport—was due to land ten our time and was coming straight

35

here, which means she should have been here about eleven. Hmm . . . A secretary for her, a chauffeur for him, and that big house. They're living pretty high on Catherine and the Judge's money, which leads to an interesting question—if *they* get a divorce, how will they split up all that Tracy community property?"

"Don't trouble your little head, Sammy dear. Babe's marriage is as solid as a brick wall."

"But even brick walls start to go when the mortar starts to crumble. Of course it all depends on how good the mortar is to start with, and I'd say—"

"I'd love to discuss bricklaying with you, but Babe's long overdue. We have to find out if her plane landed on time."

"I'm way ahead of you," Sam said, already dialing. It took only a minute to establish that Babe's plane *had* landed on time.

Honey sighed. "I guess there's nothing to be done, then, but for me to call Catherine." She made the call while Sam went back to the bar to refill her glass. After volleying with Catherine for a bit, Honey reported: "It seems she hasn't heard from Babe in *weeks*, even *months*."

"See? She always says that. You didn't tell her we expected Babe almost four hours ago?" Honey shook her head and Sam said, "Good, not that she doesn't deserve an anxiety attack herself."

"But what do we do now?"

"*Nada.* Maybe Babe decided she didn't like what she was wearing and went shopping instead of coming straight here."

"Shopping for four hours after she got off a plane?"

"Why not? You know Babe was always a Rodeo Drive freak."

"I think we should call Babe's secretary back. Maybe they'll want to start checking from their end."

"We're talking four hours here, not a missing person! Maybe Babe needed time to herself or took the opportunity to check into a motel for an off-the-record dicking, and the least we can do for her is not turn her in to the cops."

"Very funny. So, what *shall* we do?"

"We'll sit tight and wait for Babe to show up in her own

time." She locked the door. "If anyone comes knocking, don't make a sound, and in the meantime, how about a refill?"

Honey shook her head, thinking about the times they'd locked themselves in this room to hide from the world. Often they'd sat for hours no matter who pounded on the door while Sam calmly read aloud from a magazine. Still, no matter how frequently they'd done this, she herself had always been shocked anew by Sam's indifference to the order: "Open up!," while Babe, her black-cherry eyes sparkling with nervous excitement, was enthralled by the show of disobedience. But while Babe found Sam's audacity awesome, she would have been terrified to pull a stunt like that in her own home, which was something Honey understood. The Tracys' silent treatment and "confinement to quarters" discipline *was* inhibiting.

"But what if Nora comes to the door, Sam? You're going to *have* to open up. You're not a rebellious kid any longer. Well, not a kid, anyway. And this *is* her house."

"Tell me about it!"

"In all fairness, Nora has given you a home here anytime you wanted regardless of how——"

"Sure, as long as I remember that it's *her* house, just as Grantwood Studio is *her* studio. Besides, she only wants me here so she can remind me of what a fuck-up I am, not to mention that she wants to control me just like she did Daddy."

"The truth, Sam, is that Nora controlled your father as much as he *let* her control him. He was a very strong man."

"He was putty in that manipulative hand of hers. Why else would he have left her *my* studio and *my* house, damn it?"

"Oh, Sam! It was his studio and he chose to leave it to the woman who made him happy. Sooner or later you just *have* to come to terms with that, not keep tearing yourself apart."

"But I can't bear it!" Sam cried, throwing herself down on the sofa. "I'm his daughter! It's his blood that runs in my veins just like making movies ran in his. That studio belongs to *me*! You know she doesn't give a damn about it. It never meant anything to her except for the money it made."

"But she's always been willing for you to work there. She urged you to——"

"Oh, sure. She wanted me to work at the studio as a gofer. But what she really wanted was to humiliate me."

"Come on, Sam. The problem was you wanted to start off producing fifty-million-dollar pictures and she wanted you to learn the business thoroughly. She thought that—"

"How do you know *what* she thought or why she tried to make my father hate me or why she sent Hubie away? And you don't really know why she got me out of the way when my father was dying or why my father left everything to her, even my trust fund *to be disbursed at her discretion! Disbursed,* hell! That word doesn't even sound like T.S.! If you weren't still so blinded by all that fake charm, you'd see it all adds up to just one thing— that she's an out-and-out manipulative witch who completely snowed him, and the fact that she could fool him like that just shows what a good heart *he* had. But what's the use of talking to you? You and Babe were always fooled by her. But one of these days you're going to have to decide whose side you're on. Hers or mine."

But I've already done that, Honey ached to cry out. *I took sides a long time ago when I didn't tell Nora the truth about T.S. and I did it only to keep the truth from you.*

"Why did my father ever marry her? She's such a terrible bitch and he was *so* wonderful, wasn't he?"

Honey hesitated a moment before nodding and Sam didn't notice the slight pause. Instead, she burst into tears and Honey held her in her arms.

Never had she seen Sam like this—Sam, who had always been so strong. "It'll be all right, Sam. You'll see."

"You'll help me, then? You'll be on my side?"

"Oh, Sam, I've *always* been on your side, and of course I'll help you. That's what friendship means. The fun's the *easy* part. But you're not going to need my help. You yourself said that you think that Nora might be ready to turn the studio over to you, and if it turns out that she *isn't,* maybe she'll give you a chance at running it. Then if you proved yourself, she'd work with you to hammer out some kind of a deal—a partnership, maybe, or a trade—your trust-fund money for at least a share of the studio. . . ." She said a silent prayer that Nora *would* do the right thing. *And please, God, don't let that rumor I heard be true!*

Sam laughed harshly. "From the first day I met Nora I prayed that I'd never see her again, and now, if I finally get my hands on Grantwood Studio, my prayer will be answered."

"But all this time since your father died, ever since you've been old enough to be on your own, you didn't *have* to see her. No one forced you to keep coming back here."

"It's my home," Sam said defensively.

"Not anymore. And if you didn't want to see her—"

"There *was* the matter of my trust fund, as you well know. I had to keep after her for that, didn't I?"

"Not in person, you didn't."

"Look, when you wanted a divorce you didn't just walk *out* of Crown House and you didn't just walk *away* from Royal Productions, even though, legally, you never owned any part of it. You stayed to fight for what was yours. What makes you think I should walk away from my alliance with her without getting my fair share, without getting *my* brilliant divorce any more than you did, any more than Nora herself would?"

Honey had no answer. Maybe Sam was right. There *were* all kinds of marriages, so maybe there had to be all kinds of divorces too.

When they heard the rap on the door, Sam put a finger to her lips, but Honey felt foolish hiding from people at her own party. She rose to go to the door, but Sam pushed her back down and they tussled as Sam tried to put a hand over her mouth to muzzle her, both of them laughing soundlessly until the rapping at the door turned into pounding and they heard the ragged voice: "Open up! I know you two are in there!"

Sam raced to the door to unlock it and Babe, black hair a smooth cap with bangs cut squarely across and exquisitely turned out in a yellow suit unmistakably Chanel, came tumbling into the room, high heels clattering on the polished floor. But despite the fastidious grooming, an air of hysteria shimmered about her, and the black, hip sunglasses she wore were an incongruous note, clashing with the discreetly elegant fashion statement she presented.

"What's with the Wayfarers?" Sam asked, amused. "You

haven't worn them since you were a teenybopper."

Babe seemed surprised by the question, as if she'd forgotten she was wearing the glasses, and pulled them off to reveal wild eyes ringed with inky, smudged mascara, which struck a discordant, almost macabre note in the otherwise perfectly made-up face.

"Babe! What's wrong?" Honey rushed to her. "Where were you? We were so worried about you!"

"I had to hitchhike here from Hollywood Boulevard."

"You hitched here in your Maud Frizons?" Sam hooted, then stopped abruptly. "Honey, get her a drink. Now, sit down, Babe, and tell us what happened."

"I finally took a ride from some guy in a Brooklyn College sweatshirt in a red Ferrari. It was the first offer I received from someone who looked at least halfway normal."

"I meant why didn't you come here from the airport?"

"I needed some time to think about what I wanted to do, so I got into a cab at LAX and told the driver to drive and he drove to Hollywood. Then I got out. I thought I'd walk for a while. That's when I bought these sunglasses from a street kid who needed the money for drugs, because I'd lost mine."

"I don't believe this! Catherine Tracy's daughter bought sunglasses from a street kid who needed a fix?" Sam yelped.

"Just let her talk," Honey said, handing Babe her drink only to have her hand the glass back. "Ice, please. You know I like my drinks on the rocks," she said, sweetly reproachful.

"Oh, Lordy, I think you've lost your rocks," Sam moaned. "Will you please get on with the story?"

"Then I discovered I'd left my purse in the cab."

"You couldn't have left it in the taxi because you took money out of it to pay for the sunglasses, didn't you?" Honey asked, handing Babe her drink, now clinking with ice.

Babe took a quick gulp. "Maybe. But anyway, it was gone, my yellow crocodile purse from Paris. It was a present from my mother. She'll be furious. She'll—"

"She'll what?" Sam raised her eyebrows. "Ground you like she used to do when you were a naughty teenager?"

"Never mind that, Sam, and never mind your purse, Babe.

Why didn't you call for a ride?" Honey asked.

"There was no way I'd call my mother. Think what she'd have to say about me parading down Hollywood Boulevard. And my father would probably send me to jail for hustling."

"I see what you mean," Sam acknowledged dryly, "but you should have called *us* here. Why didn't you?"

"I didn't have any money. I told you, I lost my purse."

"You don't need money to make a call from a public phone. All you have to do is make a collect call. Or you could have taken a cab and we would have paid for it when you got here."

"I didn't think of it. Why are you grilling me?"

"We only want to help, Babe," Honey soothed. "What did you have to think about?"

But before Babe could answer, Nora flew into the room. "What's going on? They said Babe was here and—" She saw Babe then, focusing in on the glazed eyes and the smeared mascara. "Oh, love, what's wrong?"

Sam crisply filled her in on what they'd gleaned from Babe so far. "And now we're proceeding from there."

"I'm not going back no matter what anyone says! And I'd like another drink, please."

Honey went to get the drink while Nora assured her, "Of course you're not. Why would we send you back to Hollywood Boulevard of all places?"

"I'm not talking about Hollywood Boulevard!"

"What *are* you talking about?" Sam asked.

"If I tell you, do you promise not to tell my mother?"

"We won't tell your parents anything you don't want us to, certainly not until we at least talk about it," Nora said. After all, Babe was no longer a child, when she would have felt honor-bound to tell Catherine and Judge Tracy *certain* things.

"I'm not going back to Greg. You don't think I *have* to, do you, Nora?"

Nora said, "You don't have to do anything you don't want to." She was sure of at least that, but she was heartsick. What she had only suspected before *was* true. Babe was no happier than her two friends.

"Will you tell us *why* you don't want to?" Honey asked.

"I'll show you if you lock the door."

Nora told Sam to lock it, and then they watched Babe stand up to kick off her shoes as if she were ready to go into a dance, as she had frequently done for no reason at all when she was a teen. Still, they all knew that if this was to be a dance, it wasn't going to be one of Babe's usual offerings.

Babe took off her jacket and threw it aside, then unzipped her skirt and let it slip to the floor as she hummed a tune to herself, one that Sam and Honey remembered as a song Babe had always loved, though it had already been, even then, an oldie. "Take it off," Babe crooned as it dawned on them that for some bizarre reason the dance Babe was doing was a striptease.

She smiled at them coyly, sitting down to remove pale panty hose, standing up again to wriggle out of a yellow half-slip trimmed with lace, after which she leisurely unbuttoned her silk blouse and shrugged it from her shoulders, allowing it to slither down, until she was down to a yellow bra and matching bikini. When she removed the bra, first pulling down each strap to partially disclose a voluptuous breast, she coquettishly threw it at her audience. Then, when she removed the panties, she flung them up in the air. Nude, she feverishly whirled around, and Honey and Sam were so transfixed they didn't notice that Babe's ordinarily satin-smooth body was crisscrossed with a bevy of pink-and-red welts and yellow-and-purple bruises until Nora silently went over to Babe to encompass her in her arms and still the dancing.

Then Honey gasped and Sam muttered, "Jesus!" and Nora asked quietly, "When did this happen, Babe?"

"Last night. I was perfectly groomed when I left Washington this morning, but underneath this is what I looked like."

"You don't mean—?" Honey hoarsely whispered.

"Not Mr. Wonderful?" Even Sam, who had never believed Greg Ryan was wonderful at all, found it hard to believe.

"Yes." Babe laughed crazily and Sam cursed bitterly.

"Oh, my love." Nora kissed Babe, more sad than anything. So much for brilliantly happy marriages, she thought. *Sometimes all that's left to us are our brilliant divorces. . . .*

# FOUR

––––– •◦• –––––

Nora took off her red silk coat and handed it to Sam. "Get Babe into this and take her upstairs. I'll be up as soon as I get rid of that crew out there."

They practically carried Babe upstairs to put her to bed in Sam's room, still decorated as always in pink and green. Then, when Nora came up, Babe asked in a little voice if she could stay the night and Nora said, "Of course, love. Didn't I always say you and Honey were to think of Grantwood Manor as a second home?"

"Such a comforting thought on a cold and stormy night," Sam purred. "Would that some kind person had said it to me."

Ignoring her, Nora invited Honey to sleep over too and she quickly agreed. She didn't feel much like spending the night alone in Crown House with only her ghosts to keep her company. Much better to share the same room with Babe and Sam as they had so many times before, giggling and talking late into the night. *Only tonight there won't be much giggling.*

Sam cornered Nora at the windows adjusting the draperies against the late-afternoon sun. "I think we're doing the wrong thing just putting Babe to bed. How do we know she's not hurt internally? I think the responsible thing to do is get her to a hospital to be X-rayed."

"I was planning on calling Len Silver to take a look at her and let him decide if she needs to go to hospital."

"But suppose she's *bleeding* internally? By the time Dr. Silver sends her to the hospital it could be too late!"

"You're being melodramatic, Sam. I daresay that outside of the bruises the worst of it is that Babe's in a state of hysteria and

43

what she needs is exactly what we're prepared to give her—reassurance. And Dr. Silver will give her whatever it takes to calm her and provide her a night's rest."

"But it's just as easy to take her to the hospital *now*."

"Look, Sam, I know what *you're* after. You'd love nothing more than to wheel Babe into hospital and call in a bunch of reporters and photographers so that the whole beastly mess would be on the evening news and in the papers, making sure everyone took full note that Babe Tracy Ryan was beaten up by her husband. But would it be in anyone's best interest to have this thing all blown up? Would it help Babe?"

"It certainly would. After publicity like that, think how she could sail through a successful divorce. Greg could have the hottest divorce lawyer—Jeffrey Cohen or Raoul Felder—and charm boy would *still* collapse like a tired balloon."

"I don't doubt it. At the same time, the publicity would only make it that much more difficult for Babe and Greg to iron out their differences *if* that's what Babe decides to do."

"Are you *crazy*? Why would she? It's not as if she had kids or that she's some poor wretch with no means of support. She's an attractive, talented woman with rich parents to rely on *if* she had to, though who in her right mind would want to rely on the Tracys? But I don't know why we're even discussing this. She never wants to see the slime bag again. She's *terrified* someone's going to force her to go back to him."

"Really, Sam, your naïveté amazes me. How many marriages do you think break up over an isolated incident when one partner loses control for a few bad moments? Chances are, by tomorrow Babe will be happy to listen to Greg's apologies."

"Then she'd be a fool, and Babe was never a fool except for the one time she slipped and married that prick."

"Oh, Sam, haven't you learned yet we're *all* fools at one time or other? But the biggest fool is one who interferes in the relationship between two adults. There might well be extenuating circumstances here we know nothing about."

"You're blowing my mind. He beat the shit out of her and you're talking extenuating circumstances? What kind? Do you think getting slammed around really gets Babe off and he was doing her a favor? Wait, I know what the trouble was! Babe broke out into one of her tap dances and suddenly he saw red! All he knew was that he had to stop her from doing her shuffle-off-to-Buffalo at any cost! It was temporary insanity!"

"You're not nearly as funny or clever as you think you are, Sam. Most likely he was drunk when he abused Babe, and whether Babe would consider intoxication an extenuating circumstance after she's had a chance to think about it would have to be *her* decision, much as you'd like it to be yours."

For a second Sam struggled to hold her tongue, but she lost the battle and snapped, "You always have all the answers. No matter what the story is we can count on old Nora to make a reasonable analysis of the situation, giving every cocksucker the benefit of the doubt, everyone but me, that is. I remember when I came home from school complaining that a teacher was picking on me, you always said to Daddy, 'There may be extenuating circumstances here,' then you made out a case for the shit. I wouldn't be surprised if when the bombs were falling on your precious London you had something good to say for Hitler."

Nora laughed. "Hardly. When the war broke out I was barely into my teens, and my mind was on boys and clothes just like any other girl, and Hitler was just a cartoon character with a funny mustache. But yes, I believe that it's best to try and find equitable solutions—that's just common sense."

Smiling falsely, Sam pantomimed holding a microphone up to Nora's mouth. "Would you tell our audience, Ms. Grant, if this *teddibly* sweet philosophy of yours is the secret of your phenomenal success in the marriage marketplace?"

"Gladly." Nora went along with the gag. "It's my belief that if one keeps a level head and one's sense of humor, it's the rare relationship that must end in bitterness and strife."

Sam's grin disappeared. "I'm sure you're right if you're Nora Grant, who always ends up with everything one can squeeze out of a relationship. Like, you ended up with Grantwood Manor and the studio and I ended up with a big, fat—"

Nora cut her off. "Let's not get into that again. It's hardly the time. Right now we have to try and help Babe."

"Sure. There's always *someone* who's getting the benefit of your loving ministrations, *anyone* but me!" Sam could almost taste the sour tang of bile on her lips but she couldn't stop. "The truth is it was never *my* turn with you. Just like it was never my turn at the studio that—"

"Enough! All that will be settled once and for all, I promise you, and sooner than you think. But right now we must concern ourselves with Babe, who's in immediate need."

"I'll say she is! She might even die on us because you wanted to spare her the publicity of being an abused wife," Sam spat out, needing to have, if nothing else, the last word.

*   *   *

Nora told Babe that, just to be on the safe side, she was calling her own doctor, Len Silver, to come to the house.

"No! No doctors!"

"But he's a friend and we can count on his discretion."

"It's either the doctor or the hospital." Sam backed Nora up this time. "Take your choice."

"But nothing *really* hurts me and nothing's broken. And I can't see a doctor or go to any hospital! I went once when I thought my arm was broken and Greg started in again on me when I got back before I had a chance to explain that I told them at the hospital that I'd fallen down the stairs."

Stunned anew, Honey and Sam stared at one another while Nora sank to a sitting position on the bed, asking: "You *do* mean it has happened before?"

Babe only moaned in reply.

"How many times?" Honey asked in an agonized whisper.

"Many . . ." Babe mumbled, burying her face in a pillow.

"How many?" Sam demanded, forcibly turning Babe's face around with her hands.

"Twenty, thirty . . . After the first time, when I couldn't leave the house for days, he never touched my face again."

*He never touched my face again.* . . . It took a few seconds before the full implication of Babe's words sunk in. Then Honey had a mental image of Greg—tall, tanned, his muscles rippling as he beat a tiny Babe while retaining so much control that he remembered to spare any part of her visible to the eye. That seemed even more grotesque than the beatings.

"And he only did it when he was sure there was no one in the house to hear," Babe whimpered. "No servants."

"And what did *you* do when he was beating you?" Sam asked.

"Why, I tried to get away from him, to lock myself in a room. Sometimes I managed to do it, but it was worse when I came out, or he broke the door in. Sometimes I tried to fend him off and begged him to stop, but— What *could* I do? He's over a foot taller than I am and a hundred pounds heavier."

"Didn't you ever think of calling the police?" Honey asked, bewildered by what seemed a stoical acceptance on Babe's part. Babe, who was . . . *who used to be* . . . so spunky and full of life, who had a funny quip for every occasion.

"I called the police once, but they wanted me to swear out a complaint. And how could I have Greg arrested? It would have been in the papers . . . all over Washington. His career would have been ruined! So I never called the police again."

"*His* career ruined?" Sam sputtered. "What about *you*? He was ruining you and by doing nothing you were guilty of complicity—a co-dependent, I believe, is what they call it!"

Babe broke out into wrenching sobs and Nora said, "That's enough! I'm calling Len Silver, and in the meantime, I'm declaring a moratorium on all discussion. Babe's going to rest and that means there'll be no more questions and answers. Do I make myself clear?" Honey mutely nodded and Sam only watched Babe's narrow shoulders heaving under the comforter.

Still, a last unasked question hung heavy in the air: *But why didn't you leave him before this, little Babe?*

\*   \*   \*

Once Dr. Silver left, after having verified that Babe's injuries *were* only external and prescribing a sedative, Sam asked Babe one more question. "There's still one thing I don't understand.

How could the prick—drunk enough at least to beat the hell out
of you—still be so much in control as to remember not to hit
you in the face?''

"Drunk? He doesn't drink! His father was an alcoholic. The
most he ever has is a glass of wine with dinner.''

"So what you're saying is that he always beat you while he
was stone sober, in cold blood, so to speak. But why? What
horrendous crimes did you commit?'' Sam asked.

"But that's it. I don't *know*. I used to try to figure out what
I did to get him so mad, and then I'd just not do *it* ever again,
but there was always something *new*. There was no way of
knowing beforehand what'd set him off. Sometimes it seemed
like such a *little* thing, like the time I forgot to order a special
wine he wanted to serve at a dinner party. Well, I *do* understand
why he was so upset *that* time. Secretary of State Wilson was
our guest of honor and it *was* a coup to get him to come to our
party at all, so it was only natural that Greg wanted to impress
him by serving a special wine. It was—'' she faltered. "Oh, God,
I can't remember— But anyhow, when he first found out we
didn't have the right wine he didn't make a fuss, so I thought it
was all right. But then, after the guests went home and the
caterer's people left, he threw me against the wall and—'' her
voice broke off.

It was so perfectly still in the room then that when Sam
finally broke the silence, her voice sounded like shattering glass.
"So, which was it *that* time, Babe? A *little* thing or one of the big
ones?''

"I'm not sure—it wasn't like with the tie. Once I said I didn't
like his tie and he got ticked off and wrapped it around my
neck— Well, I guess I *was* being critical that time, and he does
have this thing about criticism.''

"You know, you actually sound like you're *defending* him—
this sadist! What's wrong with *you*?'' Sam screeched.

"I guess I do sound like I'm defending him, but I'm just
pointing out that I *did* criticize him, so in some way I did bring
the beating on myself. . . .''

"God!'' Sam was so furious with Babe for accepting that she
was to blame that she felt like beating her herself. Instead she

turned to Nora: "So what do you have to say? Is it the duty of
the perfect wife never to criticize? In all your many marriages,
did *you* criticize your man or were you always the good little wife
seeing only to his comfort and keeping your mouth shut?"

"I always *tried* to be a good wife if that's what you mean,"
Nora said, "which also means giving as good as one gets. But
we've talked about this enough now. As Scarlett O'Hara once
said, 'Tomorrow is another day.' I think what we need now is
a bit of supper and a sip of the old vino."

"Vino . . ." Babe repeated, breaking into a grin. "Oh, I
remember—the name of the wine we were supposed to have. It
was a Beaujolais Nouveau, and the night we had the party was
the first day of the season the new wine was ready to drink."
Now that she remembered she settled back as if to pleasantly
reminisce. "It happens every fall. They ship it from France so
that it arrives in time for wine lovers all over the world to take
the first sweet taste of the season in tandem."

"That's lovely, but now you have to rest, help the sedative
along," Nora said as Honey and Sam exchanged looks of bewil-
derment. Babe sounded as if her mind had been affected.

"But I want to tell you about it so that you understand how
*important* Beaujolais Nouveau day is . . . a tradition. And Greg
*knew* that Secretary Wilson was a wine lover, you see."

"Well, that explains it all," Sam snapped. "Undoubtedly
you *deserved* to be slammed against a wall."

But Babe was oblivious. She had a bemused smile on her
face and repeated to herself: "The very first sweet taste of the
season . . ."

\*   \*   \*

Nora had dinner sent up on trays, but no one ate more than a
few bites and Babe, depressed again, kept repeating, "This time
I'm not going back, no matter what."

"Of course you're not," Honey soothed, but Nora said:
"There *is* one thing. Before, I said I wouldn't call your parents
until we discussed it, but under the circumstances I think I
should call them *now* so that they can see you, hear how all this

has been going on for so long. After all, your father is a judge—
he'll know what steps must be taken."

"But they've seen and they've heard and they've always
made me go back. Each and every time!"

Sam and Honey—their faces mirrored images of one another's horror—and even Nora stared at her in disbelief. "But
that can't be true," she said. "Your parents would never send
you back to a man who beat you. You're upset—"

"I'm upset but I'm telling the truth. So you *can't* call them.
They'll make me go back and I can't anymore," she said as if it
were a matter of her just being too tired. "I think I might do
something really bad . . . set Greg on fire like the woman who
spilled kerosene around her husband's bed, or maybe I'll just
kill *myself*. It would probably be easier."

"Babe!" Honey cried. "How can you say such a thing?"

"She doesn't mean it," Nora soothed, holding a cup of tea
to Babe's lips. "You mustn't say such things. Killing's so messy
and unnecessary. In this day of the easy divorce, no one has to
kill anyone, least of all one's self. One divorce and you'll be a
free woman. Free to start all over."

Babe repeated her words: "Free to start all over," and began
to relax until Honey said, "But I don't understand. *Why* did they
want you to stay? *Why* did they make you go back?"

Babe's eyes widened, surprised that all of them still didn't
understand. "Because they think that one of these days Greg's
going to be president and they want me in the White House with
him! The First Lady of the land! You know how Catherine
always said that the most important thing was to be a lady and
who could be more of a lady than *the* First Lady? Now I'll be a
divorcee and you know what *that* means?" She giggled before
she began to cry. "I'll be a little nobody again, the silly little fool
Catherine always said I was."

Now there was another question hanging oppressively in the
air. Was the fragile, nearly broken woman Babe was now strong
enough to survive not only the rigors of a divorce battle but the
united front of Greg and the Tracys? If she hadn't been able to
resist them before, when there'd been remnants of the old Babe,
how could she resist them now?

Nora wished she had the answer, but she didn't . . . not yet, but she sure as hell intended to work on it. "Everything will look better in the morning," she said. "Then, who knows, you might even *want* to see your parents and tell them your decision straight out so that they know you mean it. Now I must go see about a few things, but I'll be back in a little while to say good night."

Sam, already in an emerald-green satin nightgown, pacing back and forth and brushing her hair, held the door open for her. "And we'll be here waiting for you with bated breath."

"And well you should, my dear," Nora smiled, exiting.

" 'And *well you should, my dear*,' " Sam aped, closing the door after her. "What do you think she meant by *that*? I just bet it has something to do with the studio. I'm sure of it!" Then she began to beat at her hair so hard with the hairbrush, Honey thought that most likely she was pretending it was Nora she was beating. . . .

# FIVE

——————•◦•——————

Finally they were in bed—Sam and Babe in the king, Honey on the daybed—but they didn't turn off the lights. They waited for Nora to do that when she came back to make her good-nights, part of the ritual they'd always followed at a sleepover at the manor. First she would open a window wide. "It's the fresh air that puts the roses in the cheeks," she would say before she tucked them in, kissing them lightly, with Sam making a big thing out of shrinking back. But even that had been one of their bedtime rites, though Honey had always suspected it was mostly pretense on Sam's part. No matter how she felt about Nora, how could Sam *not* crave a motherly touch as she went off to sleep, as much as Babe craved it . . . as much as she, who had never experienced it, did.

Then Nora would turn off the lights and coo, "Sweet dreams," Honey believing the words to be more promise than mere wish. Occasionally Nora would say instead, "Nighty-night, now, don't let the bedbugs bite," and she and Babe would giggle, but not Sam. Rather, she would recite one of her silly rhymes:

> The only thing that's bound to bite
> In the middle of the night,
> With great pleasure and delight
> Is Nora, the dirty, rotten blight.
> That, you see, is my plight
> Because no matter how I fight,
> In the end she'll surely bite.
> Alack and alas, I know I'm right!

But Honey doubted that tonight Sam would recite or that she and Babe would laugh. They *were* thirty-something, chastened and subdued, and of all the specters that might haunt their dreams tonight, bedbugs would be at the bottom of the list.

*   *   *

"Are my little chickadees ready for the sandman?" Nora—burnt-orange taffeta peignoir rustling, her face lit up by a brilliant smile—asked when she returned.

Sam chirped, "All your chickadees are ready, Mommy Hen, and don't you look purty? How about a peek at the nightie underneath?" and Nora parted the peignoir to reveal a satin-and-lace confection.

"But surely all those peek-a-boo glimpses of creamy-skinned, rosy-tipped titties can't be all just for us chicks. Is there, perchance, a lover or a new candidate for the Nora Grant matrimonial sweepstakes already panting in your bed?"

"Forsooth, no. It's just a precaution—you wouldn't believe all the attractive men I keep meeting in my dreams," Nora joked as she opened a window, moved on to the tucking in, stooped to kiss Honey's and Babe's brows, but this time not Sam's, whose eyes narrowed at the omission, though she kept her tone playfully arch: "What? No bedtime kiss for Sammy girl?"

"Oh, I have something even *better* for you, Sam."

"You do?" Sam, caught off guard, sat up straight.

"Oh, yes, an announcement about the studio," Nora drawled. "As you've probably sensed, Grantwood Studio has been much on my mind of late. What to do with it since I never had the inclination or the skills necessary to run it, and none of the arrangements I've made have worked out satisfactorily, and—"

"Oh, for God's sake, Nora"—Sam's voice was ragged with tension—"will you get on with it?"

"You've waited so long for this resolution, Sam, I'm sure

you can bear with me for a few minutes more. As I was saying, I was cautious about making a decision, considering all the possibilities since it wasn't only I who would be affected by my decision. There was Hubie to be considered—"

"Hubie?" Sam was astonished. *What did Hubie have to do with the studio?*

"Of course, Hubie. It *is* my studio and he *is* my son."

"Isn't it a bit late for you to start remembering that little incidental?" Sam asked dryly.

Ignoring the question, Nora went on: "And then there was you, Sam, and your bloody conviction—how making moving pictures was in your blood as it was in your father's."

Sam grew unbearably impatient. It was on the tip of her tongue to remind her that there was also the matter of her trust fund to be taken into account if she was considering the possibilities, but she made herself hold back. Nora *was* smiling very sweetly, so who knew what she was going to say?

"And while I was considering the options, perplexed as to what to do, something quite extraordinary happened! Out of the blue I received an offer from an unexpected quarter!"

Honey's pulse quickened. Then the rumor she'd heard about an offer being made for the studio was true!

"What quarter?" Sam demanded, inner antennae quivering.

"I'm afraid that will have to remain my little secret."

"Did you tell them what to do with their offer?" Sam's voice was a hoarse whisper. "That they could stick it—?"

"Of course I didn't! It was an excellent offer and— Well, I'm talking to my lawyers about drawing up the papers."

"But the studio is *mine*! My sweet dream!" Sam cried.

"*Your* sweet dream!" Nora sneered, her smile disappearing. "We orchestrate our own dreams and they're only as sweet as our imaginations, and your dream was so sweet you assumed you were entitled to it without lifting a finger. All you ever did was demand and complain. What made you think that when it came down to choosing between *giving* the studio to you and getting a pile of money for it, I'd choose you? Because you're a charity and I'm a philanthropist or because you've been so loving a stepdaughter? Don't you know that there are *no* sweet dreams? There's only reality, just like in a marriage. We dream of how it will be, but then comes the real thing, and what it boils down to is how we deal with what *is* instead of how we dreamed it'd be. Isn't that right, Babe?"

Not expecting to be drawn in, Babe cried out, but Nora went on: "But in both dreams and marriages there's always a bottom line, and sometimes the bottom line is only a row of dollar signs as there might be in a divorce. Right, Honey?"

Honey stared at Nora. *How had they gotten from selling Grant-wood Studio to Babe's marriage, then to her own divorce?*

"*Your* bottom line might be a row of dollar signs, but there's another bottom line here," Sam burst out. "That the much-married Nora is the greedy whore I always knew she was. And I have a couple of questions for you. How greedy *exactly* is a greedy whore, and *where* is my trust-fund money?"

"You know the terms of your father's will. It's to be disbursed *when I think you're ready*. In the meantime, keep on dreaming. Who knows? One of these days you *and* your two friends here might wake up with the right answers."

"Go fuck yourself!" Sam spat out.

"Surely I taught you better manners than that, Sam," she chided. "Besides, it would be so much more fun to find a man to do that for me, and possibly more financially rewarding."

When she went to the door, Honey waited to see what she would say, having already dispensed with sweet dreams for all three of them. Then, as if ritual were too strong to break, she bid them: "Nighty-night, now, don't let the bedbugs bite."

"But *you're* the fucking bloodsucker and you've already done your biting," Sam said tiredly, spent, and when the door closed, the silence was broken only by Babe's whimpers.

Honey felt incredibly cheated. She had *believed* in Nora's sweet dreams. Yet the truth was that life's rich and early promise *had* eluded all three of them. Was it because Nora herself had never truly believed? And what about the ultimate question—could they still reclaim the promise of their youth, or, still so young, had they already run out of time?

*    *    *

For better or worse I've dropped my bombs, Nora thought
when she was back in her room. Now all that remained was to
wait for the fallout in the morning and begin the cleaning up,
just as they had in London during the war when she'd been but
a girl, half the age her three girls were now. But she was tired and
so afraid. Well, nobody ever said war wasn't hell. Then she went
to the phone. No girl was ever too old for reassurance, a bit of
warmth, and a few loving words. . . .

# SIX

———— •• ••• ————

earing Sam tossing, Honey called out, "Sam," in a whisper, not wanting to wake Babe, who had finally fallen asleep.

"Go to sleep, Honey. I don't want to talk."

She sounded so defeated, Honey thought miserably. Had Sam, like Babe, run out of steam? After all, Sam's mother had run out of steam early in the game. Was it possible that a propensity for that sort of thing was transmitted in the DNA and carried in the bloodstream just as Sam claimed the genius for making movies was? Was it possible that Sam would follow in her mother's footsteps? Like mother, like daughter . . . Isn't that what they said about her when she became the Honey Rose, TV's sex kitten? Like mother, like daughter . . .

But following in her mother's footsteps had always been the last thing she'd wanted. Her friends knew it; her father knew it. Why hadn't the man she married known it?

Then her thoughts, like mice scurrying around, switched back to Sam. How she wished she could help Sam, whose love had never faltered. Wasn't that what life's sweet promise was really all about? Love? Oh, Josh had promised her love along with a glorious future, but then he'd delivered only on his *own* version of love and a future that was hardly the future she'd envisioned for herself. He had promised her babies and a palace to live in, but the palace turned out to be only an empty house no matter how grand, with no babies to fill it, and now there was no future for them at all . . . not together.

She wondered if he too was lying awake tonight, contemplating the future, or was he too mourning the past? Or was he only

57

worrying that she was going to walk away with that quarter of a billion dollars, going to snatch his beloved Crown House away? Or was he asleep dreaming of the woman who'd been his wife, or was it the woman who'd been his star? Was he holding her in his arms, burying his lips in her throat, fondling her breasts, kissing her moist thighs, calling out her name in ecstasy? But was the name Honey, my sweet love, or Honey Rose, my lovely golden goose?

Oh, God, how he had cheated her! More than Nora had cheated them with *her* false promise of sweet dreams. Well, at least there would be the money. What had Nora said—that the money helped the pain go away? She hadn't said money was love. Still, if you used the money to make the pain disappear, why, then, it was *almost* as good as love, and if it couldn't make her *own* pain go away, it *could* help Sam's disappear.

"Sam," she whispered again.

"Why aren't you sleeping?" Sam grouched.

"It's not over, Sam. The business with the studio."

"Forget it. You heard her. My studio is gone."

"Not yet. A deal's only a deal when the names are on the dotted line. If you offered her as much money as those other people, why wouldn't she sell it to you instead?"

"Because selling the studio to them is as much about *getting* me as it is about money. She'd *prefer* to sell it to them. Besides, where would I get the money? From my trust fund she won't give me?"

"You'll get the money from me."

"You mean your settlement money? Are you crazy? I couldn't ask you to do that."

"You're not asking. I'm offering. Besides, I'm not *giving* you the money. We'll be equal partners—you'll make the movies, but I get to do the movies of my choice."

"Oh, Honey, I appreciate what you're trying to do, but owning a studio wasn't part of your dream for a new life."

"Dreams are like wardrobes, Sam, sometimes they need updating. And I *liked* what you said this afternoon—about owning my own studio and picking my own projects."

"Don't you know you can't go by anything I say? Suppose

I lost the money which represents fifteen years of your life? Suppose Nora is right—that I'm just an arrogant bitch who *thinks* she can run a studio, but who actually has a lousy track record when it comes to success."

"But I trust you even if you are an arrogant bitch."

"In spite of all my fuck-ups?"

"In spite of every last one."

"Hey, there weren't *that* many," Sam said then, and Honey could tell she was perking up.

"I know it's a risk, Sam, but so's living and loving and trusting someone enough to be your best friend. Besides, I told you—I don't care about the money as money. What would I do with it but put it in banks and live off the interest? Not nearly as much fun as owning a studio. And this way we both get a new deal."

"You almost have me convinced, but it won't work. For one, Nora won't sell it to me . . . to us, for the same price she's getting from that unexpected quarter. She wants to break it off in me. We'd have to offer her a hell of a lot more money than they are. At least a half—"

"A half of a billion dollars? Why, that's a fortune!" Honey cried, and Sam laughed, "If anyone should know it's you."

"But I guess it sounds about right. Grantwood Studio has to be worth at least as much as Royal Productions, and that's what the accountants figure *it's* worth, which is why we're asking for half of that as my community property. But no matter how much I end up with, the banks will lend us the rest. Josh always says that if you already have plenty of money, banks will kill themselves to lend you more of it."

"Yeah, but who knows what figure Nora will come up with. It could be one that might mean committing financial suicide before we even made our first movie—"

"Look, you're tired now. But in the morning you're going to be my old Sam, ready to come out fighting. We both will and we're going to make Nora an offer. I'm counting on you not to let me down, Sam. You won't, will you?"

"Well, if you put it that way—okay, it's a deal! We'll pitch the bitch! And who knows, before night falls I might end up being the president of Grantwood Studio, and then I can tell her where to stick it. Right, Honey Bunny?"

"Wrong, Sweet Sam. By nightfall, *I* might end up being the president of Grantwood Studio and you its VP."

"I might have known! Already the power and the money's gone to your head!"

# SEVEN

Babe moaned as she came awake, and Sam, switching on the bedside lamp, said, "I guess we woke you. I'm sorry."

"I'm not. I was having a nightmare. It was morning and Catherine and the Judge were here and they were yelling—"

"Is it *so* much worse for you to tell your parents than Greg that you're leaving him?" Honey asked, though she *knew* it was—telling them *anything* had always been hard for Babe.

"Well, they'll be so mad and Greg won't be—not at first. Each time afterwards, he's sorry and tries to make up, swearing it'll never happen again. He's very sweet then and always makes love to me."

"Makes love to you? You *do* mean sex?" Sam demanded.

"Yes, of course, sex."

"And you *let* him screw you right after he beat you up?"

"Well, not *right* after."

"But as soon as he says he's sorry?"

"Yes . . . I suppose."

"You suppose? Either you did or didn't. Which is it?"

"I don't know," Babe groaned. "Does it matter?"

"Yes, it *matters!* How do you think it sounds that you want a divorce because your husband beat you, but right *after,* you let him prong you? Does that sound like a woman who's been degraded and abused? It sounds like a woman who's turned on by the beatings. *Hurt me! I love it!*"

"But it wasn't like that! It was more like—like a woman who's about to be raped but it's hopeless to resist so she decides to lean back and enjoy it."

"Oh, my God, that's *revolting!* Insulting to any woman who's

61

ever been abused. And tell us, *did* you enjoy it? Did you love getting screwed by the man who'd just beaten you?''

"Of course not! It's just an expression. Accepting the inevitable. I was only trying to explain an attitude a helpless woman can assume. Why are you being so mean to me?''

"Yes, Sam," Honey said. "What was the point of Dr. Silver giving Babe sedatives if you're only going to upset her?''

"I'm just trying to get things straight in her own head.''

"But I told you, it's just an expression. Why would you assume that I enjoyed it?''

"Oh, Babe! We all know how you are when it comes to sex," Sam said, her voice gentle now.

"How *am* I when it comes to sex?" Babe's voice was ragged. "Go on, I want you to say it!''

Honey's heart beat fast. They were on dangerous ground here. Sam pushing, Babe on the defensive. Too much might be said and the secret that she and Babe had kept so long from Sam and Nora would come out and then there would be no going back.

"You were always so *greedy* for sex!" Sam's voice was soft despite the harshness of her words. "We always made a joke of it but the truth is that you *always* wanted to get laid, and you didn't care who, where, or how. . . .''

Honey held her breath, waiting for Babe's denial of what was essentially the truth—while Sam had always *talked* a good game of sex, it was Babe who *had* embraced it greedily. But Babe didn't answer and Honey was filled with relief and gratitude. She was sick to death of denial. What had it gotten them but membership in the club, the Hollywood Exes?

She looked at Babe then, so miserable, and at Sam lying next to her looking just as miserable, remorseful that she'd probably driven Babe further into depression. What had Nora said? That she'd always tried to maintain her sense of humor. She got out of bed to go sit on the edge of theirs and laughed.

"Oh?" Sam said. "Have I overlooked something even slightly humorous here? If so, I'd love to be filled in.''

"I was just thinking about that time Babe and I slept over when there was a big party going on. Cary Grant was here that night and Henry Fonda, and we decided to smuggle some bottles of wine upstairs. Remember?''

"Do I! How about you, Babe? Do you remember?'' Sam tapped her on the shoulder insistently until Babe gave her an angry shove back.

"Remember? How could I forget? You made me carry one of those bottles between my thighs and I couldn't even take a step, much less go up a flight of stairs. Then all of your folks' company came out into the hall to say good night as we went up to bed.'' Now she was struggling to choke back the laughter. "Nora thought something was wrong with me and kept asking if I was all right, and I kept saying I was fine but I was unable to move. Then your father gave me a boost from behind, half pushing, half picking me up, and then it was all over. I'll never forget that bottle slithering down, then rolling down the stairs with everybody's eyes glued to it until it landed right side up unbroken with everyone clapping like it was a feat of magic! Even Cary!

"Still, I was sure your father was going to send me home and Nora would write a note to my parents denouncing me as an alcoholic, and then the Judge would send me to that home for bad girls he was always threatening me with. But your father laughed and said he was going to stick that bit into one of his comedies and Nora said, 'You wouldn't have enjoyed it anyway. I sampled some of the same bottling and it was bloody sour.' But I still can't imagine how you thought that I'd make it up the stairs with that thing between my thighs.''

"You can't blame me for thinking you could,'' Sam said. "You always were a champ at managing big things between your thighs. I guess it's a knack some girls are born with. But seriously, I thought you could do it because you were always doing all those splits and things, that you had control of all those muscles. But fortunately, I already had a couple of bottles of wine stashed away in my panties drawer.''

"Speaking of panties, what about the bottle of wine you made me stash in *my* panties?'' Honey demanded. "And I had to walk up the stairs in front of everyone looking like I was pregnant. And I wasn't worried so much about the darn bottle falling out as I was that it would leak and Cary Grant wouldn't only think I was peeing in my pants, but peeing *red!*''

"If only it had happened like that!" Sam howled.

"Oh, yeah?" Honey cried. "What about me getting sick from the wine and throwing up in your closet all over your shoes? You really didn't think that was so funny at the time."

"No, I didn't," Sam admitted. "But how was I to know you'd get so polluted you'd mistake my closet for the bathroom and my boots for the toilet bowl? Now, Babe was a much-nicer-behaved drunk. All she did was dance for us in the buff."

"But she wasn't *completely* naked. She was wearing a scarf as she did her bumps and grinds against the hat stand."

"Of course I was wearing a scarf! I was doing my imitation of Isadora Duncan."

"Only I doubt old Isadora had a pair of bazooms like yours to wave around in the breeze," Sam snorted.

"It wasn't my fault if I was well developed. As a matter of fact, Sam, you were always insanely jealous of my tits."

"Actually, I feared that being so short you were top-heavy—that you were going to fall over flat on your face."

"At least I didn't have to wear padded bras like some very tall but underdeveloped individuals," Babe retorted.

"Of course you didn't wear a padded bra—how could you, when what you wore resembled a harness more than a bra?"

But instead of volleying, Babe turned morose again. "Catherine was always *so* embarrassed by my tits. She said it was déclassé to have so large a bosom . . . that only Jewish women, country singers, and actresses flaunted their obscene chests. She always made me get the bras that minimized."

Now Sam was sorry she'd brought up the topic. "Look, the truth is that that bazoomless barf bag was always a shit!"

"But if *she's* the shit, how come everything *I* touch turns to shit?"

"But we've *all* had our share of bad experiences, Babe," Honey said sadly. "Our soured marriages certainly."

"But whose marriage is *quite* as sour as mine, or as shitty? Sam's weren't and neither is yours."

"No, but *any* marriage that fails is soured," Honey said.

"And consider the statistics," Sam added. "Fifty percent of

marriages end up in divorce, and how do you know how shitty all those marriages are? So stop thinking you're the only one who steps into it. And we're not going to dwell on the past. We're going to forge on into the future, heads high. Remember our old pledge that we'd always stick together and emerge victorious because our hearts were strong, innocent, and pure? Are we going to lose the faith now?"

"Hell, no, we still go!" the three of them shouted in unison, another bit of their teenage ritual.

"Okay, put it there!" Then Honey stuck out her hand palm up, Babe put her hand on hers palm down, and Sam put her hand over both of theirs, and it was a pledge renewed. But then, as she went back to her own bed, Honey realized that the pledge no longer applied. Their hearts might still be strong—that was yet to be proven—even pure (and that was open to debate), but they were hardly innocent . . . hadn't been for a very long time. Not since they were fourteen and experiencing that first sweet taste of their season. . . .

# EIGHT

————— •••• —————

Babe had fallen asleep again, but Honey heard Sam still tossing restlessly. Then she heard a peculiar sound coming from the courtyard below. "Did you hear that noise, Sam?"

"No, but don't worry. The security alarm would have gone off if someone was out there."

"Listen, there it is again."

"It's the garage door closing. It makes a whooshing sound going up and down. But who—?" Then they heard the screech of tires, and Sam leaped from the bed to run to the window with Honey fast at her heels in time to see Nora's silver Jaguar rounding the curve before disappearing down the driveway.

"I wonder where she's going this time of night," Honey mused. "She was dressed for bed a couple of hours ago."

"I bet I know," Sam hissed. "Remember when she came back in her nightgown and I asked her if she had a lover or potential husband waiting in her bed? Well, I guess he wasn't in her bed or she wouldn't have to drive to get to him. Where else would she be headed at this hour in full makeup and a peek-a-boo nightie with her tits spilling out all over the place unless, of course, she's turned pro?"

"I'm sure I don't know," Honey said, "but I'm heading back to bed. We've got a big day ahead of us tomorrow."

They were back in bed only a minute or so when Sam said, "It's not a lover. It's her next husband. I'm sure of it!"

Honey sighed. "How can you be so sure?"

"Because everyone has a pattern, and a woman who's been

married so many times has to have one all her own. And what
has been Nora's pattern? Not that bull she spouts about the first
time for love, the second time, blah, blah, blah. Still it's a
pattern by the numbers.

"One, she marries a rich and important man; two, she
sheds him by one means or another; three, she picks up all the
marbles before moving on to the next sucker to repeat the
pattern all over again. And that's what she's doing now. After
marrying my father and disposing of him—I'm still not convinced she didn't murder him—she's picking up the marbles
by selling off the studio, and probably the manor too. I
wouldn't be surprised if she already has it on the market. Anyway, you can see the pattern—she's already picked out her
next husband."

"And who might *he* be?" Honey asked, not ready to accept
Sam's theory. As usual, she was letting her imagination run
wild. "Do you have any likely candidates in mind?"

"Well, I do, kind of, but I'd rather not say since I'm not sure
if the person I have in mind is rich enough for her."

"In that case, once and for all, *I'm* going to sleep."

Still, she couldn't stop thinking about Nora—how she'd
said that there were no sweet dreams and that one of these
days not only would Sam wake up to reality and the right
answers but she and Babe as well. It was as if she'd suddenly
*turned* on them at a time when they all were particularly vulnerable. *Why?*

She thought of all the charges Sam had made against Nora
through the years. *"She's a witch who manipulates everyone. She
wants us all to fail so then she can play savior—God! She's as avaricious for love as she is for money. She wants everyone to love only her,
and if you don't, she punishes you. She's a vampire who lives by sucking everyone's blood dry. . . ."*

She and Babe had never taken Sam's melodramatic charges
seriously. They'd put it down to a natural enough jealousy of
any woman her father might have married. Also, Sam *was* the
girl who had always believed in fairy tales, in enchanted castles
and princesses, and what was a fairy tale without a wicked

stepmother? They'd always felt that Nora really loved Sam as
they themselves loved and trusted Nora. Even her own father,
Teddy, whose judgment she trusted, had always said Nora was
a woman you could believe in. But tonight, Nora had acted in
such a fashion as to change all the rules.

So what *was* the truth? Was she the witch who manipulated
the people around her, even programmed them for failure—all
three of them had certainly failed at marriage—so that she could
save them and earn their slavish love? Only Sam had resisted,
and Sam *was* indeed being punished now with the loss of the
studio and maybe the manor as well. . . .

And there was the mystery of Hubie. *Had* he been punished
by being banished from the magic kingdom for loving someone
more than his mother, as Sam always claimed? It was true that
he had never so much as visited at the manor in all these years
as far as she knew. What kind of a woman could so exile her
own child? *Not* a truly loving one.

Once one started doubting, the possibilities were infinite,
she reflected.

Why *had* Nora turned on her and Babe tonight for no appar-
ent reason? Was it a warning? *Love me more than Sam or off with
your heads.* Or were they being punished too? Was it possible
that Nora was jealous even of her love for her father, Teddy, or
was she still angry that she had loved Josh too much?

Was Sam right about where she was headed tonight? On the
old marriage hunt again and with what goal in mind, considering
her by-now-infamous quote? And *what* about those marriages?
Even if they weren't *all* conceived in greed, as Sam contended,
they couldn't have *all* been only for love either. How many of
them had been approached *only* with cold calculation? Indisputa-
bly—at least as far as her marriage to T.S. was concerned—Nora
*had* ended up with all the marbles. . . .

So, who was she? Warm and loving woman or manipulator
without peer? Surrogate mother or avaricious whore? Or was
she but a charming fraud like so many others from whose lips
flowed lies, sometimes sweeter than truth and sometimes as vile
as a good marriage gone bad?

Somehow she had the feeling that if they only knew the truth about who Nora truly was and the real truth about all those marriages, she and Sam and Babe might find the answers as to why their own lives had taken so wrong a turn. They might even find a way to go so that they could once again savor that first sweet taste of the season. . . .

# PART TWO

# THE FIRST TIME AROUND

London, 1943–1951

# NINE

————— •◦•◦ —————

Blond, blue-eyed, and curvaceous, with a good nature and an eye for the lads (and they for her), pretty Natalie Hall changed her name to Nora (thinking it more sophisticated) when she left the Cotswolds to go to a London at war soon after her mother, her last loved one, passed on. It wasn't so much a matter of employment. She was more concerned with having a lively time of it—there were no young men left at home.

Part of the baggage she carried to London was her virginity, which would have stunned her old neighbors, who would have wagered that the high-spirited eighteen-year-old crumpet was a bit of a tart. But the truth was, Nora had always coupled her love of a good time and admiration of men with a healthy self-respect, holding neither her person nor virtue cheaply. Also, she was a romantic. She wasn't waiting for marriage to yield up her virginity, but true love.

Untrained for most work but with a repertoire of bawdy songs (her sole legacy from her mother, the barmaid), she found a job singing in a second-rate cabaret, which suited her fine. Realistic about her limited talents, she wasn't looking for a career. But making up for her only fair voice with flair and enthusiasm, she was a big favorite with the boys in uniform, including the handsome Captain Hubert Hartiscor, with whom she fell in love at first sight. Then she was grateful that Hubert's job organizing entertainments for the fighting men precluded his leaving London. He wasn't about to kiss her hello only to kiss her good-bye a fortnight later.

She was told that he was of an artistic bent with an eye for the look of the thing and an intuitive sense of what was in good

73

taste and what was deplorable. But all she really knew about him was that she had never known anyone as charming or as beautiful, and if she had known how to, she would have written an ode to his beauty: the mane of yellow hair waving back from the manly brow, the chiseled nose, the square jaw, the cleft chin, the dimples that in no way took away from his masculine image. The odd thing about her finding him so beautiful was that anyone seeing them together always remarked how much alike they looked, down to the exact coloring, so much so they might have been brother and sister. Then Nora always said: "But there's nothing sisterly about my feelings."

Nora also knew that Hubert talked as sweetly as he appeared, with the kind of manners and style she'd never before encountered, and that he enjoyed a good time and seemed to find her as attractive as she found him. What she didn't know about him would have filled a book.

While she recognized that he was upper class—only a nit couldn't see that—she had no idea that his father, Lord Jeffrey, was the twelfth Earl of Hartiscor and one of the richest men in the country, the family's landed estate exceeding a hundred thousand acres of fertile countryside and a few hundred acres of even more fertile London brick and cement. She also wasn't aware that, in addition to being a member of the House of Lords, Lord Jeffrey was a prestigious member of society on many different levels and the intimate of every person of consequence in his radius, even the prime minister himself.

But it didn't take long before more knowledgeable friends filled her in, warning her that she was wasting her time if she was silly enough to fall in love with the likes of Hubert Hartiscor. "If you believe there's a chance in hell he'll marry you, then you'd believe that I'm the queen," one friend told her. "And what's more, laddie doesn't have a shilling. Without an allowance from the old boy he can't set himself up in style, much less a girlfriend. And what do you think would happen to that allowance if Da got wind that he's mucking around with the likes of you—a barmaid's daughter?"

The consensus of opinion among her friends was that she should sleep with Hubert if she must, but that she shouldn't expect anything but a few nights of rolling around in the sack, after which he would most likely give *her* the sack, which was what men like Hubert Hartiscor always did with girls like her.

But Nora was too young and enthralled to listen to any cautionary advice. While a more experienced woman might have recognized certain flaws in Hubert, Nora had never even heard of a flawed diamond, much less a flawed character. But at the same time she had too much common sense to have expectations of marriage. Besides, what she felt for Hubert was wildly beyond the consideration of whether he would marry her, and, at this point, hardly her dilemma. Her problem was that while she ached to surrender herself to Hubert, yearned for the very feel and smell of him, for the swell of him pressing against and into her, he himself had made no move in that direction.

Not that they weren't friends. She thought she would never again have such a wonderful friend. They always had so much to say to each other and enjoyed each other's company to the exclusion of everyone else's. And not that there weren't intimate moments—murmured conversations, heads close together; laughter, lips inches away; long walks, fingers interlaced; dancing, cheek-to-cheek, thigh-to-thigh, even belly-to-belly; friendly hugs and sweet kisses, occasionally even hungry kisses and lingering good-nights, as if the nights themselves were too good to let go of.

Yet, that was as far as it had gone. There'd been no foreplay, no entrance, no final thrust, no cries of joy and release, and Nora—craving sexual fulfillment until she was almost ill with it—came to the conclusion that Hubert was just too much the gentleman to make the first move. Then beyond caring about ladylike delicacy, she decided that she herself would make that first move and invited him to her flat for dinner, which she'd often done before but in a casual way. This time it would be a very special dinner.

By trading away her meat rations for months, she was able to dig up a decent roast, and on the big night she set the table with a lace tablecloth and pink candles in Bristol blue candlesticks. As for herself, her blond hair was freshly washed and set—a wave dipping over one eye like a film star—her eyebrows darkened with brown pencil, her lashes twice coated with cake mascara, and her mouth painted a shade of lipstick called Raven Red. And underneath a gossamer negligee, she wore the kind of intimate apparel no decent shop carried—lingerie that left nothing to the imagination—just black-lace scraps and a shocking-pink garter belt that held up the last pair of black net stockings she owned.

When the buzzer sounded, she rushed to the door, at the last second thinking that their dinner would, after all, wait, and she didn't give a bloody damn if the bloody roast dried up like a bone. She herself had already waited far too long.

She flung open the door and, without even giving Hubert a chance to take a good look at her in all her glory, threw herself at him, causing him almost to drop the bottle of wine he was carrying in one hand. (He *did* drop the bunch of flowers that he held in the other.) But when he drew back, she laughed, thinking that she had really knocked him for a loop. She picked up her posies and pulled him into the room, slamming the door shut after him. But then he stood unmoving, his eyes hooded so that she couldn't read them, taking all of her in. Naturally he wanted to savor the look of her, she thought. That *was* the idea, and any second he would move to touch her, say something, embrace her, crush her in his arms.

She laughed again, removing the wine from his inert hand to place the bottle and the flowers on the table. Then she shrugged off the negligee and went to him, standing only an inch or two away, the better for him to take in the full image of her in her high-heeled pink marabou-trimmed slippers, breasts spilling from the inadequate bra, thighs emerging from the lacy scanties, garters meeting stockings with a creamy expanse of flesh in between. But Hubert remained mute and, unable to bear his silence another moment, she cried, "Don't you have anything to say? Have you been struck deaf and dumb? Oh, say something, Hubert! Say something wonderful!"

Still, rather than coming toward her to take her in his arms, to mash his lips against hers, to force her mouth open with a demanding tongue or run his hands down her body, he remained motionless as if he had turned into a pillar of salt.

Was he petrified with desire or simply terrified by her bra-
zenness? Nora agonized. Then, when she saw a look of intense
pain cross his beautiful face, she herself grew terrified. "What
is it, love? What—?" In a frenzy she slid her arms around his
neck and, placing her hands on the back of his neck, rubbed her
body against his. Then she drew his head down to hers so that
she could press her lips to his, attempt to force his lips open
with her tongue. When that still didn't make him move, she ran
her fingers over his groin feverishly, groping to find an erection
. . . *which simply wasn't there.*

"Oh, my sweet Nora," he finally spoke. "I'm so sorry."

"What are you sorry about, love?" she asked quickly, smiling, trying to hide her disappointment. Her friend Rose, who
had been around the block more than a few times, had told her
that this sort of thing happened frequently—blokes getting so
excited that instead of a hard-on they had a limp-on. "These
things happen, Hubert love . . . but we'll take care of that in no
time." She reached for his testicles again—to cup them, mound
them, squeeze them. And then she felt for his penis, to fondle
it, rub it persuasively with the heel of her palm. When she still
didn't feel it respond, she took his hand and placed it between
her breasts so that he could feel their heat and then between her
thighs so that he could feel their wetness, and when he only
threw his head back, not in exultation but in a gesture of defeat,
she placed his hand under her panties and forced it to rub
against her there.

"Don't," he muttered as if in profound distress.

"Shh!" she whispered, unzipping his fly to find the opening
in his shorts to free his penis so that it could emerge in all its
fiery tumescence . . . but then she found it wasn't tumescent at
all, but *flaccid.*

She fell to her knees to wet it with her kisses, to caress it with
her lips, to make love to it with her tongue, to take it in her
mouth, to suck on it, to lick at it, to tease it gently with her teeth,
but the only thing that happened was that he put his hands to
either side of her head and forced it back, and she fell back on
her heels to look at him pleadingly. "What am I doing wrong?
Tell me what to do!"

He looked down at her, his eyes filled with tears. "It won't help. Don't you understand? *Nothing* will help!"

"But why not?" she raged. "Why don't you want me like I want you? Aren't I good enough for you just to *want* me? I never asked you to marry me or even to love me. I just want you to *make* love to me. Aren't I good enough for that?"

"Too good," he whispered. "I thought you understood."

"Understood what?"

"Understood that I have never in my life loved a woman . . . made love to a woman. . . ."

At first she was bewildered, but when she finally understood, she felt humiliation coursing through her. She struggled to her feet from her kneeling position and stared down at herself—at the absurd underwear, the silly suspender belt and obvious net stockings, the foolish satin mules. Never had she felt so pathetic.

She kicked off the slippers, tore at her stockings, tugged at the garter belt until its fastenings gave way and she pulled it off, still grotesquely attached to the torn stockings. But her rage was unabated. She ripped off her bra, pulled at her panties until they were in tatters. "I'd like to kill you!" she screamed, moving to the table to pick up dish after dish and send it crashing to the floor.

He rushed over to pull her to him to comfort her somehow, but it was so far from what she needed that it only enraged her further. "What were you doing? Playing with me? Laughing behind my back with your fairy boys at the barmaid's daughter who was mad about the elegant gentleman and just grateful for his attentions? How could you be so cruel to someone who loved you so? Why, in God's name, did you do it?"

"Because I love you, Nora."

"Oh, no, don't you dare say that to me!"

"I love you," he said again. "And I tried *so* hard! I wanted so much to love you like a real man. You're such a wonderful woman—a woman any man would die to make love to. And I thought that if it could happen with anyone it would happen with you," he cried, the tears rolling down his cheeks.

She believed him, and that was the worst of it—the feeling

that she'd been cheated of the greatest love story ever told. She
fell into his arms to sob against his chest, and he picked her up
and carried her into the bedroom, laying her naked body tenderly on the bed. Then he undressed and kneeled over her to
lower his head to her there and made love to her with his lips
and tongue. It wasn't *quite* the same as man-woman love, but it
*was* love—a gift of love, she thought, and when she climaxed she
cried out before she cried real tears. Then they licked the tears
from each other's faces and spent the night in each other's arms.
In the morning they swore the eternal love of best friends. Still,
Nora wondered, would she ever love another man like she had
... *did* ... love Hubert Hartiscor?

# TEN

———————— ••••• ————————

Only a week after she and Hubert had spent the night in each other's arms, Nora, in a knockout satin gown, was singing the first verse of "Roll me over," when Corporal John Wayne from Butte, Montana, loped into the Cock 'n' Bull with his buddies. Johnny, whom his pals referred to as "the Duke" because that was what the movie star with whom he shared his name was called—encouraged by dares from his fellow Yanks—asked Nora if she would like to do some rolling over in the clover with the best cocksman in the whole U.S. of A. "It'll be an experience you'll never forget," the Duke promised. But then he almost dropped in shock when she invited him to go home with her to prove it.

\*   \*   \*

Waiting for him to come out of the lavatory, Nora lay on top of the chenille bedspread still in her dress and sandals, more nervous than aroused, thinking that the Duke would want to undress her himself. This was the big moment. Before morning came she would know what it meant to be made love to by a real man—an expert "fuck artist," as the corporal himself had bragged. And at last it would be over. She would be virgin territory no more, and what was still a mystery would all become clear.

Then she remembered her stockings. Johnny, in the throes of passion, might remove them too roughly and she couldn't risk a ladder. She sat up to remove her shoes, stockings, and suspender belt, then lay back again and tried not to think of Hubert, with the tears rolling down his cheeks.

80

Finally, the Duke emerged and she was shocked to see that his upper half was still fully clothed, his tie only loosened, which made his exposed penis—as long and lanky as the Duke himself, but standing at attention—seem ridiculously out of place. And she thought that if Hubert were there, they would both probably laugh at how silly it all was.

But Hubert wasn't there—only she and the Duke were, and she waited for him to approach her, to kiss her and fondle her, to murmur sweet nothings in her ear before he took off her clothes. But as he loped over to her on his bowed legs, he said, "Pull up your dress and take off your panties."

*He wasn't going to undress her, after all!*

Well, he should know, she thought. He was a real man, a cocksman by his own admission, and thoroughly experienced. Maybe it *was* sexier this way, he still in the upper pieces of his uniform, she in her dress, so she wriggled out of the pink step-ins, throwing them to the floor, and pulled her dress up to her waist. Then, quickly, he was on top of her, crushing her, each of his hands mauling a breast through the satin, and she thought that this must be what was called foreplay and how lucky it was that a man had two hands and a woman two breasts to make everything work out so evenly.

But the foreplay was over by the time she even finished thinking the thought, and his penis was masterfully attempting to find its rightful home, straining against her virginal membrane but getting nowhere. "Jesus!" he muttered, the sweat dripping from him and staining her dress. "Don't you English girls even have a hole? Maybe you'd better blow me."

Something clicked inside her head then and she wanted to tell *him* to blow it . . . right out his barrack bag. But in for a penny, in for a pound, and he was already on top of her and she was already lying under him, and her dress was probably already ruined. She might as well get it over with.

"Oh, we English girls have holes all right—if we get a real man with a real cock who knows how to fill it!"

"I'll show you a real cock!"

Straining with frustration and panting, he pounded away unmercifully, the thrusting growing more furious and vicious with each shove until she could feel herself tearing and him entering. Then, as if the sound were far away, she heard a groan and realized that it was *hers*, one of pain. Moments later, she heard another—the Duke's—as he erupted within her, and she groaned again as he collapsed on her chest, his weight crushing the breath from her. She waited a few polite seconds while a line of a ditty danced in her head:

> Thank you kindly, sir, she said,
> As he broke her maidenhead.

Then she said, "Would you be so kind as to get off? You're crushing me."

He rolled off. "Did you—?"

She guessed at his meaning. "Not really, cocksman."

"I'll finger-fuck you if you want," he offered generously as befitted a Duke, a bit of *noblesse oblige*. "Personally, I don't go in for diving the muff, if you get my meaning."

"I do and that's all right, I don't go in for it myself. And I'll pass on being fucked by a finger, if you don't mind, since if that's what I *had* in mind, I've got ten of me own."

\* \* \*

When Nora discovered that she was pregnant and pondered her options with Hubert, he asked her if she really wanted the baby, and when she said yes—that she was already filled with love for it—he proposed a "marriage of sweet convenience."

"A marriage of sweet convenience . . ." she rolled the phrase over her tongue. "But who am I going to marry? You don't mean the Duke? He's long gone. Besides, I wouldn't marry him even if he was a real duke or even a king."

"Marry *me*, Nora."

She looked at him in shock, then in bemused sorrow, before she asked, "And who would it be convenient for, besides me?"

"For the baby, of course, and me . . ."

"You?" she scoffed. She didn't believe he really meant it. He was just being kind and talking nonsense. "I can just picture how convenient it would be for you to marry me, two months' preggers with the bastard of a Yank."

*God, what a nit I was! For the same results, I could have picked a nice Yank.*

"What would your father say . . . *do* if you married a girl who sings at the Cock 'n' Bull even if he didn't know she was already two months gone? He'd more than not have a stroke."

"No, not really." Hubert's laugh was just barely bitter. "Perhaps if it were my brother, Rupert, he who is beyond reproach, Father might be put off somewhat. After all, the woman Rupert marries will be the future Countess of Hartiscor. But his younger son, the charming but very black sheep in the family—? He probably won't turn a hair."

"I don't believe you're serious."

"But I am. Very serious. Even sincere."

"Well, even if your father didn't perish from shock, he'd cut you off without a quid. . . ."

"Look, when I proposed a marriage of convenience I meant exactly that—for both of us. The old boy is quite on to me and more than fed up with my little . . . er, shall we call them peccadillos? Actually, he's been threatening to cut off my allowance for months now. But if we were to wed and you were pregnant with my child, he'd be reassured. Who could doubt the manhood of a chap lucky enough to be married to a lusty woman like Nora Hall? Especially when the chap's already planted the noble Hartiscor seed in the rich, luscious loam of her? What I suspect will happen is that Father will be so thrilled he'll give me an allowance three can live on very nicely. Do it for us both and for the baby," he begged, gazing into her eyes the exact shade of blue as his own. "And who knows—maybe you'll even make a real man of me."

That was the clincher. "Oh, Hubert, do you mean it?" she screamed in delight. "I warn you, I'm not a quitter."

He laughed. "That's exactly what I'm counting on."

It was an offer and a challenge that Nora couldn't refuse and she vowed to herself that she would do everything in her power to make the marriage work. A marriage of sweet convenience was already all the sweeter when you loved a man *so much* you'd be willing to die for him, much less just live for him.

Still, much as she hated the idea of lying—passing off the baby as Hubert's—it bothered her even more to tell Lord Jeffrey that they were just now getting married when she was already pregnant. "It's embarrassing. It makes me look like a you-know-what."

"All right. We'll just tell him we're getting married and won't say a word about your being preggers. We'll wait a couple of months and then we'll announce it. You won't be the first bride who ever gave birth to a seven-month baby."

"That'll be even worse. In a couple of months I'll be showing, then I'll not only look like a liar but an idiot too."

"In that case, there's only one thing to do—tell Father that we were married three months ago. Then we can say you're already two months gone with no problem."

"I guess that'll have to do, only I hate all this lying."

"You *are* an old-fashioned girl, my darling. Don't you know that a few lies keep things interesting?" Hubert laughed. "But since we *are* going to tell Father that we're already married, we'll tell him right away. Then we can get married later, secretly but leisurely."

Later . . . secretly . . . leisurely . . . It didn't matter. All that mattered was that she and Hubert loved each other and would be united both spiritually and legally. And the rest would follow as surely as the night the day. . . .

# ELEVEN

⸺•◦••⸺

Dressed in her best—a two-piece pink rayon with hat to match—and quaking in her four-inch heels, Nora was ready, though their appointment with Lord Jeffrey was still hours away. She couldn't have been more nervous if they'd been going to Buckingham Palace to take tea with the queen.

Hubert tried to reassure her that things would go smashingly. "You'll see. In his way, Father's a man with a very clear vision. That's why Churchill depends on him so, even had Father along when he met with Roosevelt to draw up the Atlantic Charter. He'll see clear to your heart and then he'll love you almost as much as I do."

Since Hubert didn't love her the way she yearned to be loved, what did it matter if Lord Hartiscor loved her as much? she wondered. But she couldn't say this to Hubert. It would only bring that look of helpless pain to his face, and since neither smiles nor tears would change anything, she preferred to see him smiling. She herself felt enough pain for two.

"Why would he love me as much as you do? Is he *daft*, then, like you?" she teased. "But it must be me who's daft even going there today."

"Don't worry so. We have an advantage. You're the picture of my sister, Anne, and he adored her."

"I didn't even know you had a sister."

"Yes. Five years older than I, so I was still a boy when she ran off to Australia. She married a chap from the outback and we never saw her again."

"Oh, that's awful. And your father? What did he do?"

"He tried to be in touch, but Annie said she was no longer

85

a Hartiscor. We should just *consider* her dead. After that, Father refused to talk about her even after Mummy died. But she'd always been his favorite, and I know he still thinks about her. I've seen him staring for hours at the old snaps of her he keeps locked in his desk."

"That's so sad. But why did she run off like that? Wanted the family to think of her as dead?"

"I'm not sure, but there was always bad blood between her and Mummy. Anne always thought Miranda—that was my mother's name—was jealous of her and hated her because Father favored her. It *did* seem as if Mummy couldn't stand the sight of Anne."

"Still, she must have been crushed when Anne ran off."

"Actually, she seemed relieved," Hubert laughed. "But then she still had me, *her* favorite. Looks went a long way with Miranda, you see, and she always said I was the most smashing of her litter, as well as the only one who was full of fun, just like her. Father always claimed she was spoiling me rotten, not that he did much to stop her. But I suppose he wasn't that wrong. I *am* a bit of a rotter, you know." He smiled at her beguilingly.

"Oh, hush. I don't want to hear you say that, not even in fun. But what about your brother, Rupert?"

As always, when she questioned him about his older brother who was off fighting the Germans, his face closed up. "What do you want to know about Rupert?"

"Well, you said your father was crazy about Anne and your mother favored you over Anne. Did she favor Rupert too?"

"Hardly, but she didn't dislike him the way she disliked Anne—it was more that Rupert wasn't her cup of tea. He never laughed, was more brooding than cheerful. Miranda always said Rupert was born old, without a bit of charm. And while he was the good son, very well behaved, Mummy just didn't give too many good marks for those qualities. No, it was I who dear Mummy always took into her bed to tickle and giggle with and play little bedtime games."

"And your father? Did he treat you and Rupert alike?"

"He tried, but it was pretty clear whom *he* preferred. Not

that I blame him. If you were Father, a man of accomplishment boasting one of Britain's greatest fortunes and everyone's respect, whom would you prefer? The good son or the one that's not only a black sheep but the family clown?"

Nora protested, but Hubert hushed her. "It's true and I'm the first to own up to it. But Father tries to make the best of it—*me*, that is. Stiff upper lip, you know, and he keeps trying to find a niche for me so that I won't be left entirely in the cold when he chucks it and Rupert becomes the Earl of Hartiscor, unless, of course, I get lucky."

"What do you mean—*lucky?*"

"Well, I'm next to inherit if Rupert buys it in the bloody war. . . ." Hubert grinned.

"Oh, Hubert, that's a terrible thing to say . . . even to joke about!"

"It would be if I didn't hate Rupert's guts quite so much."

Nora dropped the subject. *Poor Hubert!* It must have been terribly hard for him to be the black sheep or even the family clown when there was another son whom his father respected, the very same son who would inherit. On the other hand, it had to be hard for Rupert too to have been the one second in his mum's heart—the son she never tickled or took into her bed, with whom she never played little bedtime games.

*　*　*

Lord Jeffrey, taking both her hands in his, held Nora's eyes with a sharp, shrewd gaze and Nora's heart dropped into her stomach. While she hadn't expected him to love her, as Hubert had said he would, she had hoped that he would accept her. But the way he was looking at her now, she was afraid he knew instinctively that she was an impostor.

But shockingly, Lord Jeffrey kissed her on both cheeks. Then he said that he was delighted that she and Hubert were married and that soon he would be a grandfather. Then, even more shocking, he not only granted Hubert a generous increase in allowance, he also asked them to make their home with him.

"This is a very large house, my dear, and of course Hartiscor Castle is even more enormous, and both homes are very, very empty with everyone gone—"

When his voice drifted off, Nora presumed that he was thinking of his late wife, the cheerful Countess Miranda, and Anne, the daughter he had loved so much, but he went on without mentioning either. "It seems like years since Rupert went off to war and Hubert moved out to live on his own the way children will. And with so much of my staff—they were like old friends, really—off to do their bit for the effort, I really am at a loss. You'll be doing me a great favor, Nora, gracing my home with a real family again. Oh, yes, I'm in great need of a woman's presence, to organize things and create a warm atmosphere. And there's always so much entertaining to do. Beyond me, really. What a relief it will be to have so charming a young woman as my hostess."

Nora noted that he had said *"will be"* instead of *"would be"* . . . as if it were all settled.

"But you have to understand, Lord Jeffrey, that I know nothing about these things—about grand houses like this." She gestured wildly at the opulent furnishings, the crystal chandeliers, the walls hung with tapestries and paintings. "Why, this house is practically a palace. And I couldn't know less about entertaining the kind of people who—" she stopped abruptly and smiled. "Oh, you're just twitting me, Lord Hartiscor, like Hubert is always doing, aren't you?"

"But I'm quite serious. And you must call me Jeffrey."

"But I wouldn't even know what to say to the kind of people you entertain. They would most likely laugh at me . . . at my ignorance, at the way I speak. And to tell you the truth, Lord Jeffrey, I don't even know a port glass from a sherry glass. As for my clothes, I might have some idea of what I shouldn't wear, but not what I *should*—"

Lord Jeffrey waved his hand. "Mere trifles. I won't take no for an answer. I already consider the matter settled. My only regret is that by marrying in secret you two cheated me out of the pleasure of a grand wedding. Still, we must toast your marriage and drink to the marvelous coming event—the birth of your and Hubert's child."

He pulled the bell cord, and when an elderly man answered the summons, he introduced Nora as proudly as he might have introduced one of the royal princesses before telling the old gentleman, "We are making *two* toasts today, so be sure to bring both a port *and* a sherry. And Edward, you sly dog, be sure to bring out those bottles I know you've been hoarding, waiting for this bloody war to be over. I have a strong feeling victory is at hand. Don't you think so, Hubert?"

"Oh, positively, Father," Hubert agreed, puffing on a cigarette contentedly. But to Nora it seemed almost as if he were, by some invisible line, removed from the proceedings.

Then Jeffrey called after the butler, "Oh, Edward, be sure to bring glasses for yourself. You must join in our toast to the new Lady Hartiscor."

*Lady Hartiscor!* Now Nora really felt the impostor and regretted having told Jeffrey that they were married—it was bad enough to be passing off Duke Wayne's child as a Hartiscor. They would have to get married in a hurry so that at least they would have only one lie on their mutual conscience.

As Edward filled first the Waterford port glasses and then the sherry, Nora could hardly fail to get her father-in-law's point. This was her first lesson. The port glasses were tall and long-stemmed with a small bowl on top; the sherry glasses had shorter stems and were tapered. And, of course, she would never again *not* know the difference between the two. Simple. If only all of it were as simple.

Lord Jeffrey chuckled, as if reading her mind. "Nearly all problems are solvable for a bright young woman. Before you know it, you'll know everything Edward knows, and you'll soon discover that that in itself is no small accomplishment. As for Hubert, don't let him deceive you. He's fond of hiding his lights under a bushel, but he knows more than he lets on about many things—art, literature, decoration. Miranda always said Hubert's eye was infallible. When she herself was in doubt about what gown to wear she often consulted him, and he a mere boy then. Rupert, on the other hand, has no eye at all. Before he went off to war his only interest was the business of money. 'Money is what makes the world go round,' he said even when he was a very young chap. But be that as it may, you must get Hubert to advise you on your wardrobe.

"And when it comes to charities, Hubert will be able to help you out there too. He's always been good at running things for various charities. Fund-raising efforts, you know. Everyone assumes this success is due to Hubert's inestimable charm, but I believe he has a remarkable flair for organization even though he'd be the last to admit it. And it's a shame to let all his talent go to waste. You'll have to get him to share it all with you, my dear. Left on his own, Hubert has a tendency to slack off, but you mustn't let him—you must persevere so that Hubert will. And I'm sure you're a young lady with talents of your own. You and Hubert will each teach the other. That's only as it should be in a good marriage."

Suddenly, Hubert—silent the whole time his father had discussed him, as if he weren't in the room—drawled, "Was that how it was with you and Mummy, Father? Each teaching the other as it should be in a good marriage?"

Jeffrey acknowledged this question with a dark look before he remembered to smile. "Oh, I think Nora and I are in agreement as to what constitutes a good marriage, my boy."

While Nora took note that Lord Jeffrey hadn't really answered Hubert's question, she realized that one way or another, she and the Earl of Hartiscor had already made some kind of a pact. Then she remembered her own mother advising her, "Be careful who you be making your bargains with, me girl . . . that it isn't the devil himself."

But Jeffrey was no devil—he was not only younger than Hubert had led her to believe, he was much warmer, and she reflected how really fortunate she was to have not only Hubert but Lord Jeffrey as her friend. Really, more than she had bargained for . . . much, much more. . . .

# TWELVE

N ora and Hubert moved into Hartiscor House and immediately Nora's lessons in being a proper lady began. Soon after that, Lord Jeffrey insisted on giving a reception to introduce his new daughter-in-law to his friends and associates. What with one thing or another, by the time they had a chance to slip away to tie the knot in secret, Nora's pregnancy was already obvious for all to see. Then she was too embarrassed to show up at her own wedding with an extended belly, and they decided to wait until after the baby was born.

Bright if uneducated, Nora was a quick study, and in only a few months she was (with Hubert's assistance) involved in various war charities, and—attired in tasteful maternity dresses (Hubert's fine hand again)—playing the hostess at Lord Jeffrey's dinner parties (with him at her side to guide her) when he entertained some of London's most powerful men, like Sir Winston and Martin Cantington, the American ambassador.

She performed surprisingly well, utilizing her natural wit, charm, and good humor. By the time she was about to give birth—having learned a little about politics, the arts, and philanthropy, and quite a bit about how to walk, talk, dress, give a party (all under Hubert's guidance), and run a great household (this last with Edward's devoted assistance)—it was as if she'd been born to be Lady Hartiscor.

While thrilled with her success, Nora insisted that she couldn't take the credit. "It's one part your doing," she told Hubert, "and two parts your father's."

"There you go," Hubert pretended to pout, "giving me just a little credit while giving the other side most of it."

"But your father's not the *other* side. You and he and I are all on the same team, like the Allies. Besides, I can't give you as much credit as your father because you already believed in me while your father took me on faith. That's a wonderful thing to do for someone—it makes you strong because then you feel you *must* live up to their expectations."

"Yes, I suppose," he said thoughtfully. Then he laughed abruptly. "I can't say anyone ever had that kind of faith in me. Certainly not Father."

"But your mother? You said that—"

"That I was her favorite, her adorable pet, her playmate. I never said she *believed* in me."

"But she loved you so much."

"But it's not the same thing, is it? Loving someone and believing in them?"

"I can't imagine loving anyone and *not* believing in them. I can't imagine not believing in you." She cradled his head against her breasts. "I both love and believe in you."

"And I believe that you believe because while it takes a liar to know a liar, by the same token it takes a liar to recognize the truth. Oh, Nora, I'll try to live up to your belief in me, I swear it!"

"Oh, Hubert, I believe in that too!"

*   *   *

Little Hubie was born just days before the war was over. Hubert took one look at the baby and told Nora, "Our son's the most beautiful thing I've ever seen besides you," and Lord Jeffrey, dubbing Hubie "the Victory Baby," said, "Remarkable. He looks exactly like Hubert did when he was born!"

Then he produced several photograph albums to illustrate his point, and Nora saw that there *was* a marked similarity between the two Huberts. But it was more luck than remarkable—everyone always said that she and Hubert bore a strong resemblance to one another. The luck was that Hubie resembled her rather than his father, the Duke of Butte, Montana.

With the war over and Hubert a civilian again, Nora believed things were falling into place. One of these days they would manage to find the time to go out of town to be married quietly, and in the meantime, all she had to do was to be patient, put her faith in God and Hubert, and then, if her luck held, she and Hubert would be living and making love as they were meant to, and all of them would live happily ever after.

*Everything she had bargained for and more . . .*

But the one thing she hadn't bargained for was that Rupert, home from the wars, would take up residence again in his ancestral homes, Hartiscor House and Hartiscor Castle, and that changed the family portrait quite a bit. Where before there'd been a doting grandfather, a proud daddy, a loving mummy, and a bouncing baby boy, there was now also a brother and an uncle who, by his mere presence, cast the dark shadow of old hostilities, spoiling the cheery picture.

Of the two brothers it was Hubert who was openly hostile, whereas Rupert adopted a proper if less than warm manner. Nora couldn't blame Rupert for his reserve in the face of Hubert's open animosity. On the other hand, *did* she detect a certain snideness in Rupert's every chance remark, each glance? *Was* Rupert subtly condescending toward Hubert, or was she imagining it? *Was* his attitude toward *her* patronizing, or was she imagining that too? She wasn't sure. Still, sometimes she could *feel* Rupert's eyes burning into hers, even boring into her back. Was he taking her measure? But wasn't that a natural enough curiosity about the woman of common background who had married his brother? Did he picture her as a trespasser, an opportunistic poacher? Or was it but a manifestation of his resentment against Hubert?

Then she wondered about his feelings toward Hubie. Did Rupert see him as an encroachment on his ancestral terrain, resenting Jeffrey's affection for the baby, thinking of how Hubert had once displaced him in his mother's affections?

Still, Rupert *did* say the right things—that Hubie certainly looked the healthy specimen, that he had a good nature, always gurgling and cooing, just as he remembered Hubert had as a baby. Sometimes his comments were even accompanied by the rare smile. But then Nora had to ask herself: Was it a forced smile, or not a smile at all but a smirk . . . a sneer, as if he *knew* that Hubie weren't Hubert's son? Or was it that she herself was projecting, sensing an attitude that wasn't there—her *own* sympathetic reaction to Hubert's hostility?

Actually, from everything Hubert had said, she had had a mental image of Rupert completely different from the reality. She had imagined him as darkly brooding—a kind of aristocratic Heathcliff, the churlish gypsy boy out of *Wuthering Heights*, the movie she'd seen at least five times as a teenager, entranced by its romantic, if tragic, qualities. (She had even visualized Rupert looking like the handsome Olivier.) But while Rupert *was* seemingly humorless, it was more that he was distant than brooding. And while he wasn't as good-looking as Olivier, if one wanted to stretch a point there *was* a slight resemblance—the elegant nose, the smoldering eyes, an almost palpable pent-up intensity. This intensity was Rupert's most disturbing quality, Nora thought. Yet at the same time, she had to admit, it was his most compelling . . . even attractive, feature.

Nora's main concern was how they were all going to continue living under the same roof under the circumstances. How could she raise Hubie in such an oppressive atmosphere and expect him to grow from a contentedly cooing baby into a happy boy? Something had to be done to bring about a reconciliation between the brothers, and while she wished Jeffrey would take the initiative, he obviously had no such intention. It was as if he were either oblivious to the situation or deliberately choosing to ignore it. If this was how it had been when the Hartiscor children were growing up, with Lord Jeffrey seeing no disharmony and the Countess Miranda showing such poor judgment as to make a pet of Hubert at the expense of the other two, no wonder Anne had fled . . . had run for her very life.

Then it occurred to Nora that maybe Jeffrey was simply waiting for *her* to effect a reconciliation. Perhaps that was part of the tacit bargain they had made that day when Jeffrey first met her. If this was so, she could hardly let him down.

Since she could scarcely approach Rupert, and it *was* Hubert who was the openly hostile brother, she begged him to take a more conciliatory attitude toward Rupert. But Hubert smiled at her tightly, going to the drinks table in the library to pour himself a whiskey, and said, *"Et tu, Brute?"*

"Don't make a bad joke out of this, Hubert, and at the same time imply that I'm being disloyal to you. I am *not* taking Rupert's side and I'm not asking you to love him. All I'm asking you to do is act a little bit nicer and friendlier. Then Rupert will respond and act nicer and friendlier too."

Hubert tossed off his whiskey and poured another. "So little Nora Sunshine thinks that's all it takes, does she?"

"Please, Hubert. I'm not trying to make *little* of how you feel about Rupert. I'm sure whatever your resentments are, they're well founded. But they *are* a hangover from your childhood, and probably neither you nor Rupert is responsible. The responsibility lies with your parents and the British system of entail and primogeniture that—"

Hubert's eyes slitted. "Look at little Natalie Hall from the country now. She's using words like *entail* and *primogeniture*, words she probably never heard of before she came to London and got herself an education by marrying into the brilliant Hartiscor family. Oh, we've schooled you well, little Nora, haven't we? Now you can bounce phrases off Hubert's little pointed head with the best of them."

It was the first time Hubert had been even a tiny bit sarcastic, but she forgave him. In pain, he was just lashing out blindly. "It's not Rupert's fault that he's the older son . . . that he's going to inherit. How can you blame him?"

"You don't know anything about it, Nora, so the best thing you can do is keep out of it. Don't ask me to kiss his bloody ass and don't talk about things you don't understand!"

"But Hubert, I *want* to understand."

"Then understand *this*. Remember when I told you that if I got lucky, Rupert would get himself killed off in the war? With your innocent little heart you thought I was simply making a joke, one not in the best of taste, but still a joke. But it wasn't. It was my fondest dream, my most fervent wish. And then I cursed God the day Rupert returned from war. You see, I had prayed to Him at least a thousand times that Rupert wouldn't live to walk through the door again."

Nora was shocked into silence. But then, a few days later, she felt she had to try with Rupert. But not wanting Hubert or Jeffrey to know that she was appealing to Rupert for his cooperation, she chose a time when she knew Rupert would be at home and *they* wouldn't—at six, since this was the time Jeffrey could usually be found having a whiskey and soda at his favorite gentleman's club, the time Hubert was most often making the rounds of *his* favorite hangouts ("just keeping my ear to the ground for an interesting project . . ."), and the time Rupert invariably returned home from his office, where he administered to the various Hartiscor enterprises.

Accordingly, Nora was lying in wait for Rupert with the fire lit, radiating a cheery glow, and the tea table set in the Venetian sitting room (so designated because it was dominated by several Turner paintings from the artist's Italian period). She had chosen this room as her setting because Rupert had once idly mentioned that it was his favorite room—that he found its pale-yellow and robin's-egg-blue color scheme restful—and she wanted Rupert in the best possible frame of mind when she prevailed upon him to extend his hand in friendship to his younger brother.

\* \* \*

Rupert permitted himself a tiny smile as he sipped from the delicate Spode teacup. "Forgive me, Nora, but aren't you being a bit presumptuous?"

"Perhaps I am, but you'll have to forgive me. When so much is at stake—a pleasant home for my child to grow up in—I can't afford to stand on ceremony or worry if I'm so rude as to violate the boundary lines of what you consider proper."

"Well, yes, I can see that you have a problem. And yes, I can understand that you're too upset to—as you put it—stand on ceremony. But this is a complicated matter between my brother and me. Did it ever occur to you that the easiest solution would be for you, your son, and your husband to simply clear out? I know it will be difficult for Hubert to provide for his little family and that certainly must appear to you as a

major problem . . . as if there weren't already *enough* problems
for you to face, being married to our Hubert. But we don't
have to talk of them since we're both well acquainted with *all*
of them, aren't we? But don't worry, my dear, Father will always take care of Hubert's charming little family."

Despite her declaration about not standing on ceremony or
caring if she were so rude as to be presumptuous, Nora felt ill.
She'd made a humiliating mistake in approaching Rupert. He
was being every bit as hateful as Hubert thought him.

"You're right, Rupert," she said, fighting to retain her dig-
nity. "I have been presumptuous, but not in the way you mean.
I was presumptuous to think that you, as the older brother, were
big enough to overlook childhood grudges. I was presumptuous
to think that you—the brother who will eventually inherit everything—might find in his heart a generosity of spirit for a
younger brother who's less fortunate than you."

"Less fortunate?" Rupert sneered. "You make Hubert
sound like a character out of Oliver Twist. Does Hubert have
you reading Dickens now as part of your ongoing education?"

She could feel herself losing control now. No wonder Hubert despised him.

"Don't you patronize me, you arrogant son of a bitch! I
might be an uneducated barmaid's daughter and you *want* to
*think* that I married your brother for the name and the money,
and the privilege of living in this house and wearing dresses like
this"—she tugged at her dress, a Lanvin—"but it just isn't so.
Yes, I have a wardrobe fit for a queen, and yes, it's pleasant to
take tea in a lovely room like this, but believe me, this is not the
essence of a good or rewarding life. Your father told me that as
a child you used to say that money was what made the world go
round. I guess that was a clever thing for a little boy to say, but
as an overbearing, nasty adult, I can see you haven't learned a
bloody thing!

"It's *love*, Rupert, that makes the world go round, something
you know nothing about. But you believe what you want. Because *you're* such a loveless bastard I guess it makes you feel
better *not* to believe that I married your brother because I loved
him! And you don't have to concern yourself with my problems

with Hubert. The truth is I pity *you* because while you'll have the prestige and the fortune and the title, you'll never be the sweet and loving man your brother is or experience the kind of love Hubert and I share."

Despite her fierce words, she was on the verge of tears. How could she have shamed Hubert like this, gone behind his back to beg this unfeeling bastard to be *nice* to him, as though Hubert himself were nothing but a petulant child who had to be indulged. But then she looked up to see that the cold, hateful Rupert actually had tears streaming down his cheeks. *What in God's name?*

He leaned forward to grasp her hand, to hold on to it tightly. "Forgive me, Nora, I beg you. Everything you said about me is true. I *have* been an impossible, insufferable bloody bastard! But I beg you to understand. The truth is I've always been jealous of Hubert. You see, I *do* know that love is what makes the world go round, at least it's what makes life worth living. And no matter what he did or didn't do, Hubert was the one everyone always loved. Oh, how Mother loved Hubert! And even Father after Anne left. It's me he respects, but it's Hubert he really cares about, whom he worries about. Even Anne—it was Hubert she always confided in. And now there's *you*. Who wouldn't be jealous of a brother who's lucky enough to be loved and so well by a woman like you? Can you understand, Nora?"

She nodded. How could she not? Rupert was still the little boy who had been "tolerated" by his mother, not taken into her bed to be cuddled, coddled, and loved.

"So, will you forgive me?" he begged.

Her first tendency was to cry out, "Of course!" But *was* it her place to forgive him or was it Hubert's? And if she herself forgave Rupert, would Hubert ever forgive *her*? Or would he forever see it as an act of betrayal?

Then she was startled to hear, "Ah! What do we have here? And who's holding whose hand?"

It was Hubert, standing in the doorway with a funny smile. She dropped Rupert's hand to run to him. "Darling, Rupert and I have been having the most wonderful talk. About how sorry he is that you and he haven't been friends all these years and how it could be different now. He *wants* to be your friend . . . our friend. We could all be one, happy family. If only you'll agree."

Hubert smiled and shrugged. "Only an Englishman who's no gentleman could refuse so generous an offer, and never let it be said that Hubert Hartiscor is no gentleman."

At first Nora suspected that Hubert was a bit swizzled. But then she wasn't so sure about that when Rupert came over to extend his hand to Hubert and he lifted his right arm high, placing his hand out of Rupert's reach and wiggling his fingers, laughing. "Oh, you don't want to shake this hand, big brother. I just soiled it doing something with it that I shouldn't. You know how it is. But it's no matter since you've already shaken hands with Nora, and God knows, she's a better man than either one of us."

And then he laughed so hard that one would have thought he had just told the funniest joke on earth. He laughed so hard he had to wipe the tears from his eyes, and then Nora was left to wonder how slender, really, was that thin, invisible line that separated laughing from crying. Probably no thicker than the line that separated love from hate.

For the second time that afternoon, she wondered if she had done the right thing . . . wondered if all this was going to end up being much more than she had bargained for . . . much, much more. . . .

# THIRTEEN

Although tonight they were throwing a second birthday party for Hubie, it was Nora who received a spectacular present from Jeffrey, a diamond and ruby tiara. "I wanted you to wear it to the party tonight, my dear."

"It must be the loveliest thing I've ever seen!"

"Yes, it is a beautiful piece. It was created by Cartier in 1925 here in London, and these are Burmese rubies, which are considered the finest in the world."

"But Jeffrey, what have I done to deserve such a magnificent present?" she protested. Still, she ran over to the gilt-encrusted pier mirror to try it on.

"You've wrought a miracle, undone all the harm that Miranda—" He broke off and began again. "I don't know how you did it, but you've brought Rupert and Hubert together."

Nora sighed and put the tiara down on the console table as if it were very heavy. "Not *together*, not really, though Rupert's been wonderful. He's trying *very* hard. He's even getting down on all fours to play horsie with Hubie." She smiled, thinking about Rupert in his banker's gray down on the floor with Hubie yelling, "Giddy-up!" and digging his heels into Rupert's sides, whipping at him with a sofa pillow.

"And I suppose Hubert's trying too. He says 'Good morning' to Rupert every day at breakfast and even discusses sports with him. Yesterday he even asked Rupert what he thought of Dior's New Look, and poor Rupert was quite thrown—he'd never heard of a New Look. But the thing is, when Hubert speaks to Rupert there's a big grin on his face, and I suspect that this friendship business is a huge joke to him. That he's having us all on. So you see, I haven't really earned the tiara. Maybe it's a little too grand for me anyway." She smiled wistfully. "It's a tiara fit for a duchess."

"In that case, it's not grand enough. *You* should have a tiara that's fit for a queen."

"Oh, Jeffrey, you *are* sweet. But if you really want to give me a present, I'll trade the tiara for—"

Jeffrey was alarmed. "Nonsense! The tiara is yours. But what is it, my dear, that you want? What can I give you?"

"You can give *Hubert* something . . . something meaningful to do with himself, to give purpose to his day, rather than squandering it at the bookmaker's or Claridge's bar or—"

"I see. Do you have something specific in mind?"

"Well, Rupert has all the financial companies to run. I think it must be something on a par with that."

"But what? The mines? The farms? I hardly think Hubert would be interested."

"No. It has to be something suited to his talents."

"But we've tried various things with Hubert, Nora," Jeffrey said wearily. "Nothing's ever worked out."

"That doesn't mean we can just give up. It only means we haven't hit on the right thing. And I've been *thinking*—a foundation might be the answer. *The Hartiscor Foundation,* to endow various endeavors for—" She groped for the right words. "For the good of mankind. And Hubert will head it."

"That sounds like an excellent idea, but perhaps we should be more specific as to what kind of endeavors we're talking about. Medical research, endowments for the arts, what—?"

"We leave that to Hubert. He must make the decisions, be completely in charge. He's a man in his thirties, not a child, and you must start treating him like a man."

*As she herself was trying damned hard to . . .*

"Very well, it will be as you say. We'll get started on it at once. I'll speak to Rupert about it and—"

"Rupert? I'm not sure that's the best way to proceed."

"I'm afraid you don't understand how these things work, dear Nora. A foundation must be funded, a great deal of money allocated. A trust must be set up and Rupert's the person to see to that. It's not like we can say to Hubert, 'Here's the cookie jar, help yourself to whatever you need and when the jar is empty, let us know—we'll bake up a new batch.' "

It was a joke and Nora smiled politely. Still, she knew Hubert would be put off if Rupert held the purse strings, but she didn't think she could argue with Jeffrey. As he said, she really didn't understand how financial things worked.

"Then it's all settled," Jeffrey said. "And just think, with Rupert and Hubert working together, they might even get to be real friends. Now you must go upstairs to get ready for the party. Our guests will be arriving soon. I hope that you're wearing a gown that will go well with the tiara? We must show everyone what a *real* countess looks like."

Nora was startled. *A real countess?* The late Miranda had been the real countess, and she herself wasn't even a sham one. It was a funny slip of the tongue for Jeffrey to make and she chided him, "Am I being demoted so quickly? Only a bit ago you mentioned a tiara fit for a queen, or at least a duchess. Now you're relegating me to a mere countess."

\*   \*   \*

As Hubert in his white tie and tails did up the hooks of her wine-red evening dress, Nora exulted over its color. Even if she'd known that Jeffrey was going to give her the ruby tiara, she still couldn't have made a better choice.

"While I'm about it," Hubert said, brushing the nape of her neck with a kiss to send goose bumps running down her spine, "I might as well fasten your necklace in place too. Are you going to wear your pearls? I think they'd be exactly right nestling in that glorious cleavage."

He buried his lips in the valley between her breasts and she bit her lip as the familiar tingling of desire coursed through her body, but she only smiled teasingly at him. "I know *you're* the fashion expert around here, m'lord, but I think I won't wear any jewelry except for the ring you gave me for Christmas." She wanted the tiara to be a surprise, and she didn't plan on putting it on until after Hubert went downstairs. "Between my ring and this gown I think I'll be quite fancy enough, no?''

"Quite!" He rolled his eyes appreciatively. "You're right. Why clutter up the effect of that exquisite view with any distracting note?" He kissed each breast in turn. She shivered at the caress and thought that, if nothing else, Hubert *was* a gentleman. Even if he didn't follow through, at least he always said the right thing and went through all the right preliminary motions.

"Are you ready, then? Shall we go down?" he asked.

"No, Jeffrey's plan is for you to go down ahead of me. He wants to handle the reception line along with you and Rupert, and then, after everyone's here, I'm to come down with Hubie. Poor baby. It's his birthday party, but at least half of adult London is going to be here. Your father's invited every last lord in the House but not another child, and we're serving only refreshments unfit for two-year-old consumption. I'm sure Hubie would gag if we tried to feed him an oyster."

"But why did you allow Father to take over the guest list? The whole party? You must take a firmer stand with him. Miranda would never have let him get away with that."

"But I'm *not* your mother. And do you really think I'd get into a row with your father over Hubie's party? I think it's sweet of him to take such an interest. He's so proud of Hubie, I'm just happy he wants to show him off to his friends. Besides, I'll make another party for Hubie, with little boys and girls and all the proper birthday-boy treats."

"I'm relieved to hear it. But why don't you let Nanny bring Hubie down so that you can receive the guests too?"

"No, that would spoil the effect of the grand entrance your father wants us to make. You see, Hubie and I are going to match. Me in this dress and Hubie in his little red velvet suit. Won't that be a spectacular entrance?"

\* \* \*

Poised at the top of the staircase, tiara in place, and with Hubie clutching her hand, Nora was unprepared for *how* spectacular an entrance they were making. First a buzz swept through the assembled crowd, and then there was a hush, followed by a total silence with all eyes fixed on her and Hubie as they descended the stairs slowly, each step a major accomplishment for Hubie's stubby little legs.

There wasn't a sound until they finally took the last step onto the black-and-white marbled floor and Jeffrey broke into applause. Then all his old friends came rushing up to wish the birthday boy happiness, but with all eyes focused on *her tiara.* And then it hit her! When Jeffrey had said, "We must show them what a real countess looks like," it had been no slip of the tongue. *It was the Countess Miranda's tiara she was wearing!* Then, when she saw Hubert's paper-white face and Rupert's stunned look, she knew that not only was she wearing their mother's tiara but that it was an electrifying jolt.

* * *

As she and Hubert prepared for bed, Nora set the tiara down on the dressing table. Grimacing, Hubert nudged it with a finger. "Shouldn't you put that thing away in the safe in Father's study or call Rowens to do it?"

"It's so late and Rowens must be exhausted. It can wait until tomorrow morning. Unless the sight of it upsets you?"

When Hubert didn't answer, she went on: "Is it because it reminds you of your mother? It *was* hers, wasn't it?"

This time Hubert answered but barely. "Yes . . ."

"I'm so sorry. It must have been a shock, so painful for you to remember your mother wearing it. Sometimes the most wonderful memories are the ones hardest to bear."

"What are you talking about? What wonderful memories?"

"When your mother was dressed up for a party, wearing her tiara. She was probably so happy and looking very beautiful. Remembering her that way would be a wonderful memory for you but it would hurt at the same time because she's gone. . . ."

"It wasn't that way. There *was* a party that night but—"

"What night?"

"The first time Mother wore the tiara. It was her birthday and Father had just given it to her. Most of the people here tonight were there that night too. And yes, Miranda *was* looking very beautiful, standing at the head of the stairs ready to descend. But that was the first and only time she wore the tiara. It was the *last* time. . . . That was the night Miranda fell down the stairs and broke her neck."

"My God, I didn't know! You never told me how she died!"

"You never asked."

"But when Jeffrey gave me the tiara I didn't know that it had been your mother's. All he said was that it came from— If I had known I never would have worn it. You must believe me! I don't even know why he gave it to me under the circumstances. It must be a terrible memory for him too."

"One would think so, wouldn't one? Especially since he was standing right next to her when she fell, and if he'd reacted a bit quicker perhaps he could have—"

"Oh, dear God, how awful for him! I wonder why he even *kept* the tiara—why he didn't sell it or something. Why do you think he gave it to me?"

"Perhaps he wanted to pretend . . ."

"Pretend *what*? That I'm your mother?"

"Hardly," Hubert laughed hollowly. "If it came to that, he'd much rather pretend you were Anne. Maybe he just wants to pretend to himself that you're the Countess of Hartiscor."

"What does *that* mean? You're not making any sense."

The whole thing didn't make any sense. How could Jeffrey have been so insensitive? It was so unlike him. She picked up the tiara as if it burned her fingers and put it away in one of the vanity drawers to get it out of sight. "I'm going to give it back to him tomorrow. Then he can sell it or lock it away in a vault or give it to Rupert's bride when he marries if Rupert doesn't mind."

"*If* Rupert ever marries, which I doubt he'll ever do in *my* lifetime," Hubert muttered, sitting down wearily on the edge of the bed to remove his shoes. "But you won't give it back."

"Why do you say that?"

"Because Father would be upset and you're Miss Sunshine. You wouldn't do anything to upset Father, now, would you?" he asked bitterly. "Any more than you'll stop trying to fix

Rupert and me up in your other role as the Happy Match-maker?''

Nora bristled, but she knew he was right. And suddenly she understood why Jeffrey had given her the tiara. This afternoon he'd said it was in appreciation of the miracle she had wrought undoing all the harm Miranda had precipitated between her sons. In Jeffrey's mind the gift constituted some kind of convoluted trade-off—an evening out of the score. But it had been a beastly bad idea.

"Oh, Hubert, I'm sorry about everything. I was just trying to help. . . .''

"I know, Nora, I know," he said tiredly, dropping a shoe as if it were too heavy to hold. "And I'm sorry about what I said. You're the last person that I want to hurt. But there are some things . . . some people, even *you* can't help. Sometimes, even you must throw in the towel.''

*Does he mean that I have to give up on him too?* It was true that he never mentioned their getting married anymore, and she tried to remember when it was precisely that he had stopped.

"Sorry, mate, but I'm fresh out of towels." She grinned at him and kneeled to help him remove his socks.

"What are you doing now?" he asked in exasperation.

"You seem so tired. I'm just helping you out.''

Right now she had a concern that took precedence over everything else, and any talk of matters irrelevant to that concern was an intruder in the night. Tonight, just like nearly every other night, she would try again to transform her sweet, loving friend into her passionate lover even though it often seemed she was losing ground rather than gaining it. But how could she give up? That was part of the original bargain she'd made with him when she accepted his proposal of sweet convenience—that she would never give up on him.

It was also part of the implicit bargain she had made with Jeffrey. And now there was little Hubie to fight for too, since he was part of the same bargain.

She turned on the radio so that there would be music to make love to, or at least music for her to dance to. Then she was whirling about, a nude nymphette in a dreamlike trance, caught up in the hope that somehow, suddenly, Hubert would be entranced—at last seduced, set on fire with a burning desire. Oh, yes, any moment now he would call for her to come to him, to impale herself upon the erect and throbbing symbol of his manhood. . . .

# FOURTEEN

I t had been on Nora's mind for some time that she *could* seek outside help for her and Hubert's problem—a medical solution. She was aware of hormone therapy, had even heard of a serum made from bulls' urine (or was it live cells extracted from the testicles of unborn bulls?), and had read of tonics that wrought miracles. In addition, she had listened to the gossip continuously making the rounds at parties about what was going on in those infamous Swiss clinics.

A typical story: "Did you hear about Ronnie Ashton? He hadn't had an erection in his entire life until he went to the Weiner Institute in Lausanne where they pumped his ass so full of monkey glands with a horse-sized needle, the next thing anyone knew he was under arrest for trying to rape a woman on Kingsbridge Road in broad daylight! He was walking around so horny the damn fool couldn't even wait for the cover of dark."

Another story related that a cousin of Fruity Marlowe, who was related to Lady Stilton on his mother's side, who lived in a pink chalet just above Vevey to escape the taxes, was given a potion at some *clinique* that was made from grinding the horns of rhinos into powder. It was evidently so powerful that his wife had to be "sewn up" to repair the damage (the operation was performed by a London surgeon who was known on the q.t. to work on women who needed to present themselves as virgins).

Then again, if one had *any* flagging organ in need of revitalization, there was a spa in Zurich where they injected a mysterious formula directly into the organ itself, which was awfully convenient if one wanted to visit one's money stashed away in one of Zurich's banks at the same time.

But she could hardly ask Hubert to go to Lausanne to submit his bum (as well as his tender sensibilities) to the horse's needle on the off chance that he wouldn't turn into a monkey, or to Zurich to have his prick pricked.

Then there was the analyst's couch. She knew that if she insisted, Hubert would agree to undergo psychotherapy, but the idea of *forcing* Hubert to expose his problem . . . his inadequacies . . . to a third party was repugnant. What good could come of coercion? As her mother had always said, "You could lead a horse to water but you couldn't make him drink." Or as Hubert put it, "You could lead a hor-ti-culture but you couldn't make her like it."

No, theirs had to be a private battle, and as far as she could see, seduction was her only weapon. Accordingly, she tried various costumes: barmaid, French maid, little country maid. She tried being luscious siren, shy siren, depraved siren—satin on her body, filthy words on her lips. She even tried dressing up as a little girl in white socks and Mary Janes, having read that "doing it" with little girls was a fantasy that appealed to many men. A nanny with a sharp voice, ruler in hand, was another fantasy she tried, but Hubert only burst out laughing. "Sorry, darling, but it just isn't *you*." Then she laughed too, grateful that at least they could still laugh about it all.

Occasionally she won a skirmish, and then for a couple of days she went about her routine bubbling over with hope, singing bits of happy tunes. But mostly nothing worked, though it was the most intense kind of effort—humiliating, frustrating, anything but sexy. And while she knew that it wasn't the way love was supposed to be, it didn't make her love Hubert any less. Sometimes she thought it only made her love him more, the struggle intensifying her own passion.

Then, when even the tiniest of victories became only a distant memory, she decided to develop more expertise, consulting various manuals. Still, she came up with very little that she didn't already know or hadn't already tried. The only dividend of any significance was that her vocabulary became more extensive. But what good did it do her to know that the technical term for a blow job or *going down*, which she had already tried many times (a thousand times?) was *fellatio*? Or that its reverse—that which the Duke of Montana had called muff-diving and which Hubert had often administered to her as a kind of consolation prize for her efforts—was the act of *cunnilingus*, also referred to as *sitting down to dinner*?

Did it really help her to know that there was *anilingus* as well as something called a *three-decker*, or that urinating on a sexual partner was considered stimulating in some quarters? Or was it an aid to learn that a combination of *fellatio*, anal, and straight-arrow sex, and an all-around going over with the tongue, was referred to by women in the trade as a "trip around the world" (though in her extreme youth she had heard it referred to as a Cook's Tour)?

The terms only filled her head with questions and certain pictures that increased her agony all the more. Hubert refused to hold still for *fellatio* as performed by her, forcing her to speculate if *fellatio* was more acceptable to him when performed by a man, and *why*? Did it really make any difference who the perpetrator was? As for anal penetration, why was it that *her* anus was less acceptable, less interesting to him than a male lover's? Weren't her buttocks as lovely as any man's, and could the male organ really differentiate between male cheeks and female cheeks?

Her desperation increased by the day, but she would *not* give up, and she went back to reading whatever she could find, discovering something called urethral masturbation, which she had never heard of before but which was considered highly effective in stimulating carnal passion. True, it sounded bizarre, but perhaps bizarre translated into exotic, which could translate into erotic, which could translate ultimately into plain lovemaking, neither bizarre nor fancy but fulfilling.

In urethral masturbation, she read, the passage from the bladder to the outside was stimulated by inserting objects into the urethra and moving them about gently, a form of stimulation more effective in women since an object so small as a hairpin or even a rubber band (*a rubber band? What did one do, precisely, with a rubber band?*) could be the tool of insertion, a woman's urethra being extraordinarily sensitive, situated as it is between the clitoris and the vagina with nerve connections to both. But with a man, a longer object was needed—a piece of tubing, a length of wire—

Then she could bear it no longer and flung the book against the wall. Was she going mad even to think of teasing the man she loved into performing sex by sticking a piece of wire up his willie? What would she be willing to do next? Dress up like some ruddy bloke, hook up a dildo (one of those kinky Japanese ones with two heads) to her snapper, and stick it up his arse? Or sneak a few dashes of Spanish fly into his brandy and make him so crazy with the itches that he would be so mad as to have the itch for the likes of her?

She buried her face in her hands and sobbed helplessly. All she wanted seemed like such a small thing, a simple thing. Nothing bizarre, hardly exotic, not extraordinary in any way. All she wanted was for him to love her like any plain and simple man might, and not like his best friend.

\* \* \*

The possibility that she was fighting the wrong enemy became a suspicion only when the Hartiscor Family Foundation blew up, in a manner of speaking, in their collective faces.

In not quite a year the foundation, funded with an extraordinary amount of money—two million pounds—was bankrupt, the last drop of its life's blood exhausted, and the hundred or so recipients of its scientific grants (such as a Dr. Milton Crawford, who was conducting a study of *The Sex Life of the Tussah* in a posh flat in Mayfair) were left high and dry with their studies incomplete. There wasn't one finished report, nor was there a shred of evidence to be found anywhere that humankind had benefited in any way, manner, or form.

Jeffrey was, of course, furious, not so much with Hubert as with Rupert, whom he had charged with the administering of the trust. *Why hadn't Rupert better supervised what Hubert was actually doing with the money?* But all Rupert would say in his own defense was that he'd tried to endow Hubert with as much responsibility, fiscal and otherwise, as possible. He did *not* reveal that he had done this at Nora's behest, that she had implored him to employ a *laissez-faire* policy with Hubert. But when Nora herself told Jeffrey as much, he scoffed. "Rupert had no business listening to you. His conduct was reprehensible. All he did was give Hubert enough rope to hang himself. *You're* blind to certain facts about Hubert, but Rupert knew he wasn't to be trusted."

"Why isn't he to be trusted?" Nora demanded angrily, defensive as always when it came to Hubert. "Because he's a fool or because he's a cheat?"

Jeffrey only said that the whole topic was too painful to talk about and begged her to desist. Then, when she went back to Rupert to recount her conversation with Jeffrey, Rupert smiled sadly. "I could have told you what he'd say. But what conclusion *have* you come to after talking with him? Who is to blame for this two-million-pound fiasco? You, because you're an innocent and asked me to give Hubert a free hand, or me because my conduct was irresponsible—that I gave Hubert autonomy when I knew he couldn't handle it? Or is Hubert to blame because he's a fool or a cheat, or a little of each?"

"You tell me, Rupert. What do you think?"

"I think the fault rests with a *what* rather than a *who*— something called a lack of moral fiber."

"You're referring to *Hubert's* lack of moral fiber, I take it?" she asked resentfully, defensive again.

"I think we must start with Hubert's since his *is* outstanding, but then we must proceed to yours since you too display a lack of moral fiber—a weakness of character—when you refuse to admit that Hubert has this lack. And then I must confess to my *own* weakness of character."

"Oh, I'm glad you're not letting yourself off the hook," she said caustically. "So tell me, Rupert, how did you display *your* weakness of character?"

"I didn't have the strength to resist giving Hubert his head when I knew very well that I shouldn't."

"And is that what your father meant when he said your behavior was reprehensible?"

"I suppose, but Father's not one to talk. He displays his own lack of moral fiber when he tries to get others to do what he doesn't have the taste to do himself, or tries to lay off his guilts on others."

"Now, what does *that* mean?" Nora was losing her patience. They were getting nowhere with this philosophical discussion. "What guilts are you talking about?"

"You know how Father always makes it sound like we'd have been one happy family if not for Miranda. As if *everything* was her fault. Well, it wasn't—not *everything*."

The last thing she wanted to get into now was a discussion about Jeffrey and Miranda's relationship. She had enough trouble dealing with hers and Hubert's. "Well, who knows about these things? I'm sure that in any family there are always resentments. But speaking of resentments—your father said you gave Hubert enough rope to hang himself. That sounds like he was implying that you did so deliberately, knowing that Hubert would make a mess of things. Is *that* true?"

Rupert laughed. "Oh, that. Father has this thing about people having enough rope to hang themselves. You might say it runs in the family. There was an Earl of Hartiscor back in the seventeenth century who hanged himself from the rafters, and then in our own century, there's my sister, Anne."

"Anne hanged herself?" Nora was stunned. "But I thought she was in Australia, only considered herself dead to her family."

"Father didn't tell you that. His way is simply to refuse to talk about unpleasant things, especially Anne. It must have been Hubert."

"Hubert *did* say something about Anne being dead, but I guess I misunderstood. I thought he was talking figuratively."

Had she misunderstood? But what did it matter? It was only Hubert who mattered, and there was much she still didn't understand. "So finally we're down to the bottom line," she said. "Considering your family's predilection for hanging themselves and knowing that giving Hubert complete autonomy might well be a disaster, you still did it, and I want to know *why*. Why, Rupert, why?"

"But I thought you understood. I went against my better

judgment and my father's specific orders for one reason only—
because *you* asked me to." He gazed into her eyes. "Don't you
know, Nora, that I would do *anything* for you?"

Yes, she knew it, had taken advantage of it, had manipulated
him into doing what she wanted, and Jeffrey too. Ironically, the
man she'd manipulated them for was the only man in the family
who was resisting her manipulative efforts.

\*   \*   \*

But Hubert's resistance didn't stop her from going to Jeffrey
with a new proposal soon after. "The problem with the foundation as far as Hubert was concerned was that it was more a
matter of administration than something really suited to his
talents. But an art gallery would put all his best talents to use. I
think that's the answer and it would require a very small invest-
ment compared to the foundation."

Jeffrey quickly acquiesced. "Of course. Anything you want,
Nora. I'd do anything for you."

Then she only wished that what he'd said hadn't been the
same thing Rupert had, and that he was doing it for Hubert
rather than for the woman he believed was Hubert's wife. . . .

# FIFTEEN

With her and Hubert's supposed fifth anniversary only a week away—feeling like the worst kind of fraud as well as a desperate fool—Nora planned one more seduction scene. Maybe this one would be a triumph, the *pièce de résistance* that Hubert would not be able to resist. Then maybe they would be able to look one another in the eye when the subject of their getting married came up, rare as those occasions had become.

\* \* \*

A black mask covering half her face, she was nude except for black shiny boots. In one hand she held a whip, in the other a black scarf and a white silk handkerchief, and in a clipped, cold voice, she whipped out her orders: He was to undress himself and kneel before her so that she could blindfold him with the scarf and gag him with the handkerchief, after which he was to lie facedown on the four-poster bed with his legs spread. Hubert's eyes turned to the bed to see that ropes were already attached to all four of its posts. Then, when he looked back at her, she saw the expression on his face and it wasn't one of sexual arousal—it was a look of horror and then *she* was filled with horror.

*Doesn't he know that this is only one more of my silly fantasies? That even if I blindfold him, gag him, flay him with the black snake, I couldn't really hurt him. How could I when I love him so?*

Seeing his tears, she tore the mask from her face. "Why are you crying? Don't you know how much I love you?"

"I do. And I see what the love of me has brought you to.

115

This final degradation! Isn't that reason enough to cry?"

She dropped the whip as if it were burning her fingers. "Hubert, no! Please, don't! I—"

"All these years you've played the masochist so well. No matter what I did you kept loving me while I kept breaking your heart. But you went on trying to make me into something I can't be. And now this! *You, of all people, a sadist?* Why can't you get it through your head? I'm a poof, a fag, and I'm never going to love you the way you want to be loved, and your turning yourself into less of a woman with these grotesque charades isn't going to make a better man of me. All you'll succeed in doing will be to defile yourself more than I've already defiled you."

"Stop, Hubert, stop!"

"No, *you* stop! Stop debasing yourself. How humiliated you must feel dressing up like a trick dog in the circus, trying to win my sexual favors. And for what? Why don't you know what everyone else knows? That I'm not worth it."

"Hubert, please! I'm so sorry!"

"But do you even know what you're sorry for? Oh, my sweet, warm, loving girl! If you love me, then don't let me do this to you! You think it's only another trick that you're willing to try in the name of love, but what you don't know is that it corrupts the soul. If you won't give up for your own sake, then do it for mine. Don't you understand? You make me feel like I can't sink any lower. Let me put it this way—if you're a real sadist, then you'll go on with it, but if you really love me, you'll give it up!"

She rushed to him to press his face to her. "I promised you I'd never give up!" But even as she spoke she knew that she had to break her promise. She had no choice.

He gently pushed her away. "For once, *I'm* giving the orders, and what we're going to do is get married finally so that Hubie has the Hartiscor name legitimately, and then we're going to get a divorce."

"No, I'll marry you but I'll never divorce you!"

"Oh, for God's sake, Nora! Get on with it and get yourself a bloody lover!"

She looked into his eyes. "Is that what *you've* done?"

"Not yet. Not once since the day we've been together."

She believed him. "But you *want* to? *Yearn* to . . . ?"

"*Need* to . . ."

"I see." And she did. "Well, then, you must."

There was a great silence as he fully absorbed her words— that she had, at last, released him.

"And you'll marry me, then, and divorce me?"

"No. Marry or not, I'll never leave you."

"But if we stay together, you *will* take a lover? Tell me you'll take a lover! I want you to!"

She shook her head sorrowfully. "I don't know if I can. Maybe someday . . . after I've learned how to love you less. No, I take that back. I will *never* love you less. Make that when I learn to love you like my best friend." She smiled at him even as she licked at the tears salting her lips.

*Will the ache ever stop?*

His lips twisted into a grimace of a smile. "Some people would say what a lucky man I am with a sweet little boy for a son and a woman who loves me so much she won't even cheat on me when I beg her to."

She wiped at the tears with the back of her hand. "Well, even a charmer like you can't have *everything* you want, my darling. But one thing you must promise me and *mean* it. You *will* be discreet in taking a lover, won't you? For Hubie's sake, for your father's."

"For Hubie's sake, anyway. But what about you, Nora? What do I do for *your* sake?"

She sat down on the edge of the chaise to look up at him. "You can continue to try and get along with Rupert for every-one's sake, even if it kills you," she said, trying for a light note.

He sat down on the floor next to her. "You may think you're joshing but it probably will—kill me. They're both so clever, Father and Rupert. I wouldn't be surprised if one of them was plotting how to kill off this fool of a black sheep this very minute."

He was kidding, of course, a bit of black humor. "Why would they want you dead?" She smiled sadly.

"Maybe because I'm a dark blot on the family name or

maybe because they're both in love with the fool of a black sheep's wife and each one wants her for his very own."

More black humor. "Really, Hubert, you *are* a fool!" she chided, leaning wearily back in the chaise. Only then did she remember that she was still done up for the farcical seduction scene that had been scheduled to take place and, feeling ridiculous, she sat up to remove the black boots.

But Hubert pushed her back against the pillows. "Here, let me." He pulled off each boot, kissing each toe in turn, and she bit her lips not to let a moan escape her lips. Then, after tenderly covering her nude body with the pale-pink cashmere throw, he asked, "What else can I do for you? And don't mention Rupert's name or Father's again, I warn you."

"You can try very hard to make a go of the art gallery. Its success will please me more than you can imagine."

"Granted. I will try very hard to make the art gallery a brilliant success. What else?"

"Set an example for our son. Be sweet and kind, good and true, strong and brave."

"I swear I will to the best of my ability. You know I love him *almost* as much as I do you and I'll do everything I can to see that nothing bad ever happens to him. But you. I must do something specifically for *you*."

"All right, then." She tried to make a joke of it. "Swear you'll never love anyone as much as you love me."

He got up from the floor to lean over her. "Oh, Nora, *you're* the fool. Don't you know that no matter with whom I *make* love, I'll never love *anybody* the way I love you?"

She felt as if she were breaking apart inside.

"Oh, Hubert, kiss me! Kiss me quick! Kiss me and tell me you love me over and over and over again! And then, just this *once*, make love to me . . . the very best way you can!"

First tearing off his clothes, then stripping away the cashmere throw that separated their bodies, he did all of these things—he kissed her quickly, he told her over and over again that he loved her, and then he made love to her the very best way that he could. . . .

Later, as Hubert slept in her arms, Nora thought that as

pure sex the lovemaking hadn't been brilliant, but at the same time it had been an exquisite act of love. And whether or not they ever legally married, that was something to hold on to . . . because whatever else it was, this act of lovemaking was the last time she and Hubert would ever again share an intimate physical expression of their love. This part of their lives was over forever. . . .

# SIXTEEN

◆·••·◆

For a long time Hubert was so discreet that Nora had no idea if he had one lover or several. They never discussed it. Part of their tacit understanding was that it was not a matter for discussion. But one day, dropping by at the gallery on the off chance Hubert would be free to take her to lunch, she discovered him in a back room making love to an assistant, Pepe, a small black man from the Indies.

Heartsick (would she ever be able to erase the study in black and white from her mind—the weird juxtaposition of the main elements of the composition against a blurred background), she spoke only of discretion. He *had* promised to be discreet. But incredibly, Hubert insisted he *had* been. After all, he *had* used the back room.

She was infuriated. How dare he laugh off his outrageous behavior, treating it as a joke? Her hand reached out with a will of its own to crack his face, but immediately after she burst into tears, not sure why she was crying. Because she had lost control, or because, while she *had* given him consent to take a lover, the reality of it was too much to bear?

"Oh, very well," Hubert said in the face of her tears. "I suppose it *was* a bit of poor timing on my part, but at the time, the timing seemed perfect."

*Another joke . . .* Again rage engulfed her, and when he smiled at her, showing her his dimples as if this would assure her not being able to stay angry with him, she ached with the urge to crack his face again, but she resisted.

"And now, what about some lunch?" he asked. "The Savoy?"

*Lunch? The Savoy? He is incredible!*

Her arm swung up again but he caught it in midair. "All right, it was *definitely* a bit of poor judgment. Satisfied?"

Her anger was replaced by despair. *A bit of poor judgment? A weakness of character?* Was it possible Hubert had never known the difference between what was and wasn't outrageous behavior?

"Are you upset because of the gentleman's color?"

"Oh, Hubert, this has nothing to do with anyone's color! It's this whole sordid affair—carrying on with an *employee* in a place of business, never mind the back room or the front. It's in the worst possible taste and the Hubert that I know and love was *famous* for his taste. I don't pretend to understand the manner of your passion, but surely you can confine it to what's fitting, or are you so far gone you have no sense of what constitutes appropriate behavior?"

"What makes you think I ever had?" he asked soberly.

She was taken aback by the question. *What, indeed?*

But what was the point of going on with this? Nothing she could say would change anything. Accordingly, she pasted a smile on her lips, redid her face, and they set off for the Savoy, where, over an excellent filet of sole and a fine Sauterne, a subdued Hubert promised to do better, for whatever his promise was worth.

\*   \*   \*

Hubert's promise was worth about six months' time until he was arrested in a public washroom in Victoria Station for behavior best described as unbecoming an English gentleman. Nora's heart was broken all over again, but she was grateful that at least the whole business never made the tabloids, thanks to the Hartiscor influence and a lot of hush money.

When a silently contemptuous Rupert brought a shamed Hubert home from the lockup, she took him to the room they still shared. There, instead of lecturing him, she took him into her arms but only to comfort him, much as she did with Hubie when things didn't go his way. Still, she wondered: A lack of moral fiber? No sense of appropriate behavior? *Or is it a defi-*

*ciency of will?* An inability to make the required effort to curb one's excesses, no matter how excessive . . .

Then she realized that *all* of these flaws—*flaws of character in an otherwise perfect physical specimen*—had always been there, existing as a completely separate entity from his sexuality, plain enough for anyone with a grain of sense to see. Only *she* hadn't been in full possession of *her* senses. She had been too absorbed in her own obsession—her pitiful quest for a Hubert Hartiscor who never existed. All this time she'd been fighting for a Hubert who could never be when she should have been battling to save the Hubert who *was*.

But it was too late to think about that, too late even for self-recrimination. It was only the end result that counted now, and how it affected the people she loved—Jeffrey . . . Hubie . . . her poor darling Hubert himself. She had to do something to keep him from slipping down the drain, the victim of his own flawed character.

She decided that it was time for the psychotherapy that she had once resisted because she couldn't bear for Hubert to be forced to expose his inadequacies. But that had been *her* weakness, *her* flaw, *her* own inadequacy.

At first mention of undergoing analysis, Hubert drawled: "Is this your idea or Rupert's? Dada's? Little Hubie's? Or is it a consensus of opinion?"

She ignored the sarcasm. "I haven't discussed this with Rupert or your father. You know I wouldn't do that, Hubert. It's totally my idea."

Then he was only sad. "So, Nora, you haven't given up? I should have known. Still think you can turn me around?"

"No, Hubert. I've made my peace with your sexuality. What I'm concerned with is how you're throwing away your life—all the wonderful things you can still be. Please, Hubert, do it for me, for Hubie, and no one else has to know. Just promise me that you'll seek help."

But then, remembering that Hubert had a problem with promises, she herself went to consult psychiatrists and, feeling a certain sympathy flowing from one James Webster on Harley

Street, set up the first appointment and followed up by checking to see that Hubert kept it. After that, she left it to Hubert to make his own appointments, always inquiring how things were coming along but only in a general way, knowing that Hubert wasn't supposed to talk about his sessions with the doctor. Still, she was gratified that Hubert *elected* to discuss his treatment with her so vividly that sometimes it seemed as if he were recounting their fifty-minute conversations almost word for word.

\* \* \*

"You know, I think Dr. Webster and I really had a break-through today."

"Oh, Hubert, really? So soon? How wonderful!"

"Yes, old Jimmy seems to think that most of my problems probably relate back to my childhood when Mother preferred me over Rupert, and Father, Rupert over me. You see, I *respected* him more than Mummy, and when he rejected me in favor of—"

"But I'm sure Jeffrey never *really* rejected you, Hubert."

"Dr. Webster seems to think he did." Hubert took a chiding tone. "Now I know that you've come a long way from the girl that you were, Nora—one who didn't know a port glass from a sherry or a Renoir from a Picasso—but do you presume to question the judgment of the good doctor who spent years training and accumulating experience in the field?"

"No, of course not."

"Well, then—" He spread his hands eloquently.

When next he told her of the recurring dream he had recently related to the doctor about Rupert sneaking into his bed at night and buggering him up the asshole as he slept, she was appalled. *What a horrid dream!* But out loud she only made objection to his choice of words: "Surely you didn't use that language when you told the doctor about the dream?"

"But I *did*. I can see you don't know how analysis works. You don't soft-pedal the facts. It's *supposed* to hurt. The important thing is to get it all out—a verbal regurgitation of all the muck. But you're focusing on the wrong thing. Don't you want to hear what Dr. Webster *made* of the dream? He thinks it *really* happened!"

"You don't mean that? I can't believe that the doctor actually—"

"But it's true. Dr. Webster believes that when we were young lads Rupert actually climbed into my bed at night and gave it to me up the old bunghole. And then I didn't tell Father about it either because I was afraid he'd call me a liar because he never believed *me* when it was my word against Rupert's, or I *did* tell him and he *did* call me a frigging liar. Either way, I repressed all memory of the incidents, which is the reason I'm having the recurring dream."

"But I can't believe it of Rupert! Besides, Dr. Webster can't be *certain* this really happened—that it's a dream that has a basis in reality."

"No, he can't know for certain. He can only draw conclusions, as we all do. But *his* conclusions are based on objective, scientific observations that are more trustworthy than *our* subjective nonscientific ones, wouldn't you agree?" he asked reasonably. "Besides, if we can't accept their professional judgments, why should we consult these head doctors in the first place?"

"I don't know," Nora agonized. "It's so difficult to know what to believe. But what does Dr. Webster think you should do? Confront Rupert?"

"No, he said that would be the worst thing I might do . . . for the present, anyway."

"But you must do something to come to terms with this—"

"Yes," Hubert laughed. "And do you know what the good doctor suggests? That I get more exercise and fresh air. I haven't gotten much of either lately since I've been so busy with the gallery. I haven't been riding in ages. Not since the hunt at the Athertons'."

She was bewildered. "I must be missing something here.

What does fresh air and exercise have to do with your dream? With what Rupert did? With your problems?"

"Old Jimmy believes that the better one takes care of one's body, the healthier the mind. It's quite progressive of him, really, for a psychiatrist. You know how most of these doctors are. If they're medical, they totally ignore the head, and if they treat the mind, they don't even acknowledge the body's existence. All in all, I think Webster was an excellent choice. Thank you so much, Nora darling."

"For what?"

"For everything. But especially for choosing James Webster as my shrink. I'm sure it wasn't pleasant for you interviewing all those doctors, washing our dirty linen, so to speak, so many times before you settled on him."

No, it hadn't been pleasant. And while she *was* pleased that Hubert was pleased, she found it difficult to accept the doctor's theory that Rupert had sodomized Hubert. At least she had her doubts, but she didn't want to argue the point with Hubert—he had to believe in the doctor if his therapy was to work.

All the same, it was difficult for her then to look at Rupert without wondering . . . without an involuntary repugnance. . . . Sometimes her eyes followed Rupert so intently that he couldn't help but notice and comment. Once, when Jeffrey was in the room too, Rupert, smiling enigmatically, observed, "You watch me so closely, Nora. If I didn't know better—if I didn't know how besotted you are with Hubert—I might think you were falling in love with me. . . ."

She didn't honor *that* with an answer but looked away and then felt *his* eyes burning into her. But when she looked up again, it was Jeffrey's eyes that were fixed on her and she wondered what *he* was thinking—if Jeffrey had any more idea than she what Rupert was really all about . . . if he knew how to distinguish truth from dreams. . . .

Months later she would think that if there hadn't been so many details, so many obscure embellishments . . . if Hubert hadn't gone on and on repeating at length each weekly dialogue between doctor and patient, she herself wouldn't have been so blind to the truth.

*   *   *

Hubert's birthday was coming up, and she was at Blackley's trying to choose a new riding crop for his present since he had taken up riding again with a vengeance, when she spotted Hubert's psychiatrist.

"How wonderful that I've run into you, Dr. Webster. Since you're responsible for Hubert's renewed mad interest in riding—he hardly misses a day—you're just the person to advise me. You must help me choose the most beautiful, elegant crop ever for Hubert's birthday."

James Webster blinked, totally at a loss, and she thought, of course he doesn't recognize me. They had only talked in person that once. She reintroduced herself.

"Yes, of course I remember you, Lady Hartiscor, and your husband from the one time I saw him, but as for my being responsible for his renewed interest in riding, I have no idea—"

"You mean you *haven't* been seeing Hubert regularly?"

"No, I'm afraid not. After that one time he never returned, but that's not unusual. It often happens, for reasons best known to the person himself. But I trust that you've both been well." He smiled and moved on rather hurriedly.

*Dear God! All this time! All those lengthy discussions about all those sessions that had never taken place. . . .*

And Rupert! How could she look him in the face after she had half believed Hubert's fabricated description of his brother's incredibly perverted behavior? She should have taken into account Hubert's cynical view of lying. *There's nothing like a few little white lies to keep things interesting. . . .*

Still, what would be gained by telling Hubert that she had run into Dr. Webster and knew the truth? He would only look charmingly hangdog for a moment or two, then he would not only make new false promises but would probably throw in a few more lies, white or otherwise. And she couldn't bear to listen to the lies anymore—it was as painful for her to hear them as it was demoralizing and degrading for Hubert to be telling them, even if he didn't know it.

She told Hubert it would be best if they no longer discussed his therapy since the sessions were supposed to be confidential, only between patient and doctor. Then, even when Hubert persisted, insisting it *helped* him to go over it with her, she forced herself to turn a deaf ear to him. That was a first for her, and it was hard, but she knew it was time. . . .

# SEVENTEEN

———◦•◦———

It didn't really come as a shock to Nora when the Hartiscor
Art Gallery was finally forced to close its doors. Clearly
Hubert hadn't intended to defraud anyone, but the fact was
that many of the artists the gallery represented had never received the payments due them on the sale of their paintings. The
money had simply vanished into that place where misappro-
priated funds usually went—thin air. She was only grateful that
Rupert and Jeffrey were there to take care of the details and to
make good on the monies due the artists.

Though the proceedings resulted in much less adverse publicity than they'd anticipated and Hubert acted properly repentant, she saw that there truly were no more avenues to be
explored with Hubert, and that the time had come for another
first in their relationship—detachment. Not cold-blooded—it
could never be that—but a *firm* one. It was necessary for her
own survival, and she had to survive for Hubie's sake; the
Victory Baby who'd been born only days before the war was
over was going on six and needed . . . was entitled to . . . a
mentally healthy mother's devoted attention more than that of
a child-man whose fate had been sealed long before she met him.

As for her poor Hubert, he would have to sink or swim on
his own, and she could only pray that he was a stronger swimmer than any of them assumed—that he could at least go the
distance. But then Hubert proved a far weaker swimmer than
she could have possibly anticipated. . . .

\*    \*    \*

When a stunning female impersonator—those who had seen his act swore one couldn't tell the performer from the real thing—was found dead in his flat with his lovely torso methodically slashed in geometric pattern, his testicles separated from his body and his penis stuffed into his mouth, the police immediately perceived that he was the victim of a jealous lover. Then, when it became known that the scion of one of England's foremost and wealthiest families had been the entertainer's most frequent and dedicated lover and, even more pertinently, was the last person to be seen with him the night of the murder, Hubert was taken into custody.

Nora's belief in his innocence was absolute. While there was that void in his character, she knew that he was the most gentle of men, incapable of committing so heinous a crime, and that it was only a matter of time until everyone knew it, including the police. But as the days slowly passed and the unbearable tension mounted, Hubert remained in custody while the family was literally under siege, held hostage by a hysterical media and a horde of curiosity-seekers who kept a constant vigil outside their iron-picket gates.

Still, Nora fought to keep her anxiety at bay by busying herself with keeping Hubie's schedule as normal as possible, though at this point her most acute fears still centered around Hubert's immediate fate. Then, one morning, Nanny took Hubie outside to ride his trike in the courtyard, and only minutes later she heard the woman's outcry.

She ran to the door to see that, incredulously, one of the Fleet Street reporters had actually scaled the gates to accost little Hubie as he played. She tore out of the house in time to hear the odious brute ask a bewildered and frightened Hubie, "Are you worried about your daddy being in jail, laddie? That they say he killed a man?"

Before it was all over, Nora literally had to be pulled from the man she was furiously assaulting, with the result that the next morning there were pictures of the incident taken from outside the gates in various papers. One accompanying headline read: LADY HARTISCOR VICIOUSLY FIGHTS BACK.

While Rupert hired private security guards to make sure there was no recurrence, she still felt that she could no longer allow Hubie to set foot outside even within their own grounds. She also forbade the servants to discuss the case among themselves under threat of dismissal in fear that Hubie would overhear. Still, she had something else to worry about in addition to her anxiety over Hubert—Hubie's vulnerability. Who knew how far the tabloids would go to dig up more scandalous dirt and what they would unearth besides, possibly, a sordid string of Hubert's former lovers? That she and Hubert were never married, stigmatizing Hubie as a bastard?

Also, she was concerned about Jeffrey, who, apparently immobilized by *his* anxiety, relied on Rupert to act as the family's liaison with the police, lawyers, and the media, while he barely left his study. Mostly he sat silent, staring into space, stirring himself only to pour another whiskey. But she was grateful that at least when he did speak, he affirmed his belief in Hubert's innocence. "Preposterous!" he would mutter.

To make matters worse, she hadn't seen Hubert since the police had taken him away. If only she could see him, comfort him, tell him that everything was going to be all right! But while she wasn't actually prohibited from seeing him, Rupert thought it unwise: "The leeches from the tabloids will make it appear as the visit of the wife calling on the husband who has already been tried and *convicted.*"

Then Rupert urged her to take Hubie and leave London for their country estate, leaving him to deal with the mess. "Here you and Hubie are prisoners. There Hubie would at least be able to go outside to play, and if you got Father to go with you, it would be even better. I'm concerned for his health," he pressed, ever the dutiful son so unlike his brother.

"Jeffrey will never leave London while Hubert's under suspicion and neither will I. When the police release him we'll all get away for a while until things quiet down. But tell me, Rupert, why *haven't* they released him? They haven't charged him. How can they continue to hold him?"

"They say it's only for questioning, but I must remind you that they do have eyewitnesses who saw him and his murdered boyfriend leave the Pink Fly together that night. At any rate, the solicitors and I believe it's wiser not to lean on them too hard at this stage of the game."

"At this stage of the game?" Her voice rose. "You sound as if you expect things to get worse!"

"I have to be honest with you. It doesn't look good."

"But *you* believe in Hubert's innocence?"

He smiled at her enigmatically. "I do if you do."

"That's no answer!" she raged. "You must believe in Hubert on your own!"

"I'm doing whatever I can." He shrugged. "Does it make any difference if *I* personally believe or disbelieve?"

"Yes. You're the one who's fighting for Hubert, who's talking to the police and the lawyers. How can you fight for a cause you don't truly believe in?"

"Mankind has been doing it for centuries."

"And *winning*?"

Rupert shrugged. "Sometimes . . ."

"*Sometimes* isn't good enough! Hubert's life is at stake—not some vague cause! For his sake you must fight to win, harder than you've ever fought for anything! And for my son's sake! Think of what his life will be if his father is convicted of murder!"

"Oh, I'm fighting to win, Nora. But as for whose sake—? Let's say it's for *all* our sakes and leave it at that. . . ."

But *could* she leave it at that with the future of the two people she loved most hanging in the balance? Especially since she was no surer than before about Rupert's belief in Hubert's innocence, and, more frightening, she wasn't really convinced that he was doing his utmost for his brother. *Was it the ghost of old hostilities rising up to haunt them once again?*

She would talk to Jeffrey, she decided. Try to rouse him into action. There was a vast difference between fathers and brothers, after all. Surely the father's heart would be more responsive than the brother's, his fighting spirit more easily ignited. If not, they were all lost. . . .

# EIGHTEEN

———•◦••◦•———

N ora, in the sitting room adjoining Jeffrey's study, had the door between the rooms not quite closed so that she could listen in on Rupert and Jeffrey's conversation.

"It's intolerable. Hubert can't be detained any longer," Jeffrey began. "What do the police have to say?"

"They're still not ready to charge him. Pity really. At least if they charged him we could get on with it—the trial and our lives," Rupert said coolly. Too coolly for Nora's taste, and she waited for Jeffrey to blast him, but all he said was, "The reason they're not charging him is because they don't have any *hard* evidence."

"True," Rupert agreed. "I'm surprised anyone even thinks Hubert has the guts for this kind of crime. Lesser ones, yes. Embezzlement as in the case of the gallery. But most of all I'd say what Hubert has a taste for is disgracing us all."

She hoped Jeffrey would at least remonstrate with Rupert, but he only asked, "But what's their justification for detaining him? They *have* to give a reason."

"They're vacillating. Yesterday they said it was for questioning. Today they said it was for his own protection. That *if* the killer is still at large, assuming Hubert *isn't* the killer—they're being cagey about their language—then there's the possibility Hubert might be next on the killer's agenda since he was the murdered man's number-one lover."

"Absolute rot! Everyone who's arrested has the right of bail, but *my* son, a Hartiscor, is sitting in jail without any rights? We must insist he be released at once! You know how to lean on people, Rupert, how to exert influence. Do it!"

"But they're not about to listen, no matter how hard we lean or exert, Father. My guess is they're stalling for time hoping to find more solid evidence. The murder weapon, who knows? It's always possible that even without sufficient evidence, they still want to make an example of Hubert. Show the public that even the son of a wealthy member of the House of Lords is not above question . . . will be held accountable—"

"How dare they pick on my son for their bloody example? And what are the lawyers doing? Why aren't they getting Hubert released? I won't have it! Hubert sitting in a cell when he's no more guilty than a babe in arms!"

"He could be sitting in worse places, Father."

"What's worse than sitting in jail?"

"Sitting in that special place they reserve for those destined for the gallows."

Nora heard Jeffrey gasp as she herself did, then fall silent. It was obvious that her plan to get him to take charge of the situation instead of leaving it to Rupert, whose motivation she suspected, wasn't working. Either Jeffrey was physically incapable of rallying to the task or emotionally incapable of summoning up enough strength of will, or perhaps even—God help them—sufficient interest, considering how Hubert had shamed the family. But she couldn't just let things go on, leaving Hubert to dangle helplessly in the wind. . . .

She rushed in to accost Rupert, "How can you talk of gallows? Don't we have enough to deal with?"

"*We? I'm* the one who's dealing with the cesspool Hubert has pulled us into. It's I who's trying to keep the press off your and Father's back, and it's I who has to issue statements when nothing I say doesn't leave people snickering. All of London is snickering! And who has to *beg* the lawyers—your *supposed* friends, Father—to take Hubert's case, and why do I beg? Because this mess is so filthy they don't want to befoul their hands—they're afraid the stink will never wash off. And who's *trying* to throw the weight of the Hartiscor name around while they're laughing behind my back, and who can blame them? They already *know* what the name Hartiscor stands for! Everybody knows! Faggot! Bugger! Cocksucker!"

Jeffrey covered his ears with his hands while Nora lunged at Rupert, but he caught her arm. "Don't hold *me* responsible for what Hubert has wrought, Nora. Yes, I believe he's innocent of murder, but he's guilty of other crimes, isn't he? Guilty of placing himself in a situation where he *can be* suspect, of bringing this offal down on us until we're smothering in it! But my concern isn't even for Father or myself. *We* can survive this scandal with our money and our standing. But when I think of what Hubert has done to *you*—how you suffer, how you bleed! And Hubie—so young, so innocent. When I think of how this'll affect him, oh, I bleed too—but for Hubie, not for Hubert." Now tears escaped his eyes. "Don't you know I'd do anything for you and Hubie, Nora, and therefore for Hubert? That in the final analysis, I know that I *am*, after all, my brother's keeper. . . ."

When she saw the tears, heard the sincere concern in his voice when he spoke of Hubie, heard him say, "I am my brother's keeper," Nora thought that she had misjudged him, and under the circumstances, had to forgive him his harsh words. "I'm sorry, Rupert. It's this nightmare. It's making us all crazy. But we *must* have a real plan of action!"

"I know what we must do," Jeffrey said, as if to appease her. "We must hire private inquiry agents to find the killer."

"Yes, I've thought of that," Rupert said. "In fact, I've arranged for it," he added, looking at Nora for approbation. "But all this time I've been mulling over another idea—a plan that can save Hubert in case everything else fails."

"Yes? Quick, Rupert! Tell us," Nora cried.

"We have to have Hubert declared incompetent—of unsound mind as evidenced by his degenerate life-style, unable to distinguish between right and wrong."

"You mean we should *ask* to have Hubert declared *insane* because of what you call a *degenerate* life-style?" she demanded, horrified.

"The term I used is *of unsound mind*. It's not quite the same thing."

"But in effect it will be exactly the same!" She turned to Jeffrey, expecting him to tell Rupert that his idea was outrageous. But, shockingly, Jeffrey didn't; incredibly, he appeared *interested*, ready to discuss it.

"Must we use the term *degenerate*, Rupert? Another word, perhaps. And we don't *know* that they're going to accuse Hubert of murder. Isn't it precipitous to do it now?"

"If we wait until he's formally charged it will be too late. No judge would go along with it then, willing to dispense with a trial to simply place him in a facility for treatment. No, once Hubert is charged he'll have to stand trial and take his chances with an insanity plea."

"But he's innocent!" she cried. "Why would he have to enter an insanity plea? Besides, how *can* they indict him? Both of you said that they don't have enough evidence."

Then both Rupert and Jeffrey smiled sadly at her as if she were a naïve child, and Rupert said, "Believe me, Nora, men have stood trial with less hard evidence against them and have been convicted. And the times are such—ever since the end of the war—that there's a lot of strong feeling against what our working classes call the landed and *decadent* gentry. And there's a lot more of *them* than there are of *us*. Even the lawyers believe it will be difficult to find twelve good men who haven't already made up their minds that Hubert's as guilty as hell. Don't you understand? They *want* to believe he's guilty. It's class resentment."

"No, I won't accept that!" Nora cried.

"But you might have to! The barristers might insist their only chance *is* to plead Hubert not guilty due to insanity. Then everyone will assume he's *so* guilty that the insanity plea was the only defense we could come up with and give it little credence. But if we move *now* to have him declared of unsound mind we might have enough influence to find a judge willing to go along with it."

"But if we do it before he's even been accused, it will look like his *own* family believes he's guilty, then everyone will think that if *we* do, why shouldn't they? And suppose we *do* do it now? What will happen to Hubert?"

She asked the question of Rupert but it was Jeffrey who answered. "It means that, aside from the question of whether or not Hubert committed murder, we who ask that he be declared of unsound mind must also ask that he be confined. Otherwise, there'd be no point to have him declared of unsound mind in the first place."

"No, I won't stand for it!" she began to cry.

"Oh, Nora, Nora, do we have a choice?" Rupert asked sorrowfully. "Don't you see, once Hubert's been declared mentally ill and confined to an institution, everyone involved will be able to tell himself justice *has* been served and will then be willing for the whole thing to be dropped. It won't be the first time it's happened, believe me. In the final analysis, who *really* gives a damn that Hubert disposed of some filthy scum society is better off without?"

"But they'll lock him up and he's innocent! We can't do that to Hubert!" *It will kill his soul. . . .*

"Having a person committed doesn't mean it's forever. When the doctors feel he's ready—is repentant, if nothing else—he'll be forgiven all his sins and allowed to return to society, who will grasp him to its bosom. There's nothing the world loves more than a penitent." Rupert smiled cynically. "Am I right, Father? Tell Nora I'm right."

"Yes, Nora, I think Rupert is quite right," Jeffrey said, finally decisive. "We *must* do what is necessary. . . ."

Then Nora saw that between them the matter was already decided, and that no protest from her, a mere woman and commoner, would carry any weight. *The lord who would one day be in charge had proposed and the lord who was still in charge had disposed and who dared question the ways of the lord?*

She was powerless and, if it came down to it, had no legal rights. She wasn't even Hubert's wife.

*But why are they doing this, the father and the brother?* It was almost as if, with only a very weak legal case against Hubert, they wanted to hedge their bets—*assure* that he was out of circulation for a long, long time. Had the black sheep so blackened the Hartiscor name that no less an exile . . . no less harsh a punishment . . . would do?

Suddenly, she remembered the conversation she and Hubert had had about how his brother and father felt about him: "I wouldn't be surprised if one of them was plotting to kill off this fool of a black sheep," he had said, and she, not thinking he was serious, had asked why. "Maybe because I'm a dark blot on the family name or maybe because they're both in love with the black sheep's wife and each wants her for his very own. . . ."

*Oh, my God, Hubert! What have I done?*

# NINETEEN

---

The whole matter became academic a few days later when another female impersonator, one quite butch with a heavy body, hirsute legs, and considerable expertise in wielding a knife—butchering had actually been his occupation before he traded in his knives for high heels and lipstick—was apprehended fleeing the scene of a second killing only minutes after he had duplicated the first murder down to the last gory detail. With the bloody murder weapon still in hand—a butcher knife—he confessed to both crimes, and a rail-thin, ghastly pale Hubert came home to his family.

Rupert was actually very sweet to him—there wasn't a word of recrimination, only sympathy for what he had suffered—and Jeffrey broke down and cried. Then Nora was ashamed that she'd thought the worst of both of them—she'd been so distraught, she had let her imagination get the worst of her. But now that Hubert was free and the family was again a unit, perhaps they would all be able to put the past behind them and get on with their lives. Maybe they would even be a reasonable facsimile of a happy family, with Hubie the beneficiary.

But the tabloids chose to go on exploiting the case—the sheer scandal of it still having popular appeal—and they continued to make Hubert the main focus of their sensationalism, the Hartiscor name carrying more weight with a public avid for lurid details of life among the sordid rich than a few female impersonators outside of even the fringes, whom no one would miss.

These publications managed to keep the public interest at a feverish pitch by running a series of daily segments on the degenerate life and times of Hubert Albert Hartiscor, who, while married to the former cabaret singer Nora Hall—"notorious" for her voluptuous charms—sought more exotic thrills among the freaks and perverts of London's netherworld. Whatever dirt they managed to dig up was eked out by sheer creative invention and supplemented by interviews with several of Hubert's lovers, who came crawling out from under the rocks to tell their own tales in sordid detail.

The pain of it was excruciating and a frantic Nora tried to keep the tabloids out of the house, forbidding the staff to bring the noxious publications into even their own quarters, but, an unsmiling wraith, Hubert himself went forth every day to buy the papers himself.

"You mustn't, Hubert darling," Nora remonstrated. "It will all die down soon. You know how it is—nothing is as cold as yesterday's news unless it's yesterday's mashed potatoes. And that's how it will be in a few days. It can't go on indefinitely."

But again Hartiscor House was under siege—the Fleet Street reporters taking note of their every coming and going, the photographers going into action every time a maid as much as stuck her head out the door—and an emaciated Hubert forbade Nora to allow Hubie to leave the house.

*Oh, dear God,* Nora prayed, *let it end!*

\* \* \*

The tabloids were fortunate in that when, inevitably, public interest began to wane, the story regained its potency when Hubert took his own life. . . . Of course, they would have preferred that he'd committed the act in grislier, more dramatic fashion, shooting himself in the mouth perhaps, or in his sexual parts, allowing himself to bleed to death. But Hubert passed on these methods. Rather, he went up to the attic and quietly hanged himself. As Rupert had once told Nora, the Hartiscors had a taste for death by hanging.

On the attic floor stood a nearly empty bottle of Jeffrey's finest brandy but no suicide note. But there *was* a note in a special place that only Nora knew of—she and Hubert had frequently left notes for one another in an illustrated volume of human anatomy, a kind of private joke. And while the note tore at her heart, she mused that no poet out of all the poets Hubert had familiarized her with could have said it all as eloquently as her sweet Hubert.

The moment she began to read, she knew this wasn't really a suicide note but only a very personal farewell. It began by asking her forgiveness while attempting to assuage the terrible sorrow with which he anticipated she'd be consumed:

> Don't ever feel that in some way *you* failed, darling girl. Only true gamblers know that sometimes the odds are too great even for the most daring and loving of betting men and only God knows how cruel a joke fate played on us. . . . But perhaps in the grand scheme of things there *will* be a time for us and we'll meet in another lifetime and it will be the way it should have been the first time around. . . .
>
> But in the meantime, in this lifetime, know that whatever true happiness I experienced was at your hands and therefore you are obligated to me as is one who saves another's life. Thus I charge you: live and be happy and do not cry for me. Find a man who will love you in the way you deserved to be loved and take care of our 'sweet convenience' and provide for him the way I yearned to, but could not find the strength to make a good job of it. And no one knows better than you that I am not talking about the fripperies of life such as money or titles but of its very heart. . . .

*I'll try my best, dear love.*
But there was one thing that Hubert asked that she *couldn't* do—she could not *not* cry for him. It was quite possible that in her heart she would cry for him till the end of time. She kissed his signature and blurred it with her tears, thinking that this was not so much a suicide note or even a note of farewell as it was a love letter.

But the following day, another written document—a legal notice, properly notarized, placed and paid for by Hubert Albert Hartiscor just before he took his life—appeared in all the newspapers, including the tabloids, which featured it on their front pages. It stated that the woman Nora Hall, commonly known as Lady Hartiscor, the wife of Hubert Albert Hartiscor, was not and had never been his legal wife, and that her issue—the male child commonly known as Hubert Winston Hartiscor—was not of his loins.

Nora knew then that this public disavowal, which branded her as a woman who had lived a lie and Hubie as a bastard, but meant only to free them of what the world would view as a much more damning taint—being the widow and son of a moral degenerate—was the true love letter. By disavowing her and the boy he had always loved as a son, Hubert had also forfeited his only claim to immortality.

# PART THREE

# ONCE FOR THE NAME

England, 1951–1955

# TWENTY

"I feel so guilty," Rupert told Nora after they returned from the private gravesite service. "As if I could have done more to save him—"

"We all did what we could, Rupert, and you mustn't blame yourself," she said, making an attempt to comfort him, though her own grief was overwhelming.

"But it was *my* responsibility as head of the family."

She was startled. It was an odd thing for him to say. "Your father may be shaky at the moment, but he's still the head of your family." *At least, what remains of it.*

"Of course. What I meant to say was that it was my place to look after my younger brother. Besides, you know how Father is about assuming responsibility."

"No, I don't. How *is* he about assuming responsibility?"

"He *doesn't . . .* ever."

Then she remembered. This wasn't the first time Rupert had mentioned Jeffrey's dislike of accepting responsibility. But she was hardly in the mood for this conversation. "Personally, I think your father was wonderful with Hubert, always trying to help him, always forgiving him no matter—"

"But that was *after* the fact, that was *his* guilt!"

The last thing she wanted now was to discuss Jeffrey's possible guilt. All she wanted to do was to go to her room to be alone with her thoughts. "I'm exhausted, Rupert, but tell me—what did your father have to feel guilty about?"

"He *knew* what was going on with dear old Mummy and little Hubert and he didn't do a damn thing about it!"

Her heart skipped a beat. "What are you saying, Rupert?

*What* went on with Mummy and Hubert?"

"Didn't Hubert ever tell you about the games Mummy played with him in her bed? How she sucked on his little tippie?"

She was appalled rather than shocked. "Stop! Hubert never told me any such thing and I refuse to listen to it now." She started for the stairs but Rupert ran after her.

"It's true! I swear it!"

"I don't want to hear this. I'm going upstairs and—"

"But that *was* what was going on! Why won't you believe me?" Now Rupert was actually crying.

*Oh, God! Will it never end?*

She sat down on the bottom step of the stairway wearily. "Frankly, I don't know *what* I believe. Maybe it happened and maybe you only *thought* it happened because you were sick with jealousy and that was your mother's fault because she played favorites. But to think that Jeffrey knew and didn't do anything about it? *That's* unbelievable, and you can't fall into the trap of not being able to separate truth from fancy."

Rupert sank to the marble floor at her feet and buried his face in her lap. She could feel the dampness of his tears through the silk of her dress and her heart went out to him. He was still the little boy whose dutiful behavior hadn't earned him any points with his mother. She smoothed the dark hair back from the troubled brow. "But it doesn't matter anymore. Your mother's dead and Hubert's dead and no one will ever really know the truth and probably it's for the best. As for your father, you must be very kind to him—he's lost a son and that has to be one of the worst things that can happen to a father, even—" *Forgive me, Hubert, for what I'm about to say.* "Even if the lost son was only *second* in his heart."

"What do you mean—second in his heart?"

"Well, Hubert always said *you* were your father's favorite . . . told me how much Jeffrey loved you, how you always came first with him." *A half-truth. But would it help anyone if she told him that what Hubert had really said was that after Anne he came first?*

Rupert straightened up. "Hubert really said that? It's hard to believe. But Father—what does *he* say?"

"Oh, he's implied that he loved you best many times."

*Once you told a half-truth, what difference did it make if you embellished on it so that it became a little white lie?*

Then an overwhelmed Rupert so forgot himself that he kissed her most inappropriately, full on the lips. But she didn't reprove him. At best, they were all caught up in a highly inappropriate situation in the most inappropriate of times. . . .

\* \* \*

The next day, she, Hubie, and Jeffrey left London for Hartiscor Castle. Rupert, acting as if the previous evening's conversation between him and her had never taken place, reassured them that he would "sweep up" as much as possible in their absence and hopefully by the time they returned, the worst of the gossip would be over.

Nora didn't believe it. Really nasty gossip had a way of lingering on for years. But she wasn't so much concerned for herself as she was for Hubie and Jeffrey. Hubie had such a long time to live under its dark cloud, and Jeffrey perhaps didn't have enough time to get out from under it. . . .

Still, though she didn't find Hartiscor Castle the idyllic haven Jeffrey thought it—to her it was more gloomy than peaceful—she and he were able to share several weeks of serene if not completely healing respite. They spent most of the day with Hubie, who was so sweet he made them forget for a little while that they were in mourning, and their evenings in isolation with no visitors and no newspapers. Rather, they took comfort in their quiet companionship, playing a game of chess, discussing the novel *From Here to Eternity*, which they were reading simultaneously, listening to the latest records—"Be My Love" was a mutual favorite—or chatting about all manner of things from gardening to the U.S.S.R. exploding an A-bomb.

But the day arrived when Jeffrey told her they would have to start thinking about returning to London to "get on with it."

The sooner they resumed the routine of daily life, the sooner they themselves would be on the road to recovery.

Nora turned away from the window where she'd been watching Hubie play with the caretaker's little boy under the eye of the governess, to face him and see too clearly how their tragedy had aged him. It was as if in a matter of weeks he had grown small and frail, where before she had always thought of him as a vigorous figure, a tower of strength. "You do understand, Jeffrey dear, that under the circumstances, Hubie and I won't be living with you at Hartiscor House for too long? It's time we were moving on."

" 'Moving on'?" he scoffed. "What kind of fatuous phrase is that? It makes you and Hubie sound like a couple of vagrants, or two adventurers on the loose. No, I won't hear of it. As far as I'm concerned, your home will always be with the Hartiscors. At least until you consider marrying, which, I suppose, eventually you will, but—" his voice trailed off.

"I appreciate your generosity, especially after I deceived you so badly, pretending that Hubert and I were married, that Hubie was his son. That's probably the one thing I regret the most— having taken advantage of your kindness."

She went over to where he sat on the rose velvet Victorian sofa and, seating herself on the floor, took his hand and pressed it to her cheek. "I hope you've forgiven me."

"But you didn't deceive me. Not about the boy, at any rate. Somehow I always knew, *felt*, right from the beginning that Hubert wasn't Hubie's father."

"But why, then, did you accept me? You've always been *so* good to me. Why?"

"Because, no matter what else, Nora, *you* always gave as good as you received. And you and I have always understood each other, haven't we?" He stroked her hair as she leaned her head against his knee.

It was true, she thought, they *had* always understood each other. She thought back to the day when Jeffrey had toasted her, how she had felt that they had made an unspoken pact.

"Let's not talk any longer about the past, Nora, except to say that in my heart you were Hubert's wife and Hubie was his son.

More importantly, I can still give you and Hubie the benefit of my protection and the privileges of my position and wealth. I will not only provide for Hubie, but I will watch over him, present him with opportunities, open doors for him. For Hubie's sake if not for your own, you must stay."

"Oh, Jeffrey, I don't think I can. Not that I don't appreciate everything you've done. And no matter how it all turned out, I still think I got the best of that bargain we made. Between you and Hubert, I learned how to be a much more accomplished person, and I had the love of *two* good men and the privilege of loving you both in return."

"Ah, Nora, you talk of love—of my loving you and you loving me, yet in the same breath you talk of deserting me."

"Deserting *you?*" How could Jeffrey construe her leaving as something she was doing to *him?* "I never thought of leaving your household as desertion. First of all, there's the scandal. Much as we'd like to pretend it doesn't matter, we know it does. You know the way people are. They'll always refer to Hubie as 'the Hartiscor bastard who's no Hartiscor.' As for me, I'd be lucky if all they called me was 'the Lady Hartiscor who was no lady much less a wife.' But if we go abroad to live—say, Paris—and start all over, Nora and Hubie Hall will more than likely melt into the crowd."

"Nonsense. It's a small world and the scandal will follow you, and the people you'll meet in Paris won't be any different from the people you know here. They'll relish the malicious gossip just as much."

"But if we stay you'll—"

"I'll what? I'll stand my ground, that's what, and dare any man to sneer. But you—if you run like a coward, you and Hubie will forever be sneaking around corners, ashamed of who you are. What kind of a way is that to raise your son?"

She started to protest, but he put a finger to her mouth. "If you stay and get some steel into your backbone, we can face down the gossip together and hold ourselves proud. Then you'll not only be accepting the challenge, it will be Hubie who'll be the victor."

*Run like a coward . . . Get some steel into your backbone . . .*

Jeffrey *was* a sly old dog. How well he knew the phrases that were guaranteed to ignite her fighting spirit.

"I wasn't going to run like a coward," she said stiffly. "I was just going to face the facts and protect Hubie."

"That's exactly my point—protecting Hubie. *I'm* the Earl of Hartiscor who commands one of the largest fortunes in England. and we Hartiscors go back a long way, and with a few exceptions, like poor Hubert, we're a tough and hardy bunch. It can rain bloody hell and we survive, while our detractors live to eat their words. And that's the kind of protection I wish to provide you and your son, and if you're the wise woman I always thought you were, you'll accept, at least on Hubie's behalf."

"I don't know, Jeffrey. There's Rupert and—"

Jeffrey's eyes slitted. "What about Rupert?"

"Well, Hartiscor House *is* his home, and while he doesn't appear to have any interest in any particular woman now, the time will come when he'll want to marry and have children of his own, and what then? No matter how fond we all are of each other, Hubie and I will be in the way. You know no house is large enough to accommodate two families. Hubie would be relegated to the status of some kind of a stepchild without a legal name to call his own. And what would be *my* status? No, we'd both be in an untenable position."

"Ah"—Jeffrey fingered his mustache—"a point well taken. But no one could question your position if you were already the *Countess* Hartiscor, could they? Or Hubie's, if he were once and for all time legally a Hartiscor?"

She looked at him, puzzled. "What does that mean?"

"It means, my dear, that it all boils down to that I could care less about whom or when Rupert marries or how he and his future wife may feel about you and Hubie. Do I owe it to him to give up everything to him even before I die? It means that you and I must think only about Hubie and *us*. What we want and what we owe one another. And that means that you must marry me!"

Nora's brain reeled. *Marry Jeffrey?* It was inconceivable!

Without waiting for her response, Jeffrey went on, his enthusiasm mounting with every breath: "Yes, it's exactly what you must do! Actually, considering everything, it's fortunate that you and Hubert were never legally married. Then, according to the civil laws and the laws of the church, it would have been impossible for me to marry you. But now I'll be able to take care of you and Hubie properly, adopt him as my own, and if Rupert doesn't like it, well, he will just have to lump it . . . clear out himself."

This was insane! Mourning had apparently addled Jeffrey's brain even as it had aged his body and his spirit! But then she saw that even that was no longer true. She could see his former vigor and vitality surging through him, his former larger-than-life presence taking over, the high color flowing back into his face. While it had taken three months for him to age prematurely, it was as if she were watching him take back the years in a matter of seconds. It was amazing! It was *all* so amazing. . . .

It wasn't that during these weeks of mourning she hadn't thought about marrying . . . hadn't daydreamed about what kind of a man she would want . . . hadn't tried to visualize him in her mind's eye. She would have been inhuman if she hadn't—she was twenty-six with a son of six and not a quid to her name, and she had been masturbating herself to sleep for years. But she had thought that when and if she married, she would marry a virile man with an urgent need for her, one who would love her in the way she yearned to be loved—madly, passionately, with a burning desire. But then, looking at Jeffrey, reenergized by his proposal, she realized that he loved her in just that way—with an urgent need, madly, passionately, with a burning desire. . . .

*Oh, dear God, what am I to do?*

She heard Jeffrey say, "We will wait a few months, of course, for appearance's sake, and then we'll be married." Then he rose from the sofa to extend his hands to her and pulled her to her feet from her position on the floor.

"But Jeffrey! I haven't agreed! It's not settled! I—"

"Of course it's settled! It's the only decision that makes sense!" He laughed as happily as a schoolboy. "You said you loved me before, did you not?"

"Yes . . ." She nodded tentatively. That was undeniable.

Caring about someone *was* loving them, even if it weren't how she yearned to love.

"And I love you. Do you accept that?"

"Yes." To say otherwise would be a lie.

"And our marriage will mean a secure future for Hubie. Is that not true?"

She nodded again. It was undeniably the truth.

"Well, there you are. It's settled, then! Am I right?"

She owed Jeffrey so much. He'd been so good to her. How could she deny him? And she owed Hubie even more, and how could she deny him his own good name?

Maybe it had always been meant to be this way, an evening out of the score. Hubert had told her that *their* marriage would be one of sweet convenience, but being Hubert he had gotten it wrong. It had been for love . . . would have *always* been for love. Love for him and love for Hubie. But then they had never married. *This* marriage, then, would be the one conceived in convenience and out of duty, but still it would be for love too—Jeffrey's love for her and hers for Hubie.

"Yes, Jeffrey, you are right," she said finally, offering her cheek for his kiss.

But he took her face between his hands and kissed her hard on the lips, then kissed her again, crushing her to him, crouching to match her body to his so that all the parts of one fit into the other. "I have loved you *always*, Nora," he muttered into her throat, kissing her again fervently and pressing the lower half of his body against hers convulsively.

*Always.* The word made her sad. *Always* would *always* be the way she had loved Hubert. But what had Jeffrey said when they had started this fateful conversation: "*You* always gave as good as you received, Nora." She liked that. It had a fine ring to it. And she would try to make it true again in every way.

She tipped her head back away from him to smile deeply into his eyes and then pulled his head down to hers to return his kiss, hard at first, then softly as she parted her lips to draw his tongue into her mouth. Then, as he groaned softly, she took his hand to insert it into the *V* of her dress, and as she felt the heat of his fingers touch her flesh, a flash of pain pierced her breast as she remembered. . . . No, she would never forget Hubert and she didn't want to. And though Hubie wasn't Hubert's son, it didn't matter. The best part of Hubert would live on for her in Hubie, their shared sweet convenience.

Then she smiled into Jeffrey's eyes again as she lowered herself onto the sofa and pulled him down over her so that his body covered hers.

# TWENTY-ONE

———•◦•◦—————

When they returned to London, Nora was surprised to find that as scandal, the Hartiscors were old hat. Intelligence's Guy Burgess and Donald Maclean had defected to Russia, for whom they'd been spying since university days, and the tabloids were devoting all their energies to their story instead.

Now the only thing she was nervous about was how Rupert was going to react to the news of the impending marriage. She'd asked Jeffrey to delay telling him since the wedding *was* several months away, but Jeffrey wouldn't hear of it. "There's no reason to procrastinate with Rupert. *He's* not a child who might have reason to be upset. Besides, you're making a fuss over nothing. Probably he'll be delighted."

\* \* \*

They were having tea in the salon when Jeffrey made the announcement, and for a brief moment Rupert's face went blank before he found his voice: "Well, this *is* a surprise! May I offer you both my congratulations? No, that isn't quite right, is it? One offers the groom congratulations and wishes the bride good luck. Isn't that how it goes, Nora? I was never good at these small social graces. That was more Hubert's department, he having been trained so well by our mother, the countess. But now that *you're* going to be the countess, we'll have to look to you for guidance. So, what do you say—do I wish you luck or do I merely kiss the bride?"

Pouring, she said, "Though I'm not yet the countess, I believe I can make a ruling. I think it would be quite nice and proper too if you were to offer your congratulations to us both, along with your best wishes. Don't you agree, Jeffrey?" She passed him his cup of tea.

"Whatever you say, my dear." Having made his announcement, Jeffrey was now immersed in the correspondence he had brought to the tea table—he'd been away from London so long that he had a great deal to catch up on.

Rupert took his cup. "But *do* I get to kiss the bride?"

"Hardly"—Nora smiled—"since I'm not yet a bride. That's still several months off. Probably not until the beginning of next year."

"Of course. Stupid of me, really. But very wise of you to wait. We wouldn't want people to get the wrong notion."

Nora glanced at Jeffrey to see if he would react to that, but he was concentrating on his mail and paying no attention. She sighed and asked, "What wrong notion, Rupert?"

Rupert took a sip of tea. "Oh, I say now, Nora, you added my slice of lemon cut paper-thin, just the way I like it, but you forgot to put in my two lumps of sugar." He held his cup out so that she could deposit the requested lumps.

"Two to be sure," Nora said, dropping them in with the silver tongs, then held up the plate of biscuits for Rupert to choose one. "Now that we have your sweetness quotient taken care of, Rupert, why don't you tell us what you meant by people getting the wrong notion if we married right away?"

"Well, we wouldn't want people to think that you two were so hot to trot you couldn't wait until the body was cold." He laughed then in the face of Nora's frigid stare. "Just a small joke, you know." He stirred his tea. "Oh, dear, Nora, you *are* scowling. People are always saying I don't have a sense of humor and when I try—well, I've offended you. I guess I'm just not as good at it as Hubert was. Mummy always said Hubert could make a statue laugh."

He tasted his tea and made a face. "Oh, my, Nora, this tea is quite tepid. You'd think the very least we could expect of the kitchen would be *hot* tea. Very, very hot."

Nora agreed. She only wished the tea were hot enough to

scald him if she did what she felt liked doing—pitching the contents of her own cup of tea in his face.

"Don't *you* agree, Father?"

Jeffrey looked up. "Agree? With what?"

"Don't you agree that the tea is quite cold?"

Perplexed, Jeffrey took a swallow of his tea. "I don't know what you're talking about. My tea is sufficiently hot."

"You're lucky, Father, because we all like it hot." He set his cup down with a clatter. "It just struck me—you're going to be my stepmother, Nora! Isn't that amusing?"

Nora shrugged. "Not particularly."

"But it does give me certain privileges. Prerogatives, you might say." Abruptly he rose from his chair. "Like kissing the bride *before* the wedding." Then, before she knew what he was up to, he was standing over her and swooping down to kiss her full on the lips.

Then she was startled to hear Jeffrey chuckling. "Good show, my boy! There, Nora, I told you he'd be delighted."

\* \* \*

Clearly it was going to be an early evening. After dinner and many glasses of wine, Rupert was drunk, and when Jeffrey retreated to his study with his paperwork, Nora decided to retire to her room. But Rupert pleaded with her, "Please don't go yet, Nora. I know I acted rather badly at tea today, but you must give me a chance to make amends."

"It's not necessary, Rupert. I can understand that our news was something of a shock and that naturally you reacted." She pushed her chair back to rise, but Rupert rose to speed around the table to put his hand on her shoulder, pressing down hard to hold her fast to her chair.

"You know, you should have waited, Nora."

Resigned then that she was going to have to listen to him but that she wasn't going to hear anything she wanted to hear, she asked wearily, "Waited for what?"

"For me to ask you to marry *me*."

She didn't look at him. "It was never a question."

"But I was going to, you know. As soon as a decent amount of time elapsed. I did so want to do the decent thing. That's my style and I thought you'd appreciate that quality—decency. Still, you must have known how I felt about you."

She wouldn't respond, she thought. It was foolish to respond to a man as drunk as Rupert. But she *was* upset. While she had suspected that Rupert might react badly to her and Jeffrey's news, she had never expected *this*. She hadn't dreamed that Rupert might be thinking of *her and him*—a couple. But actually, Hubert had warned her. And for the second time she thought of Hubert's words that night when she had at last given up on their being lovers:

*I wouldn't be surprised if one of them was plotting how to kill off this fool of a black sheep. . . . Maybe because they're both in love with the fool of a black sheep's wife and each one wants her for his very own.*

*Oh, no fool, Hubert, but very much dead just the same.*

She shook off the pressure of Rupert's hand on her shoulder. "I'm going to bed now and I suggest that you do the same. After a good night's rest I'm sure you'll feel differently about things."

"I doubt it but I just realized. *Of course* you wouldn't wait for me to marry you. Why would you? It wasn't so much a husband you wanted, or even a father for Hubie. It was that you couldn't *wait* for me to make you the Countess Hartiscor. . . ."

\* \* \*

Lying in bed, unable to sleep, she decided that the only solution was to insist that Jeffrey ask Rupert to take up residence elsewhere, even if this meant revealing to Jeffrey what Rupert had said and how much hostility simmered beneath the surface. It was not what she wanted at all—to come between father and son—but she didn't know what else she could do.

But then, in the morning, a roomful of flowers arrived with Rupert's profuse apologies, professing how much her friendship meant to him and how much he wanted to play the good uncle to Hubie. And she decided that it behooved her to forgive him his lapse. She had had a few lapses of her own and she had forgiven Hubert so many. Besides, she owed it to both Jeffrey and Hubie to give Rupert the benefit of any doubt.

\* \* \*

A date was set for the wedding in early March. Rupert insisted that a grand celebration was in order—one that would set London on its ear with a reception for a thousand guests—the aristocracy from the Continent as well as Britain's own, plus all Jeffrey's American friends, including Harry Truman and Ike. They would show the world that they didn't give a bloody damn for any still-circulating gossip. Nora was touched, though she said she had wanted a much smaller wedding.

Still, Rupert was so enthusiastic, insisting on orchestrating the proceedings, that she let him take over. She knew it was his way of making up to her. Then, as it turned out, the wedding came off beautifully, there wasn't nearly the amount of dread coverage by the press that she'd anticipated, and the only shadow hovering over the celebration was the king's death a month earlier—Jeffrey had been very fond of King George.

In fact, every detail of the reception was so perfect, Jeffrey said that even Hubert, who'd been so good at these things, couldn't have done it better. Then Rupert smiled, gratified, and Nora was pleased. It looked as if there were smooth, if not exhilarating, sailing ahead. . . .

# TWENTY-TWO

O nce they settled down to a routine, Nora discarded any
lingering doubts she had about Rupert. His attitude was
splendid, and if Jeffrey's age and position rendered him
too remote to take the place of a father, Rupert was the right age
and willing. He was very good with Hubie, playing games with
him and reading him bedtime stories. Also, he was good to her,
offering escort service whenever Jeffrey was unavailable, and his
time and advice for her various philanthropies.

When Nora said as much to Jeffrey, he blustered: "He *better*
behave himself or I'll send him packing. I'm still the lord and
master around here, not some impotent old dotard."

"*Hardly* impotent," she laughed. It was true. When it came
to sex, Jeffrey was insatiable. Merely seeing her *begin* to disrobe,
removing nothing more seductive than her pearls, was enough
to put ideas into his head, and the sight of her in a negligee was
enough to inspire an erection of enormous proportions. Then
he would lead her to bed, where he unfailingly proved a lusty
lover. And if she weren't thrilled by the incessant lovemaking,
regarding it as only one more of her obligations as Lady Hartiscor—overseeing the running of the house, attending and hosting
private and public functions, and heading up various commit-
tees for different causes—she nevertheless threw herself into the
job of satisfying his every sexual demand with vigorous, if simu-
lated, enthusiasm, pleased that she could please him. It was the
least she could do for the man who was so good to her, who was
forever presenting her with some gift: a gold bracelet set with
sapphires to match her eyes, a painting she admired, even an
estate in the Cotswolds—Merrillee Manor, which he called her

159

dowerage—because she'd told him how much she missed the countryside of her youth. He even allowed her to hire a tutor for Hubie rather than send him off to boarding school, though it would have pleased him more to have all her attention himself.

No, she couldn't complain, she told herself, and she had to be grateful that life was proceeding smoothly if not excitingly. The only thing that really disturbed her was that as time went by it became increasingly evident that Hubie, who had the attention span of a gadfly, needed a firm hand.

Rupert tried to console her: "A short attention span is a sign of the quick intelligence." She, already convinced that no little boy was sweeter, was thrilled to hear it, but she was also convinced that no boy was ever lazier. Whenever she told him to pick up his clothes or his army of lead soldiers, he would smile at her winsomely and tell her he was too tired. "Can't Mary do it? She *likes* to do it, Mummy." When she insisted, his bottom lip would quiver adorably and he would complain that his arm hurt, or his stomach, and he would get down on the floor and lie there moaning as if in terrible pain. Or he would retch all over everything, making a clean-up at someone else's hands an absolute necessity and she would end up marveling at how he was able to vomit at will.

He was also determined to get around her rule about limited amounts of sweets. He would go into the kitchen and plague Cook for the biscuits she'd been instructed not to give him unless Nora gave a specific order. While this was what any child with a sweet tooth might do, it did seem that Hubie was willing to go a bit further than the average boy. He would plead and whine so long until poor Cook lost her wits, or he would charm her with kisses and tell her how much he loved her until the besotted woman handed over the whole biscuit jar. And when he found it impossible to move her with either tears or kisses, he would simply wait until her back was turned and *steal* the biscuits. But once confronted with his theft he would admit his guilt and say, "I'm sorry, Mummy, I didn't *mean* to take them. It was just that I was so hungry, and they were my favorites—the big ones with the raisins—that I forgot I wasn't supposed to take them without permission. Don't be mad at me, Mummy. I won't do it ever again!"

But he did, and would think up new excuses each time. Once, after hearing Molly, the parlormaid, telling Mary, the chambermaid, that the reason she had given in to temptation with a certain gentleman was that "the devil made me do it, whispering in my ear," Hubie batted his long lashes at Nora and blamed the devil for whispering in *his* ear.

Rupert laughed heartily at that one. "We best be keeping a sharp eye out for that old devil. Either that or make sure those maids are making their confessionals where Hubie can't hear them tell what *else* the devil made them do."

"Don't laugh, Rupert," Nora protested, trying not to laugh herself. "It's really not funny, you know." The truth was, she was more disturbed than entertained.

Jeffrey told her she was overreacting. "What little scamp hasn't nicked a few sweets? Hubert, in his time, made the pilfering of biscuits a major occupation. When he wasn't actually caught with his fingers in the cookie jar, he'd deny he was the culprit, and when he *was* caught, he'd just promise that he wouldn't do it again, but of course he did."

"Of course," Nora smiled grimly. "But what about Rupert? Did he steal sweets?"

"Certainly not. I've told you Rupert never misbehaved. But sometimes when Hubert wasn't actually caught red-handed, he'd try his ruddy best to lay the blame on him."

"And Rupert was punished?"

"No, even Miranda didn't swallow Hubert's lies."

"What happened then? Did she punish him for lying?"

"I suppose you could call it a *kind* of punishment. She'd make him apologize to Rupert, and then, when it was time for treats, she'd give Rupert two sweets instead of one to make up for his having been falsely accused. But then Hubert got two sweets too, his reward for having apologized. I wouldn't be surprised if he got three. Miranda just couldn't bear for Hubert to do without." He sighed. "But I daresay, in the long run it didn't matter."

"While I know it's in bad taste for the second wife to be

critical of the first, I think that it *did* matter, that it was deplorable. It was reinforcing Hubert's unacceptable behavior pattern. If he knew that he could steal sweets, put the blame on Rupert, then be made to apologize because no one believed him, and *then* be rewarded for apologizing, he was receiving a negative message. As for Rupert, he was getting a negative message too— being rewarded just for being falsely accused."

"I'm sure you're right but you're making my head spin."

She suspected that she was making Jeffrey's head spin only because he wasn't really interested. Rupert's words rang in her ears: *When it comes to family problems, Father tries never to assume responsibility.*

"So why didn't you step in?" she persisted. "At least tell Miranda that you thought what she was doing was wrong?"

"Miranda and I didn't get along very well as it was, and I hesitated to interfere in matters that were her domain."

"But Hubert said there was bad blood between Anne and Miranda. Didn't you feel that you *had* to step in there?"

"Anne?" His voice froze her. "I don't discuss Anne. Her name is not to be mentioned in this house."

He's furious with me, she thought. Never before had he been really angry with her. "I'm sorry," she said, and she was. Still, she couldn't help thinking that if he had at least *tried* to reconcile mother and daughter, maybe Anne would never have run off to Australia, would never have succumbed to the Hartiscor disease—death by the rope.

But then Jeffrey smiled. "Such a sad face, my dear," and kissed her. "Do you know what I think the problem is? You've been reading too many books on child rearing. And my advice is just be glad Hubie is a high-spirited young boy and concentrate on *this* old boy's high spirits."

He took her hand and pressed it to his erection. "Now, isn't that much more demanding of your attention?"

*   *   *

She finally decided that Hubie had to go to school instead of being tutored at home with a houseful of adults dancing attendance on him. What he needed was the company of friends his own age, the give-and-take of playing with other boys, learning to get along in the real world. Since she still couldn't bear the thought of sending him away to boarding school, she enrolled him at the Treadwell Academy, only a fifteen-minute ride from home, traffic permitting.

But almost immediately there were negative reports that he was a disruptive force. He was inattentive and frequently disobedient, albeit charmingly so, and always seemed to be in the center of all the little disturbances. Nothing monumental. A schoolyard scuffle or a small prank—a professor's notebook disappearing to be found in an unpopular boy's desk or a paper-ball fight as soon as the instructor's back was turned. According to Hubie, he was almost always innocent—the other boys made him do it or, if it was a fight, the other boy pushed first.

She was upset, but Jeffrey always came to Hubie's defense, especially if it was a fight. "What would you have the lad do? Stand there and take it on the chin? Do you want to turn him into a bloody pacifist who won't defend himself?"

"Of course not. But how do I know he was only defending himself? You know how Hubie always—" She broke off. She had almost said, "You know how Hubie always lies and blames others." She was falling into the trap of thinking that if Hubie lied once, he was lying again. . . .

Even when Hubert had lied about having all those sessions with Dr. Webster, even when he had made up that dream about Rupert sodomizing him . . . one truth had slipped through the barrage of fabrications. *Dr. Webster says I'm having this dream because it all really happened and I suppressed it because I knew that if I went to my father, he'd never believe me. Or I suppressed it because I actually did go to Father and he called me a bloody liar.*

Poor Hubert. Even in his fantasized dream, that truth had emerged—that he would be branded a liar automatically. Well, she wouldn't make that mistake with Hubie—call him a liar without giving him the benefit of the doubt. And if she found out he *was* lying, she would try to teach him that truth brought its own rewards and convince him that lies were the refuge of the weak and the cowardly and brought only misery. And someday, when he was older and she herself was stronger, she would tell him how she attempted to shroud his own birth in a lie and how it all turned out. . . .

# TWENTY-THREE

Since Hubie already had a tarnished reputation at Treadwell, Nora transferred him to the Wheaton School and tried to impress upon him the importance of starting off on the right foot. He was to follow the rules, pay strict attention to his teachers, and not do any old thing that popped into his head before thinking about it twice.

"I know what you mean. Like looking before you leap."

"Exactly!" She was delighted that he grasped the concept.

But then, like a self-fulfilling prophecy, only a few days later, when confronted with a big puddle in the schoolyard, he and another boy jumped right into the middle of it. They not only drenched themselves with filthy water, they splattered six other boys *and* the irate assistant headmaster, who insisted that they had jumped with malice aforethought, displaying a reckless disregard for the health and comfort of others, and the school asked that Lord and Lady Hartiscor come in to discuss the matter. But Jeffrey refused to go, calling the whole thing poppycock, and advised Nora to forget about it too.

Disappointed, she turned to Rupert for counsel. "Do you think the school's making a fuss about nothing?"

"Of course, and the conference with the little hellions on the carpet will turn out to be a junior inquisition, but—"

"Hold on. *Hellions?* That implies guilt and—"

Rupert caught her hand affectionately. "It's just a term, not an indictment. And I still remember Mummy saying how she couldn't *abide* a boy who didn't have a touch of the hellion in him," he laughed. "I don't believe she really ever forgave me for being better behaved than Hubert."

"Oh, poor Rupert. That must have been so difficult for you. And I'm convinced that the traumas of childhood are never really outgrown. That's why I want to be very careful to do the right thing now, and I especially don't want Hubie to get the reputation of being a troublemaker or a liar. Once he gets the name—well, you know how it is. He'll think if he has the name, he might as well have the game."

"You're absolutely right. Besides, guilty or innocent, how would it look if you didn't go and defend Hubie?"

"I have no intention of defending Hubie if he's wrong."

Rupert smiled sadly. "That's what you say now, but once you get into that room with those prune-faced Wheatonites and the other boy's parents you'll defend him, just like Miranda always defended Hubert. If anyone dared attack her darling, she stood ready to pluck out the offender's eyes."

"But Rupert, I'm not Miranda and Hubie isn't Hubert."

"Of course not. It's just that—well, Hubie *is* so much like Hubert, they really *could* have been father and son."

"Oh, really?" she said frostily, though it was the same chilling thought that had occasionally flashed through her own head. "Because there's a physical resemblance—because Hubie's so handsome and so was Hubert? Half the people in the world probably have blue eyes and blond—"

"But you can't deny that there's more than a *physical* resemblance. That there's a similarity of personality—"

"Hubie is as charming as Hubert was and, like Hubert, loves a good time, if that's what you mean," she said coolly.

"I can see you're annoyed. Let's drop it, shall we?"

"No, I want you to say what's on your mind. I insist."

"I don't want to offend you, Nora, but it's as if Hubie were really Hubert's son and inherited his most significant characteristic—that lack of moral fiber we once discussed."

Oh, she recalled all right—the lack of moral fiber he had called a weakness of character—and she felt like slapping him. *How dare he?* But she *had* insisted he say the damning words even though she knew beforehand what he would say, and she knew only because the same thought sometimes crept into her head to bedevil her. *A significant characteristic.* She herself thought of it as an affliction. *Flaws of character in an otherwise perfect physical specimen.*

"But I know that's foolish," Rupert said now, repentant. "Hubert was a grown man and Hubie's only a little boy, just full of the devil. I'm sure he'll grow out of whatever— Will you forgive me for for saying that? I was just—"

"Just trying to be helpful?" She tried to smile.

"Something like that. You must know by now that I only want to be your and Hubie's friend and I want to help in any way that I can. Will you let me?"

She thought of how Jeffrey had backed away from her problem. "Of course. I wouldn't dream of turning down a good offer, even from the devil himself." But then she laughed at how the words sounded. "Sorry, I didn't mean to imply—"

Rupert laughed too. "I know. But we do have a deal? And when you go to that beastly conference at Wheaton, why don't I go with you to lend my support?"

"Thank you, Rupert. That *will* be a help."

\* \* \*

She went into Hubie's room to get his side of what had now become the infamous puddle-jumping caper, but he was already asleep. She looked at him in the dim glow of the night light: his yellow hair curling on the blue pillow slip, the long lashes curling in shadow on his pink cheeks, the lips—still a baby's rosebud—curved in a smile as if he were dreaming the sweet dreams of angels. She smoothed the pure brow gently, leaned down to kiss it lightly.

How *could* Hubie's character be a carbon copy of Hubert's? Wasn't a flawed character something that would have to be transmitted in the genes? Could it come into existence by some mysterious form of osmosis? Was it contagious, its bacteria floating in the air ready to infect the vulnerable young in close proximity? Could a boy who looked like an angel and was as sweet as one catch the disease simply by being given a name that didn't belong to him? And if so, what other manifestations might appear? Would he grow up another sweet ne'er-do-well, a charming charlatan, a foolish rogue, a man who loved all too well but unwisely?

As she had wondered in the past, she wondered again about what kind of a man Hubie's genetic father, Duke Wayne of Butte, Montana, had really been. Other than that he was a boorish oaf, she knew nothing about him. It had never even occurred to her to try to find out anything. Did he lie? Could he be sweet? Did he pilfer? Did he love his mother? Did he cheat at games? Did he know right from wrong? Had he made callous love because he was a callous man, or was it only that he had been indifferent to *her*? Had there existed in the man a wellspring of love waiting to be tapped by the right woman, another man perhaps, or his very own child? Had the battlefield somehow made a better man of the man she had known only for a few hours? Had he *survived* the battle? Was he alive and well in Butte, Montana, living a far better life than he himself had ever dreamed possible? Should she make it her business to find out for Hubie's sake?

She dismissed the thought. Johnny Wayne had planted the seed, but a man could sow thousands of seeds and scatter them to the winds. It was those who cultivated the soil and nurtured the plantings who had to take responsibility for the eventual harvest. Johnny Wayne was as much a stranger to Hubie as he was to her. No, she had to put her trust in the people who knew and loved her and Hubie and served them well—Jeffrey and Rupert, who had given her their pledge.

\*   \*   \*

Rupert proved his worth as an ally when he accompanied her to the meeting at Wheaton. Amazingly enough, he put the whole matter into perspective quickly with charm and humor.

First, he got the two boys to admit that they *had* jumped deliberately, but only for the sheer joy of jumping, and then he pled their case so eloquently before the stodgy Wheaton bunch. *Who was so old that he had forgotten the pleasure of jumping for joy into a puddle and who was so hardened that he could punish a boy simply for being so joyously young?*

Before the meeting was over, both boys swore that they would think twice before they leaped the next time, and all the adults were pleased, though no one quite believed them. Then everyone was laughing, saying things like, "Boys will be boys," and, "Would we want them to be any other way?"

Then Rupert brought tears to everyone's eyes when he suddenly bent down to hug Hubie to him. "He's my brother by adoption, you know, and he's quite a boy, the very best, and I couldn't love him more even if he were my very own."

\* \* \*

On the way home Nora suddenly took Rupert's hand and pressed it to her cheek. "You were wonderful!"

"Much as your praise is music to my ears, I really didn't do very much."

"I think you did and I think that, after all, blood *will* tell. This afternoon for the first time I could see that you and Hubert shared two very significant characteristics."

"In that case I think you'd better tell me quickly what these two characteristics are."

"Oh, no cause for alarm. They were two of Hubert's best qualities, those that I hope Hubie will always be blessed with too—his charm and his loving ways." Then, seeing Rupert's face darken, she asked, "Does that upset you?"

"No. Who wouldn't be thrilled to be called loving and charming by the lovely Nora? Actually, I was marveling at what an extraordinary man Hubert really was."

"Yes, he was, but extraordinary is like beauty, in the eye of the beholder. Why do you see him as extraordinary?"

"Because out of all the *un*charming and *un*loving things Hubert was, you remember him best for his loving and charming ways. I must say that takes an extraordinary man," he said bitterly.

She turned away to look out the car window at the darkening day, depressed that so much bitterness still rankled in Rupert's heart for his dead brother. Then she saw two lovers kissing on the street and another thought, even more disturbing, popped into her head. Was it only bitterness that rankled, or was it *still* jealousy? But she was no longer his brother's love. She was his father's wife. . . .

She turned to look into Rupert's face to try to read his heart, but his eyes were burning into hers and she had to look away again. Then the car pulled into the courtyard and Parks opened her door and she gently touched Rupert's arm. "Come, let's go find Jeffrey and tell him how wonderfully it all went and how it was *you* who won the day."

# TWENTY-FOUR

"Don't go, Mummy. I have a stomachache and my head hurts too," Hubie begged piteously for at least the fourth time when Nora, dressed and ready to leave for that night's reception at the American embassy—a farewell party for Ambassador Martin Cantington, who had served at the Court of St. James's for more than ten years—went in to say good night to him.

After speaking with the doctor, she went down to tell Jeffrey that he should go on to the reception without her. "I think I'm going to stay home with Hubie. He's not feeling well and—"

"Did you call the doctor?" he asked severely.

"Yes. He said it was probably a flu that's going around and that we should keep him in bed, give him an aspirin and lots of fluids, and check back with him in the morning."

"Well, *has* Hubie had his aspirin?"

"Yes, but—"

"And you *can* leave instructions with the staff that he's to be given fluids frequently and checked on constantly?"

"I suppose," she said reluctantly.

"Well, then, that's all that's necessary, isn't it?"

"But you know how Hubie's been lately. When he's feeling sick he wants only me."

"I know all too well. You're spoiling him, Nora, giving in to his eternal complaints just like Miranda did with Hubert. At one point it got so bad it took a reception at Buckingham to get her to leave the house. You're not doing Hubie any good giving in to him. Besides, Martin will be deeply disappointed if you're

171

not there tonight, and Rita will take it as a snub. You know how she is."

"But with five hundred guests there tonight, neither Martin nor Rita will notice if I'm not there. I think this time Hubie's *really* sick. He's even running a slight fever."

"I'm sure he is," he snorted. "There isn't a schoolboy living who doesn't know more than a few ways to raise the temperature artificially, and I assure you that rascal probably knows every one of them. Now, will you say good night to him and get your wrap? You know I detest being late."

She really couldn't blame Jeffrey for being annoyed. But Hubie had been in tears and he hadn't been himself for weeks now. "Why don't you go on ahead, and then later, if—"

Rupert walked into the library. "I'm planning a quiet evening at home and I thought I'd find myself a whodunit. But I see it's top-ho for you two, and I must say, you look spectacular in that gown, Nora, even more so than you did at the Coronation Ball. So, where are you chaps off to?"

"It's the affair at the American embassy for Martin Cantington if I can get Nora to tear herself away from Hubie."

"Oh? What's the problem with Hubie?"

"He's not feeling well," Nora said, "and I thought I'd stay home with him, but your father is much put out with me."

"And well he might be. You look far too smashing and I think he wants all the men there, including old Martin, to ogle you and eat their hearts out. Isn't that right, Father?"

Jeffrey permitted himself a smug smile. "I do think Martin is a bit soppy for Nora, but a lot of good it will do him."

"Oh, stop it, both of you. What utter rot."

"Well, you really will be a rotten sport if you spoil Father's good time when there's no need. I *am* staying in and I'll keep an eye on Hubie. First, we'll watch *I Love Lucy* on the telly, then I'll challenge him to a game of Scrabble, which he loves since I allow slightly naughty words, and then, for every one he uses, I teach him another, even *more* vulgar."

"Oh, wonderful!" Nora giggled. "Just what any eight-year-old really needs in the way of vocabulary training."

"Sounds like a splendid offer to me," Jeffrey said, "and

Nora accepts. Now, may we please get going?"

"Are you sure, Rupert? You really are a dear!"

*　*　*

Dancing with Martin Cantington, she felt self-conscious remembering Jeffrey's "I think Martin's a bit soppy for Nora."

"I'm going to miss all my English friends," he smiled at her wistfully. "But no one more than you and Jeffrey."

"And we'll miss you." He *was* holding her a bit close.

"You must plan on visiting us in the States."

"That would be fun. I've never been to America." She was having difficulty concentrating. She couldn't get the picture of Hubie sobbing out of her mind.

"In the summers we go to Cape Cod. We have a place there right on the beach."

"Oh, lovely." *I shouldn't have left him, no matter what.* "You must be eager to get home."

"Yes and no." She felt the pressure of his hand on her bare back increase. "But I expect to be busy. Ike's asked me to take a cabinet position. I told him no but that I'd be happy to serve his administration in an advisory capacity."

"Oh, how interesting!"

"So, you *will* visit?" He tightened his hold on her hand now. "Perhaps you'd prefer to visit us on Cape Cod instead of in Washington? Our compound, oddly enough, is right next to Joe Kennedy's, my esteemed predecessor."

"Oh, that's nice. Are you friends or simply neighbors?"

Martin laughed. "Hardly friends. We did have a bit of a row over certain of his anti-Brit sentiments."

"But that's a long time ago. Surely you've made up by now?" This had to be the most inane conversation she had ever had, but she wasn't really up to small talk.

"Well, we act civilized . . . naturally. . . ."

"Naturally . . ." Wondering what they would talk about next, she smiled into Martin's face, but all she saw was Hubie's face, flushed and frightened, the tears rolling down his cheeks in torrents when she'd gone upstairs to tell him that Rupert was going to stay with him until she returned. He had clung to her convulsively. *What am I doing here having this silly conversation with Martin Cantington when Hubie needs me?*

She pulled away abruptly. "You'll have to excuse me, Martin. Hubie was ill when I left. I *must* go! Will you tell Jeffrey that I left? That I'll send the car back for him?"

But Jeffrey came running out angrily just as she was stepping into the Rolls. "What is this sudden madness, Nora?"

"I want to go home to Hubie, but you don't have to leave."

"I insist you come back inside with me."

"I can't. I have this feeling that Hubie needs me! I should never have left—"

"Very well," he said huffily. "I'll return home with you so that we may both attend to this terrible emergency."

*   *   *

Nora raced up the stairs with Jeffrey close behind. She supposed he wanted to be in position to turn to her the moment they saw a peacefully sleeping Hubie to crow: "There, are you satisfied? Pleased that you forced us to leave the party?"

But he never had the opportunity to deliver those words, for when she opened the door very quietly so as not to wake Hubie in case he was sleeping, what they saw by the scant light in a room full of shadows was a silent Hubie lying completely naked in his bed, facedown, his legs spread apart. Then it took another moment to register that Hubie was gagged and that astride him was Rupert, his nude body glistening with sweat as he thrust and shoved, thrust and shoved. . . .

Then, as she screamed out, she heard Jeffrey gasp, "Oh, my God, it *was* true!" And she knew then, as she ran to the bed, that this wasn't only Hubie's nightmare they were living, but Hubert's as well. . . .

# TWENTY-FIVE

Nora stayed on at Hartiscor House for several months until Jeffrey was well, grateful for both their sakes that his stroke had been a minor one. Then, his first week out of bed—she had just wheeled his wheelchair out to the garden—she told him that she was leaving him for good.

"But why?" He clutched his chest.

"Please don't do that. The doctor said there's nothing wrong with your heart. And do you have to ask *why?*"

"But Rupert's gone!"

"Living at the Savoy, taking care of Hartiscor business as usual, is *not* gone. It's beside the point in any case."

"But it isn't! Rupert's the reason you're leaving and I have a plan that will take care of him! Listen!"

"No. While Rupert has been the catalyst, he's not *the* reason I'm leaving. Hubie was the reason I joined the family Hartiscor in the first place, and he's the reason I'm cutting my ties now. Frankly, I can't get away fast enough. This is a haunted house—full of deadly ghosts."

"I know what a terrible thing happened here, but we *can* put it behind us! We *will!* I tell you I have a plan!"

"I don't want to hear it. I just stayed until you were well enough for me to leave with a clear conscience."

"*Clear?* To walk out after all I've done for you?"

"Remember when you asked me to marry you? I said that you'd been *so* good to me and you said that I had always given as good as I got. But I felt I owed you so much more and I agreed to marry you for *that* reason, and for Hubie's sake because you were going to adopt him. But they were the *wrong* reasons and

175

I got what I deserved. But Hubie didn't deserve what *he* got. He still wakes up in the middle of the night crying and so do I. Crying for Hubie *and* for Hubert."

"You blame *me* for what Rupert did? Is that fair?"

"Did Hubert come to you, a terrified little boy, to tell you that his brother was buggering him?"

"Yes, but—"

"Were *you* fair? Did you try to find out what the truth was or did you call him a despicable liar?" Jeffrey didn't answer and she said, "Then I *must* blame you, mustn't I?"

"But who would have believed Hubert? Would *you?*"

It was a question she'd asked herself many times, but how could she answer for that period in Hubert's life? When she'd met him his future was already a foregone conclusion.

"I think I would have *tried* to find out the truth as I would have *if* Hubie had come to me. But he didn't because he was afraid—Rupert had him convinced that no one would believe him. He was *so* persuasive only because it had all happened before exactly the same way. Who'd believe Hubie over Rupert, who will be the thirteenth Earl of Hartiscor?"

"But he won't be!" Jeffrey cried. "Let me tell you my plan! I'm not going to let Rupert go unpunished!"

"My point's not whether Rupert's going to be punished. It's that what happened with Hubert and Hubie could only have happened because you and Miranda had already created a hell, a place where something so evil *could* occur. You made it all part of the Hartiscor legacy and history. And history always repeats itself. Well, I'm getting Hubie out of here before any more bad things happen to him . . . before he too is laid to rest in the Hartiscor mausoleum of dead souls."

Jeffrey smiled slyly. "Would you call Hubie sitting in the House of Lords being confined to a mausoleum? And do you consider it a *bad* thing to inherit the Hartiscor fortune? What woman would turn down such a legacy for her son?"

"*This* woman can when that legacy includes a killing hostility bred into the bone. And I have another kind of legacy in mind for my son—decency and good character, and the ability to appreciate the important things in life like love and laughter and hope. What hurts me so is that Hubert knew this—knew what the important things in life were, was reaching out to find them but never had a chance. He was already too crippled by the past.''

"Empty words! Do you think when Hubie is grown he'll thank you for denying him his peerage and his fortune?"

"Are you offering Hubie what is already Rupert's? Do you think he's so contrite he's going to step aside for Hubie?"

Jeffrey leaned forward eagerly, thinking he had her hooked, after all. "That's what I've been trying to tell you, that I'm going to go to court to have Rupert's rights abjudicated on the same grounds he wanted to incarcerate Hubert with—moral turpitude, degenerate behavior."

She was astonished that he believed it would be that simple. "Don't you know Rupert will fight you every inch of the way? Or do you think, even *pray to God*, that he'll just crawl away to hang himself from a rafter at Hartiscor Castle?"

"Are my sins so great that I deserve that from you?"

"Great enough," she said, hugging herself, suddenly cold.

"What do you mean—'*great enough*'? Yes, I made a mistake with Hubert. But that was an error in judgment, not a crime!"

She hadn't intended to get into this—Jeffrey's crimes. But he was forcing her hand. "Crimes? What about the fall that ended Miranda's life? Was that a crime? And what about Anne? Wasn't that a crime?"

"What are you talking about?" he shrieked at her.

"I know, I know *everything*. I've already been to see Rupert, you see, and heard everything he has to say."

\* \* \*

Rupert had been lounging on a gold velvet sofa when she entered his suite at the Savoy, very much in control of himself and at first as correct as he was icy. He stood up as he asked her to sit down, took a cigarette from a gold case, lit it with a gold lighter, exhaled a stream of smoke, offered her a cigarette, which she refused, and then asked her to have lunch with him in the Grill. "It's that time of day and the food is superb."

She had promised herself that she wouldn't lose control, wouldn't fly at him with her nails to rake his arrogant face, would restrain herself from calling him all the names that were on the tip of her tongue, burning to be shouted. All she said was, "Yes, I know. Hubert and I often lunched here."

"I should have known. If nothing else, Hubert always lunched at the best places in town."

"I didn't come here to discuss Hubert."

"Of course you didn't. Still, why *not* have lunch while you're about it?" He bared his teeth in a grimace of a smile.

"I didn't come to have lunch with you, either."

He considered a moment. "I suppose not, and now that we have *that* established, why don't you tell me why you *did* come so that I, at least, can go down to the Grill to have *my* lunch. Personally, I'm famished."

"I came to tell you that I intend to file charges against you so that you'll be prosecuted for what you did. That I'm going to demand that you be arrested and put away for—"

"No, that's not why you came here. If it were your intention to have me arrested, why *tell* me about it? Why not simply do it? Do you know what I think?" His eyes were slits. "I think you came here because you're a bitch in heat! My brother's slut! My father's whore!"

*Oh, my God, he's mad! And I was mad to come here!*

She started to rise, intending to make a rush for the door before he could say another filthy word. But before she could straighten up, he was pushing her back down on the sofa.

"Where are you going so fast, whore bitch? You just got here and you didn't get what you came for. We both know what you want. What you never got from either Hubert or Father!"

He unzipped his trousers.

"Get out of my way! You're not stopping me from leaving! *I'm* not some frightened little boy!" She started to get up again, but again he pushed her back down, then took his penis out of his trousers, but she tried not to look at it, kept her eyes pinned to his face instead, figuring out her next move.

"Oh, yes, we both know you're not some frightened little boy, Nora. What you *are* is a hot, panting cunt who first married a pansy and then an old man. Poor Nora, she never did get a proper fucking, did she? Well, that's what you came for and that's exactly what you're going to get!"

Then he was on top of her, one hand reaching under her jacket to tear at the buttons of her blouse, ripping it open to expose her breasts, barely covered by a lacy bra, while his other hand groped under her skirt. When she opened her mouth to scream, the hand mauling her breast formed a fist that he jammed between her lips, and she bit into it, tasting blood. But instead of yowling with pain, Rupert laughed, his face glistening with a fine layer of sweat. "So that's the way you want it? I should have known you'd like it rough!"

He slapped her, first one side of her face and then the other, and, realizing that she wasn't going to be able to stop him from doing whatever he wanted—he was simply too strong for her—she grew panicky and for a few moments lay there without moving, eyes closed, trying frantically to think what to do as he pulled off her panty hose and then her panties, taking her silence and motionless state for compliance . . . mute desire, and she could feel his hot breath on her face.

Then she remembered the advice of the bouncer at the Cock 'n' Bull, a burly ex-sailor named Barney. "When a matey gets too big for 'is britches, if you get me meaning, and too hard for a little bird like you to handle, you give 'im the old one-two-three. First you grab 'im by the ears, smashing 'is nob with your own, and as 'e's seeing stars, you're letting go of the ears to thumb 'im in the eyes, at the same time bring up your knee to wallop 'im in the old bollocks as wiciously as you can manage. It's guaranteed to knock the wind out of any bloke's sails, but mind you, you got to take 'im by surprise and be quick about it!"

"You know what I'm going to do?" she heard him grunt. "I'm going to give you what Hubert got, what sweet little Hubie got, since that's what you *really* want and I'm too much the gentleman not to oblige. So flip over!"

*Take him by surprise and then be quick about it. . . .*

"Oh, yes, that's what I want! Oh, yes!" Now she made her eyes shine with lust and licked at her lips lasciviously. "But first there's something I want to do. Something I *must* do! Stand up, Rupert, so that I can kneel at your feet. . . ."

She wriggled off the sofa to stand over him as if in eager anticipation as he struggled to get to his feet. But before he could straighten up, she delivered a vicious knee to the groin, causing him to howl in pain before falling back on the sofa, clutching at what her mother, the barmaid, used to call the family jewels, or, sometimes even more inelegantly, his nuts. Then, taking full advantage of the moment and his incapacitated state, she picked up a small bronze figurine and gave his jewels another whack, ensuring that he would be incapacitated for, she hoped, a couple of days.

At least he was disabled enough so that she could take a few minutes to make some hasty repairs to her appearance, enough to get her through the lobby. But she did it in front of him so that she could keep an eye on him as he dragged himself over to a table to grab at a bottle of Napoleon brandy. At least now she was positioned close to the door so that she could make a fast getaway if he managed to pull himself together. But she doubted it, watching him drink his brandy straight from the bottle. In fact, he didn't even look at her, hardly seemed to be aware that she was still there.

Still, he'd been right about one thing. She hadn't come simply to tell him that she intended to swear out charges against him. As he had said, why bother to tell him about it rather than just do it? What she had come for was to ask him a question—get an answer that would enable her to close the Hartiscor chapter of her life forever.

Now, positioned at the door with hose in place, shoes on, the torn, blood-specked blouse discarded, her jacket buttoned to the neck to cover her breasts, she asked the question: "Why, Rupert, why did you do it?"

He looked at her with contempt. "I gave you more credit than that, Nora. A simpleton could figure it out. There are acts of love and there are acts of hate—what the pros call acts of hostility." He held the bottle of brandy up to the light. "And you know what they say—the line between love and hate is so thin, so fine, one is hard put to separate the two. Now, I loved my mummy, but she chose Hubert over me to play those little games with when I yearned for her to play them with me. So I performed an act of hostility against Hubert, but it was really an act of hostility against Mummy. That should be perfectly clear even to one as naïve as you."

"But why Hubie? Surely he was innocent and he loved you! Trusted you. He didn't deserve your act of hostility!"

"But *you* did!" His look was pure hate. "I loved you, but you loved only Hubert and Hubie, and then, with Hubert dead, I thought you would love *me*. But you didn't, you chose Father."

"So, what you did to Hubie was an act of hostility against *me*?" she asked, the horror of it seeping through her.

"*Now* you've got it! So, you see, Nora, you aren't so simple or naïve after all. And you must understand that if you try to have me prosecuted, I will have to fight back."

"But how can you? There were two of us who *saw* you— your father and I. Two witnesses and Hubie. We'll support each other's testimony."

"I know you—you'll never allow Hubie to go through that. And Father will never testify against me either."

"He will!"

Rupert smiled coolly. "He won't. He can't. He'll never testify against me because if he does I'll expose *him* and then he'll have no choice but to go hang himself."

She was afraid to ask but forced herself to, her hand reaching out for the doorknob. "*How* will you expose him?"

"Haven't you guessed? The night Mummy fell down the stairs, Father *pushed* her. No one else saw his hand on the small of her back as he pretended to put his arm around her in affection, but I was standing behind them and I saw!"

"I don't believe you! No one will believe you."

"I'm prepared to swear to it in court and to testify *why* he did it, and then they'll *all* believe. It will be *their* pleasure to believe," he laughed.

She turned the knob. She didn't want to hear any more but Rupert went on: "Don't you want to know *why* he pushed her? But you already know, don't you? Father pushed Mummy down the stairs to *silence* her. You see, *she* was going to blow the whistle on him—that he'd been fucking my sister, Anne, and had been doing it for years! Why do you think Anne ran away, and even after she ran away, couldn't live with it and ended up hanging herself from a tree? Poor, little Anne. As I heard it she botched the job and lingered for hours. . . ."

*   *   *

This was the moment of truth and she could not shrink from it. "If we go to court, Jeffrey—I to press charges against Rupert for what he did to Hubie or you to have his right to inherit ab-judicated—Rupert is prepared to make countercharges. He's going to swear that you *pushed* Miranda down the stairs the night she fell to her death."

She watched him closely to see if he would register shock at being so accused, but Jeffrey only sneered, "Let him swear! He has no proof!" Then, feeling sick, she thought that while she couldn't be sure, the charge was probably true. If he were inno-cent he would have simply protested rather than talk about no proof.

"And he's prepared to swear that the reason you pushed Miranda was because she was going to reveal that you and Anne were—" she forced herself to say the word, "lovers."

She prayed Jeffrey would sneer again, would cry: "Let him swear!" Then at least she wouldn't be sure. But this time he only bowed his head and began to sob.

She held out her hand to make certain. Yes, it was beginning to rain and she wheeled her husband into the house. He was convalescing and she didn't want him to catch cold.

# TWENTY-SIX

———◦•◦———

When time dragged on and Jeffrey remained adamant that there would be no divorce and that adultery was the only real grounds for divorce, she knew she had just one option. She was only sorry that Jeffrey was forcing her to make the proceedings more painful than they already were.

\* \* \*

She checked into the pretty little inn in Stratford-upon-Avon in Warwickshire with her friend Mick Nash, but they were early. The detective her lawyer had hired to document her act of adultery wasn't due until two hours later.

"You must have more experience with this sort of thing than I do, Mick. What do we do until Mr. Humboldt arrives?"

Mick, testing the bed by bouncing on it gingerly, laughed, which was the thing he did best as an actor who played romantic leads since he had perfect white teeth. "Experience with this sort of thing? I've never been a correspondent in a divorce before, if that's what you mean. This is a new, though entirely delightful, role for me."

"But you *have* checked into a hotel with a lady who wasn't your wife?" she asked archly, inspecting the bathroom. It was small but adequate with a large tub on clawed feet, though she doubted she would be there long enough to take a bath.

"Of course I have, especially since I've never had a wife. But I've never before checked into a lovely country inn with so lovely a lady on my arm."

Nora laughed. "Really, Mick, you sound just like one of

those silly charmers you're forever playing in your films."

Mick pretended to be offended. "What kind of role would you have me play? No one's exactly proposing *Macbeth*."

"What a shame!" she said in mock sympathy. "But tell me, Mick, how is it you've never married?"

Mick stretched out on the bed with his hands folded under his head. "For the same reason I've never done *Macbeth*. No one's ever proposed. But that doesn't mean I'm not prepared to entertain an interesting proposal. And I can tell you what we can do while we're waiting for Mr. Humboldt to smash down the door." He fluffed up the bed pillow next to his and patted the empty space beside him. "We can rehearse."

Then she wondered if she had made a mistake in allowing the elegant and dashing Mick with his upper-class accent to play her lover instead of the stranger her solicitor had suggested. She'd known him for several years now, ever since they'd both served on a committee for the Dramatic Arts Council—she really loved the theater—and had hit it off instantly. They were both about the same age—he a couple of years older, which she always teased him about since he had the vain actor's usual thing about age—and they both liked to laugh, finding the same things funny. The best thing about Mick was that he had a knack for making a woman *feel* like a woman, wondrously attractive and desirable.

But was he the right man for the job? He had insisted that he would love to help her out . . . that it would be marvelous fun. "And who can fill the bill better than I? I'm tall, dark, and handsome, a most devilish rake—everyone says I would have made a damn fine Rhett Butler—and I've been in bed with the best of them. And I must say I hope this all makes the tabloids. I'd love nothing better than to have people sit up and take notice that old Mick is as hot between the sheets as he is on the screen. It would probably do wonders for my career. I ask you, who has better credentials?"

"No one," she had laughingly agreed, thinking that posing with an old friend like Mick would be less awkward than with a stranger, and that his celebrity might even prove helpful. But she had never imagined that there might be a problem with him forgetting that they were only *pretending*—not once in the years they'd been friends had he made an overture that might have been construed as overly familiar. He was much too stylish for that, but then, again, he had never before had reason to believe that she would be receptive to such a move. But now, under these circumstances, there was no reason for him *not* to believe it.

She went over to the bed to tug at his arm. "Come, old chum, on your feet. Let's take a walk around town while we're waiting. We can visit the Royal Shakespeare Theatre and the house William was born in, and who knows? Maybe you'll grow so infused with the spirit of the Bard, some great director will take one look, snap his fingers, and say, 'Mick Nash, I always thought you'd make a great Rhett Butler, but I was wrong! What you are is perfect for my production of *Macbeth*!' "

"Oh, very well, let's take a walk if we must." He grinned at her engagingly, stood up, then bent down to kiss the crown of her upswept golden-blond hair. "But are you quite certain that's the best suggestion you can come up with?"

Now that he mentioned it, she wasn't all *that* certain. Mick *was* supremely attractive, and she was experiencing an odd sensation—as if an exotic butterfly had somehow flown into her vaginal orifice and was fluttering its wings. . . .

\* \* \*

"It's only necessary to bare the upper part of the body, Mr. Nash. If you will, please remove your coat, tie, shirt, and undervest and pop under the covers. And you, Lady Hartiscor, if you'll remove your blouse and join Mr. Nash under the covers, we can commence."

Elston Humboldt was hardly the type of man Nora would have envisioned in this line of work. He was slight, sported a small, neat mustache, and wore rimless spectacles and a black suit—the sort of man she would have taken for a mortician, or even a vicar. But, then, he did appear to be taking a conservative approach.

"Masterful direction," Mick muttered as she followed instructions, shushing him, saying, "Let's give the man a chance."

But it seemed Mr. Humboldt required only staid and static poses: the two of them sitting with their backs upright against the bed's headboard while they looked straight ahead directly into the camera; another with Mick's arm draped halfheartedly about her shoulders; then the two of them lying supine, their arms languidly at their sides, doing nothing more than staring listlessly into the camera.

A shot of Mick kissing her ear was as passionate as the proceedings got.

"Can't I at least *bite* it?" he begged, but Mr. Humboldt remained unmoved.

"Not at all necessary."

"Oh, hell, foiled again!" Mick grumbled, withdrawing his mouth from her lobe. "I must say, Nora, this afternoon's a big disappointment. Doesn't it get any hotter than this?"

"It will," she whispered. "I promise."

"When? Oh, God, when?"

"Soon," she giggled as the detective frowned, but soon he was finished. "That should do it. I'll be in touch with your solicitor when the photographs are ready."

But then she told him that she required *another* set of photos—this time in total undress and in more *explicit* positions, and Mick enthused, "I say, that's more like it!"

But the detective blinked and said stiffly, "I beg your pardon, Lady Hartiscor, but the pictures I have already taken will satisfy the courts as evidence of misconduct. Strictly routine in matters of this sort. It's not necessary to be more, as you say— *explicit*. No need for what may be construed as pornography," he clucked, turning to pack up his equipment. "No indeed, that wouldn't do at all."

"I'm not asking you to take *dirty* pictures, Mr. Humboldt. All I require is . . . well, shots of what just *look* like compromising positions, but pictures no judge will ever see."

Mr. Humboldt didn't respond, but they could see even the hairs of his mustache bristling.

"Listen here, old boy, the lady says she needs more compromising positions and it's making me cross that you seem to have a problem with that. Believe me, you *don't* want to get me angry," Mick growled in imitation of a Hollywood tough guy, elbowing Nora in the ribs, enjoying himself thoroughly.

"Hush, Mick," she whispered. "This isn't a joke. You'll really spook him. Can't you see how nervous he is about getting involved in something other than just taking routine divorce stuff? He's afraid we're up to something else—something nefarious, hard-core stuff. . . ."

"Some kind of blackmail?" Mick suggested, eyes sparkling.

Blackmail's not far from it, she thought, whispering: "I really *need* these pictures, Mick. We have to manage to talk him into taking them or this whole thing's been a waste."

"Don't worry, if you *need* those pictures, you're going to get them! I have the perfect convincer."

A *convincer!* For a crazy moment Nora thought Mick was referring to a gun, but he jumped out of bed to go to the Queen Anne desk to retrieve his wallet. Then, winking at her, he counted out several banknotes and handed them to Mr. Humboldt, and when the detective silently accepted and pocketed them, Mick winked at her again and proceeded to divest himself of his remaining clothing. And then, still under the covers, she removed her chemise and panties.

\* \* \*

They remained in bed until Mr. Humboldt left. Then, suddenly embarrassed, she wrapped herself in the crumpled sheet and got out of bed, leaving Mick fully exposed. Then, self-conscious, she tried to avert her eyes from that which was very much in evidence—Mick in a state of arousal, a condition, she discovered, she shared. There was that sensation again—the beating of butterfly wings—and she could feel her inner thighs growing moist.

"That *was* fun," he said, but he wasn't so much as smiling.

Hoping to break the tension that was as thick as fog, she teased, "If it was so much fun, why aren't you laughing?"

"Because I'm sad."

"Oh, poor baby. Why is it sad?"

"Because I'm thinking how much *more* fun it would have been if we'd been doing it for real instead of faking it. . . ."

First, she thought: He's absolutely right. It would have been lots of fun. And then she thought: It's *supposed* to be fun and never had she done it strictly for the fun of it. Then she allowed the sheet to drop to the floor.

*At least once, just for the fun of it.*

\*　\*　\*

Nora spread the first set of photos, the relatively inoffensive poses of Mick and her, out on the library table for Jeffrey to examine. "You can use this set of pictures to sue for divorce and it will be relatively simple and painless. But if you choose not to—" She held out the envelope containing her second set of photos. "Then I'll have to take these to the tabloids. And I *will* do it though it will cause me as much shame as it will you."

He snatched the envelope from her, tore it open, ruffled through the pictures—Nora lying spread-eagled with Mick on top of her, his mouth to her breast; another of his head buried in that space between her thighs; another, she kneeling on the floor as Mick sat on the edge of the bed, her mouth somewhere in the vicinity of his groin—all a medley of avaricious loins, of breasts and buttocks and tongues, of frank abandon, lust, and fulfillment. Then Jeffrey allowed all the pictures to drop to the floor before he began to weep. At that point she knew that she had her divorce.

\*　\*　\*

The afternoon deepened into a melancholy twilight, but neither of them made a move to turn on the lights.

"What kind of settlement do you expect?"

"I don't expect anything."

"You do understand that Hubie will get nothing? That—"

She cut him off. "That was my intention."

"Still, I'd like to give you and Hubie something."

"I can't accept anything."

"What will you live on?"

"I haven't sorted it all out yet but we'll manage."

"Where will you go?"

"To Merrillee." When Jeffrey had given her the country manor he had called it her dowerage; now it would be her refuge. "It will be peaceful for a bit. Eventually I'd like to go out into the world and bend it to *my* will for a change."

That was true enough. She'd been only a girl when she'd come to London and entered the world of the Hartiscors, letting her emotions rule her heart, and the Hartiscor men her life, but that was more than ten years ago and she was a woman now, fully seasoned and hopefully able and ready to get on with it. And she would like to have a bit of fun too along the way. *I haven't had much of that.*

She got up and turned on the lights. "I'll ring for your tea," she said, and he looked at her beseechingly.

"Will you stay?" he asked, and she hesitated. Having tea with Jeffrey seemed like a small favor to grant, and he had, in his fashion, loved her and been good to her and Hubie. But once she started making room in her heart for pity, she would be lost in the past again.

"I'm sorry, Jeffrey, but I have an appointment."

*At least once in a while, just for the fun of it. . . .*

# PART FOUR

# AND ONCE FOR THE FUN OF IT

England and Hollywood, 1957–1958

# TWENTY-SEVEN

———•◦•———

When Mick came down to Merrillee Manor for the weekend Nora assumed it was only for the pleasure of her company, but he soon confessed he'd come with an ulterior motive in mind—to ask her to tag along with him to Hollywood.

"You're going there to do a film? That's wonderful!"

"*Hopefully* to do a film. Grantwood Studio—one of the biggest in the States—has asked me to test for a very famous role in a sequel to a very famous film that's in the works and you get three guesses as to which film it is."

She thought for a few moments. *"Gone With the Wind?"*

"You witch! How did you know? Someone told you!"

"No, no one told me. I was just gazing into my crystal ball and I saw you playing Rhett. I must say you made a dashing Rhett, but something was odd—"

"Odd? You thought I looked too young for the part?"

"No," she said thoughtfully. "Maybe more like too *old*."

"May I remind you that Clark Gable was older than I am now when he played Rhett almost twenty years ago?" he huffed.

She laughed. "I wasn't serious, you nit. I don't even *own* a crystal ball." Apparently she could tease Mick the man and Mick the lover, but she should have known better than to tease Mick the actor. When it came to age and looks, an actor's ego could brook no nonsense.

"Well, all right," he said, only partially mollified. "But *I'm* quite serious about your coming along with me to Hollywood. We'll really have a time of it!"

"It sounds exciting, but no. I'm not ready."

193

"Why do you have to be *ready*? I'm not asking you to marry me, after all. All I'm asking you to do is come along for a bit of fun. You certainly could use a little of that and this is your chance, all expenses paid."

"Oh, Mick, I'd love to, but I *can't*. I need time to—"

"What? You've been here a year, hiding out like a nun except for those times I took pity on you and came down."

"But I haven't been hiding out. I've been renewing my energies, making plans for the future. I can't make any rash moves. I'm a single woman with responsibilities, as a mother and a breadwinner, and I just can't pick up and go running off with you, especially now that I'm on the brink of—"

"On the brink of what, for God's sake?" he demanded. "A nervous collapse? Suicide? Middle age?"

"Middle age?" she shrieked. "If you recall, I'm only thirty-two. And who'd know that better than you, you rat, since you're the one I celebrated my thirty-second birthday with at the film festival in Cannes. Did you forget? You know, on second thought, considering that you *are* older than I and already beginning to grow forgetful, maybe you *are* too old to play Rhett. It's possible senility is already setting in and how will you even remember your lines?"

"I may be senile, m'dear, but that doesn't change *your* condition. You may be only thirty-two but your state of mind is at least twenty years older, not to mention that you're not exactly basking in the glow of virginal innocence either. Some would even say Nora Hall Hartiscor is damaged goods," he retaliated for the crack about his possible senility.

She threw a sofa pillow at him.

"And as such," he continued, "you'd do well to take my offer seriously and consider yourself fortunate that a handsome, incredibly sexy, tremendously successful, eligible *young* bachelor like myself is giving you this opportunity to have a high old time. Besides, you're no longer a countess and that does reduce your eligibility somewhat more."

"I think I'll manage to cope," she laughed.

He studied her for some seconds over the rim of his whiskey and soda, then, as if startled by an upsetting thought, he put down his glass. "Tell me, if it's *not* middle age, suicide, or a mental collapse, what *is* it that you're on the brink of—another marriage?"

She threw a second pillow at him. "If you must know, I was going to say that I was on the brink of making the manor a paying proposition. That I've just leased two parcels of land to two tenant farmers."

"Fine. But does that mean you can't take a few weeks off? It might not even be for that long. The whole thing could just fizzle out. These Hollywood chaps *are* notorious for starting projects then abandoning them. And there's the possibility that I'll test for the role and not get it."

"Never! Once you test for the part, it's yours. These American filmmakers are devilishly clever. They know a Rhett when they see one no matter how old and senile he might be."

This time, Mick advanced on her with a sofa pillow of his own, but suddenly they weren't laughing but kissing. At first they were tiny, tender kisses, but soon they intensified to the point where lips, mouths, and tongues weren't enough and they began to tear at each other's clothing, hungry to get to each other's parts, all of them. When they were finally naked they rolled around on the carpet in front of the fire, first she on top of him, then he on her, rolling ceaselessly about, over and over, as if this would somehow better fuse their bodies into one, until she couldn't wait any longer to lower herself onto him, he raising his hips to meet her. Then she moved herself up and down the length of him, slowly tightening her thighs and inner muscles to grip and then release him, until the pressure of his hands on her buttocks was so great she could no longer move and only he could thrust, and then, seconds later, they both climaxed. But then, when she moved off him to lie next to him, their breathing still ragged, they began to kiss, again softly and tenderly, before his tongue traced downward on a treasure hunt, finding her breasts, her belly, the soft flesh of her inner thighs before she felt it enter her, its entrance as sweet as his entrance before had been fierce. And as she felt herself exploding again in a frenzy of joy, she thought of what she had missed all those years of loving Hubert and living with Jeffrey, feeling no passion for him. And she swore to herself that no matter what the future held for her, she would never do without this kind of love again.

\* \* \*

"Come with me!" he urged again. "We're good together!"

"I'd love to, but Hubie's finally doing well in school. He's been at Mayberry's for eight months now and we haven't had a single problem. I'd hate to take him out of school."

"But you don't have to take him *out*. All I'm proposing is a *brief* holiday while he's safe *in* school so you can go with a free mind. If I get the role we'll proceed from there. Did I tell you that they're paying for a bungalow at the Beverly Hills Hotel? It's their ultimate in star treatment."

Why not? she argued with herself. Hubie *was* in school with no problems and the manor *was* in fairly good shape. It was the perfect time for fun. *Once just for the devil of it!*

\* \* \*

After taking two hours to dress, his hair perfectly arranged in a wave curling rakishly over his forehead, Mick announced that he was off for his test at Grantwood Studio.

"But you haven't had breakfast," she protested. "How are you going to test on an empty stomach?"

"They rang while you were in the shower. The test has been rescheduled for this afternoon."

"Then, why are you leaving now? We can breakfast here in the Polo Lounge. I'm told that's where Hollywood people have what they call a power breakfast. Doesn't that sound exciting . . . unless, of course"—she smiled provocatively—"you think breakfast in bed sounds even more exciting?"

"Mmmm, it does, but I'm breakfasting at the studio with T. S. Grant himself." He sounded extremely pleased.

"Well, that certainly sounds more exciting than breakfasting in bed with little old me. But really, Mick, I think that breakfast with T. S. Grant sounds *very* positive. A good omen."

She knew how upset he'd been that, while they'd arrived

three days before and been wined and dined, even taken to a wild party in Hollywood and a more formal one in Beverly Hills, he had yet to meet the head of Grantwood Studio.

"I'd better dash. They've sent a car for me," he said with satisfaction. "Now, *that's* what I call star treatment. Do you know no one ever sent a car for me before? I really like how they do business in this town. Now, if you need anything while I'm gone, just pick up the phone and ask for it."

"Yes, Mick," she laughed. "While this *is* my first time in the States, I *have been* in first-class hotels before and I know all about how one picks up a phone to ask for things."

"Yes, of course you do. I just want to be sure that you know how to announce yourself when you do pick up the phone."

"What's gotten into you? Has all this sunshine gone to your brain so quickly? I'm a big girl now and I *think* I've known how to properly announce myself for years now."

"Yes, of course, but I want to be sure that you call yourself the Countess Hartiscor."

"Look, Mick, if it weren't for Hubie, I'd stop calling myself Hartiscor altogether, so can we drop the countess business once and for all?"

"Sorry, old girl, but you're *already* registered here as the countess. Titles knock the stuffing out of Americans. It impresses them no end. Do you understand?"

"What I *don't* understand is why it's necessary for me to impress the staff of the hotel. Do the desk clerk or the waiter really care if I'm of the aristocracy?"

"Maybe *they* don't, but the reporters they rang up the minute we checked in do. Now it's in all the dailies and on the grapevine that the hot English star Mick Nash is doing the local scene with the ravishing Countess Hartiscor. As a result, do you know what is on everyone's lips?"

"I'm sure you're going to tell me, so—"

Mick put a hand on his hip and dangled the other from a very loose wrist: "They say the countess is mad about him, darl-ing, and she, being as dee-vine as *she* is, she must know the truth—that *he's* absolutely dee-vine!"

She giggled. "I'm sure they're absolutely right."

\* \* \*

She lunched in the Polo Lounge by herself, amusing herself by watching all the milling and table-hopping going on, with people constantly being paged to the phone. But while it was fun, the din of it all was exhausting, and she went back to the bungalow to change into her swimsuit, thinking she would relax by the pool—a seemingly tranquil oasis of bright-blue water, tropical flowers, and tall palms. But no sooner had she finished oiling herself down with lotion than she heard the Countess Hartiscor being paged to the phone.

"Really, Mick, you *are* naughty," she said, trying to keep the annoyance out of her voice. "I thought I told you that— Oh, never mind. How did the test go?"

"It didn't. It's been rescheduled for tomorrow."

"Oh, that's a shame. But how did your breakfast meeting with T. S. Grant go?"

"Not bad," he laughed ruefully. "He sat for as long as it took him to drink a cup of coffee before he had to leave. But he seems a nice chap. Laughs a lot. And he said that he really felt great about having a star of my stature testing for the role, and then he left a couple of his people to finish having breakfast with me, and *that* was informative."

"Oh, good! What did you learn?"

"Well, I finally found out what the T.S. stands for—Thomas Samuel, or, if you prefer, tough shit."

"But what does *that* mean?"

"I think it's supposed to describe his down-to-earth quality. That he says what he means and doesn't pull his punches, and if you don't like it, well—tough shit! I guess that's okay. At least one knows where one stands with him."

"And where do you think you stand with him other than that he feels good about your testing for Rhett?"

"*That's* my problem—I'm not sure. But he wants to meet *you*, so we're having drinks with him at five and maybe you'll help me sort out where I stand. They're sending a car for you, so just climb into your sexiest getup and—"

"Sexiest?" she laughed. "Why? *I'm* not trying out for a part. Besides, the sun will still be high in the sky at five. Don't you think I'd look a bit odd in clinging satin and a plunging neckline before sundown?"

"This is Hollywood, silly, the sun never sets. Besides, we'll probably be going on to dinner with him. Oh, and don't be surprised when I introduce you as—"

"The Countess Hartiscor! Mick, I'm going to brain you!"

"I was going to say—the loveliest woman in the world."

"Oh, Mick, that's sweet."

How could she ever be mad at this man? It was so much easier to be mad *about* him. . . .

\* \* \*

When she stepped out of the limousine dressed for evening but circumspectly so in a cocktail suit, Mick was waiting for her on the sidewalk in front of the Tropical Flower Lounge, all alone, immersed in melancholy. "What is it, Mick?"

"It's T.S. He isn't here."

"Is he delayed or what?"

"He isn't coming. He had to go down to Palm Springs."

It was foolish, she knew, but, then, *she* was disappointed. She'd been looking forward to meeting the famous T. S. Grant. Actually, she was more than disappointed—she was annoyed. She knew how silly it was, even odd, considering she didn't know the man, but somehow she felt as if he had stood *her* up.

"Well, these things happen, Mick, but never mind. We'll have drinks and then we'll have dinner, just the two of us."

"Oh, no," Mick brightened. "There's a gang inside. Some of the other people T.S. asked to meet him for drinks. After that we're going on to the Cocoanut Grove. It'll be lots of fun and that's what we're here for, isn't it?"

And it *was* fun, lots of fun. Still, when they returned to their bungalow at four in the morning, she turned on Mick accusingly. "How could you introduce me to those people as your fiancée? A total lie."

"It just kind of popped out. I suppose it was wishful thinking on my part." He grinned at her, but his eyes weren't smiling and she realized that he was quite serious.

"Oh, Mick! You made it very clear that my coming along was just a fling. You can't change the rules in the middle of the game. It's just not fair."

"You're the one who's not playing fair. All my life I've been told that it was the female's prerogative to change her mind. Well, who says a man can't change his mind too?" His lips grazed her eyelids, her mouth, her throat. "I love you, Nora. Isn't it fair that I tell you *that*?"

"It's late, Mick, and you have your screen test tomorrow. You must get some sleep or you'll have bags under your eyes, and who ever heard of a Rhett Butler with baggy eyes? We'll talk about this tomorrow. Tomorrow *is* another day."

"Yes, Scarlett, tomorrow is another day, but tonight is tonight and this is the night I swoop you up in my arms to carry you up the stairs to make love to you against your will. But after—ah, *after* you realize how much you really love me." And he advanced on her.

She backed away. "Mick, you're being silly and there are no stairs here." She ran to stand behind a chair.

"A good actor can always improvise!" He laughed menacingly and kept coming to shove the chair out of the way, to swoop her up in his arms and carry her into the bedroom . . .

*   *   *

As the sun began its ascent in the East, Mick asked, "Now, what do you have to say, Scarlett, my love?"

"I always said you'd make the most marvelous Rhett and I'm not about to change my mind." And she didn't even smile.

Two hours later, the studio called to announce that they had to cancel the screen test for that afternoon. This time Mick said, "Perfect," and an hour later they flew to Las Vegas to be married in a wedding chapel that offered either a plain ceremony without music and flowers that took five minutes or a deluxe one that included both and took fifteen. They opted for the latter, and as the groom kissed the bride, he murmured, "These

Yanks! They sure know how to expedite a situation before a chap has a chance to change his mind."

"Or a woman . . ." she murmured, and congratulated herself that this time around she had married a darling, amusing, and very dear man for the best of reasons—for the sheer pleasure of it—and that *had* to be a brilliant marriage!

# TWENTY-EIGHT

———— •••• ————

"What do you think is going on?" Nora asked after four weeks had passed and Mick still hadn't had his screen test.

"Who knows?" he shrugged. "But what do we care? We're having fun and they're paying the bills."

"But how long will they *continue* to pay the bills?"

"You worry too much. You have to learn to relax and go with the flow."

" *'Go with the flow?'* Where'd you get that?"

"From T.S. I finally managed to get him on the phone and asked him what was happening with the picture, and he told me that if I wanted to survive in Hollywood I was going to have to relax and go with the flow, and he should know if anyone does. That man has *real* problems, but you'd never know it."

"You never told me. What kind of problems?"

"I just found out. It seems his wife's in a private sanitorium in Palm Springs—some kind of a mental disorder—and there's a baby, a little girl."

"Oh, that's so sad. How bad is his wife and how's he managing with the baby?"

"They say she's pretty badly disturbed. That's why he's always running down to Palm Springs. As for the baby, she's with her maternal grandparents in Pasadena—what they call California's old-money crowd."

"Poor man. Sounds like he has his hands full. No wonder he's not able to concentrate on your project."

"I don't think that's the problem. Actually, I think they're having trouble with the screenplay."

"I didn't even know there was a screenplay."

"Of course there's a screenplay, at least in development, I *think*. There's *usually* a screenplay before they start casting. Anyway, it seems that they have a Pulitzer Prize–winner working on it, but he's a novelist, not a screenwriter. His name's F. Theodore Rosen."

She tried to concentrate. "The name *sounds* familiar."

"That's probably not because of what he's written but because who he's married to—Mimi L'Heureux."

"You mean the French actress?"

"I mean the French *sex goddess*. I met her once in Cannes, and to meet the gorgeous Mimi is not to forget her."

"*That* sexy? But what's the problem with the screenplay?"

"I don't know, but I'm going to try to find out today. I'm lunching at the Brown Derby with Bob Rankin. He's the head of publicity. Care to tag along?"

"No, I don't think so."

"Oh, come on," he urged. "It will be fun to see how much studio gossip we can bleed out of the bloke."

"No, Mick, I'm really not in the mood."

He studied her for a moment. "Something's bothering you. Is it that letter you received yesterday from the headmaster at Hubie's school?"

"Yes. How did you know?"

"Elementary, my dear Watson. The only thing that really upsets you is anything to do with Hubie. Now, *your* problems are *my* problems, wifey dear, so why don't you tell me what's wrong while I dress for my lunch date?"

She followed him into the dressing room while he selected what he would wear. "The point is that I'm not sure *what's* wrong specifically. You know how vague these academics can be. He just referred to certain difficulties—"

"That's all?" He held up a tie for her approval and she nodded. "In that case, what you should have done was gotten on the horn this morning and called the bloody school and found out what difficulties they're referring to."

"But that's what I did do! At five this morning."

"And—?" He went into the bathroom to shave.

"It seems that Mr. Haskell, the headmaster, won't be back until it's two o'clock in the morning here."

"Why didn't you ask to speak to someone else?"

"I did—the assistant headmaster, but *he* said he wasn't at liberty to talk about a matter of this nature and that I would have to wait for Mr. Haskell."

"And you couldn't manage to worm anything out of him?"

"Oh, Mick, *that's* one of the problems. I *did*."

Mick laid down his razor. "And—"

"He said the problem was of a *sexual* nature."

"But that's ridiculous!" Mick laughed, picking up his razor again. "How old is Hubie? My God, the boy's not thirteen yet. What kind of a problem can he have that's of a sexual nature when he's at school where there's *only* boys?"

When she burst into tears, he said, "Oh. I see." He put the razor down again to take her in his arms. "But Nora, you can't— You mustn't! It really can't be a case of history repeating itself, so why assume the worst?"

"But there *was* that experience with Rupert, and Hubert had the same experience. Oh, God, will the curse of the Hartiscors never end?"

"That sounds like the title of a twenties' film. *The Curse of the Hartiscors.*" He kissed the top of her head. "Look, why assume anything until you get to speak to Haskell? What probably happened was that they found the kid masturbating—what twelve-year-old boy doesn't play with himself? And they can't hang him for that. They can't even expel him for it or they'd have to expel half the school."

She wiped at her tears with a sodden handkerchief and tried to smile at him, though it was the *other* half of the school that she was concerned with. If they weren't masturbating, then what of a sexual nature *were* they doing?

*   *   *

So many emotions played across Nora's face as she talked to the headmaster, Mick couldn't tell whether she was exhilarated or crushed at what she was hearing, and the moment she put the phone down he begged: "Is it good news or bad?"

"You won't believe this! Hubie was caught having sex with the mathematics professor's eighteen-year-old daughter!"

"But that's marvelous! Aren't you pleased?"

"Of course I'm pleased! I mean, I'm *relieved*. It *is* good news, isn't it?"

"Good news? I think it's *extraordinary* news. Our little Hubie fucking an eighteen-year-old woman! Amazing, really. Nora, you should be proud of the boy!"

But then she reproved him. "Really, what's there to be proud of? That my son is precociously promiscuous?"

He followed her into the bedroom, where she began to throw things into a suitcase. "What are you doing?"

"I'm doing exactly what it looks like I'm doing. I'm packing. I have to leave for home immediately."

"Why? Everything's fine. Hubie was fucking a *girl*."

"No, everything's *not* fine. You men think all is well as long as any male—even a boy of *twelve*—is screwing a female. They've expelled him and they're keeping him confined to his room as if he were a threat to national security until I come to pick him up. Can you imagine? I have to go back and transfer him to another school immediately."

"But the planes don't leave in the middle of the night. You're losing your perspective. You're acting hysterical."

"Am I? It's just that— Oh, Mick, I can't tell you how relieved I *really* am! I know I'm acting crazy, but I thought that—" She sat down on the bed and he sat down next to her.

"I know, Nora, I know what you thought. I understand."

"Do you know that I blame myself for marrying Jeffrey?"

"*For marrying Jeffrey?* Don't you mean you blame yourself for taking up with Hubert?"

"No, I would never blame myself for taking up with Hubert. I've never regretted that. I *loved* Hubert! Oh, how I loved him! I loved Hubert so much that—"

"So much that what? That you'll never love anybody as much as you loved him?"

Mick looked as if she had stuck a knife in his heart, and then she was filled with remorse. He was so sweet and they laughed so much and they made such wonderful love together. "Oh, no, Mick, I wasn't going to say that. I was going to say that I loved Hubert so much that sometimes I forget that Hubert wasn't really Hubie's father. That sometimes they just merge into one. Hubie and Hubert. Sometimes I imagine that Hubie *is* Hubert. Does that sound ridiculous?"

"No, of course not," he soothed her. "But now I think we should go to bed and in the morning—"

"In the morning I *must* go home and see to Hubie."

"Are you sure you have to go? I forgot to tell you. We've been invited to a very chichi party in Malibu at the home of our esteemed screenwriter and the sexy Mimi."

"Oh, Mick, I'd love it but I have to go."

"I know. But maybe I should go with you?"

"And miss that chichi party with the sex kitten? Heaven forbid! And besides, I can't let you leave without having your screen test. I'd never forgive myself if you missed out on the role you were born to play. I'll go home, arrange for Hubie to go to another school, then I'll come back, and by that time the cameras will probably be rolling. I bet they won't even bother with a screen test anymore."

"Do you really think so? And you'll rush right back?"

"The very second I can, I promise, cross my heart."

"Well, jolly well, then. You know, none of this is any good without you."

"I know, and just *you* remember that."

"And now that that's settled, shall we go to bed?" he leered. "You might be gone a week and look at all the fun we'll be missing. We have to make up for the lost time starting right now!" But then he showed no hurry as he undressed her tantalizingly slowly, kissing each square inch he bared. And she, giving herself up totally to the exquisite pleasure of his lovemaking, reflected that some men were born to laugh and to love and to make love. . . .

*And who would be so foolish as to love them less than the ones you loved who loved you back but still managed to break your heart?*

# TWENTY-NINE

———·••·———

"It really wasn't my fault, Mummy."

Hubie looked so forlorn, it was hard for her not to just take him in her arms and forget the lecture. But it was her job to help him grow into a good, strong man.

"You're growing up and there are certain urges you might feel—well, we all feel them—but we have to learn to hold them in check until the proper time, when the circumstances are right." Oh, God, I'm making a mess of this, she thought, and wished that Mick were there to talk to him. At times like these a boy needed a father more than a mother.

"Do you understand what I mean, Hubie, about waiting for the proper time and circumstances?"

He was confused. "You mean like Rupert should have?"

Oh, dear God, what do I say to that? "I've explained all that to you, Hubie. That Rupert's a very sick man . . . that what he did was a criminal act."

"Then, why isn't he in hospital? Or in prison?"

Why not, indeed? "I know it's hard to understand, but sometimes things aren't the way they should be and we just have to trust that time will make them right. But we have to talk about you. You have to learn that, along with the pleasures of being a man, there are responsibilities."

"But I told you, it wasn't my fault. She made me do it."

"Part of growing up, Hubie, is also learning to take responsibility for your actions instead of blaming others. That's what little boys or men who refuse to grow up do."

"But she tricked me into going to the boathouse, and when I got there she was naked and she—she touched me there!"

She sighed. While Hubie might appear to be physically mature, tall, and well built, he was still an innocent and he probably was telling the truth, that the woman—a girl of eighteen *was* a woman—had seduced him, was to blame. But what had the girl been thinking of? Had she been so sex-starved as to pick on a boy who simply didn't know how to deal with her except to do what came naturally?

She kissed the angelic face. "All right, we shan't talk about it anymore. I've enrolled you at a new school. We'll be driving up next week. And you have to try to stay out of trouble. And if it should happen that you *do* get into trouble—I know that sometimes it happens no matter how hard we try not to—well, just face up to it like a man and not try to lie your way out of it or put the blame on others." Then it occurred to her that she had another rule to add to the list: Avoid all sex-starved young women. But she didn't dare. He was such an innocent, he might misunderstand and run in the opposite direction.

After depositing Hubie at Brewster, she called Mick to tell him that she would be another week. She wanted to be sure Hubie was adjusting to his new school before she left England.

"Don't you think you're overdoing the protective-mother bit? And aren't you afraid you're neglecting this old boy?"

"No. That's what's nice about marrying a *man*. He's mature enough to know that a young boy's needs come first."

"Oof!" he said. "That pointed arrow really hurt."

"Good, and you be good and don't get into any trouble, at least not until I get there and can properly attend to you."

\*   \*   \*

It was by chance that she picked up a copy of the international edition of *Variety*. She was meeting Sally Whitehead for lunch at Claridge's, and while she was waiting in the lobby—Sally, as usual, was late—a man seated near her left his paper behind and she glanced through it to spot the death notice of T. S.'s wife, Elise Parker Grant, twenty-three, who had died suddenly in a sanitorium in Palm Springs. The only details were that the deceased was survived by her husband, Grantwood Studio's T. S.

Grant, a young daughter, and her parents, and that the service
would be held at Forest Lawn Memorial on Friday, the twenty-
seventh, at two P.M.

*How terrible for them all! The parents, T.S. and his baby, as well
as the poor woman who had barely tasted of life.*

Then she thought of Mick. She recalled his telling her that
he couldn't *bear* funerals—they actually made him ill—and that
he never attended them if he could help it. But under the circumstances, he couldn't help attending this one.

*And I should be there by his side.* She had intended to fly back
Sunday after seeing Hubie on Saturday, but it really wasn't
necessary. She'd seen him just yesterday, and he seemed to be
doing fine and Mick really needed her. She rushed to find a
phone to call the airlines. If she could get a plane out this
afternoon, given the time difference and even with a wait in New
York for a connecting flight, she should land in California in
time for the funeral, with a couple of hours to spare as far as she
could figure it.

She was racing out the hotel door just as Sally Whitehead
came sailing through it. "Nora! Where are you going? We're
supposed to be having lunch!"

"Sorry, darling, but you were *so* late and I grew *so* bored that
I decided to fly back to Hollywood immediately. Ta-ta!"

\*   \*   \*

When she arrived at LAX at eight in the morning, she decided
that there was no point in calling Mick to come pick her up. She
would just grab a taxi and surprise him by jumping into bed with
him before he even opened his eyes.

But then, when she walked into the bedroom, it was *she* who
was surprised as the camera in her brain went *click!* to add
another picture to join in aching infamy with two others: Hubert
making love to his assistant in his art gallery and Rupert sodomizing Hubie. But she had to admit even as she stood struck
dumb—the dashing Mick Nash and the breathtakingly lovely
Mimi L'Heureux made for a much more attractive photo than
the other two. In an exhibition of photographs it might even

have had as its title, "Sex as Poetry in Motion."

Mick looked as shocked and as shattered as she herself felt, but the sex kitten was as slick as perfumed bath oil and as cool as iced champagne as she slithered out of bed and undulated across the room. As gracefully as a jungle cat, she picked up her discarded white slip of a dress and pulled it on in one motion as she thrust her feet into high-heeled mules, then moved sinuously to the dresser to pick up Mick's silver-backed brush and pull it through the incredible wild mass of blond pillow-rumpled hair. After finishing with the brush, Mimi tossed it to Mick, still lying silently distraught in bed, then glided over to the bedroom door, where she—the betrayed wife who was also silently distraught—moved hastily out of the way to allow the star to make her exit unimpeded.

But before she left, Mimi tossed off as spectacular an exit line as Nora had ever heard in any play or film. First she flashed an incredibly white smile at her, and then, in that throaty voice, said: "Not to worry, *ma chere.* . . . *C'est magnifique, mais ce n'est pas la guerre.* . . ."

With that, she was gone, leaving a chagrined Mick muttering, "What was that bloody remark?"

"That bloody remark was 'It is magnificent, but it is not war.' I think it was a French officer who said that watching the charge of the Light Brigade at Balaklava. But what I think Mimi was doing, *mon cher*, was rating *your* performance—something like, it was good but not sublime."

\*   \*   \*

She was disappointed in Mick. She would have thought he would be more original than to spout all the old clichés: *It doesn't mean a thing.* . . . *It's just one of those things that happen.* . . . *It has nothing to do with us or the way I feel about you.* . . . *A onetime thing that will never happen again* . . .

And then he began the "it wasn't really my fault" routine, in which he tried to make *her* feel guilty: "A chap does get lonely, you know, and I was upset by this funeral business. I don't understand why it took you over two weeks to see to

Hubie's ridiculous little scrape. Good God—you'd think the problem was that the Empire was crumbling! What the hell *were* you doing there all this time? If you had been here, where you were supposed to be, this never would have happened. . . ."

And then came the next stage, in which he attempted to lay all the blame on the sex kitten while at the same time belittling her character as well as her attractions, probably thinking that this would both please and appease Nora.

"She's no more than a slut. She came creeping around at the crack of dawn, practically breaking down my door with some kind of a crappy story—she was supposedly breakfasting with a producer in the Polo Lounge, but the bloke was overdue and she was hungry and did I want to join her in a spot of breakfast? Three guesses as to what the tart was hungry for. Well, before I knew it, she'd pulled off her dress—the French cow wasn't even wearing so much as a pair of panties and what was a man to do? But believe me, she was a big disappointment in bed—she just lay there like a sack of beans, and where she got this reputation for being the sexiest woman in the world is beyond me. Even her body's been overrated. She's too wide in the bum and her boobs are already beginning to sag—"

The last few sentences of his statement—obvious misrepresentations of the truth—told her that his whole story about Mimi pounding on his door that morning was a lie. The goddess of cinematic sex had hardly been lying there like a sack of beans when she'd first opened the door but delivering an act that easily lived up to her reputation. And as sick as she'd felt watching Mimi slither across the room, she hadn't failed to notice that the actress's flawless body was every bit as extraordinary as her performance.

*   *   *

After Mick settled down sufficiently to offer a graceful apology, to take responsibility for his misconduct and promise sincerely that it would never happen again, he assumed that the matter was over and done with. Then Nora told him that it was their marriage that was over.

"Over *one* little incident? You have to look at the broad picture. Weren't we having a wonderful time? Jolly good sex and lots of laughs? We did have loads of fun, didn't we?" he appealed to her beseechingly, much as Hubie was wont to do.

"That's the problem, Mick—the fun's gone out of the thing, or maybe it's that the fun of it was a success but the marriage itself is a failure. But I blame myself. I should have known better. I should have known that one really can't marry just for the fun of it. Marriage is, after all, serious business. Much more serious than even divorce. . . ."

# THIRTY

She'd been back at Merrillee for more than three months before she was able to work through her pain over her quick marriage and even quicker divorce—Mick had obtained a six-week decree in Las Vegas just as she'd suggested he do before she left California. It was an easy and practical solution to the divorce problem, since he dearly loved Vegas—the shows and the slots and even the neon lights—and he would still be only a fast flight away just in case anything happened with his film. Besides, it made some kind of crazy sense that the marriage that had been born in Vegas should die there.

In the meantime she had been doing a lot of thinking about where she would go from here. When she had first come to Merrillee she'd had it in mind that after a while she would go back to London to make a niche for herself, thinking that there were several things she could do to earn a living. She could set herself up as an interior designer or a professional party-giver. She had even thought about her first love, a career in the theater. She certainly hadn't planned on remarrying, or at least, not so quickly. But she certainly had been busy. Once she'd found herself immersed in trying to make the manor earn her and Hubie's keep, she'd been determined to make a go of it and, in the process, had practically exhausted her resources—the jewelry that she'd been selling off piece by piece. Not to mention having married and divorced again!

Well, she was still determined to make the manor a paying proposition, and that was what she would concentrate on. As for men and marriage and that sort of thing, the best thing she could do was to put it all on hold and let things come naturally.

213

And as far as her recently exed-husband was concerned, she was ready to be friends again, which delighted Mick, who—newly back from Hollywood—came to visit carrying two bottles of California champagne.

"Don't tell me you brought that champagne all the way from the States? And what are we celebrating—our divorce?"

"Hardly, but I thought it only fitting that we toast the end of my California debacle with California wine instead of French. Besides, you can understand why I'm a little wary of anything French these days." He grinned and she grinned back.

"So tell me all about it—the end of the debacle," she said after he popped the first bottle of wine.

"You go first. What's happening with you and Hubie?"

"I've been busy trying to make ends meet while I get the barns back in shape. I thought I'd keep a few jerseys. As for Hubie, he's in a bit of a jam *again*. He and his friends at school sneaked into town to carouse at the local pub."

"Ah, Nora, when are you going to learn that no matter what *you* do, boys *will* be boys?"

"I'll try to keep that in mind if you'll tell me what happened with my overgrown boy in Hollywood."

"Would you believe Grantwood Studio never *had* the rights to make a sequel to *Gone With the Wind* in the first place?"

She was astonished. "But how could a major studio do a thing like that? Hire a screenwriter, bring you over to test, and all the rest of it without securing the rights first?"

"It seems that T.S. ordered his people to get the rights, and then everyone thought someone else had."

"That's incredible."

"Not as incredible as it gets. Remember when we used to lie in bed at night speculating—among other things to be sure—as to whom they were going to get to play Scarlett? Well, three guesses as to whom they had in mind for Scarlett the whole time— No, you'll never guess."

"No, don't tell me!" she shrieked. "Not Mimi L'Heureux?"

"But how *did* you guess?" he demanded, seemingly crushed.

"Not difficult, really. First I thought of the most incongruous casting imaginable—the sex kitten with the French accent as the quintessential Southern belle—and then I thought of the screenwriter—her husband—and it just popped into my mind. But tell me, *before* they found out they didn't have the rights, did Mimi *agree* to play Scarlett? I'd think that *she*, at least, would have had more sense."

"Well, it seems that since our star was barely out of her nappies when they made the original and had never seen it, even with French subtitles, much less heard of the Civil War, they took her into a screening room so that she could take a gander at Vivian Leigh playing Scarlett, and I went along too.

"Well, Mimi sat through nearly the whole first half of the film in complete silence, and everyone figured she was enthralled and were already congratulating each other that they had found their Scarlett. But then came that scene in the railroad depot when the Southern boys, thousands of them, are lying on the ground wounded and dying as far as the eye can see. A really impressive shot if you recall? And Mimi stands up, sticks her retroussé nose disdainfully in the air, and, just before sweeping out of the screening room, she says, 'Gentlemen, it is magnificent but it is not war.' "

Nora stared at him, shocked, until she realized she'd been *had!* Mick had set her up, making up the whole story, knowing exactly *who* she would guess, just so that he could deliver that punch line. She burst out laughing. She could marry a million times, but she would never again marry anyone who was as much fun as her own dear Mick.

"But seriously speaking, my dear, there's more to this story than meets the eye. The literary genius? It seems they were never really interested in *him*. It was Mimi they were after—they wanted *her* to come over from France to do a film for them, granted it *wasn't* the sequel to *Gone With the Wind*—and they only took him when Mimi made them a package deal."

"But why would *he*—a fine writer, a Pulitzer Prize-winner— want to do a screenplay, a sequel no less?"

"Because *she* wanted him to do it for the money, they say. Why have one salary when you can have two for the same trip? It seems the sex kitten's the sort who keeps an eye on her bank account even as she keeps her ass busy in bed." Then he flushed, realizing that, under the circumstances, the remark was a *faux pas*, but Nora merely smiled and urged him to go on.

"Besides, it seems his literary career wasn't doing so well. The story goes that he was only twenty-one when he won the Pulitzer, fresh out of Princeton, and went to Paris to write his second novel, met Mimi, fell crazy in love, and before the week was out, they were married."

"How romantic. Was she as crazy in love as he?"

"Who knows? One has to keep in mind that while they're the same age there was a world of difference between them when they met. She was a Parisian—you know there's no one more sophisticated than a Parisian—and he was a small-town American boy, and she'd been this amazing film star ever since she was seventeen and had dozens of men—"

Again he looked sheepish and she laughed and told him to continue, but then he turned serious. "It never happened again, you know . . . with her." He took her hand in his.

"Let's not talk about it, Mick. It's over and we have to get on with it. Now, please get on with the story."

But Mick had lost his zest for the tale and tried to sum up quickly. "Well, once they were married it was the high life à la Scott and Zelda Fitzgerald and lots of bubbly flowed, and when the second novel finally got finished it was a terrible flop, and then came a baby and most of the esteemed writer's time was taken up with playing nursemaid to the baby as well as to Mimi and her career. So, when Hollywood beckoned they packed up baby and Mimi's hundreds of trunks and—"

"The rest, you might say, is history," she finished for him. "Did he ever complete the screenplay?"

"It doesn't much matter at this point, does it?"

"I suppose not. But it *is* sad about his literary career. And what about the American film she was supposed to make?"

"I don't know. The last I heard was that she was hot to go back to Paris, that she hated *everything* American."

"Let's hope that doesn't include her husband," she said dryly before asking about T.S., who had so recently lost his wife and then had a big disappointment with his movie. "How're he and his baby doing?"

"The baby's still with her grandparents and he's keeping busy making other movies. You know what they say, you can't keep a good man down," Mick said, smiling again and leering at her suggestively. "He always rises to the occasion."

She managed a laugh to please him, but her thoughts were still on two seemingly very interesting men she had never met.

\* \* \*

Mick came down to Merrillee about once a month to stay for the weekend, and occasionally Nora went up to London to meet him for lunch and a matinee of one kind or another if he wasn't working, or to spend the evening with him if he was. But it was always a lovely time, Mick taking the trouble to make their time together special, filling his flat with flowers to welcome her, getting tickets for a show she'd been dying to see, taking her to the hottest new club, or discovering an Indian restaurant in the West End he knew she would like. He even listened sympathetically when she talked of her problems with the manor or with Hubie and his little scrapes, and kept offering her money to help out with the bills, which she steadfastly refused, much as she had refused to accept any when they divorced. Most of all, he told her over and over again that she worried too much and that she was too beautiful to risk getting worry lines, and she told him over and over again that she didn't know why she had ever married him, considering he was so much better a best friend than he'd ever been a husband.

It had become a ritual, one she treasured as much as she treasured his affection, though when he proposed once again she told him that it was impossible.

"But why? I don't understand why you refuse to give us another chance."

"Because no matter how much I'd love to, I can't *afford* to."

"If you're talking about money, you don't have to worry. I am *not* a poor man," he reminded her.

"I'm *not* talking about money. Well, not primarily, though I won't say it isn't a consideration. But Hubie *needs* a father, and if I marry again I have to be sure it's right."

"And I don't fill the bill as a father, is that it?" Though his tone was jaunty she knew he was hurt.

"It's not that you're not a fine person with lovely qualities, Mick, but Hubie needs a more *serious* man—"

"A man of substance and stability, of sterling character? A man full of true purpose who has never yielded to temptation and who knows duty comes before a good time?"

The ironic part, she thought, was that Mick thought *he* was being ironic, but the fact was that if she'd tried to describe the man she had in mind, the description wouldn't have varied much from the man he'd just described. Oh, she could have enhanced it a bit. She could wish for the man to be young, rich, handsome, fascinating, and sexy . . . to come riding up to Merrillee Manor on a white steed to swoop her and Hubie up and carry them off to some wonderful never-never land where women loved madly and were so loved in return. But that was too much to hope for . . . too much even to dream about. No woman had a right to expect it all.

"And what about what *you* need, Nora?" Mick startled her by breaking into her thoughts, and then she tried to break his somber mood by flirting with him. "Right this minute *you* are exactly what I need, my dashing Micky Nash."

But then, when he turned up again only three days after she'd just seen him, she demanded to know why he was there again so soon and he parried, "Such a tepid welcome and after I brought you a present—a jar of that bilious green chutney from Fortnum's you're so fond of." He reached into the pocket of his Burberry to bring forth the jar, but then held it a few inches out of her reach.

"Really, you're *such* a child," she said, grabbing for it, and after a few moments of grappling, he let her have it. "But it's such a tiny gift. What *else* did you bring me?"

"So greedy, and you haven't even offered me a drink."

"It's only eleven—you don't get a drink until noon."

"Not only are you greedy but cruel as well."

"Mick, I'm warning you. If you don't tell me what else you have for me, you're not going to get any lunch either." But then she realized that he was stalling for time rather than simply clowning. "What is it, Mick? Is something wrong?"

And then he pulled out a newspaper. "When I read this, I thought you could use a little company when you heard. Or have you already—?"

"Heard what?" She pulled the paper from his hand, and as soon as she saw the headline it took her only a few seconds to absorb the import of the story: After Lord Jeffrey Hartiscor had accidentally but mortally wounded his son and heir, Rupert, at a duck shoot at Hartiscor Castle, the grief-stricken father had taken his own life by hanging.

"Shall I get you a drink, Nora?" Mick asked anxiously. "I know that this must come as a terrible shock."

"No, not really. The only surprise is that it took Jeffrey this long to take that shot." Still, she sunk into a chair, shaken. "I guess it's really over at last."

"Not quite. You've forgotten one important detail. Since Jeffrey adopted Hubie and Rupert is dead, Hubie's now the Earl of Hartiscor and sole heir to the Hartiscor fortune."

"No, he's not."

"Nora, what are you talking about? You must be in shock! With Jeffrey and Rupert both dead—"

"No. When Jeffrey divorced me I signed affidavits agreeing to have the adoption nullified, relinquishing Hubie's claim to the Hartiscor title and estate."

"But how could you have done that? Look, I'll talk to my solicitors. You'll file to have those affidavits declared invalid. You'll say you signed them under duress—that Jeffrey forced you to."

"But that's not true, Mick. I signed them willingly and I don't want anything declared invalid."

"But the Hartiscor fortune! Are you mad? How can you do that to Hubie? Rob him of his legacy?"

"What legacy—the Curse of the Hartiscors? There are more important things than titles and fortunes. In fact, I was thinking that Hubie and I would be better off if we dropped the name Hartiscor altogether. But there *is* something you can do for me, Mick."

"Anything . . ."

"I must go to the funeral and Hubie must go too. He was my husband and he did adopt Hubie. We owe that much to him. And it would be a big help if you went with me, though I know how much you dislike funerals. I need a friend to lean on."

"Of course, Nora."

*   *   *

It was going to be a tremendous funeral, with anyone of any importance in London gathering to pay their last respects to Lord Jeffrey, including the prime minister and Prince Philip as well as friends and emissaries from abroad. All week long they had flown in from all parts of the world. Nora was pleased for Jeffrey's sake—he'd been a proud man—only she didn't know how she was going to get through the strain of the service and the reception that followed with only her terrible memories for support. She wasn't even sure she would be able to climb the steps of the great cathedral. Not alone, and that's how it was going to be, after all. . . .

Even Hubie, not understanding how important it was to her that he be at her side, had deserted her, pleading an important soccer match, and she'd been too disheartened to argue with him. And then, only last night, Mick had begged off—he was flying to Rome to do an Italian movie. "But couldn't you leave the next day?" she'd begged him, but Mick, being Mick, had only murmured something about how she knew how Italians were—very, very emotional.

For one of the few times in her life she broke down and cried, just as she was ready to go out her door and into her car to drive herself to the funeral. *God, did she have nothing in her life but boys?* How tired she was of them. But then she couldn't believe what she saw in the distance, coming down the lane. No, it wasn't a white steed, but it *was* a white Bentley, and once the car came to a stop in front of her door she saw that, while it wasn't a young, handsome, sexy prince who would make her heart beat madly who stepped out, it surely was not a boy but a *man* . . . a gentleman of substance, who had come to offer her his support through a trying time.

And though it had been several years since she had last seen him, she recognized him at once—just the hero she needed, arrived in the nick of time, the man who, as her late former husband and stepson claimed, had always nursed a secret yen for her—the recently widowed Martin Cantington, former ambassador to the Court of St. James, distinguished elder statesman and adviser to presidents, possessor of one of America's great fortunes, and, not incidentally, the father of four grown, successful sons.

Oh, yes, Martin Cantington was not a boy but a man. . . .

PART FIVE

# THE ONE THAT REALLY COUNTS

Washington, D.C., 1958–1968

# THIRTY-ONE

———◆•◆———

The plan was for Martin to precede Nora to Washington so that he could fill in his four sons and two daughters-in-law on his marriage plans while she told Hubie and made her arrangements to leave. Then, after spending a couple of weeks in the capital, they would all go down to Palm Beach for the wedding.

"I assume your children will all be interviewing me for the position of your wife," she'd joked with Martin the night before he left. "Suppose they decide I won't do? Will you throw me over?"

"What a thought!" he'd laughed. "Besides, they're going to love you as much as I do. How could they not?"

But then, no sooner than she and Hubie stepped off the plane, she discovered that this wasn't so when Peter and Paul, Martin's twin younger sons, met them at the airport instead of Martin. While they were polite and efficient, taking care of all the business with customs and the luggage, they weren't exactly warm. As for Hubie, eager to meet Martin's sons—he'd been so excited when he heard that he was going to have *four* big brothers—Peter and Paul barely looked at him. But she wasn't worried—she would wear them down with her own warmth.

"It was naughty of your father not to come and meet us," she said cheerfully when they were settled in the limousine. "I'm going to have to give him a piece of my mind."

The young men exchanged looks before Peter said, "Dad's waiting at the house with Billy and Bobby and their wives. We thought it would be best this way—less excitement for him."

"Less excitement? Isn't Martin feeling well? He was glowing

when he left England." More than glowing. Once she'd agreed to marry him they'd celebrated by making love over and over again, and he'd been almost lyrical.

Peter smiled tightly. "Our father's not a young man, Mrs. Nash, and we're concerned that he doesn't overdo."

"Call me Nora." She thought of telling them to call her "Mummy," just to shake them up a bit, but then decided to behave herself until she got to know them better. Probably it was as difficult for them to accept a strange woman as their father's wife as it would be for a small child.

"Patty, Bobby's wife, says that getting married at Father's age is bound to be a strain, especially when he's marrying a much younger woman," Paul said.

"Mummy's not so young," Hubie commented. "She's thirty-three," and then Peter said, "Our father's *sixty-three*," and Hubie conceded, "That really *is* old. I'm only thirteen but Mummy says your father's not *too* old to be my father and we'll get along fine. I think it's keen we're going to be brothers. Then, if your father can't play games, *we* still can."

Peter and Paul exchanged raised eyebrows and Paul said, "Patty said we had to be sure that Father doesn't overdo."

"I'm sure Patty's right." She nodded. "I'll certainly have to see to it that he doesn't."

Then Hubert chortled and Peter and Paul looked at him as if they were thinking: *What is this idiot kid laughing at now?*

"What's funny?" Peter asked, and Hubie said, "That you chaps are in your twenties and I'm only thirteen but I'm taller than both of you already," and she could see that the brothers didn't find that amusing at all.

But it would all work out. It was just a matter of everyone getting used to one another, and that was *her* job—to see to it that they were one happy family. And she thought she had the answer to that—the perfect link in the chain that would bind them all closer—a baby brother or sister that would be half Hubie's and half the Cantington boys'. What could be a stronger link?

Then the shocks came, thick and fast.

For one, the enormous house on R Street was incredibly *shabby*. The front lawn was brown and patchy, the marble floor in the entry scarred and cracked, and in the drawing room, where she and Hubie were left to cool their heels while the twins went to fetch Martin, the tabletops were unpolished, the upholstered chairs threadbare, and the down pillows in need of re-stuffing. There was only one conclusion she could come to—that even though Martin was a very rich man with most probably a huge staff, what he really needed more than a wife was a good gardener, a capable housekeeper, and a talented interior designer, all of whom he was clearly doing without.

Hubie repeatedly asked her when were they going to eat when Peter finally reappeared to take them upstairs to where his father and the others were waiting. Of course! she thought, this explained it all—why Martin hadn't come to the airport and why he hadn't been waiting for her downstairs. They had a party waiting with banners and a table full of party food. She whispered to Hubie, "I have a feeling you're going to get something to eat any minute now."

"Good! I could eat a horse!"

"Don't be silly, darling, they don't eat horses in America." She giggled happily. "All they eat all day long are bonbons, ice cream, and chocolate cake."

But then, what greeted them upstairs was not a party but a family gathered round as if to take a family portrait, with Martin, the aged patriarch, sitting with his sons and daughters-in-law grouped about him. In his arms he held a crying baby while a little boy was trying to climb up a leg and one of the daughters-in-law was attempting to sit a girl of perhaps five, fat and kicking, on his knee.

*Martin was a grandfather!*

Delighted, she rushed to him while he tried to rise to greet her, still holding the baby in one arm and attempting to push the kicking girl away with the other. But the child at his leg defeated him and he fell back into the chair. Laughing, she took the crying baby from his arms and handed it over to Hubie—he loved babies, "even beastly ones," he'd once confided—and she leaned over to give Martin a kiss as he whispered, "Now, if you can get rid of that monster trying to amputate my leg, I'll be able to reciprocate properly."

Once this was accomplished—she plucked up the boy to give him a kiss before setting him firmly on his feet, and the baby stopped crying because babies always responded to Hubie—they embraced and the introductions were made. And if the sons and the daughters-in-law were cool, Hubie made up for it with his enthusiasm. He thought the big family scene was good fun and she thought that once she won Martin's children over, what a wonderful time they were all going to have.

She could picture the big family dinners they would have at least once a week and, of course, at Thanksgiving and Christmas. And on the Fourth of July they'd have picnics with fireworks, and on Easter Sunday they'd have their very own egg hunt, with the very youngest Cantington—hers and Martin's— given a head start because it was the baby. And the master of the hunt would be none other than Hubie Cantington, the eldest of the younger set of Cantingtons, at long last part of a big, happy clan. She and Hubie had really lucked into it this time, she thought, and anything she had to do to make the dream a reality she would do most gratefully.

Then, *sotto voce*, Martin asked *her* to ask his children to go home so that they could be alone.

"But Martin, it's not *my* place to send them home. I can send Hubie to look around or something so we can be alone, but I can't ask *your* children to leave. I have my work cut out here just getting them to like me. Naturally enough, I suppose, they think I'm nothing more than a fortune hunter and I—well, I don't want to get off on the wrong foot. I think that it would be better if *you* asked them to leave."

"No, *you* must. It's the only way you're going to establish any authority. If you don't, all is lost." He smiled but she could see that he was in dead earnest.

"But dinner—? Weren't they planning on us all having dinner together here?"

"I'm sure they were," he chortled. "And they were probably planning on feeding me pablum along with that wretched baby.

Now, Nora, you must be firm or they'll walk all over you just like they've always managed to do to me.''

She couldn't argue the point with everyone pointedly waiting for their private conversation to end, and then there was nothing else for her to do but tell them that their father was as tired as she was, and that perhaps it would be best if they came back tomorrow when everyone was feeling fresh.

"Of course he's tired,'' Bobby's wife, Patty, said severely. "But before I leave I'm going to see to it that he eats something—he's on a special diet, you know—and then I'll settle him properly in bed—''

*Be firm,* Martin had said. Nora set her face in so firm a smile it made her jaw ache. "Oh, I know *exactly* what to feed him, and if there's one thing I'm *really* good at, it's seeing that a man is properly settled in his bed. So, all of you can run along and see to your kiddies while I see to mine and tomorrow we'll have a proper get-together. I'll have Cook prepare a real English feast, roast beef and Yorkshire—''

"But that's exactly what Dad *shouldn't* be eating,'' Patty said, horrified, and Daisy said, "And you'd better not be upsetting the cook. She doesn't like any interference. Right, Billy?'' and Billy said, "Right. She might get miffed and walk out, and then where will poor Dad be?''

"With a new cook in *his* kitchen, I daresay,'' Nora laughed, shooing them toward the door, and they reluctantly departed as Martin cheerfully waved. Then he suggested that since it would be some time to dinner—if one could call the pap they would be served *dinner*—Hubie should go down to the kitchen and see what he could scare up while he and she got reacquainted.

"But you heard what Billy said—that Cook might become annoyed enough to leave and where would that leave us?''

"Yes, but I also heard your answer—that it would leave us with a new cook. That was inspired!''

"And that's what you really want?'' she asked, sending Hubie off to find his way to the kitchen.

"My God, yes! I'm sick to death of her food and her sullen ways!''

"Then, why haven't you simply given her the sack?''

"But *I* couldn't do that. The woman's been here for thirty years. I can't fire her any more than I can fire the rest of the menagerie that work here."

"But you're quite willing that she or the rest of them *quit* if things around here become not to their liking?"

"Willing? I'm *counting* on it. I'm damn tired of having the worst-run house in Washington and serving up the worst meals in town. Even before Rita became ill, an invitation to dine at our house was enough to send people into paroxysms of laughter. You can't imagine how I felt when I was in England and we'd go to your and Jeffrey's home for dinner—"

"How?"

"Jealous to the core. Not only did Jeffrey have you—the beautiful and desirable Nora—in his bed, but also the hostess with the most illustrious salon in London."

She realized that though Martin was smiling, he meant every word he said. "But you're an important, wealthy man with a distinguished career. Why *didn't* you have things the way you wanted them?"

"It was Rita. She hated my being a public figure. If it weren't one thing she was complaining about it was another, and it made no difference if we were here or abroad. Why do you think we left England when we did? All she wanted was to be at home with the children, and when we *were*, the children always came first—certainly before me or my career. And if I told her we had to do something about the house because its deplorable condition was an embarrassment, she said only the *nouveau riche* worried about those things. As far as *old* money was concerned, shabby was a badge of honor. But the truth was she acted out of spite. She tried to smother me with those children just like those children are trying to smother me now—trying to make an old grandpappy of me with their brats crawling all over me, telling me I mustn't overdo, feeding me milk toast, trying to relegate me to a rocking chair on the back porch. They want to take over not only the family fortune but my very life. They're jealous of my position, just like their mother was. Do you realize if it weren't for Rita I could have been president?"

*I could have been president!*

But she had had no idea this was something Martin had wanted for himself. She studied him now, mesmerized by the harsh look of frustrated ambition that shot from his eyes like fiery sparks. This was *not* the winsome, dignified, unfailingly pleasant Martin Cantington she knew, a man content to rest on his laurels . . . the man she *thought* she was marrying . . . the man she'd assumed was marrying *her* only for her own winsome charms.

"But it's not too late, you think?" he asked, his eyes pinned to hers with an urgency. "For the presidency?"

*Ah, he still wants it. . . .*

She spoke slowly then, choosing her words carefully. "I'd say sixty-three is the perfect age to be president if a man has his vigor, his health, and his wonderful capabilities."

These were the very qualities she'd been considering when she thought that they might have a baby. But now she saw that what Martin envisioned for their shared future was something else altogether, and that there was no room for a baby in *that* scenario. Still, she was willing to do her part. Whatever role Martin wanted her to play, she could learn the lines. If nothing else, she was prepared to give at least as good as she got.

"Now, what presidential-election year are we talking about?" she asked thoughtfully. "And the campaign we're going to wage—when does it officially begin?"

"The actual election year is '60, but I think the campaign has already started," Martin cried joyfully. "It began the moment you stepped off that plane."

"In that case, we're wasting time," she said enthusiastically. "What's the best restaurant in town where Washington's most elite will be dining tonight?"

"By elite, do you mean socially or politically powerful?"

"Both, but with the emphasis on the latter, to be sure."

He considered. "It's been a while since I've even been out to dinner. My jailers, you know. But I would say the Vendome would be as good a choice as any."

"Then, I'll call for a reservation and then I'll go collect

Hubie so we can change into our very best."

"You mean we're going *out* to dinner? But you must be tired. You just got off the plane—"

"But we *have* to eat, and you yourself said the food here is beastly and you haven't been out to dinner in ages. If we go out to dine you'll be sure to meet old friends, and besides introducing everyone to your future wife, you'll be reminding them that Martin Cantington's still around, by God, and a force to be contended with! Now, doesn't that sound sensible?"

"It sounds wonderful! I'm in your hands and I *am* a shrewd old goat. I *knew* you were going to make things fun."

She went downstairs to find Hubie, hoping he hadn't stuffed himself so that he wouldn't be able to eat dinner, but she needn't have worried. He hadn't made it to the kitchen after all. It seemed that first he'd been ambushed on the way, then detained in a parlormaid's bedroom in the basement.

"What *were* you thinking of, Hubie?" she demanded. "How could you—?"

"But she said I had a beautiful body and she just wanted to feel my muscle," Hubie grinned beatifically, and then she didn't bother to ask which one. Sometimes it was better not to ask too many questions but to just go with the flow. . . .

# THIRTY-TWO

＊•＊

N ora was up at dawn though the wedding guests wouldn't
start arriving until at least one, an incredible one thousand
of them—political bigwigs and governors from all over
the country; *anyone* of importance in Washington, Republicans
as well as Democrats, even the Eisenhowers complete with Secret Service. There would be dignitaries from abroad, society
people and money people from New York, a movie crowd from
California, sports heroes and media stars, as well as local neighbors like the Kennedys, who were also their neighbors on Cape
Cod. Friends, family, and power brokers . . . anybody who was
anybody . . . because she and Martin were not only getting
married today, they were also privately at work on their campaign to garner support for Martin's try for the presidency.

She went to the window to observe the day. So far it was
overcast, though the weatherman had promised an exquisite
day, the sun shining bright and clear and the temperature at an
ideal 72 degrees, perfect for a Palm Beach wedding. And after
three weeks of exhaustive work—the Cantington waterfront estate had been as badly neglected as the Washington house—the
grounds at least, if not the house (its refurbishing would have to
come later), were ready to serve as the perfect setting.

She saw that the catering people were already setting up their
buffet tables under the white-and-pink-striped tents, the florists
busily arranging thousands of deep-pink roses, pale-pink tulips,
and fragrant gardenias, the musicians arriving early to go over
their arrangements, workmen laying a dance floor over the carpet of green lawn. And soon their beautifully attired guests
would be milling, sipping champagne, dancing to Meyer Davis's

orchestra, and aahing over the five-feet-tall wedding cake. Yes, today she was having a very grand wedding, but it was *hard* not to think of the previous ones—the one she'd never experienced with Hubert, the proper one with Jeffrey but shadowed by scandal and tragedy, the giddily garish one she and Mick had shared. . . .

Then she reminded herself that she had no time to stand at the window dwelling on the past. This morning, only a few hours before she and Martin joined hands, she had an important meeting about the future, hers and Hubie's. When Martin's sons had arrived yesterday, along with the wives and the children, they had brought a mass of papers for her to sign. . . .

* * *

Martin had looked over the batch of papers. "You have to understand that the boys are all lawyers, though they don't practice so they have a tendency to overdo these things. Most of it doesn't amount to much—insurance forms, licenses. . . . There's only one *important* document here—the marriage contract which they've taken the liberty of drawing up. It spells out what you *will* get and what you *won't* under various circumstances and contingencies. But if I were you I wouldn't sign it as is." He smiled. "The thing to remember is that everything's *negotiable.*"

"I'm not worried. I assumed there'd be a marriage contract and I can understand that they want to protect their inheritance. But since it is *our* marriage contract, it means that we both have to agree to the terms and sign it, and I know that you wouldn't sign any contract that wasn't fair to me. And I'm sure *you'll* negotiate for me since *you're* the diplomat—*the* great negotiator."

"But I'm going to do something better than negotiate for you. I'm going to teach you how to *negotiate for yourself*, which will serve you well even after I'm gone. And the secret is to give a little here to get a lot more there, and to watch out for those contingencies. And if the opposition takes a rigid position, don't be afraid to walk away from the deal."

"Walk away? But I'd be walking away from you! How could I do that with the wedding only a few hours off?"

"That's what they're counting on—you panicking."

Martin had made it all sound like some board game . . . she and his sons playing at war. "But I don't want to play games and I don't want to think about contingencies. I'm not marrying you to divorce you but to have a good life with you, and I hope that I'll be such a good wife you wouldn't dream of divorcing me. And I refuse to even think about your dying!"

"That makes you a fool, and I'll be damned if I'll marry a fool. I want to marry a winner! And if you refuse to think about your own future, what about Hubie's? How do you think *my* sons will feel about my adopting *your* son, who *you're* going to *insist* is cut in for his fair share of the loot when their old man takes his swan dive? You're going to have to fight them tooth and nail, and you're going to have to be tough."

"Oh, Martin, you mean you haven't told them yet that you're adopting Hubie?"

"No."

"But why not?" *It was the least he could have done. . . .*

"Because it's *you* who must do the negotiating, and so it must be *you* who lays the cards on the table. But cheer up, my dear, you're going to learn enough about negotiating and politicking to last you a lifetime."

"But Martin, I don't even to know what to ask for. You have to give me some guidelines."

"Follow your heart, but don't let it impair your good judgment. . . ."

She had promised that she would follow his advice and that she would be tough, but the one thing she was determined to be was fair. . . .

\*   \*   \*

She'd better go down to meet with the boys now and get it over with so that she could dress for her wedding. Put on her pale-pink wedding gown, the tiara of orange blossoms and pearls, and Martin's wedding gift—a necklace composed of diamonds and pearls in the shape of flowers. Then she would put on her biggest and best smile.

But just as she was about to turn away from the window, the sun showed a happy face and she *knew* it was going to be a fine day. The she spotted Hubie, already dressed in his white usher's cutaway, racing across the lawn toward—*what? Life just for the joy of it!* She almost called out to him, to stop him in flight, to caution him *not* to go down to the beach, *not* to soil his white suit, *not* to fall and break his leg. But he was so beautiful with his yellow hair catching the sun that she couldn't bear to stop his poetry in motion, and then her own feet barely touched the floor as she danced, humming to herself.

# THIRTY-THREE

———— •••• ————

In January Nora sent Hubie away to boarding school feeling much like a mother sending her son off to war. She knew she was being silly, but he was so new to being both a Cantington and an American, she'd thought that in the beginning she would keep him with her. But Martin had insisted that, since Hubie was now a Cantington, he had to be educated as a Cantington, which meant an excellent prep school and, eventually, Harvard. "The Cantington men have always gone to Harvard. In fact, there was a Cantington in the first Harvard commencement class in 1642."

"I doubt that Harvard will ever accept Hubie."

"That's a negative attitude and not what I'd expect from you, Nora. You've been so positive and enthusiastically optimistic about *my* chances for the presidency."

"There's an absurd comparison. You have this strong will and determination, and people who *know* always talk of your sterling character and how you're entirely presidential material, and no one—not even I—would say Hubie's Harvard material."

"Don't count Hubie out yet. He's a fine boy and between us we're going to see that he *does* fine." He took her hand to bring it to his lips, and she sighed. Martin was so sweet and loving, he made it almost impossible to argue with him.

"But you have to realize, Martin, Hubie's scholastic record is *not* good and there's always been a behavioral problem."

"Then, that's all the more reason to send him to the best schools, so that he'll do better all around, plus he'll be better able to develop self-discipline away from his oversolicitous

237

mother and his doting dad, because I warn you—I intend to be most doting.

"Besides, if I'm to announce my candidacy by the end of the year, we're going to be busier than ever running around the country gathering support and making me a really viable contender. Then, once I do announce, we'll have to start stumping for the primaries right off, and *if* I get the nomination, the really hard campaigning will first begin. So, that makes almost two years, during which you'll be much too busy for this hands-on supervision that Hubie is better off without. But in the end it will all have been worth it. I'd like to see them try to keep the president's son out of Harvard."

As it worked out, it was just as well she didn't keep Hubie at home. Before the month was out, Martin proposed that they take their delayed honeymoon trip to, of all places, the Soviet Union.

"But Martin, we have so much work to do here, and it will be *so* cold in Russia this time of year."

"Exactly. I thought that you and I might drop in unofficially and warm things up. I think 1959 might well be the year of the big thaw with Russia—heal the breach—and the man who starts the icicles melting might end up a hero. Even Eisenhower is sending Nixon to Moscow on what he calls a courtesy visit, but I have a feeling he and old Khrushchev will lock horns, whereas I think *I'll* do much better—my field of expertise *is* foreign relations, besides which I'll have you by my side. We'll be an irresistible combination. Then, if I do get the party's nomination and run against Dick in '60, I'll already be one up on him. What do you think?"

"I think I'm married to a very wise man," she said, and spent the days before they left boning up on Mr. Khrushchev, which amused Martin no end.

"I'm taking you to Moscow to *charm* Khrushchev, not to write a paper on him."

"You said we were going there to warm things up. Well, how can I do that if I walk in *cold?* I may not be the wise man my husband is, but I do know that the best way to charm a man is to talk *to* him *about* him even if it is through an interpreter. Now, don't you think I'm right?"

"I think that the wise man married a woman infinitely wiser than he, not even to mention her considerable charm."

*   *   *

Nora managed to be so charming that when Khrushchev toured the States as the year waned, he not only demanded to see Disneyland but the Cantingtons as well. And while he wasn't permitted to go to Disneyland for security reasons, the house on R Street was sufficiently secured (and by now sufficiently beautiful, with its pale chintzes, gleaming Georgian silver, and awesome art collection) for the Cantingtons to host a reception for the chairman that was viewed by Washingtonians as the coup of the political season. Even the Eisenhowers felt compelled to attend, which made it a double coup despite the necessity to beef up the security twofold as well, and there were at least twenty Kennedys on the guest list.

"Do we really have to invite the whole tribe?" she asked, trying to cut down on the numbers.

"Afraid so. The word is that Jack's about to announce his candidacy, so he'll be my chief competitor in the primaries, and it's a good rule to keep in touch with the competition so you can better gauge what they're up to."

In the end, the guest list grew so extensive that they purchased the house next door (which was opportunely for sale) to accommodate out-of-town guests and even some of the Khrushchev entourage at the behest of the Soviet ambassador. She then had a little bridge constructed to link the two houses, which was facetiously dubbed in the press as the Cantington link to the Kremlin. While this delighted Martin, she only hoped this so-called link wouldn't come back to haunt them.

As extensive as the guest list was, it did *not* include Martin's sons and their wives. She'd wanted to invite them, but Martin refused to allow it because of their hostility, which had begun with the haggling over the marriage contract and the fact that

Martin was adopting Hubie, and was intensified by their disap-
proval of his political ambitions and the trip to Russia, for
which they blamed her. *Was she trying to kill him?*

But when Hubie was sent home from school on suspension
pending the results of an investigation into a rash of petty thefts,
Martin had no problem with Hubie being at the party, though
she herself did. "I'd hate for him to get the idea that he's being
rewarded in some way for—"

"Rewarded? The poor boy's been maligned, and under no
circumstances will I even allow him to return to St. John's. And
before we send him off to another school I think we should do
everything to make his stay at home a pleasant one. I'm really
surprised that you don't agree with me."

"But we don't have all the facts yet," she protested weakly
in the face of Martin's vigorous championing of Hubie. "He *is*
friends with the boys who seem to be the culprits."

"So, are we, his parents, to pass judgment on him and con-
firm that he's guilty merely by association?"

How was she to explain to Martin, who had promised to
"dote" on him, that Hubie could never resist temptation and the
wrong sort of friends? But, then, how could she not take pride
in their son when everyone at the grand reception was so taken
with the charming and handsome Hubie Cantington, even the
dour Mrs. Khrushchev?

But that was in November 1959, when Martin was still a
hero to the public for helping to forge a dialogue with the
Russians, what with a summit conference coming up in May in
Paris that included Eisenhower, Khrushchev, De Gaulle, and
England's Harold Macmillan and looked so promising for world
peace. But then in May, just before the conference was about to
convene, Martin—who was sweeping the primaries—suddenly
ceased to be a hero when a Russian rocket shot a U-2 out of its
skies, and in the ensuing days Khrushchev denounced the Americans for treachery and spying and relations rapidly deteri-
orated, with Russia once again the villainous foe.

Then Martin was only a *tired* presidential hopeful who had
bet on the wrong horse, and just weeks away from the Democratic National Convention he withdrew from the race and she

was devastated. "But you can't just give up."

"But I don't intend to just give up. I'm going to ask my supporters to swing their backing to Kennedy at the convention, and then I . . . *we* . . . will work for his election. He's young and strong, full of vigor, and that's what our country needs right now. Jack Kennedy is the voice of the future."

"But we've been on the campaign trail all this time campaigning *against* him."

"That's politics. The *important* thing is the welfare of the nation and the party. You know what they say—'Now is the time for all good men to come to the aid of their party.' That means it's time to heal the breach so that what's really important can survive."

*Heal the breach* . . . That was the second time Martin had used that phrase. And of course he was right. That was what was truly important, and the least she could do for the man who had given her his love and her son his name and both of them a sense of identity was to heal the breach and give him back his natural sons so that *all* of them could survive in the best possible way—as a family.

\* \* \*

She started her personal campaign that summer by inviting the children up to the Cape even though Martin was resistant to the idea. She was determined to do it for him no matter how much he objected, and it was something she needed to do for Hubie too, to make him part of the whole.

First came Bobby and Patty and Billy and Daisy and their assorted kids, and there was a lot of cheerful confusion as well as picnics on the beach, with Hubie building castles in the sand with the small fry. There was even a birthday party for Billy and Daisy's daughter, herself and Hubie canvasing the neighborhood to round up children to fill out the guest list. All in all, the visit was *fairly* harmonious, and when Martin complained that there was no peace and quiet, what with the elder children's harping and carping, she told him that it was good for him—it would keep *him* from getting old and stodgy.

After the two families left, the twins came for their visit, each in a separate quandary. First Paul confided that though he was with the State Department along with Peter, he was more interested in the administration of the family's financial interests, which was Billy and Bobby's territory. He would like to switch over, but one, he didn't want to impinge on Billy and Bobby's domain, and two, he was afraid that Peter would feel abandoned because they'd always been inseparable.

But when Peter confessed *his* problem—that he was involved with a very pretty but shy, unsophisticated girl, Chrissy by name, whom he wanted to marry but was afraid that his overwhelming sisters-in-law would scare her off—Nora had the obvious solution to everyone's problems since she was already armed with the one factor missing from the equation. From recently listening to Patty and Daisy's carping, she knew that Billy's ambition was to get into Virginia politics, but he felt obligated to help Bobby oversee the family's business.

Now Billy could leave the family business office to go into politics with a free heart because Paul would take his place alongside Bobby without having to feel bad about abandoning Peter, because Peter had Chrissy. All that really remained for her to do was to try to instill some self-confidence and backbone into the girl so that she could fight back when the sisters-in-law got out of hand, since she already knew from experience that everyone had to do their own fighting.

She invited Peter to bring his girl to the Cape and urged Martin to welcome her warmly and cultivate her so that she would feel less shy and more self-confident. If anyone could do it, he, the great diplomat, could. Martin resisted, claiming that it was not that the physically well-endowed Chrissy herself was shy but that her head was—shy of intellect. But Nora wouldn't take no for an answer. "If you go for long walks on the beach with Chrissy, it will not only make her feel that you like her, giving her a lot of self-confidence, but it will provide *you* with exercise and her with the benefit of your brilliant conversation so that she won't be all *that* shy of intellect."

Then she finished out the summer season by giving Peter and Chrissy a huge engagement party (with *all* the Kennedys from the neighboring compound present), which brought the family together in what she hoped was an act of solidarity guaranteed to make Chrissy feel "at home." As for keeping Daisy and Patty from overpowering Chrissy, there were some things people had to learn for themselves or their character would never develop along with their intellect.

In November they all returned to the Cape to celebrate a truly wonderful Thanksgiving, and Martin's boys even bent sufficiently to include Hubie in their rough-and-tumble touch football. But for her, the highlight of the four days they spent together came after Martin gave the Thanksgiving blessing and she suggested that they go around the table, with each family member telling what he or she was most thankful for.

Hubie was first and he looked around the table with a glowing face. "I'm thankful that me and my mum are sharing turkey dinner with all of you, but most of all I'm thankful we all share the same name and the same dad, who's the greatest!"

Nora had to bite her lip not to cry, and the table went quiet except for the baby, who banged the tray of his high chair with a spoon. But when Martin walked from the head of the table to where Hubie sat at the foot and placed his hand on Hubie's shoulder to say, "Son . . ." she did cry and pretended not to hear Patty stage-whisper to Bobby, "I bet *she* put him up to it just to impress your father."

The Christmas holiday was spent in Palm Beach again with the children, with Martin complaining, "I hope that this family gathering will suffice until at least the first of April." But she paid him no mind, convinced that everyone was enjoying the togetherness despite the few, inevitable discordant notes.

First, Daisy complained about her children's accommodations—it seemed they weren't used to sharing a room. Then Patty wondered aloud if a fifteen-year-old boy who was failing physics (Hubie having confided this himself) really deserved a state-of-the-art telescope from Martin, which had to cost in the thousands as a Christmas gift, and demanded to know why Martin had not seen fit to select comparable presents for his *real* flesh and blood who *never* failed to excel. (No one gave her an answer.)

There was a bad moment when Hubie took a couple of the younger kids sailing and didn't come back until well after dark and Bobby called him "an irresponsible jerk." Nora could scarcely blame Bobby. She was furious with Hubie herself—it was such a thoughtless act and had caused all of them so much anxiety. Still, Martin defended Hubie. "He's a competent sailor who always has the situation well under control."

It seemed that nothing could deter Martin from his defense of Hubie. Not even when she and he, and luckily no one else, discovered Hubie and Chrissy on the back patio in what could only be described as a *clinch* ten minutes after midnight on New Year's Eve. Martin said this was excusable since it *was* New Year's Eve, and probably Chrissy and Hubie—though *he* had been forbidden more than one glass of the bubbly—had too much champagne, and it was best not to make a fuss.

"Hubie's only a teenager with a healthy dose of male hormones, and she—? Well, I hate to say that I told you so, Nora darling, but I *did* tell you that that girl, even with her healthy pair of boobs, is a total nincompoop."

Still, all things considered, she felt that they had made some headway in healing the breach. . . .

# THIRTY-FOUR

N ora would always remember the day of John Kennedy's inauguration—Friday, January 20—as vividly as most people would remember the day he was shot. She and Martin were scheduled to attend the inaugural, their places on the stand with JFK assured by the prominent role they'd played in his election. But the day before the inauguration, following a week of bitter cold, a fresh snow had fallen, covering Washington with a frozen white blanket, accompanied by an icy wind blowing in from the Potomac and the Tidal Basin. On Friday morning, though the snow had stopped falling and a cold sun shone, the temperature still hovered below freezing and the frigid winds continued to blow, and she decided it would be better if they watched the proceedings from the warmth and comfort of home. Martin hadn't been feeling well for a couple of weeks, and he'd been coughing for the last few days.

At first, he objected. "Do you propose to start treating me like an invalid as my children tried to do? I warn you, if you do, I'm going to have to turn *you* in for a new model."

"And I warn you: Just try it and see what you get. More trouble than you ever bargained for. But seriously, Martin, tonight's going to be a really long evening, what with the dinner we're giving before we even start out for the Inaugural Ball. It makes more sense for you to take it easy during the day so you'll be rested and ready to charm your dinner guests off their feet and able to keep up with me later on at the ball, where I propose to dance your *feet* off. So, you see, I want to keep you at home for purely selfish reasons. Besides, I myself dread sitting out there in the beastly cold."

"When you put it that way, I have no choice but to cave in to your bullying as gracefully as possible." Having said that, he flicked on the television in the study and sat down in the big leather easy chair by the fire to watch the preinauguration coverage. Surprised that he hadn't put up more of a fight, she wondered if he were secretly relieved that she'd made the decision to watch the event on television. He *did* seem really tired and he did have that persistent cough.

By noon the temperature had risen somewhat, but still it was below freezing, and she knew she'd made the right decision.

At 12:20, JFK made his appearance on the stand, hatless and coatless, and Martin smiled sadly. "See, Nora? Twenty degrees above zero and Jack's not even wearing a top coat. Who could take that punishment except a *young* man with an iron constitution?"

"What rot! Who ever said the ability to freeze was a qualification for the presidency?"

They watched Richard Cardinal Cushing give the invocation, after which Robert Frost rose to read a poem, but the glare of the sun on the snow was so blinding that he had to recite a poem from memory. Finally, at 12:51, Justice Warren administered the oath of office and the new president began his speech: "Let the word go forth from this time and place, to friend and foe alike, that the torch—"

It was then that Martin cried out softly and slumped over in his leather chair.

\*　\*　\*

She didn't know if it really took so long for the ambulance to get there or if it just seemed that way, knowing that it had to be a terrible day for ambulances, what with that icy blanket covering the city and the impossible Inaugural Day traffic. When the ambulance finally did arrive, they tried futilely to dissuade her from riding along with Martin, but she knew she should when Martin, regaining consciousness, gripped her hand as if holding on for dear life even as they were monitoring him and administering oxygen. "*You're* my oxygen," he whispered. "Don't leave me, Nora."

She didn't, not for a moment, until he was past that critical point when life triumphed over death and he smiled up at her from his hospital bed. "We beat the rap, didn't we?"

"We did indeed," she laughed, trying not to cry, and not telling him then that the doctors had said that he would have to lead a "cautious" life and that most of his activities would have to be curtailed, and even so the prognosis was uncertain.

She only knew that she was committed to him as she had never been before, to seeing to it that he enjoyed as fulfilling a life in "curtailment" as he had in robust health. She took him home, whereupon Billy and Bobby, Peter and Paul, as well as Patty and Daisy, but at least not Chrissy, resumed their campaign to relegate him to a rocking chair, blaming his heart attack on his arduous political activities, implying none too subtly that it had been Nora, the ambitious wife, who had caused it.

But neither impressed with their arguments nor intimidated by their insinuations, she decided it was time for a new course. Much as she'd striven to reconcile Martin with them in order to improve the quality of his life, she was now as prepared to protect him from them. Trying to heal the breach was one thing, but cowardly appeasement was another and she was prepared to get as tough as she had to—it was a matter of assuring Martin's survival as any kind of man at all.

"He may be a bit more fragile than he was before, but he's still not a teacup, he's a man. And only those of you who remember that are welcome in our home."

\* \* \*

If the Cantingtons' parties had been frequent and wonderful prior to Martin's heart attack, they became even more frequent and wonderful after it, since Nora was determined that if Martin couldn't get about Washington as he had before, she would bring Washington to him.

As the profile on the Cantingtons in the October 1962 issue

of *Washington Today* put it, "Nora Cantington surrounds her husband with Washington's finest—its most brilliant intellects and its most beautiful people—so that Martin Cantington can stay at home and still feast his eyes as well as his mind, much as the fortunate guests feast their eyes on one of the town's most beautiful hostesses even as they feast at her bountiful table. . . ."

When Patty protested that Nora was wearing poor Martin out by "giving all these eternal dinner parties," she responded by correcting her: "There's really no such thing as a *dinner party*, my dear. There are parties and there are dinners, as in 'We *give* parties but we *eat* dinner.' " And when Bobby suggested that her entertaining Washington celebrities did Martin no medical good, she corrected him as well: "But you have the wrong object of the verb—we're not entertaining *Washington celebrities*; we're entertaining *Martin*."

In the fall of '63 Nora announced to the family that, just as she had brought Washington to Martin's doorstep, she wanted to bring the world to him as well. But since that wasn't possible other than by inviting the same old crop of foreign dignitaries to their home, she intended to take Martin to the world. She would begin by accompanying him to China.

"*China?*" they cried, astounded.

"Yes, China," she said blithely, as if talking about nothing more exotic or strenuous than a stroll in the garden. "Martin's never seen China and he's terribly keen on it. And you know how he feels about keeping an open mind to new ideas, how he always says, 'Rigidity's the first sign of old age.' "

After pausing a few moments to allow that nugget to sink in, she continued ingenuously, "So, while it's impossible for him to go in an official capacity—God knows it's difficult enough to go at all with things the way they are—it's been arranged for him to serve as a kind of unofficial ambassador-at-large."

"What are you trying to do—kill him?"

"Oh, not at all. In fact, I've arranged for Dr. Steinfeld to be part of our little entourage."

"*Entourage?*"

"Yes, I wouldn't dream of going without our own interpreter. We couldn't be sure of getting an accurate message across.''

"But what about the food? Suppose Dad can't stomach it?''

"Why wouldn't he? He's always adored Chinese food, and the problem's with his heart, not with his stomach.''

"Doctor or no doctor, it sounds as if Dad will drop from exhaustion.''

"Not at all. I'm taking along the best motorized wheelchair made, just in case he should tire walking about.''

"And what about the *traveling* from one city to another? Traveling conditions can be very primitive in China.''

She laughed. "The things you children worry about. We're going to be flying over in a jet, so I've decided we might as well buy our own since chartering one's so expensive anyway, and then I'll be able to keep it there, pilot at the ready. So, if we go any distance, we'll use that. As for getting around in general, I'm arranging for a couple of limousines to be at our disposal, and I'm taking along Thomas to drive to make sure Martin will be completely comfortable.''

"Is *any* of this going to be absorbed by the government or is it all going to be at Dad's personal expense?'' Paul demanded.

"*All* of it will be at your father's expense since he *is* traveling in an unofficial capacity, but why do you ask?''

"Because it sounds like a very expensive proposition.''

"But I thought we were talking about your father's health and comfort, *not* about money. Or *are* we?''

"No, of course not,'' Peter mumbled uncomfortably.

"Well, that's fortunate since it *is* still your father's money we're spending. Now,'' she said brightly, "does anyone have anything else to add to the discussion?''

"I certainly do,'' Patty spoke up snappily. "I think that if you're determined to pursue this insane course you leave Bobby and me no choice but to join your *entourage*. Then, if there are any problems, there'll be a family member present to help you cope. When you get down to it, that's all you can really count on, you know—family.''

"That's funny. Martin and I have been thinking along those same lines. But we wouldn't dream of upsetting *your* lives. *You* have the children to think of and Bobby, his work. So we've decided to take Hubie along."

"But he's only an eighteen-year-old boy and, let's face it, hardly the most mature. And while most boys his age are going off to college, he hasn't even managed to be accepted by a decent college, and why would he? He's gone through schools like they were revolving doors. What can you be thinking of?"

"Well, actually I was thinking that since he's such entertaining company for Martin and always manages to make him laugh, I can count on him to help keep his spirits up no matter what. And Dr. Steinfeld says that the spirit is as important as the body, and I couldn't agree with him more. As for Hubie's immaturity, Martin's thinking is that our counting on him might be just the answer to that problem, and as for his schooling, well, everyone knows travel is both educational and broadening. Don't you agree?"

\* \* \*

She was delighted with many things during their trip, but the main thing was how well Martin was feeling and how reenergized. It was also nice to see how thoughtful a traveling companion Hubie was proving, surely a sign of his blossoming maturity. But best of all was his devotion to Martin, and how Martin returned that devotion to a point that amazed her.

At first she'd thought that this mutual devotion just *seemed* more pronounced since they were in an exotic land, dependent on each other in a way they weren't at home, coping with all the little things that went awry and then laughing about the funnier instances later. Then she thought that perhaps the reason Martin seemed fonder of Hubie than of his own boys, and more tolerant of his failings, was that Hubie's own feelings for Martin were so uncomplicated—no sparring for power the way it often was between sons and fathers, the sons seeming to say: "Move over, old chap, it's our turn." No past resentments, no demands, only mutual admiration and respect.

Finally, she concluded that the reason Martin loved Hubie so much was because he loved *her* so much that it just kind of spilled over. Love generating love, a never-ending circle, and she knew that the love she felt for Martin wasn't diminished in any way because it was conceived in gratitude and respect rather than in romantic fantasies or sexual passion. . . .

* * *

After dinner and after being roundly beaten at chess by Martin, Hubie went back to his own room in the Peking Royale, and Martin observed, "You know, Nora, I have no regrets about Hubie not making Harvard. I'm hoping he'll attend college in Washington so that he can live at home with us."

"I'm not sure he's going to make it to *any* college," she sighed. "And what will he study if he does? Let's face it, he's never going to be a lawyer like your sons."

"What of it? They have their law degrees but not one of them actually practices law."

"But they *do* practice honorable professions for which they're well prepared. Even if Hubie gets to college, what will *he* prepare for? To be a professional charmer, or maybe one of those—what do they call them—sex surrogates?"

Martin laughed though she hadn't intended to be amusing.

"Don't worry, Nora. If nothing else, he can go to work in the family business. Public relations, that sort of thing. Or, if we can nurture him through college, we'll see to it that a place is found for him in the State Department. They can certainly use a little charm over there. But don't worry, we'll come up with *something* that will best make use of Hubie's talents. Once we get home we'll go to work on it."

*Once we get home we'll go to work on it.*

The words reassured her and she was overwhelmed with affection for her good husband. Then, after they made love and she successfully brought him to climax, she lay in bed thinking about going home. Yes, it was time to go home. She would begin planning their departure in the morning.

But that morning they woke to the news that President Kennedy had been assassinated. On hearing the devastating report, Martin suffered a stroke.

\*   \*   \*

With Martin almost totally paralyzed and completely confined to his wheelchair but still the partisan Democrat he'd always been, Nora established the Cantington Foundation for Democratic Political Action, essentially a fund-raising group and a think tank for all Democrats seeking election or reelection, on both the national and local levels. With the foundation's offices right on the premises and politicians from all over flying in for checks and consultations, and with many of the fund-raising parties taking place right there, the house on R Street was constantly filled with the excitement of people coming and going, resounding with ideas and stimulating conversation. In the center of it was Martin and that was where she intended to keep him, though there were the family's usual objections.

"What are you trying to *do* to the man, Nora?"

"The question is not what *I'm* doing but what *Martin's* doing and the fact that he *is* doing and not just vegetating."

"But he's not up to all this activity. Good God, he's almost completely paralyzed."

"Yes, his body is but his *mind* isn't. And that's what we're going to keep active."

"But you're killing him in the process."

She laughed at that. She could have told them that what she was trying to do was to help him live his life fully instead of like a man already dead, but it would have done no good. They preferred to believe that she wanted him dead so that she could get her hands on the money.

This was confirmed when Billy and Daisy came calling one evening just as Martin was retiring for the night. When they refused to be turned away by the butler, Nora came downstairs to tell them herself that it was impossible—that Martin was otherwise engaged in his bedtime activities and rituals. Undaunted, Daisy angrily demanded to know what bedtime activity the paralyzed Martin could be engaged in that precluded their looking in on him for a few minutes.

"That all depends on your attitude toward sex. Some people

like it *with* an audience, and some without. Martin prefers without, as I do. Now, if you'll excuse me—" she smiled pleasantly,
pulling her filmy negligee more tightly about her, "I'll rejoin my
husband so that we may get on with it. You know how it is. I
don't like to keep him waiting."

She left them standing there nonplussed as she turned to go
back upstairs, but not before she heard Daisy gasp and Billy
curse and Daisy say, "Did she mean what I think she means?"
And Billy swore again. Then she heard Daisy whine, "But I
don't understand. How does a paralyzed man *do it?* Will you tell
me that?"

Nora was tempted to turn around and tell her step by step,
but then thought better of it. Daisy was a big girl—she could
figure it out for herself.

Then she heard Billy say, "We were right about her. One
way or another she intends to fuck the old guy to death!"

# THIRTY-FIVE

———— •►•◄• ————

Soon after returning to Washington from Palm Beach, where they'd welcomed in the new year with a toast to "1968—the best year ever," Nora finally gave up the ghost of Hubie ever graduating from college. She discovered that, while he left the house every day ostensibly on his way to classes at American, he rarely got there, waylaid by all manner of things—trysts with women of all ages, the gymnasium where he worked out, friends who talked him into driving up to New York for a special party or sports event, or the flying field where he kept his plane (Martin's present to mark his twenty-second birthday the year before).

Oh, it wasn't *terrible* in light of what else was going on in the world, she told herself, but still it *was* discouraging to realize that the only thing her sweet son really excelled at was being an irresponsible playboy.

January was also the month when Martin became permanently bedridden, no longer strong enough to sit in his wheelchair.

A depressing beginning to the new year, for sure, and then February wasn't much better. It was the month Nixon announced his candidacy for the presidency as well as the month Hubie enlisted in the marines.

Martin tried to console her. "You must be proud of him—he did the right thing as he saw it."

But it was one thing to be proud, and another to be terrified that he would soon be going off to Vietnam. And it was hard not to speculate—had Hubie enlisted out of patriotism or out of an urge for adventure? She remembered the little boy who had always wanted to wear a uniform.

March was a little better. Bob Kennedy announced his candidacy and that was good news. If anybody could give Tricky Dicky a run for the money, it was Bobby. Then Martin even rallied a bit and sat up in an armchair for a few minutes every day for five days running.

April was the month Dr. King was assassinated, which was a terrible loss. April was also the month Hubie showed up resplendent in his marine dress blues, looking as wonderful as she had ever seen him, and for one brilliant moment the clock turned back twenty-five years and, but for Hubie's shorn yellow hair, it was as if it were the first time she was looking at Hubert Hartiscor, resplendent in *his* uniform.

She thought she might cry with pride until she learned that Hubie was AWOL. Then she was furious. He was no longer the careless boy playing pranks but a man of nearly twenty-three, a man other men under fire would be depending on. Hubie was, as ever, remorseful. "I was afraid I'd be shipped out without having a chance to say good-bye. And it wasn't you, Mum, I was so much worried about but my dad. I know I'd get to see you again, but how could I be sure I'd ever see *him* again? I just had to make sure I did. . . ."

Of course, she did cry then. And when he went in to Martin to sit by his bedside and hold his frail hand and kiss his withered cheek, they all cried—she, Hubie, and Martin. And she cried some more as she made arrangements for Hubie's immediate return to his base. Still, she felt sure things were bound to improve.

But she changed her mind about that when Hubie shipped out in May and another Kennedy warrior fell slain in June.

In July, the United States, Great Britain, the U.S.S.R., and fifty-nine other nations signed the Nuclear Nonproliferation Treaty, and that was a hopeful sign that perhaps everything in the topsy-turvy world would right itself after all. July was also the month Martin said he had to set things right and asked her to send for his old and trusted friend, the attorney Ward Prouty.

"But why do you need a lawyer?" Nora asked, anxious that Martin sensed his end was near and wanted to start setting his affairs in order. "You have four lawyers of your own that come to see you every day," she added, trying to make a joke of it, however feeble.

"They don't come to see me. They come to see *you.*"

She laughed. "Me? Have they suddenly fallen in love with me, then, after all this time?"

"Hardly. They come to see what you're up to, to see if you're wearing down a dying man to get him to turn all his money over to you. . . ."

"Oh, no, Martin," she protested, not knowing if she were protesting that she would ever think of such a thing or the fact that he was dying or that his boys came for any other reason but out of their love for him. Then she asked, though she already knew the answer, "Why *do* you want to see Ward?"

"To turn over all my money to you, just like they're afraid I'm going to do. I want to have that prenuptial set aside and leave everything to you. Then you can let the boys have whatever you think best, whatever you think fair."

"No, Martin. When we were married I negotiated a contract *under* your tutelage—all your sons, including Hubie, and I having equal shares—and that's the legacy that's fair. The boys have been your sons for most of your life, and I—"

"Have made my life a celebration," he finished for her.

She took his hand, the skin worn shiny and silky, and pressed it to her lips. "If that is true, then let it be a celebration of love, not a celebration dulled by a legacy of bitterness and greed."

It was so hard not to think of the past and even harder to think of the future.

August was the month she and Martin watched the Democrats nominate Hubert Humphrey, but then she had to turn off the TV because the riots in the streets of Chicago were too upsetting for Martin to view. August was also the month she went about the house with her portable radio in hand for constant news of the fighting in Vietnam. Inadvertently, she also heard a lot of music: the Beatles singing "Hey Jude"; the Doors,

"Hello, I Love You"; Cream's "Sunshine of Your Love," which she liked if for no other reason than for its cheerful title.

September was a month for vigils—waiting for the postman to bring a letter, fear that a terrible telegram might arrive instead—accompanied only by an almost round-the-clock marathon of reading to Martin at his bedside. She had gotten the notion into her head that reading to him was an act of faith for both Martin and Hubie. If she kept reading, death wouldn't come to claim either of them *unless* she ran out of reading materials, which was an impossibility, so the odds were with her. But while she *knew* it was a crazy notion, no telegram from the War Department arrived, nor did the Angel of Death come to call on Martin, so she kept on reading.

In September she regretted not having risked moving Martin to Cape Cod for the summer so that, even with his eyesight failing, he could have had the pleasure of once again seeing the sun rise over the Atlantic. So, in September she did just that—took him there. It still wasn't too late for him to see the rising sun one last time, and it was better than simply sitting a death watch.

Being on the Cape reminded Martin of the Thanksgiving when Hubie had blurted out that he was thankful that Martin was his dad, and the memory made him weep. "But that's a wonderful memory, Martin. Please don't cry."

"But I failed him . . . and you too, Nora."

"Oh Martin, how can you say that? You've been a wonderful father to Hubie."

"But you were counting on me to provide him with a future—to find a place for him when he comes home—and now I won't be here to do it."

She didn't protest his saying he wouldn't be there—she couldn't dishonor this honorable man with false protestations. "You gave him love and a sense of belonging and you can't do more than that for anyone."

*All you can do is point them in the right direction.*

She planned on taking Martin straight to Palm Beach at the end of October once the foliage turned, in order to bypass the gray days of a Washington November, but Martin said that he wanted to go home to Washington. "It's *our* town, the one we lived in together, and we really turned it on its ear for a while, didn't we, my love?"

So, that's what they did in the month of October. They went home.

In November, when she had despaired of ever hearing from Hubie again, she heard *of* him if not from him. The second she heard the news she rushed to Martin's room, more hospital room now than bedroom. Though the nurse told her that she had just given Mr. Cantington his sedative, she burst out, "Oh, Martin, Hubie's *alive!* He's wounded, but he's alive!"

"But what—? How—?"

"You won't believe this, but he jumped into a puddle and he came out of it not covered with mud and slime but"—her voice was full of awe—"drenched in glory! *Our* Hubie!"

"But what puddle?" Martin asked groggily.

Nora tried to explain that it really wasn't a puddle at all but a rice paddy. "There was a squad of North Vietnamese regulars holed up there and it seems after wriggling over on his stomach to be in the right position, Lance Corporal Cantington lobbed in a grenade, then jumped in to mop up with his M16, whatever that is. I think I have it straight, but I was so excited I— Well, they say he's not too badly hurt, something with his leg. . . . Oh, Martin, he'll be home before too long!" *Please wait for him!*

"Before too long," Martin whispered. "But why did you call a rice paddy a puddle?" he asked as he drifted off to sleep.

*Because once there was a little boy who jumped into a puddle just for the sheer joy of it and they made such a fuss, called him a scamp. Who would have ever thought that the little scamp would jump into a puddle again when he was all grown up . . . to emerge a hero?*

Maybe somewhere along the line she had done something right, after all. She and Martin . . .

*Or had Hubie jumped once again just for the hell of it?*

\*   \*   \*

December was the month she buried Martin.

Two weeks after the actual funeral in Cape Cod, where

Martin was buried in the family plot next to his first wife, Rita (she owed that much to Bobby, Billy, Peter, and Paul), Nora organized a memorial service at the national Cathedral in Washington. Every last seat of the cathedral's two thousand seats was filled, she having personally arranged the seating in the roped-off section so that no national or international figure was slighted. The entire diplomatic corps was accommodated, along with President and Mrs. Johnson, the defeated Hubert Humphrey, and President-elect Richard Nixon and his pretty wife, Pat. Martin would have wanted that. He believed in healing the breach.

\* \* \*

Attired in a chic black suit with only a small diamond pin affixed to its lapel, Nora walked up the steps of the cathedral on the arms of her only family—Hubie, with his campaign ribbons, and dear Mick, who had flown in for the occasion. She had shed her tears and was through with them, she thought, until Hubie limped up to the podium and held up the medal he'd been awarded for valor to say: "They gave it to *me*, but *I* didn't really earn it. My father did. It was Martin Cantington's hand that was on my shoulder, giving me a push, and it was his voice whispering in my ear: 'Do it, son, do the right thing,' and so I did. . . ." Then she wept again.

*Oh, he had jumped, but this once not just for the sheer fun of it. . . .*

\* \* \*

After Hubie went back to his base, she went to Palm Beach, not quite ready to resume life at the house on R Street, and Mick went with her so that she wouldn't be alone.

"It's so sweet of you, Mick, to stay with me."

"There's no place I'd rather be than with the charming Nora Hall Hartiscor Nash Cantington. Besides, this *is* the height of the Palm Beach season, and you know how old fun-loving Mick loves being *anyplace* at the height of its season."

"Oh, Mick, you're such a good friend. The *best!*"

"But *not* the best of husbands. What a pity. When I offered to come down here with you under the *ruse* of keeping you company, I really had an ulterior motive in mind."

"Yes?" She played along with his teasing.

"I thought that just maybe I might catch you again between husbands."

*Is he teasing? Maybe. Then again, maybe not. With Mick, it was hard to know.*

"I beg you to remember, sir, that I am a widow in mourning and not to be trifled with—"

He lowered his eyes then, realizing she was sending him a signal—a stop sign. When he raised them again he pretended to be outraged. "I beg *you* to remember, madame, that I wouldn't dream of—" Then suddenly he was serious. "*Was* Martin the best husband? I hope so. You deserve the best."

"Oh, Mick, I don't think I can define *best* any more than I can define *love.* Both come in so many forms. But I will say that Martin was the best of men and I loved him dearly."

*I married him for name and fortune and for love of Hubie and I ended up getting so much more.*

"So, what does the future hold for my friend Nora now? Will you be going back to England?"

"Sometimes I long to . . . But no, I can't do that. I'm an American now and, more importantly, *Hubie's* an American and his Cantington legacy is here and that's where I have to make a place for him as Martin would have. I'm going back to Washington to continue my work with the foundation—being a Democrat was very important to Martin and so much a part of him—and I hope Hubie will be part of that. I think that would be making the best use of his Cantington heritage."

"But *you* personally, Nora? Do you see another husband in that crystal ball of yours?"

"I don't think so," she laughed. "For one thing, I've had more husbands than any one woman deserves, and for another, I've married for all kinds of reasons, and now—well, I think I've clear run out of reasons."

# PART SIX

# THE BRILLIANT MARRIAGE

Los Angeles, 1969–1970

# THIRTY-SIX

———————◆•◆———————

L ater, she would remember all the details of the evening. The date—December 22, 1969; the occasion—a dance and silent art auction for the benefit of underprivileged children; the place—the Smithsonian; the guest list—the usual Washington luminaries: the Republicans who were in, the Democrats who were out, and a contingent of Hollywood stars to add additional sparkle to the glittery evening. The color theme was black and white, with the men requested to wear white tie and the women black, and there were gardenias for each lady, their heady scent filling the room. The flower arrangements consisted of white lilies with black-dyed bristly foxtail grass, the Dom Perignon was accompanied by black caviar, and the after-dinner brandies were served with white-chocolate mousse. She, the co-chair, wore black lace off the shoulder, a pearl choker, a big black-pearl ring, and her hair was swept back to reveal white pearls at her ears. Her gardenia was tucked into her cleavage, and she was dancing with Vice-president Agnew, who liked to dance (whereas the president didn't), and Lionel Hampton's orchestra was playing "Leaving on a Jet Plane" when *he* cut in.

She didn't recognize him, and there was no reason she would—she'd never really met him. But she went into his arms willingly, an animal magnetism emanating from his huge body though he wasn't what she would call handsome. A rugged cragginess was more like it. But when he said, "Nora *Nash* Cantington, I presume," she knew exactly who he was and said, "It's about time you showed up. How many years ago was it that you stood me up at the Tropical Flower Lounge in Hollywood?"

"I was a fool," he laughed. "That's why I'm here tonight, to rectify the error. But I must admit that I'm a fool for the smell of gardenias.'' His bent his head to the gardenia tucked between her breasts to breathe in its scent. "Intoxicating . . ." he murmured, smiling into her eyes, and, foolish as she knew it was but not anything she could control, she felt something she hadn't felt in a very long time. Those flutterings of butterfly wings deep within the core of her sexual desire had shown up again, along with T. S. Grant. . . .

\* \* \*

He showed her the painting he'd bid on—an English landscape with a manor house. It could have been Merrillee Manor and her heart quickened. "Why did you choose this particular painting? The artist doesn't have a famous name."

"I don't care about names. I don't even know anything about art. I just know what I like and I like this picture. I love the English countryside and the house reminds me of my own— Grantwood Manor. It's a grand house but rundown since I don't have either the time or a wife to see to it properly."

"You haven't remarried, then?"

He looked at her obliquely. "You *knew* my wife died?"

"Oh, yes, I was in Hollywood the day of her funeral."

"I don't remember who was there. Did you attend?"

"No. I meant to but fate intervened in the form of a woman. You see, that was the day my marriage to Mick ended."

His arm slid about her and she could feel the goose bumps. *Don't be a fool, Nora. A forty-four-year-old woman is much too old for goose bumps.*

"Mick Nash was an idiot," he whispered in her ear. "Whatever possessed him to let that happen?"

She laughed. "A she-devil . . . a very sexy she-devil."

"I bet I know her name."

"What will you wager?"

"That painting, if I get it."

"How much did you bid?"

"Fifty thousand."

"That's a lot of money for a picture painted by an unknown artist. You'll get it."

"And you? What will you put up as a wager?"

"I don't know." She already felt certain she was going to lose the bet. "What do you suggest?" In answer, his eyes met hers in a frank challenge. Then he picked up her hand, kissed it, ran his lips up her arm and across her shoulder to rest on the back of her neck, and those butterflies quickened their flutterings so violently that she looked around, sure that everyone could hear.

Then he said, "Mimi L'Heureux," and she could not but admit that she had lost the bet. But then, both of them had known that she would.

\*   \*   \*

At midnight at the Hilton, where he was staying—drenched in the sweat of passion as she sat astride his belly and his mouth moved back and forth between the breasts suspended above him, sucking voraciously—she slid farther down to grind herself into him and he bucked to enter her, thrusting and stabbing as if to pierce her body with his weapon, and she screamed out in an ecstasy she'd never known before, sexy Micky Nash not withstanding.

At twelve-thirty, *he* fleetingly thought of Mick. "I was right about Nash. He *was* an idiot. You're the goddess and Mimi— she was nothing. I've known a thousand like her."

At one-thirty, she remembered that he had a daughter and asked about her. He muttered that she was at school in Connecticut, but then he was kissing the insides of her thighs and she forgot about everything, including his daughter.

At two, she told him about how sweet and charming her son was but unfocused, and that she worried about his future. He told her that he sounded perfect for the movie business and that she could always send Hubie to him and he would make a place for him. Then—though she was gratified to hear the reassuring words—as T.S. trailed a path of kisses across her belly, she forgot about Hubie completely.

At three, they climaxed together and he groaned into her throat that he loved her, and she moaned back, "I love you too." Then, realizing that it was *really* true, she laughed in delight, and he laughed too and it was a roar.

It was nearly dawn when he said, "In one of my films the couple eloped to Elkton, Maryland, to get married by a justice of the peace on the spur of the moment and—"

*Did he really use the word* elope? *Is he actually suggesting that he and I—? But eloping's only for the reckless and the really young . . . isn't it? Besides, I've already gone the elopement route once before and look how that turned out. . . .*

"I think your screenwriter ignored the realities there," she said, playing for time while she tried to think with her head instead of her heart. "People *used* to elope to Elkton to get married on the spur of the moment, but I think they've changed the law and—"

He grinned at her slyly. "It's all in knowing the right people. What do you want to bet that I can make one call, two calls at most, and everything will be arranged."

And for the second time within a period of less than twelve hours, T.S. won his bet.

*Once for love and once for the name, once for the fun of it and great sex, and once for the money and great affection and respect. But finally—once for the best of everything rolled into one and the marriage that would last forever. . . .*

# THIRTY-SEVEN

———•◦•———

The very next day after the wedding, back at her house in Georgetown, Nora was surprised to discover T.S. packing up his one small bag, ready to go back to Los Angeles. "Wait a minute," she laughed, "aren't we moving a little quickly here? I can't simply pack up and leave on a day's notice."

"Of course *you* can't, and I wasn't proposing that you do. I have to go back to L.A. since I only planned on staying the one night for the party and I have appointments. But you stay and do what you have to. Tie up your loose ends, make your good-byes, and then, when you're ready, you'll join me."

*What's going on here?* Yesterday he had declared he couldn't live without her, and here he was traipsing off with a breezy: "When you're ready, you'll join me."

He saw that she was upset and, kissing her, he murmured, "It's god-awful being separated so soon. But what's there to do? I have to get back to the studio and you have to do your thing and get this house ready to put on the market."

She was shocked. "Put my house on the market?"

"Of course. You knew marrying me meant moving to Los Angeles. Unless you're proposing one of those bicoastal marriages, and I wasn't figuring on one of those, were you?" He chuckled, patting her rump.

"Of course not, but I wasn't figuring on selling this house either."

He shrugged. "How many houses do you need in the East? You've the house in Palm Beach and the place on the Cape—"

"But I don't. I let Martin's children have them."

She saw a look of what—*annoyance?*—cross his face.

267

"You *let* them have the houses? What does that mean? You could have kept them but you chose not to?"

"Yes. Since I had this house, I thought it only fair to let them have the other two—their family legacy."

"Playing fair is a sucker's game, but I guess it's too late for that advice. Still, I don't see any point in keeping a place in Washington." Then he smiled as if remembering to do so. "I intend to keep you far too busy for you to get to Washington much, and when you do, that's what hotels are for."

"But you don't understand. When I left England to marry Martin, I sold Merrillee Manor because it was a legacy . . . a heritage of the past, and I wanted both Hubie and me to start our lives here anew . . . as Cantingtons with no looking back. But I've always thought of *this* house as Hubie's legacy, *his* Cantington heritage. I wanted to keep it for him."

"But you said you were worried about his future. What good will his heritage do him if he doesn't *have* a future, and I told you *I'd* take care of that, that I'd make a place for him at the studio. Don't you trust me, Nora?"

"Of course I do. I'd hardly marry a man I didn't." She realized then that she would have to sell the house since T.S. was putting it like that—as an act of faith. After all, a house was only bricks and mortar, and it was the marriage and the man that were important.

"Just make sure you don't throw in the paintings and antiques when you put it up for sale. They must be worth a fortune and they'll fit right in at Grantwood Manor. Now, *there's* a house for you. It's on nine acres, a real showplace, and it's just dying for the Nora Grant touch as I am . . . right this minute." He held out his arms to her.

"Are you sure you have the time?" she asked ruefully, but going into his arms at the same time.

"For you, always. Besides, my plane doesn't leave for another three hours," he said, grinning.

"But wait—you *can't* go back today! Tonight's Christmas Eve! What about your daughter?"

He made a little gesture of impatience. "What about her?"

"She's at school spending Christmas with strangers. The

least you should do ... *we* should do ... is go up to Connecticut to take her some gifts and let her meet me."

"Out of the question. I have an appointment in L.A. Anyway, Sam's *not* at school. She's in New York for the holidays, staying with some school friend."

"But you can break your appointment—it *is* Christmas Eve. Then tomorrow we can go to New York to see her."

"You've got all the answers," he laughed. "But I bet you don't have this one—the name and address of the friend she's staying with."

"Of course I don't," she admitted. "But *you* do, don't you? At least the family's name? A phone number?"

"I *did*. I *had* the phone number on a piece of paper. I was going to call the kid to wish her a Merry Christmas, but I'm afraid I lost it, so that's that."

She was upset. He sounded so cavalier, as if it really didn't matter much. But how could a father allow a thirteen-year-old to visit with a family whose name he didn't even know. "But how could you—" she began, then saw that look of irritation on his face.

Well, why wouldn't he be irritated? She *was* being critical, and one thing she had learned from all her marriages was that *no* man enjoyed being criticized. The poor darling, he was probably feeling all kinds of guilt about his daughter, Sam, and she was just making him feel worse.

\* \* \*

She drove him to the airport, reluctant to let go of him until the very last minute. "Tell me, what is this appointment that's so important that you can't break it even for a new bride?" she chided him playfully, never dreaming that he'd say, "A Christmas Eve party in the Hollywood Hills."

Then she was so outraged that for a fleeting moment she considered stopping the car and pushing him out the door. "You mean you're leaving me for a party? A stupid party?"

"A party, yes, but stupid? No. A very important party. I don't go to parties just for a good time. Parties are where I do business, *studio* business. You ought to be able to understand that. From what I hear, you're one of the champion party-givers of all time, and I'd bet that most of them aren't just for a good time, that usually you have some kind of an ax to grind. Now, ain't that so?" He grinned at her disarmingly.

After much prodding and cajoling she had to admit that he was right, but as she accompanied him to the gate she had another thought: "If you go to parties only to do business, how come you flew across the country to attend the party in Washington? What kind of business did you think you were going to do there?"

"Monkey business." He winked, his face breaking into that craggy grin she found irresistible, and before she could think of a reply, he pulled her to him, kissed her hard, and was gone, leaving her to wonder why it hadn't occurred to either one of them that she could have flown with him to L.A., spent a couple of days there—gone with him to the party—then flown back to Washington to do what she had to do.

*   *   *

She could have gone to any number of parties herself that night instead of spending Christmas Eve alone, but too many people already knew that she'd married T. S.—Washington was a town that thrived on gossip—and would wonder why he had left her all alone so soon after the wedding. So instead she sat at home trying to figure out exactly what kind of monkey business had brought T.S. to the fund-raiser at the Smithsonian. Then, going through some bits and pieces that in his haste he'd left behind, she found the publicity piece about the coming event torn from the *Post*, a picture of her—its co-chairwoman—included, and then she knew: T.S. had come to the party only to meet her. But if that *was* monkey business, it was the nicest and most flattering kind.

The next morning she waited expectantly for the special delivery of a Christmas present, or at least a call from the Coast. Finally she decided to call him. They weren't a couple of kids playing the dating game, so why stand on ceremony? Then she realized that she didn't *have* his phone number. How could she have been so careless as to marry a man whose number she didn't even have?

Information couldn't help, since it was an unlisted number, which put her in a really foul mood. Alternately angry, despondent, and frustrated, she went to bed early, but when the doorbell rang—having given the entire staff the day off—she tore out of bed to run downstairs to get the door and she wasn't disappointed. It was the delivery of a roomful of roses, and she wondered how she could have ever doubted him. A roomful of roses was worth a dozen calls, she told herself. *Wasn't it?*

Friday, the day after Christmas, he *did* call. Or rather, his secretary, Ginny Parnis, did. "Mr. Grant was about to phone you, but he was called away so he asked me to call and tell you that he was thinking of you. And by the way, Nora, congratulations!"

She thought of telling Ms. Parnis that you congratulated the groom on his good fortune but you wished the bride good luck, and that you didn't call the boss's wife by her first name unless she specifically told you to, but what was the point in taking her frustration out on a secretary? Besides, the woman was only doing things the California way. So all she said before hanging up was, "Have a good day, Ginny," since that too was the California way, and in a couple of weeks she herself would be an Angeleno.

On Sunday he called again, this time in person. "I've been phoning day and night. Where the hell have you been?"

Should she tell him that mostly she'd been at home sorting out—deciding what to send on to L.A., save for Hubie, or give away to charities or Martin's children? Or should she really pull him up short by telling him that even if she hadn't been home when the phone rang, there was staff on hand to take messages? She didn't. A wise woman so recently married kept her mouth shut and let her husband do most of the talking, especially when he spoke such lovely words of love.

On Monday, the twenty-ninth, Mary Beth Jones, who had been in charge of the silent art auction, called to tell her that she was a naughty girl. "The whole town's talking about how you

ran off with that charmer, T. S. Grant, without so much as a
word to anyone. Is it really true?"

"True as true love."

"Oh, lovely," Mary Beth breathed. "By the way, your new
husband won the painting that he bid on. Shall we send it over
to your house or on to California?"

"You might as well send it over here since I'm having all my
paintings crated for shipping. That will save the committee a bit
of bother. And while you're at it, you might as well send your
so-delicately worded request for payment here too and I'll pass
it on."

"No problem. You married a very positive man. He was so
sure he was going to win the painting, he left a check with his
bid. He said he always gets what he goes after. So *forceful!* I do
love a man who's forceful. No wonder he talked you into eloping with him the very next day. So romantic."

Nora hung up bemused. While her elopement *was* romantic
and it was titillating to think that T.S. had flown across the
country just to meet her and had possibly even made up his
mind to "go after her," it was somehow disquieting to think
that, without ever actually meeting her, she had already been his
"quarry."

But then she chuckled, remembering how it had been with
them. Mary Beth had said, "No wonder he talked you into
eloping." The truth was, she had needed very little persuasion,
and probably if he hadn't suggested it first and if he weren't so
big, *she* would have dragged *him* off to Maryland.

On Tuesday she thought about flying out to California so
that they could spend New Year's Eve together. But then Mick
called from London to wish her good luck on her marriage.

"But how did you hear about it so soon in London? I didn't
give out any announcements to the press."

"I could say good news—or is it bad news that travels fast?
But actually I got it straight from the horse's mouth, none other
than the big man himself. I just ran into him at a cocktail party
in the West End."

*Talk about your surprises. . . . Well, as T.S. said, he did a lot of
business at parties.*

She spent New Year's Eve at home on the chance T.S. would call. He didn't. But he *did* on New Year's Day from Vail, Colorado, to make up for not calling the night before, explaining that he had been in flight on his way back from London. She didn't ask if it was a business party on the slopes that was keeping him busy today. Instead she imagined what her mum, the barmaid, would have to say: *You've got your work cut out for you keeping up with this one, m'girl. You'd best be stepping fast and fancy.* . . .

Well, lucky for her, she'd always been light on her feet.

# THIRTY-EIGHT

———•••———

There was one last thing she felt she had to do before she left for the Coast, though T.S. hadn't asked her to—go see his daughter, Sam. But realizing what a shock it would be if she suddenly appeared to announce, "Ready or not, kid, here I am—your father's new wife, your new stepmother," she called ahead to the school office, saying only that she was a family friend who would like to take her out for the day. Once she had Sam alone, she would break the news to her gently, making sure the young girl understood that she wanted to be her friend and that she posed no threat.

\* \* \*

From the second she saw the tall, slender girl enter the restaurant—she'd thought it best if they met on neutral ground—she could tell that her task wasn't going to be easy. Maybe it was the way Sam held her head, high with her nose tilted in the air, or maybe it was the surly look that sullied the fine, aristocratic features. She stood up to greet the girl with a warm smile as the hostess escorted her to the table, and though she hadn't planned on it, she moved forward to kiss her, but Sam recoiled before taking her seat, spitting out, "I don't like to be touched."

*No, not easy.* She sat down again, her smile still intact. "I know you have no idea who I am, but—"

"You're wrong," Sam said coolly. "I know exactly who you are. A liar, for one thing."

"I beg your pardon?"

Now Sam was the one who smiled as she spread her napkin

274

across her lap. "You heard me. You told the dean that you were a friend of the family, but I already know that you're the woman who snagged my poor, unsuspecting father. I heard all about the marriage while I was in New York spending the holidays with Jody Thorton. Someone from Washington called Mrs. Thorton knowing I was Jody's friend, and this someone filled her in on your background—that you've been married a zillion times and *always* to very rich men, and once you lived with a man who turned out not to be your husband and there was some terrible scandal. So you see, I *do* know all about you." She opened the menu to study it.

*No, not easy. This poor child is in so much pain. . . .*

Nora pasted her smile back on again. "Mrs. Thorton's informant wasn't *quite* correct. I've been married only *three* times, and only two of my husbands were very rich. The second one was an English actor who wasn't what you'd call *rich-rich.*" *Best to ignore the terrible-scandal part.* "But there's more to know about me than that, just as there's more to know about *you*, I'm sure, than what people might suspect at first sight."

Sam looked up from the menu warily, intrigued in spite of herself. "What might people think about me?"

"That you're beautiful, probably intelligent, sure of yourself, and physically mature for thirteen. But also that you're rude, arrogant, and closed-minded."

Sam flipped her long red hair as if to show how little she thought of that. Still, she was interested enough to ask, "And what might they find out if they got to know me better?"

"Maybe that you're as beautiful inside as you are outside and that underneath you don't really feel as sure of yourself as you pretend, and that's the reason you are sometimes rude and arrogant. And that you're capable of being a wonderful, really mature young woman, if only you'd let yourself be."

"And what else is there to know about *you*? That you really want to be a mother to me?" Sam asked with a sneer.

That was exactly what she'd been hoping to be, what she'd had in mind when she set out this morning. But she saw now that this poor little girl who was trying so hard to be grown up, sophisticated, and tough was already too damaged to accept her as a mother no matter how much love she showered on her. Instead, she would have to try for a lighter touch. "No, not a mother. But you might discover that I'll make a good friend— even a best friend—and every girl, young or old, can use one of those. Try me. What do you have to lose?"

For a second she thought she detected a crack in the hard façade, a yearning in the emerald-green eyes, even an eagerness to believe, and a wellspring of hope sprang up in her own heart, strangely like an ache.

But then Sam closed up again and the eyes turned as hard and brittle as thin green glass. Now she asked cunningly: "What's really on your mind? To try and make friends with me to impress Daddy with how wonderful *you* are while you see to it I don't get too near him?"

Nora smiled so that Sam wouldn't see how much her words hurt. But they didn't hurt so much that she was prepared to give up. Martin's sons had already been too old and hostile when she'd met them to let her into their hearts. But Sam was still young enough, so vulnerable underneath that veneer of tough- ness, that maybe it wasn't too late to go for love.

"Why don't we order now?" she suggested, picking up the menu. "We'll have plenty of time to discuss all this when you come home for your spring break."

"But I *never* go home for spring vacation," Sam said with a gleam of suspicious hope in her eyes. "Daddy never knows when he has to take off on business."

"Well, this time you *will* come home because even if your father isn't home all the time, *I* will be."

"Sure, I'll believe it when it happens," Sam sneered.

*In that case, you'd better start packing, Samantha Grant, because I intend to make a believer out of you yet.*

Oh, yes, she would try—for T.S., for Sam, and for herself— because somehow—in spite of all the anger, hostility, and arro- gance—she suspected that she'd just fallen in love again for the second time in a matter of a couple of weeks. And how many times in a lifetime did one actually fall in love? . . .

# THIRTY-NINE

From the moment she saw it, Nora fell in love with every green inch of Grantwood. It was as if she'd been transported back in time to the countryside of her youth, and the house itself reminded her of Merrillee Manor, even though it was surrounded with tropical plantings and bougainvillea trailed from its tiled roof. But, like the Cantington house when she'd first seen it, it too was badly rundown, even more so since Grantwood was that much larger and the Georgetown house, in the heart of the city, had had no grounds to speak of.

"There she is, yours to fix up to your specifications. I hereby grant you carte blanche to restore this grand old English lady to her former glory," T.S. said expansively.

"How does carte blanche translate into dollars?" She didn't want him to go into shock when the bills came rolling in. "Restoration and importing antiques from Britain doesn't run cheap, especially if you want fast results."

"The sky's the limit. Just work that Nora Grant magic."

After having said that, he removed himself from the project to devote all his energies to his studio. Even when he came home in the evenings, he didn't want to talk about fabrics or wallpaper or antiques—he wanted to talk studio, using her as a sounding board much in the manner as Martin had with politics, which was fine with her. They were, after all, life's partners. And if he was overly obsessed with his studio, obsession was something she understood too. She'd spent much of her adult life obsessed with her son. Besides, what a wonderful example of devotion to duty he would be for Hubie once he came home and went to work at Grantwood Studio.

At first when the bills came in, not wanting to bother T.S. with money talk, she paid them herself, as she did the household expenses. But when the total amount started to soar into the millions, she asked him what to do. "Shall I mail the bills to your business manager?"

T.S. grinned wryly. "You could if I still had one of those, but I fired him months ago. Who needs someone to take his cut off the top only to tell me how much money I can spend? I ask you, does that make good business sense?"

She laughed. "So what *shall* I do with the bills? Send them to your accountant?"

"Well, it would probably be easier if you paid them yourself," he drawled.

"Oh? Is there a problem with the accountant too?"

"There wouldn't be if I got myself someone a little sharper. Maybe once you finish with the house you can take care of that stuff for me. After all," he grinned slyly, "who'd know more about money than a billionairess?"

She smiled uncertainly. "Where'd you get that idea?"

"Come on," he chided. "Everybody knows Martin Canting-ton was worth over a bil and was completely devoted to you."

"That doesn't mean I was *left* a billion dollars. After several other bequests, Martin's estate was divided seven ways *after* taxes, with his four sons and Hubie and me getting equal shares."

"You mean you let them pull a number on you?" When she stiffened at the words, he explained, "It just riles me that those big-money boys took advantage of you."

"But they didn't. I got exactly what I *bargained* for and it was a *lot* of money! Hubie and I together inherited more than a quarter of a billion dollars! I wasn't greedy for more. It was important to me *not* to be. Can you understand that?"

"Sure I can, sweetheart. But you and Hubie and four sons—I'm not much for figures, I admit"—he grinned at her—"but I *can* add up to six. Who got that seventh share?"

"Charities."

His eyes opened in astonishment. "One hundred thirty million bucks left to charity? Couldn't you talk that sick old man out of leaving them that big a bite?"

"Probably. I didn't try," she said, feeling nauseated.

"Why the fuck not?"

"Because that's what Martin stood for. He believed in giving back. I'd never rob him in death of what he stood for in life."

T.S. stared at Nora uncomprehendingly, and it dawned on her that it wasn't that he wasn't a good person, or even ungenerous. He gave freely to movie-oriented causes, handed out huge tips to valet parkers, gave money to down-and-out friends, and had a staff who adored him not only because they were so well paid but because he spoke to them as if they were friends. It was that he was so preoccupied with the making of movies, both the business end and the creative, he couldn't really relate to much outside it, certainly nothing so abstract as the philosophy of philanthropy.

"I guess you'll just have to forgive me for being so ignorant about how the *really* rich do things," he said ruefully. "I'm a washout when it comes to money. If I were better at it, I wouldn't always be in a mess with the *overs*."

"The what?"

"The overs—overbudget, overextended, overdue at the bank," he chuckled. "But not to worry. In Hollywood they don't call it being broke, they call it a cash-flow problem."

She laughed. This was much better—this was the famous T.S. Grant light touch, the humor he was known for. Besides, he was a great filmmaker—a genius, and what did geniuses know of money? She was ashamed of the suspicion that had crept unbidden into her mind that just possibly he had married her for her supposed billion dollars.

"A cash-flow problem isn't unique to Hollywood, you know, not unknown even in the poshest circles. You have all your money tied up in films and they have it tied up in paper. But you were foolish to let me buy all those outrageously expensive antiques. They could have waited."

He turned serious again. "But it's a matter of *image*. You might understand about money, Nora, but image is one thing

*I* know something about. If you don't keep up the image, the word gets out that you might be *really* broke, and then you can't borrow a dime from the banks. And if *they* won't lend you money to make a movie, who will? Besides, I love Grantwood Manor and I love you. I want it to properly reflect that it's the castle of a very special lady. As for those bills, I was just kidding when I said you should pay them. Just send them over to my accountant—let him wrestle with them. That's what he's getting paid for."

\* \* \*

Instead of mailing the bills to the accountant, she made an appointment to talk to Andy Donovan.

He shook his head woefully at the bills. "No way," he told her.

Nora said, "No problem," and wrote a check. "This should take care of it for a while."

Encouraged at how quickly the check was forthcoming, Andy Donovan felt free to be frank. "The problem with T.S. is that not only is he grandiose both in his personal spending and moviemaking, he can't separate the two. But the truth is that if he doesn't have a really big winner at the box office soon, or pull off something really spectacular, he's going to lose both Grantwood Manor and Grantwood Studio."

She smiled faintly. "What do you mean by pulling off something spectacular?"

"Well, once when the studio was virtually going under, he came up with fifty million dollars like a magician pulling a rabbit out of his hat. Maybe it doesn't sound like so much today, but back in '56, it was a hell of a lot of money."

"Yes, I would think," she said, reflecting that '56 was the year Sam had been born. "And it's *still* a hell of a lot of money. But since it didn't really come out of a hat, where did it come from?"

Andy shrugged. "T.S. would never say that time. But would you believe after paying back the banks, he was back in their

debt again after only a year? And again he pulled off the spectacular, only this time he got the bank to pull *its* money out of a
vault for him," he chortled.

"Only one year later? That would make it 1957?"

*Nineteen fifty-seven was the year she was in Hollywood with
Mick.*

"If 1957 comes after 1956, then that was the year."

"But how did he do it?" she asked.

"With a really cute maneuver," Donovan said admiringly.
"First he went to the bank and pitched them with a sequel to
*Gone With the Wind.* They got all excited. Instead of asking him
if he had secured the rights, they asked who he was casting.
Well, when T.S. said Mimi L'Heureux, the French sexpot,
would play Scarlett, they went bananas. No one even asked how
Scarlett would play with a French accent. Then, when he told
them Mimi's Pulitzer Prize–winning husband, F. Theodore
Rosen, would be the screenwriter, they didn't recognize *his*
name but they did recognize the name *Pulitzer.*"

"And for Rhett Butler—?" she asked innocently.

"That was the one that clinched the deal. T.S. told them he
had an English actor panting on the line who not only was the
spitting image of Gable but who could be gotten *cheap.* And you
know bankers, their bottom line's spelled budget."

"And what spells *cheap?*"

"*That* was extremely cute," Andy laughed. "Mick Nash, the
poor fish, never did get a contract, and since the picture never
got made, Nash cost the studio only a couple of plane tickets and
a few weeks of expenses for him and his girlfriend, an ex-countess. Some creative bookkeeping, you might say—we put *her*
down in the ledger under publicity."

"I'll just bet you did."

"Then once T.S. got the bank's commitment, he flew to
France and signed up Mimi and her husband. L'Heureux was a
smart cookie—she would never have signed unless she saw that
commitment in black and white. Then, when the bank saw *her*
name on the dotted line, they forked over the cash."

"T. S. never *intended* to make the picture?"

"What do you think?" He laughed at the ridiculous notion.

"But didn't he have to give the bank back their money since the picture wasn't ever made?"

"Of course he did . . . *eventually*. But he would have had to do that in any case. The point is they lent it to him when he needed it, was desperate, which they wouldn't have done without a very *spectacular* package."

"Not only spectacular but very creative, you might say."

"That's what T.S.'s always telling me I should be—'You have to be more creative, Andy.' What a guy!"

"Yes," she agreed. "What a guy." *A guy who said he didn't know anything about money.*

"But I'm sorry if I upset you by painting a dire picture of T.S.'s financial situation. I shouldn't have done that. He's sure to pull something spectacular again."

"I'm sure," she said, rising to leave.

"It was good to meet you, Mrs. Grant."

"You must call me Nora, Andy." She smiled sweetly. "Unless you want to call me Mrs. Creative Bookkeeping."

He looked at her, puzzled.

"You know, the girlfriend, the ex-countess, the one you put down under publicity? She married the poor fish."

\*   \*   \*

"I had an interesting visit with Andy Donovan today," Nora said provocatively as she and T.S. lay in bed, she flipping through a magazine, he absorbed in a copy of *Variety*.

He didn't stop reading. "Interesting? Then, you're lucky. I find Andy pretty boring myself."

"That's mean and he says such nice things about you."

T.S. turned a page. "What kind of nice things?"

"Oh, how you're a fabulous magician and can pull rabbits out of hats. Like when you needed money and pulled out the sequel to *Gone With the Wind*. And then you looked up your sleeve and there was Mimi L'Heureux, F. Theodore Rosen, and none other than my ex-husband, Mick Nash."

He roared with laughter. "Andy Donovan's not only boring,

he's got a big mouth. All right, let's hear it. Are you worried that I pulled off a scam that the late Mr. Cantington would view as less than honorable?"

She picked her words carefully. "Well, it *was* kind of double-dealing, wasn't it?"

"Come over here," he said, drawing her closer tenderly—and as usual she couldn't resist his overtures—till she was lying in the crook of his arm. "What I did wasn't anything people in Hollywood or those politician friends of yours don't do everyday: making something work by stepping fast and talking even faster. But who got hurt? The bank got its money back with interest, Mimi made a bundle and a *different* movie, her husband got paid for a screenplay he never wrote, and Grantwood Studio is *still* here. That says it all as far as I'm concerned."

"What about Mick? What did he get besides a runaround?"

"He got better than he deserved. He got to marry you only to lose you because he couldn't resist the French slut. That makes him both a fool and a sucker, and a wise man never gives a sucker an even break."

She thought of asking him a question: If Mimi was the slut Mick, the sucker, couldn't resist, had *he*, T.S., the wise man, been better able to resist her? And she wanted to ask him if he had met Mimi *before* he signed her up, say, at one of those film festivals where people apparently spent more time flitting from bed to bed than they did viewing films. . . .

Another question she might ask was, what exactly was the spectacular trick he had performed to save his precious studio in 1956, the year Sam was born? And, most interesting of all: What spectacular feat would he, the magician, pull off this time to save his studio from the banks?

And there was one question she might ask herself: Who, really, was this man whom she had married, to whom she was committed, whom she loved with her entire being?

He slipped his hand into the valley between her breasts and she trembled. . . .

*But just as T.S. said, Martin would have seen the whole episode as less than honorable.*

His hand teased her nipples delicately and she could feel them go into erection. . . .

*But when you came down to it, was the business of politics or even diplomatic negotiation that clean either?*

His hand trailed down to part her lips with his fingers and she could feel herself moisten to their touch. . . .

*And no one really got hurt. Not even Mick. He'd had fun in Hollywood and that was what counted the most with Mick.*

Then with one violent motion he was on top of her, parting her thighs with himself, and even if her head would have told her to resist, the rest of her was entirely incapable of it. . . .

\* \* \*

Afterward, as he lay asleep beside her, she remembered what he had once advised Mick to do—to go with the flow. And it came to her who T.S. really was above and beyond everything else— lover, moviemaking genius, high liver, and good laugher, even the rascal magician and the dedicated pragmatist who would do what he felt had to be done. He was the man who went with the flow. . . .

# FORTY

———•••———

Nora gave top priority to redoing Sam's room. It had to be ready by the time she came home for spring vacation. Accordingly, she lavished attention on every detail, using Sam's favorite green as the primary color in the decorating scheme. When it was finished, only a couple of days before Sam was due to arrive, she led T.S. into the room.

He smiled patiently. "Very pretty."

"Is that all you can say?"

"What do you want me to say?" he laughed. "Tell me and I'll oblige. You know I'm an obliging kind of a fellow."

"I think you're a maddening kind of a fellow. Say it's magnificent and that Sam will adore it."

"I'll say its magnificent but she won't adore it. She's never going to adore anything *you're* connected with. She's always been jealous, terrified, that I'd marry again. Now that I have, she's going to hate your guts no matter what you do."

"Of course she's jealous. It's natural that she'd resent any woman who took her mother's place in her mother's house and in her father's heart. It's up to us to dispel her fears, you with your love and me with sheer persistence. I'm not going to give up, you know, until I wear her down."

"Don't count on it—that kid's tough."

Of course, Sam was tough, she thought. People on their own learned to be tough and Sam had been on her own—away at school and hardly ever coming home. Plus, it didn't help that her father was oddly unsympathetic. And that disturbed her more than she cared to admit, especially in light of what she'd so recently learned about the way he did business, which, much as she tried, she couldn't get out of her mind.

* * *

T.S. had agreed to go to the airport with her, but he called only ten minutes before she left to say that he was tied up. "But I'll make it home in time for dinner."

Olaf, the chauffeur, who'd been with T.S. for some years, drove her. And Sam, instead of crying in disappointment that her father wasn't there, threw her arms around him. *The poor baby.* Sam was so glad to see Olaf because at least *he'd* been a constant in her life. He'd been there each of the infrequent times she'd gotten off a plane in L.A., and Sam knew that he was fond of her.

When Nora asked Sam if she'd had a good flight, Sam answered, "Not really. They showed a movie I already saw twice, the food was disgusting, and the stewardess was fresh."

*My, is that all? That's not so bad. Just think, the plane could have gone down in flames.*

As soon as they were in the car, Sam complained that she was freezing. Nora turned down the air-conditioning, but then Sam lowered her window, declaring that she was suffocating. Then she sniffed and sniffed, her features screwed up in total revulsion, until Nora asked, "What *is* it?" and Sam answered with another question: "What *is* that nauseating scent you're wearing? You'd think that with all my father's money you could get yourself a perfume slightly less revolting. Or maybe it's just that once it touches your skin, it turns putrid." At last, she smiled—at her own malice. "That's a chemical reaction I've read about."

Nora dug the fingernails of one hand into the other while managing to smile. "Isn't that interesting?"

They were on the freeway when Sam demanded, "Why didn't Daddy come to the airport? What did *you* do to keep him from coming?"

*No, it wasn't going to be easy.*

\*   \*   \*

Nora could tell Sam loved her room from her look of delight
and the sigh of contentment that escaped her lips before she
remembered to toss her hair in disdain. "The color scheme's
kind of obvious, isn't it? But, then, I suppose a woman of your
background would hardly understand subtlety."

"My background?"

"Yes. I knew about all your marriages before, but now I
know a lot more of the scandalous *details* of those marriages."

Nora laughed. "Only a very *uninformed* thirteen-year-old
would have the arrogance to think she could possibly know
*anything* about what goes on in a person's marriage."

"But I am *not* uninformed. And it's not just gossip. I did
some checking on dates and one thing I *know* is that one and one
make two. So, I do know what was going on when you were
married to that actor and living in Hollywood." Now her tone
was more bitter than malicious.

*What was this poor, tortured child getting at?*

"What do you think was going on?"

"What was going on was that you were cheating on the poor
actor and the year was 1957—the same year my mother killed
herself, and do you know *how?* She fucking killed herself by
cutting her own throat until she bled to death, and do you know
*why?*" Sam's voice began to rise until it was a scream. "Because
my father was fooling around with another woman while she
was sick—a woman who was beautiful enough and clever
enough to take advantage of his grief over my mother's illness!"

She threw herself down on the pretty, pristine floral bedspread in a torrent of tears. Nora ran to comfort her, but Sam
shrank back. "Don't touch me! *You're* the woman who seduced
my father! Who's responsible for my mother killing herself! I
know it!"

"It's just not true, love. I'd never even met your father then.
And you don't really *know* that your father was having an affair
with *anyone*. You *can't* believe malicious gossip from schoolgirls

who got *their* information fourth- or fifth-hand from people who didn't even know your mother.''

Sam looked at her, eyes bruised with misery. ''They didn't tell me about *that*. The people who did knew my mother *very* well. Her parents . . . my grandparents!''

''Your grandparents? How could that be? They died when you were only five. How could they tell you such a thing?''

''They told me all about it just the same.'' A sick smile twisted Sam's lips. ''And don't *you* tell me that I was too young to get the facts right or to remember. It's something I remember every day of my life!''

A wave of horror swept through Nora. She didn't doubt Sam. But how could her grandparents be so brutal? Then she thought she understood. Even the nicest people could be driven to brutality by an all-consuming bitterness. A daughter's suicide . . . one generated by a husband's faithlessness . . . *could* cause that kind of bitterness.

*A woman so beautiful and so clever* . . . She knew of one woman who was around at the time who could fit that description.

''And did they tell you who this woman was?''

''No, why would they? They didn't care who *she* was. They blamed *him*. But I know better who's to blame. Oh, it must have been so easy for *you* to fool him.''

''I doubt that he was fooled by anyone. The truth probably is that your grandparents weren't lying but were, in their grief, mistaken. Your father loved your mother too much to be tempted or fooled by any woman. He's told me often how much he loved her, that he was mad about her.'' She didn't mind telling a little white lie if it helped this tormented child.

''Of course, I can't say for sure since I didn't know T.S. then. Why don't you ask him yourself tonight? Perhaps he'll even tell you how he actually stood me up the one time I was *supposed* to meet him with Mick for drinks.''

If Nora was hoping for even the tiniest response to her pathetic little attempt at humor, she was disappointed. Sam buried her face in a pillow and she decided it would be best just to let her be until T.S. came home. Then he could reassure Sam that not only hadn't he known *her*, Nora, at the time but that there'd been no other woman at all, not even a sexpot movie star.

\* \* \*

When it became clear that T.S. wasn't coming home for dinner, Nora went upstairs to suggest to Sam that they start without him in the hope that he would get home in time to join them for dessert. But Sam was asleep and Nora didn't have the heart to wake her.

Instead, she gazed at her stepdaughter. There was nothing tough or ornery about her now, with those tear-stained cheeks and her lips curling up at the corners as if she were sweetly dreaming. She carefully covered her with a comforter. Still, Sam stirred, the eyelids fluttered for a moment, and the lips curved into a real smile as she breathed, "Mommy . . ."

Oh, yes, Nora thought, Sam's dream was very sweet.

Was a needy child any less needy for being a stepchild, or a stepdaughter any less deserving of love for not being one's own flesh and blood? And if she had learned anything at all by now it was that hand in hand with love went obligation and that you didn't give up on a child no matter what . . . even if there were certain problems—certain deficiencies of character.

*No, I won't give up on you, Sam, and that's a promise. . . .*

# FORTY-ONE

.S. tried to mollify Nora with kisses, hugs, and jokes when he came home at one in the morning, but she refused to be placated. "What you did today and tonight might seem like nothing to you but it was a very cruel thing to do to Sam. Don't you realize how she adores you?"

He shrugged. "She's a hysteric just like her mother."

"Well, that's a pretty callous attitude, I must say."

She was forced to consider then if she could really forgive callousness in a man, and how could it be that she had fallen in love with and married such a callous man? She thought of the men she had loved in different ways for different reasons— Hubert, whom she had loved intensely but naïvely and romantically as only a very young woman could; Mick, whom she hadn't loved all that seriously; and Martin, whom she had; she'd even loved Jeffrey for certain kindnesses. And there had been deficiencies in all of them, but not one had been callous. And yet she hadn't loved one of them as much as T.S.—the man she'd thought she married as a mature woman for the best of everything. *I love, I loved, I have loved.* She wasn't really sure which tense applied anymore. All she knew was that even as she stood there sickened to her core, she ached for him, ached for everything to be all right between them again.

"Look, Nora, it's late and I'm tired. Let's say, I *tried* to make it but I couldn't and leave it at that."

Ordinarily she would have fussed over him if he said he was tired, and though she yearned to now, she couldn't let go of the anger. "Why *couldn't* you make it?"

"Business. Studio business," he said as if no other explanation were necessary.

"Is that the only thing that matters? That damn studio?"

He smiled wearily. "Not *the* only thing. *You* matter to me. *You* matter very much."

This was not the answer she wanted to hear right now. "What about Sam?"

"What about her?" He was out of patience. "You constantly worry about Hubie. *Is he safe? Is he keeping out of trouble? When will he be coming home?* Isn't that enough for you? Why don't you leave Sam for me to worry about?"

"But you *don't*. That's the problem. Do you know what your daughter thinks? That you and I were having an affair when I was married to Mick and while her mother was in that sanitorium, and that's the reason she killed herself."

His eyes slitted and he muttered, "That crazy kid . . ."

"That's what her grandparents told her—that you were having an affair with *some* married woman. Sam's only guessing that it was I."

When he made no response other than an expletive, she knew that the story was true, and she was incredibly saddened, but that wasn't the issue that had to be dealt with now.

"For *my* sake you're going to have to straighten her out, T.S. Convince her that you and I were not even acquainted at the time. But more importantly, you have to convince her for *her* sake that her mother didn't cut her throat because her husband was fooling around. She needs desperately to believe in you."

T.S. seemed to be almost his usual, unflappable self by now. His voice was low when he spoke, which made what he said that much more chilling: "I'll straighten her out all right, and you know how I'm going to do that? I'm going to tell her the truth, the God's honest truth, that her mother killed herself for only *one* reason—because she was *always* mentally unstable . . . off the wall . . . before and after she married me, in and out of institutions her entire life. . . . I'm also going to tell sweet Sam that she'd better watch her own step because madness often runs in the blood."

Appalled, Nora cried, "How can you even think of saying something so devastatingly awful to your own daughter?" But she was frightened too, even as she voiced the words, sensing that there would be no coming back once he answered.

"Maybe because she's *not* my daughter."

With that he smiled, albeit grimly, at her shocked expression, and she knew that, whatever he was or wasn't, T.S. *was* a man like no other. Otherwise, how could he drop a bombshell like that and smile?

"Whose daughter is she, for God's sake?"

"Your guess is as good as mine." He shrugged. "I think it was one of those society boys from old Pasadena. All I know is that she isn't mine. *The timing's off.* But what does it matter now? He wouldn't marry her and I can't really blame him, considering how many loose screws were rattling around in that pretty head."

"But *you* did?" *A foolish question, to say the least.* "Knowing she was pregnant?"

"Knowing she was pregnant."

"Did her parents know she was pregnant?"

This time he laughed. "*Did they not?* Do you think those hypocritical snobs were prepared to let their little girl marry someone in the movie business, *dar-ling*, unless they needed someone to play daddy real fast? Come on, Nora, wake up! T. S. Grant and the Parkers cut a deal."

*Of course!* The spectacular magician's stunt that had saved Grantwood Studio in 1956.

But then a year later, in 1957, the stunt got a little more complex, involving as it did one French movie star and an affair, one movie never meant to be filmed, one suicide, and a motherless year-old baby. But Nora needed another question answered. He had said that he knew Sam wasn't his daughter because the timing was off. "You married Elise in '56, but you *did* know her before?"

"I met her at a charity ball early in '55. Just cultivating the field, you might say, just in case I might want to reap a harvest someday."

"And you brought Mimi L'Heureux over here in '57? Had you cultivated *her* before too?"

He nodded. "In late '55. Once again, just sowing a little seed just in case . . ."

This man was a virtual jack-of-all-trades. As in "rich man, poor man, beggarman, thief," T.S. was lover-man, movie-man, magician, and now, apparently—farmer extraordinaire, or was he, as in a song she used to sing at the Cock 'n' Bull—*just a gigolo?*

"And what about more recently? Were you *still* casting the seed around, just in case you might need a woman to get you out of debt?"

It was a question conceived in sarcasm, but she was terrified of the answer. She was pretty sure she already knew it, but she was hoping against hope that T.S. was the magician supreme who could pull off another spectacular feat—make a believer out of her again.

He grinned at her. "If you're asking me if I married you because I loved you, my answer is that I love you more than I've loved any woman. You're *my* kind of gal."

It *was* an answer, even if it weren't the answer she was looking for, and it was, at best, one without sufficient magic. What he was telling her was that he loved her in his fashion, but he was also telling her what she already knew—that he loved his studio more. And she was filled with a bitter grief. While she believed he was even being honest in his fashion, he hadn't *quite* made a believer out of her again. . . .

"Tell me—how much did you eventually harvest from Elise's parents?"

"The fifty million I needed at the time. You *could* call it Elise's dowry. Just an advance, really, on what they were going to leave her in their will anyway. But once she was married to me they cut her out of *their* deal fast enough."

"And did they leave Sam anything?"

"Of course not. They were afraid it would end up in my pocket. They were suspicious people, you see, not really very nice no matter how la-de-da."

"Then, Sam really was left with absolutely nothing—no money, no father to love her, and a dead mother."

He scratched his head. "The hour is late and I'm a little dull. Is there a point you're trying to make here?"

"Yes, there is—the point is Sam's legacy. You got fifty million dollars and she—? She got shortchanged."

"Come off it, Nora, don't kid an old kidder. What you're trying to say is that I'm responsible for Elise's suicide and it just ain't so. She had suicide written all over her from the day she was born. Didn't you ever meet anyone like that?"

She had indeed.

"And didn't *you* ever make a deal? You know, like marrying someone to get something you want and give them back something they want in return? People marry for so many fool notions it's enough to make your head spin—some people marry for money, some for sex, and some just because they need a name for their kids. It's all okay as long as everyone knows what they're getting and what they're willing to pay. Can you disagree with that?"

She couldn't and he knew that she couldn't. She and he weren't that far apart after all. Both of them had married for love—he for love of his studio, and she for love of Hubie. But not this time. This time she had married for love of a man who, while he was so clever at so many different trades, wasn't clever enough to recognize when he was loved only for himself, and maybe that was the saddest thing of all.

But the fact remained that Sam, as well as she herself, had been shortchanged and the hour was late. Too late for all manner of things except to renegotiate the terms of a marriage contract never written out, but obsolete all the same. . . .

"All right, T.S., I already know what *you* want; now I'm going to tell you what I want. Are you ready to sit down and cut a deal?"

\* \* \*

When they were through she realized that at the very least she'd married a man who, if nothing else, was a sporting kind of fellow who didn't hold a grudge, not even when he had lost title to both his house and his studio. First he laughed, and then he shook his head in admiration. "When I married you I knew you were a beauty and a famous hostess, an ex-countess as well as a fabulous decorator, and a woman with a head for politics. What I *didn't* know was that you were one hell of a negotiator too. I'll have the papers drawn up tomorrow."

"No, tomorrow you'll be too busy taking your daughter around the studio, spending the entire day with her."

"Whatever you say. You're the boss."

"Yes, but don't forget that that's our secret. That that's part of our deal. We've bought each other's silence."

He nodded and asked with a wry smile, "But now that it's a deal and you're calling the shots, what do we do next? Do we shake hands on it? Or do we go upstairs and celebrate the way a man and woman should?"

She looked at him for a long time before answering—her body and her head, maybe even her very soul, at war. But finally she made her agonized decision—would she ever make peace with it?—and said, "Every good businessman knows that you never mix business with pleasure. . . ."

\*   \*   \*

A couple of days before Sam (almost, but not *quite*, as unfriendly as she had been that first day) was ready to go back to school, Nora told her, "I don't expect that you'll ever love me. I'm not asking you to even be my friend, though that *would* be nice. But if you would care to sign a truce, I think it can be arranged for you to spend the summer at home instead of away at camp. What do you say?"

Sam's eyes lit up with sheer joy before she grew suspicious. "What do I have to do?"

"Be civil, reasonably respectful, generally pleasant to be around, and cooperative. Nothing more than that."

"Do I have to promise to obey?"

Nora laughed. "They don't even include that one in the marriage vows anymore." Then she grew serious. "But you're right. We *will* have to have some ground rules as to what constitutes appropriate behavior. But I'll be reasonable if you will, which means that you can't be running to your father every minute to appeal some ruling of mine. You'll have to understand that he's a busy man and that he's in charge of the studio and I'm in charge of running our home."

Sam's eyes narrowed. "What about *after* the summer? You're planning to pack me off to school again in the fall, is that it? You're willing to have me around this summer so you can show my father you're *trying* to be nice, but—"

"Hold on. I was going to add that if my terms were acceptable to you, you could also stay home in the fall and go to school here. Well, do we have a deal?"

Sam was guarded but she nodded. "Deal."

"Jolly good," Nora said cheerfully. "Now, we must do something to seal the bargain."

Sam cocked an eyebrow. "You said civil and respectful, nothing about kissing. I told you I don't like to be—"

"I *know*, touched, and that was not my intention. I had something entirely different in mind. I don't know about you, but I've never been to Disneyland, and I thought that if you didn't mind we could—"

"Seal our bargain by going to Disneyland?" Sam's eyes opened wide before she rolled them. Then she said, "Well, I *did* agree to be cooperative, so I guess so . . ." And almost as if she couldn't help herself, she added: "I hope you're not a fraidy cat because they have a new attraction that's really scary that I'm dying to try and—"

"Oh, I am kind of a fraidy cat, but I think that if we do it together, I won't be *too* terrified. . . ."

Sam smiled, a smug smile but a smile, and Nora thought, *What do you know about that?*

That was what was so nice about negotiating. Sometimes there was a surprise at the end . . . a kind of bonus you weren't expecting . . . maybe, sometimes, even love.

# FORTY-TWO

———— •••• ————

Nora thought the manor looked its most beautiful—the foliage greener in the first, lush burst of the season; the flowers perkier than they would be once the summer heat set in; the pool sparkling in a somehow more brilliant sun—the day that Hubie, discharged at last, came home to Grantwood soon after Sam went back to school.

She'd worried that Hubie and T.S. wouldn't hit it off, or that Hubie wouldn't like Los Angeles. But T.S. went out of his way to be nice to Hubie, who, always receptive, thought T.S. was a great guy, especially after T.S. presented him with a gift—a red Ferrari the twin to his own bearing the license plate STUDIO 2. (T.S.'s license plate read STUDIO 1.)

She wasn't too pleased. A Ferrari was a car for a playboy, and she'd had a more "serious" car in mind for Hubie since in L.A. a man was judged more by the car he drove than by the company he kept. But she supposed it would be all right—T.S. drove the same car and everyone knew he was very serious about his work. As for Hubie, he was off and running, exploring the pleasures of his new milieu—the beaches to the west (T.S. had a house in Malibu to which he gave Hubie a key), and the Hollywood clubs to the east. He was also zipping down to Palm Springs, where the studio kept a condo for entertaining, or tearing up to Reno for a little gambling, usually in the company of a woman, each prettier and sexier than the last, a common commodity in Southern California.

After a few weeks of this Nora was impatient to see Hubie off and running into his future. With this in mind, she addressed T.S. "You've been wonderful with Hubie—"

"Not at all. Just keeping up my end of the bargain. A deal's a deal and I promised to be a real father to your boy."

"Let's not get our terms confused, T.S. For one, Hubie's twenty-five and he's *had* his share of fathers. What he needs now is a mentor and an *employer*, which is what you agreed to be since I didn't bring my son to California to be a playboy. *Sam's* the one in need of a real father, and *that's* also one of our terms of agreement. Remember?"

His smile was wily. "Of course. But I get confused every now and then with these terms of agreement. You want me to be Hubie's employer, but it's I who work for you."

"As long as you remember that, we won't have a problem."

T.S. put Hubie to work at the studio, and she soon discovered his pragmatic solution as to what one did with a handsome young man whose main assets were his charm and a talent for pleasuring women: You applied these assets to the three major P's of the industry—publicity, promotion, and public relations. Hubie's broad assignment was to influence, entertain, and gently persuade females who needed to be persuaded for whatever reason. A sideline was actresses who needed direction to wherever—premiere, party, or bedroom.

Furious, she told T.S. that the future she envisioned for her son was not that of a male whore any more than it was the life of the playboy. "Start him in production and let him learn the business from the bottom up."

He shrugged. "You're calling the shots, but I know this business—production will bore the pants off Hubie, who has problem enough keeping them on already. You'd be better off trying to make an actor out of him. He has the looks and the personality. He might even have the talent."

"No. Actors don't become heads of studios, which is my intention. Only people who learn the business properly do."

T.S. shrugged again. "I'm fond of Hubie and I too want only the best for him, but, as you say, it's *your* race."

*   *   *

The first day of summer, the day Sam was flying home, was a
scorcher, giving promise of a long, hot season. And though T.S.
had given Nora his promise that he would make it to the airport
this time, at the last moment he claimed a crisis in Burbank.
Instead, he would send Hubie as a deliberate tactic, he explained
on the phone. "Sam'll be so excited at meeting her new big
brother—as you yourself said, the poor kid's starved for family
life—she won't even notice that I'm not there."

Nora was only partially appeased. She had no worries about
how Hubie would feel about Sam—he was anticipating having a
younger sister about. Sam's reaction to Hubie was the prob-
lematic unknown. How would Sam adjust to having yet one
more person around to vie for her father's attention?

Still, she was determined to maintain a positive attitude. As
she waited for them to get there, she busied herself with the final
touches for the family party she had planned for the four of
them—a combination homecoming and birthday party since
Sam had just turned fourteen. But when T.S. showed up before
Sam and Hubie, for once keeping his promise to be home early,
he found her a nervous wreck. "The plane came in at two. Now
it's six and they're not here!"

He was unperturbed. "Did you check with the airline?"

"Of course I did. The plane landed on schedule."

"It *could* take an hour to pick up the luggage if it were a
crowded flight, especially if it wasn't nonstop."

"So that would make it three o'clock."

"Well, there could be a lot of traffic coming back from the
beaches today, it was so damn hot."

"That would take us to four. Four-thirty at the most."

"I assumed you checked for accidents and what you heard
was reassuring?" He poured himself a drink.

"Of course."

"And I daresay they didn't disappear into thin air and it's
not likely they were kidnapped—Hubie's a twenty-five-year-old
decorated marine who made it through Vietnam, and Sam *is* five

feet ten and could kick the shit out of anyone dumb enough to mess with her. So, what are you worrying about?''

*Easy for him to say. Hubie isn't his son and Sam isn't his daughter in any sense of the word. He doesn't even know what it means to love a child. Life is simple when one really doesn't give a damn. . . .*

In the end, she resisted calling the police only because T.S. told her that the Department of Missing Persons wouldn't even listen to her story of a teenager who had disappeared for less than twelve hours.

At ten they arrived, not exactly waltzing in but arm in arm, with big smiles on their freshly sun-bronzed faces. Nora's momentary relief turned to anger when she heard Hubie's ''reasonable'' explanation: ''It was so goddamn hot when Sam got off the plane and LAX is so near the beach, it seemed a shame not to take the poor kid for a swim so she could cool off.''

She was about to ask if he'd ever come across a handy invention called the phone when Sam, eyes shining with excitement, blurted, ''Then, when we were drying ourselves off, these kids on the beach were getting up a game of volleyball and they were short a couple of players so we decided to be good sports and help them out, right, bro?''

''Help them out?'' Hubie howled. ''What we did was whip their bloody asses! Little sister here didn't mention that she was a varsity champ at that school of hers.''

''That's right, I was,'' Sam shrieked, throwing her arms around the bemused T.S. ''And we sure did whip those asses!''

''Well, then the losers had to buy, and it wouldn't have been gracious not to let them.'' Hubie grinned at Nora. ''You know how you always taught me to be gracious, Mum.''

''But *I* didn't have any beer, Nora,'' Sam said quickly and primly. ''I just had a Coke. Right, Hubie?''

''Mmm . . .'' he considered. ''I guess. Well, you didn't beg for *too* many sips from my glass.''

''Oh, you,'' she giggled, punching his arm while he pretended to shield himself from her blows. ''That's a big, fat lie. Don't you believe him, Nora.''

Nora was amazed, her anger considerably dissipated. The

girl she'd seen that spring had evolved into a different person. She turned to Hubie. "Even so, that would have taken you up to what—six o'clock? And now it's past ten."

Sam giggled again. "Well, you know what they say? Time sure does fly when you're having fun, right, bro?"

Hubie guffawed, and Nora sighed. *Sam's acting like any fourteen-year-old teenager, but so is he. I guess no matter what else he is, does, or becomes—the warrior in Vietnam or Hollywood producer—he'll always remain a child at heart.*

"All right, Hubie, what *did* you do between six and ten?"

"Well, when sis here said she was famished—"

"I hadn't eaten *all* day," Sam interrupted to explain. "The stuff they pushed on the plane was totally gross."

"And I remembered that Harv Feldman had mentioned that he was having a barbecue at his place in Carbon Beach. I fully intended to call but his dumb phone was out of order."

"It was *so* super eating out on the deck and the place was crawling with movie stars!" Sam enthused.

"Stars?" Hubie hooted. "Extras and bit players is more like it, but the kid is easily impressed, 'specially since one of the jerks tried hitting on her," and Sam punched his arm again. "She's just pissed because I told him to lay off my little sister unless he really craved a bloody nose."

Sam pretended to pout. "He ruined my romance."

T.S. finally spoke up. "Sounds like the kids had a real good time, Nora, but since *they* ate and *we* didn't, do you think *we* might have *our* dinner?"

When she led them into the dining room and Sam saw the room and table decorated for her combination homecoming and birthday party, she screamed, threw her arms around her father, then around Hubie, and, finally, even Nora before declaring, "This is the very best day of my life! And tomorrow is going to be the second best."

"What's happening tomorrow?" Nora asked.

"Tomorrow my big brother is taking me to Disneyland, and then, after that, we're going to a rock concert."

She thought of reminding Hubie that he had to go to work,

but how long could she ride herd on a man in his twenties, and how could she ruin the best day of a young girl's life by nixing the plans for the second best day of her life?

\*　\*　\*

As summer wore on, T.S. observed, "I have to hand it to you, Nora, you're doing a great job. You have Hubie ensconced at the studio, and with his able assistance you've even conquered the formidable Sam. And now that we're one big happy family and everybody loves everybody else, I hope we're all going to settle down and it will be business as usual."

There it was in a nutshell, she thought. For T.S., their being a happy family was secondary, at most a pleasant detail. Business as usual—*studio* business—was the only thing that truly counted. It didn't even matter to him that legally he no longer owned the studio, that she did, so long as *he* ran it. The studio itself was *the* only thing that mattered—that it existed, that it endured, that people thought of it as the legendary T.S. Grant's studio—the rest was mere detail.

How, then, could she discuss with him the vague unease she felt about the intense intimacy struck up between Hubie and Sam, one that, considering their age difference and experience, seemed somehow unnatural? What would happen when, inevitably, Hubie tired of horsing around with a younger sister, however adoring, and turned his attention to more adult (and sexually rewarding) pursuits? Sam would be left adrift, devastated, and any progress they'd made as a family, and she and Sam as mother and daughter, could self-destruct.

But ultimately she decided that maybe T.S. was right, after all, about the importance of things settling down and getting on with business as usual. Sam would start school in the fall, and would make friends with kids her own age and develop her own teenage interests, leaving Hubie to pursue his own, more mature interests and his career.

\*   \*   \*

Summer was slowly winding to a close when things fell into the sharpest of focuses. It was a Sunday not much different from any other lazy summer Sunday. Hubie and Sam were off playing tennis in some tournament or other, and T.S. was at home reading scripts in his study as she played sounding board, he insisting she had a good ear for an exciting project. Ordinarily it was a practice she enjoyed, something that she and T.S. could do together, but suddenly . . . forcibly, she removed the script he was involved in from his hands. "I know what your problem is."

He grinned up at her. "I didn't know I had one. Now, be a good girl, Nora, and give me back my screenplay."

"No. I've figured out that your problem is that you've never stopped to smell the flowers, and who knows? If you had, you might be a better man for it. Now we're going to the beach house to relax, watch the sun set and the surf roll in."

\*   \*   \*

It wasn't the images that came into focus for her first. First there were the sounds coming from behind the door—the heavy breathing, the sighs and the moans, a male's husky groans quickly mounting, a girl's high-pitched scream of joy.

Next came T.S.'s "Shit!" as he pushed the door open to reveal the shot: three brightly-colored scraps of bathing attire lying in discard on a white-tiled floor. Pan to couple also lying on white-tiled floor, boy mounted on girl. Boy: tanned, muscular body glistening with sweat; blond head buried in girl's throat. Girl: long red hair spread out in disarray, head thrust back in abandon, eyes shut tight; long, shapely legs spread to accommodate boy's still shuddering body. . . .

Before Hubie turned around or Sam's eyes flew open, Nora heard T.S. say, "Shit," again before he said, "I hope you're not going to go all to pieces, Nora. This isn't exactly the end of the world, you know. It can be handled."

She laughed bitterly. Any minute now he would shrug and say, "Well, what did you expect? Boys will be boys and I told you right from the beginning that that girl was trouble. . . ."

It was all a matter of how one viewed the situation, she mused sorrowfully—each of the four players involved seeing this final development in a different light.

Hubie saw it sheepishly as a slip in behavior, a misstep that could be rectified with abject apologies and an honorable shouldering of responsibility: "It was all my fault."

Sam saw it as an act of romantic passion needing no defense save an equally impassioned "We love each other!"

Nora herself viewed it after the fact as inevitable, blaming herself. She'd been so relieved that Sam and Hubie had hit it off that she had closed her eyes to the obvious—that Hubie was *not* a responsible man, didn't know what constituted *inappropriate* behavior, much less a betrayal of trust, and that Sam, despite her physically ripe body and assumed sophistication, was still only a child too vulnerable in her need for any kind of love.

As for T.S., in his desire for "business as usual," he saw the incident only as an inconvenience.

Then each of them viewed the solution to the improbable situation according to his own light: Hubie presumed that his promise that it would never happen again was solution enough; Sam thought that her screaming protestation that she and Hubie loved each other madly was sufficient; T.S., ever the practical CEO, knew only that if someone became inconvenient, you rid yourself of the someone, and that if there were *two* someones, you got rid of the one most expendable. And this time Nora agreed with him—one of them had to be exiled.

She knew beforehand whom T.S. would choose. He needed *her*, and he assumed that she needed Hubie, making them a package deal. But who really needed Sam? She was extraneous baggage. *Ship her back East to school as soon as possible.*

But she knew who had to go. T.S. didn't really understand any kind of love, was unable to fathom the depth of love a woman might have for a child not even of her womb. He couldn't comprehend that sometimes a woman didn't really have a choice, as in the case of a mother who had two children whose lives hung in the balance and it was already established that only one could live . . . that she would have to choose not on the basis of love but which child had the best chance of survival.

*It is time to let go. . . .*

She had tried so hard, but now she had to let her son find his way for himself, and she could only pray that he would make it back to claim his legacy—her enduring love and his rightful place in the sun.

Yes, it might be too late for Hubie, but it wasn't too late for Sam, and this time around she wouldn't make the same mistakes. This time around it would be "tough love" so that Sam could discover the truth for *herself* . . . that she was a strong woman worthy of all the different faces of love and that her true place in the magic kingdom had yet to be earned. Still, there were certain truths she could *never* let Sam learn—not only that T.S. wasn't her blood father, but that no matter what *she* did, he was incapable of loving her.

Still, despite all her brave resolutions, it wasn't easy to let go, and it wasn't much of a consolation to know that Hubie was best off out of Hollywood—the fastest, deadliest track of all, where he was bound to stumble again and again. But then she had an idea. Perhaps Hubie would do better, after all, in the land of his birth, where she had an old and dear friend to call upon for help.

When she told Mick that she needed a really big favor, he didn't hesitate for a moment. "Of course, Nora. I always *meant* to be a good husband to you and a father to Hubie, if only you hadn't been in such a bloody rush to divorce me. Well, I'm at your service now, a little bit older, a little bit wiser, better-late-than-never Micky Nash. I will not only take Hubie under my wing and be a real father to him, I'll even show him a good time."

She had to laugh. "Hubie doesn't need any help in *that* department. What he needs is a job. I'm hoping you'll get him started in films so that he can learn the business."

*And someday—when he and Sam are both all grown up—he can come back to claim his heritage. . . .*

*  *  *

She wasn't surprised when Sam turned on her: *You were jealous . . . you wanted him to love only you . . . you wanted to break my
heart . . . you sent him away to punish him for loving me.* . . . She
even accused her of wanting Hubie's sexual favors for herself.

Nora neither defended herself nor lashed back. She didn't
even assure Sam that it only hurt for a little while before it got
better, as she yearned to do. All the old bets were off—from
now on it would be only tough love. That meant telling Sam that
she didn't give a tinker's damn whether she liked her or hated
her, but that if she wanted to stick around the place where her
father was and go to school locally, she'd better straighten up
and fly right.

Neither did it come as that much of a surprise when, soon
after, Mick called to report sadly that he had failed her again. He
had tried to get Hubie started in films and had tried to keep him
interested, but Hubie had become bored and taken off. " 'To
find some fun,' was what he said. He said to tell you that he
loved you and that he would be in touch."

"But Mick, where did he go?"

"I'm sorry, Nora, but— He joined the *Foreign Legion!*"

"That *what?*" she asked in shock. She'd thought the Foreign
Legion was extinct—an obsolete romantic notion. But after a
few seconds, she said reflectively, "Don't feel bad, Mick, it
really isn't your fault. I guess Hubie just has a few more puddles
to go."

"I don't understand. *Puddles?*"

"Puddles. When Hubie was a little boy, he loved nothing
better than to jump into puddles just for the fun of it."

# PART SEVEN

# THE FIRST SWEET TASTE OF THE SEASON

Los Angeles, 1970–1974

# FORTY-THREE

———•••———

oney sat by herself at a table in the corner of the lunch-room, taking dispirited stabs at a health salad. Since it was the first day of the semester at Beasley and she was a freshman, she didn't know a single girl, though everyone else seemed to be talking to someone else. Surely there had to be other girls who didn't know anyone. Where were they?

Just then a very short girl with dark bangs hanging low over sparkly, dark eyes bounced up. Even before she set her lunch tray down, she demanded: "Are you Playmate or Bunny?"

"I'm not sure," Honey said tentatively, not having any idea what the girl was talking about, but afraid she might just bounce off to try someone else who was more savvy. "Which are you?"

"I'd *like* to be a Playmate, but I guess I'm a Bunny."

"Well, then, I'll be a Bunny too," Honey responded quickly, thinking this was the friendly thing to say.

The girl looked at her thoughtfully: "No, I think *you* have to be a Playmate because *you're* beautiful and a true Playmate is beautiful as well as voluptuous, and therefore makes it to the pages. But I have to be a Bunny because while I'm cute I'm not beautiful. Also, I'm short and *too* voluptuous for my height. Mostly a Bunny's just cute and curvy and all she gets to do is bob her bushy tail up and down and jiggle it all around like this—" She executed a couple of fast dance steps—boogie mixed with wiggle—and finished off with an old-fashioned bump-and-grind. "See?"

Honey laughed, revealing a blindingly white, nearly rectangular smile, and the other girl enthused, "Even your smile is gorgeous. Yep, I'm cute but you're centerfold material."

*Centerfold material! Playmates and Bunnies! Of course!* The Playboy Mansion was only a couple of hundred yards down the street from Beasley in Los Angeles's posh Little Holmby Hills, and she had heard the joke that a Beasley girl didn't have to go far to get a *really* extensive education. She just walked down the street to the mansion and jumped the fence.

"You *do* mean the magazine? *Playboy?*"

"Now you've got it! That's the frame of reference."

"But I don't want to be a centerfold in *Playboy.*"

"Not even if you were Playmate of the Year? That would make you the only girl in the entire school who doesn't."

"You're not a freshman, then?" Honey asked, disappointed. If she were, it would be more likely that they would be friends.

"Fresh-man? I might be fresh but there are at least ten boys who'll testify to the fact that I'm no man. That's a joke though you're not laughing. Next time I'll do better. Actually, I *am* a freshman but I know most of these girls—we've all been on the same loop."

"Is being on the loop like being on the pill?"

The bouncy girl giggled. "Hey, *that's* funny, but being on the same loop simply means we've all gone to the same schools ever since we were little buggers. You know—the same play school, the same dancing school, the Good Preschool, Miss Way's Day School, etc. . . . Wherever our mothers thought was the right place for the right girl to be, we've all been there. And we're up to Beasley now. I recognized most of the girls even before I followed them through the door this morning. I probably can recognize almost every girl here *from* behind *by* her behind and the way she shakes it."

This time the two of them laughed together.

"Where did *you* go to school?"

"Beverly Hills. That's where we live. My father and I."

"I live in Bev Hills too. So, if you've always gone to school there, how come you're not going to Bev Hills High?"

"Well, my father went to Princeton, and now that it's gone co-ed he has his heart set on me going there too, and he thought that maybe if I went to a private school instead of Beverly Hills High I'd be more . . . well, *acceptable.*"

"*Acceptable!* That's a word my mother always uses. Mostly everything is *nonacceptable*, you understand, but I'm sure your father and my mother don't use the word in the same way. What does he do for a living?"

"He's a writer, F. Theodore Rosen. The *F* is for Franklin but I call him Teddy. He's a novelist and a screenwriter."

"That's neat. Do you know what my father does for a living *and* for fun? He sends people to jail! I'm serious. He's a judge. It's just that he really *enjoys* his work," and Honey laughed again.

"Anyway, I'm really glad your father sent you to Beasley because I just know we're going to be friends." She put down her cheeseburger to stick out her hand. "My name is Babette Lee Tracy, but everyone except my mother calls me Babe."

"I'm pleased to meet you, Babe."

"Just don't call me Babe in front of my mother or she'll have a primal-screaming fit. She thinks *Babe* sounds common. She's a Lee of the Virginia Lees who would fart Chanel Number Five if she farted at all, but she doesn't—she's too tight in the asshole department for that."

Honey didn't know if she was supposed to chuckle at that or what. "I'm Honoria L'Heureux Rosen, but I'm called Honey. And you can call me that in front of anybody, I guess."

*Even my mother, but that would be quite a trick since we don't exactly hang out together.*

"Oh, Honey's a great name for you! It fits you to a T. But Honoria? I never heard that name before. It's French, I gather, like the L'Heureux?"

"Yes. L'Heureux is my mother's family name."

"Oh, God! I *thought* you looked familiar! I mean, you look just like her! I should have known. All that gorgeous blond hair and those eyes. They're really the color of topazes. And those lashes out to there that I would gladly die for. Mimi L'Heureux *is* your mother?"

Honey blushed. "Yes . . ."

"Hey, you don't have to turn pink because your mother's a beautiful, sexy woman. My mother'd be a beautiful, sexy woman too except for one thing—she's never had sex in her life. I'm the original stork-delivered baby. I was dropped complete with a bundle of disposable diapers as part of my accessory kit! Honest! And even if Catherine did have sex just *once*, she did it with her eyes shut tight, and you know why? Because she didn't want to see my father enjoying himself."

Honey giggled. "What a thing to say about your mother."

"Oh, don't you worry about Catherine the Terrible. She can take care of herself. I'd match her against anybody's mother if it came to slugging it out. Only she'd do it with her pinky extended as if she were taking tea with the president, which, you understand, *is* her prime ambition.

"Anyway, I've seen a couple of your mother's old movies on late-night TV. When Catherine wasn't looking, natch. And I think your mom's super. Way sexier than Monroe ever was. But I haven't seen any *new* movies lately. Doesn't she act anymore?" Then, stricken, she added, "She's not dead, is she?"

"Oh, no, she's alive and well and living in Paris."

"Whew! I'm glad. I thought that maybe— Well, you *did* say you lived with your father and all. . . ."

"I know. It's just that my parents are divorced and I live with my father and *not* with my mother."

"Lucky you," a voice drawled. They looked up to see an extremely tall girl with bright-red hair licking at a spoonful of yogurt, but managing to do it elegantly. "I'm Samantha Grant and I'm a freshman, but don't ask me if I'm a Playmate or a Bunny because if another person asks me that I'll scream. *Boring!* And while I'm an Angeleno bred in the bone, I've always gone to schools in the East, so I don't know anyone here, and from what I've seen, I don't think I really want to." She sat down, crossing her long legs. "Tell you what I'm gonna do. I'm going to join you two for lunch today and, if you're very good and very careful, maybe even tomorrow."

Honey thought she'd never seen a girl as self-confident as this sophisticated Samantha and waited to see what Babe's reaction would be. Babe obliged, tinkling, "I'm Babe Tracy and my friend is Honey Rosen. But are we really supposed to call you Sa-*man*-tha? Now, my mother would gladly Sa-*man*-tha you to death, but if we're going to be eating lunch together, you'd better come up with something more informal or you'll have to call me Babette. Right, Honoria?"

"You may call me Sam," Sam said, green eyes glistening. "That's what my intimates call me. I'm named for my father, T. Samuel Grant, *the* T.S. Grant of Grantwood Studio."

"I think Sam's a lovely name," Honey said, and Babe enthusiastically agreed. "Absolutely. Sam's Jake with me."

"Good. Now that that's out of the way, how would you two like to join my club? It's called GAMS."

Babe giggled. "I'm game for GAMS. I've got the sexiest legs in the business."

"I'm sorry to say that GAMS doesn't stand for legs, sexy or otherwise. It stands for Girls Against Mothers."

Babe gave a shriek of joy. "That's groovy! I'll join, but you have to promise *not* to tell my mother."

"Who else belongs?" Honey asked.

"No one. It'll be just us three. Half the fun of belonging to a club is keeping other people out."

"Now that you mention it, I believe you're right," Babe agreed. "We'd be honored to join GAMS. Right, Honey?"

While Honey scarcely knew her mother and certainly had no reason to feel loyal, it still seemed like an act of betrayal to join a club whose main *raison d'être* was to be against her. But Babe and Sam were looking at her expectantly, waiting for her affirmative response, and she wanted them to be her friends. She just knew that if she said no to being a GAM, the two of *them* would be close friends and she would be left on the outside, looking in. "I don't know if I'm really *against* my mother. I've hardly ever seen her."

Sam shrugged. "So, what does that have to do with anything? I've never *ever* seen mine as I can remember."

"You haven't?" Honey was surprised. She had assumed that she herself was one of a tiny minority—children of divorce whose mothers *chose* not to have their children live with them.

"No. My mother—she was a debutante from Pasadena—died before my second birthday," Sam offered flatly, and her eyes were suddenly opaque.

"Oh, I'm sorry. But, then, how can you be against her?"

"Oh, it's not my mother I'm against, it's my *stepmother!* You know something? I think our meeting here at Beasley was preordained. Kismet! The second I saw you two sitting here I had this feeling deep inside that I had found true comrades in arms. Now all that GAMS stands for can be represented by just us three: you, Babe, who live with your real mother; you, Honey, who have a real mother you *don't* live with; and I, who live with my steppie, Nora, the Wicked Witch of the West."

"That's cute. Come on, Honey," Babe urged. "You heard Sam. It's Kismet! You've got to join. Okay?"

"Okay!" Honey blurted, and Babe got to her feet to do a quick-time step, ending up by throwing out both arms in an extravagant, all-encompassing gesture.

"Wonderful!" Sam said. "Now, put out your hand, Babe, palm up, and you put your hand over hers, Honey, palm down." After they complied, she put her hand over both of theirs. "Now, let's say it all together: 'Friends forever more . . .' "

They said the words in one voice just as the bell signifying the end of lunch hour rang out.

"Look, we've lots to do," Sam said, getting up. "We have to write a constitution—all the rules and bylaws and a Bill of Rights—so you'll both come home with me when Olaf comes to pick me up after school and you'll stay for dinner."

"But don't you have to ask your moth— I mean, your stepmother first?" Babe asked.

"God, no! It's my home as much it is hers, if not more. Besides, if Nora has *one* good quality it's that she loves company. It's part of the role she plays. The hostess with the mostest. She loves everyone to death . . . except me, of course." Then she added, "And probably not Hubie anymore."

"Hubie? Is that a man's name?" Babe asked.

"Yes, a *real* man's name."

"So, who's Hubie?" Babe asked as they left the lunchroom. "And why doesn't your stepmother love him anymore?"

"Because he loved *me*. But there's no time to get into that now. Now, don't forget, wait for me outside."

Babe chewed at her lip nervously. "I'll have to call my mother before I can definitely say whether I can make it or not. What about you, Honey? Do you have to get permission?"

"No, it will be fine with Teddy. I'll just call him later to tell him not to wait dinner for me."

"He must be really easy to get along with, just like my father," Sam said proudly. "Just wait till you meet him! You'll love him. Just watch out for Nora. She can charm the panties right off your butt, make you think she's mad for you, but before you know it she's taken away everything you love, including your very soul."

Honey and Sam exchanged glances. Sam *really* had a case against her stepmother.

Just before they split up in the hall, Honey asked, "Tell me, Sam, did you *really* have that feeling the minute you saw us that we were fated to be friends?"

Sam laughed so hard there were tears in her eyes. "You want to know the *real* truth? I looked over and saw you two—one cute, small, dark-haired chick and one medium-sized beautiful blonde—and I thought, add one gorgeous, tall redhead and what have you got? One dynamite trio—three enchanted princesses who'll make waves *wherever* they go with the guys standing in line to drool. But Grantwood Manor will be our home base because it's a magic kingdom."

Honey laughed at her nonsense, but then, after they went home with Sam, she both believed and disbelieved. Grantwood did *seem* like a magic kingdom, but she was convinced that Sam was all wrong about her stepmother. If she and Sam and Babe were the three princesses, then surely Nora Grant had to be the queen, and not a witch at all. At any rate, since she herself had a mother in name only, she would gladly take Nora as her stepmother. . . .

# FORTY-FOUR

———•◦•———

Two days after they'd visited at the manor, the girls got off
the school bus at the corner of Rodeo Drive and Charleville
in Beverly Hills. "That's our house down there—" Honey
pointed. "The pink Mediterranean with all the Australian ferns
and bougainvillea in front."

"Oh, it's so pretty," Sam cried enthusiastically.

"I think Teddy chose it because it reminded him of the
house in Saint-Tropez he and my mother lived in once."

"When you told me you lived in B.H. I had no idea you
meant the *south* side of Beverly Hills," Babe said as Honey fished
around in her big leather bag for her house key.

"I didn't know I was supposed to be so *specific*," she mumbled, flushing.

"Of course not. It's just that when you said you lived on
Rodeo I assumed you meant *North* Rodeo. I wasn't making a
crack because the north side's better than the south. Oh, I didn't
mean *better*. I meant—"

"More expensive?" Honey smiled faintly as she continued to
grope around in the bag for her key.

"I didn't mean that either. I just meant that certain people
*think* the south flats are less desirable but—"

"You'd better give it up before you get in any deeper, Babe,"
Sam chortled. "Besides, we understand. We know you can't
help being a snob," she teased. "After all, you are your mother's
daughter and, as they say, blood will tell."

"Just because my mother's a snob doesn't mean *I'm* one.
Besides, while we *are* north of Santa Monica Boulevard, we're
only in the eight-hundred block of Rexford at the corner of

Sunset, which is okay but not *as* good as being *north of Sunset*.
And we don't have a zillion acres in old Bel-Air like the aristocratic Grants.''

"I'd hardly call Nora an aristocrat. But *I*, who truly am one,
am not the one making snobby cracks. You are. Just listen to
yourself: *less desirable . . . north of Santa Monica . . . eight-hundred
block . . . north of Sunset . . .*''

"At least I don't go around telling everyone that my mother
was a debutante from Pasadena. Anyway, Catherine says
Pasadena is passé, that it no longer has social significance.''

"That's a hot one! Social significance! And how about your
mother being one of *the* Lees from old Virginny? If I recall my
history correctly, or at least my favorite movie—*Gone With the
Wind*—the dear old South *lost* that war. Now, that's what I call
*really* passé!''

"Will you two stop?" Honey begged. "You sound like two
alley cats and we're supposed to be best friends, remember?"
She gave up on trying to find her key and tipped back a stone
urn of pink geraniums to feel around for the house key hidden
there for emergencies. "I know you didn't mean anything by
what you said, Babe, and my feelings aren't hurt. And you, Sam,
stop teasing her. You're being mean.''

Still, as she threw the door open with a triumphant "Voilà!"
she drawled, "Welcome to the Rosens' humble abode, but keep
in mind, folks, that it's not all *that* humble. While it *is* in the less
desirable southern flats, it does have two and three-quarters
baths, including a marble bidet in the master, and it's only one
and a half blocks *south* of Wilshire, which, while not great, is not
*excruciatingly* déclassé either.''

She gave the chagrined Babe a swift kiss as they walked into
a foyer furnished only with a long Spanish table on which sat a
pottery bowl filled with an arrangement of simple garden flowers. There was a sense of tidy quiet in the dark room except for
a spill of mail on the burnished planked floor.

Honey gathered it up, explaining, "The mailman slips it
through the slot around noon, but by that time Teddy's at work
upstairs and forgotten that there's even a mailman. That's how
writers are when they're absorbed in their work—they forget

anything else exists," she said affectionately, but her attention was focused on shuffling through the mail.

"What are you looking for so hard?" Sam asked curiously. "Have you been holding out on us? Do you have a secret lover? A boyfriend in Vietnam?"

"If you must know, I'm looking to see if there are any checks here, but it doesn't look like it."

"Checks?" Babe was puzzled. "Who'd be sending *you* a check? Your mother?"

"No, not my mother, though I once got a hundred-franc note from her tucked between two sheets of stationery imprinted with her name, but not another word, although the pages *were* scented with Arpege. Occasionally she sends me a picture postcard from Biarritz or a Greek island or someplace like that; sometimes there's a card on my birthday and usually a present. There's *always* a present for Christmas. I guess it's hard to forget Christmas. . . ." her voice trailed off. "The present's usually something really lavish, like a huge bottle of ultra-expensive perfume that's sure to turn bad before I could possibly use it up. Once she sent me a satin negligee trimmed in marabou. That was the year I was eight, I think. When I was twelve, there was a pink plush elephant as tall as I was. I guess she just forgets from year to year how old I am." She shrugged. "I wouldn't be surprised if this year she sends me a walking cane or maybe even a wheelchair."

"Either that or a topless bikini," Babe suggested, trying for a laugh since Honey sounded so pathetic.

"Let's hope it's the bikini," Sam said cheerfully.

Honey placed the mail on the table, visibly disappointed, saying, "Nope, no checks. You have to understand that writers are forever rushing for the mail, hoping to find an unexpected check. Royalties on an old book or maybe an advance on a new edition or something." Still, she didn't explain why it was she and not her father who rushed to look for checks.

"You two go on into the living room while I go see if Teddy's still working. If he is I won't disturb him and you'll meet him later on."

She led them into a big curtainless room bathed in light

emanating from a skylight and a wall of glass overlooking a small jewel box of a garden. Though there was an austerity to the white room with its all-white slipcovers, there was also a warmth—in the terra-cotta floor tiles aged to a faded rose, the brightly rendered impressionist-style paintings hanging from the high ceiling, and the multicolored dust jackets of the books lying on tables in orderly stacks and lining the shelves of bookcases that formed a border around the room.

"What a super room!" Babe raved.

"It really is," Sam agreed, "though it's kind of a jolt coming from that dark room into this one."

"I know," Honey said. "That's the effect my father wanted. He says it's the way they do it in the Mediterranean. When you first come in from outside where the sun's hot and the light's blazing, you need a dark, cool room to calm and refresh the spirit, then you walk into another room awash with light to warm the soul. That's the way Teddy talks," she said proudly. "But you'll see for yourself. I'll be right back."

\* \* \*

She knocked on the closed door lightly, and when she didn't receive any response, she tiptoed in to find Teddy asleep on the daybed, his longish hair tousled, a few errant strands curling down over his boyish brow, a half-empty bottle of Scotch standing close by on the floor.

Her eyes darted to the old Smith Corona on the desk and some sheets of balled-up paper lying beside it. She could also see the photo partially sticking out from under the paper and didn't have to come any closer to see which picture it was. She knew. In the background there was the sea, and in the foreground, a young man in swim trunks with a sweet smile holding up a blond, laughing baby while a woman—her mass of blond hair whipped by the sea breeze, her body voluptuous even in a striped T and white sailor pants—sat on the sand looking up at them, her gaze inscrutable, lips set in a pout. On the back of the photo was written: "Malibu—1957."

Even though she'd pondered this photo at least a hundred

times, she wondered each time she looked at it what Mimi had been thinking. Was she wishing even then that she was free of the two people she was gazing at?

She covered Teddy with the mohair throw, then went down to tell Babe and Sam that he was deeply involved in the screenplay he was writing, which he'd promised to deliver the next day, and that if he got enough work done by dinnertime, he would join them since he was dying to meet her new friends.

\* \* \*

The girls sat at the yellow-tiled counter on white wooden stools while Honey set out cans of Coke and an orange bowl of blue corn chips and quickly mixed up a batch of guacamole. "We've an avocado tree out in back so we eat guacamole *a lot.*"

"It's yummy but I didn't know you could cook," Sam said, her mouth full.

"This is hardly what you'd call cooking, but I do cook a little. Teddy does most of it. He just got used to doing it, I guess. You know, after he and my mother split up."

"Didn't he have a housekeeper?"

"At first, I think."

"And you don't even have a maid now?" Babe was amazed. She looked at the gleaming tile floor, the shiny copper pans hanging from butcher's hooks over the polished black stove, the little pots of herbs lined up on sparkling glass shelves in front of the stained-glass window. "But everything's so clean! Everything's so perfect and neat and shining!"

Honey laughed. "Don't sound so shocked! What did you expect? A six-month layer of dust and piles of dirty dishes with cockroaches crawling all over? I bet everything at your house is neat and shining and you take it for granted."

"That's true, but my mother's middle name isn't *Immaculoso* for nothing. This woman needs resuscitation if she finds a piece of lint on the carpet, and she doesn't allow roses in the house because a petal might fall on the floor. And we have a cook and a full-time maid, not to mention the services of a professional cleaning crew that comes in to sterilize everything including the occupants every month or so.''

Encouraged by their laughter—Sam was inelegantly sputtering guacamole and corn chips—Babe warmed up. "And while *Señora Perfectionata* doesn't actually work, I have to say she *is* kept pretty busy interviewing the domestics. She *does* have a real problem with employee turnover. It's not everyone who's willing to kiss her feet first thing in the morning and her ring at noon, and it's awfully hard in this day of equality to find anyone willing to call her 'Mistress of the Universe' and the Judge 'Massa Tracy.' ''

Honey was laughing so hard she found it difficult to speak. "Well, we do have Mrs. McCarthy, who comes in every other week for half a day. And I help out a little. But Teddy does most of the work himself. He says it's good discipline and writers must have discipline, and that orderliness of surroundings is essential to promote an orderliness of the mind. But I think he's just naturally a neat person, and that my mother was *not*, and he just got in the habit of picking up after her. . . .''

She also had the impression that Teddy used his excessive housecleaning as an excuse to postpone facing his scary Smith Corona monster every day, but it would be a betrayal to tell Sam and Babe that, as it would if she disclosed her suspicion that when Teddy was scrubbing and scouring, he wasn't so much trying to eradicate dirt as the memories of past glories and broken dreams that haunted him.

Babe and Sam asked to see her bedroom, but she said they might disturb Teddy. Instead she showed them the rest of the downstairs—first the dining room with its bleached-pine floor, drenched like the living room in light and simply furnished with a pine table, matching hutch, and country French chairs with checked blue-and-white seat pads; and then the library, intensely dark with its drawn window hangings. She flicked on a lamp to reveal a room furnished with two book-laden armoires, bergères striped in green-and-white satin, a gray velvet sofa, and enameled boxes on a Napoleonic campaign table, along with bronzes and plants in porcelain cachepots. A television set was incongruously perched on a painted tea table embellished with gilt.

"I guess you'd call this our Parisian salon, though I really don't know what a Parisian salon looks like. All I know is that after my mother left to go back to France, my father bought this house and this is the stuff he brought with him from their old house in the Malibu Colony. There was a circle of French movie people and artists and writers living there, and my mother had a kind of salon—you know, all the French people hung out at their house, drank wine, and talked about how much they missed Paris. I don't like to ask Teddy too many questions about it because then he gets too sad. . . ."

Babe and Sam sat transfixed with big eyes until Babe asked, "But why *did* she go back to France?"

"Where else would she go if she was leaving? Besides, Teddy says she *hated* Hollywood. She said American directors didn't understand European actresses and they only wanted to exploit her sexuality and not her artistry."

"Too bad she didn't work for my father," Sam said. "I bet he'd have made a movie that would have pleased her."

"Not taking anything away from your father, Sam, I doubt that *anything* would have pleased her here."

Sam's eyes narrowed. "So, is *that* why she left? Because of her career? Because she didn't want to make movies here?"

"I'm not sure, but if that was the case, she wouldn't have had to leave *us*—Teddy and me—behind," Honey blurted angrily. "Don't you understand? He would have picked me up and followed her to the ends of the earth!"

"Really?" Babe's dark eyes gleamed. "But that's so romantic! Don't you think so, Sam?"

"You're incredible, Babe. How romantic can it be when obviously he *didn't* follow her. Why didn't he, Honey?"

"That's pretty obvious too. Because she didn't want him to! Because she didn't believe in husbands and daughters! Maybe she only believed in lovers. *Still* does. I saw a picture in a magazine a couple of months ago. Mimi at a Beaux Arts Ball in Paris, surrounded by all these *swains*, the magazine called them. But they were all so sleazy-looking and my father is so—" she groped for a word, "so *fine*. . . ."

She went over to the writing table in an alcove and picked up a photograph in a silver-filigreed frame. "This is a picture of my father when he graduated from Princeton."

"Wow!" Babe exclaimed. "I had no idea he was so handsome. He looks like a movie star himself."

"I think he looks like a poet," Sam pronounced. "And he does look like a fine person. Does he still look like this?"

"Of course. You'll see for yourself later." She picked up another photograph. "And this is he when he won the Pulitzer in Literature—the youngest person to win it ever!"

"*The* Pulitzer Prize?" Sam asked, incredulous.

"Of course, *the* Pulitzer Prize. How many do you think there are? He won it for his novel *In Celebration of Longing*. He won it the year after he graduated from Princeton, and the book won a load of other literary prizes too." She flipped open a big leather portfolio. "It's all here. All his reviews and interviews . . . everything. They called him the golden voice of his generation. Everyone predicted he'd win the Nobel before he was thirty-five."

"And did he?" Babe asked. "I don't exactly keep track."

Honey closed the portfolio. "No, he didn't."

"How come?" Babe looked as if she might cry.

"Really, Babe, that is a *very* dumb question," Sam said, but she looked as if she might cry too.

*   *   *

Honey came downstairs again to report that Teddy was still struggling at his typewriter. "He apologizes but he said we should go ahead with dinner without him. So, I'm just going to warm up the *coq au vin* that he prepared this morning."

"Not for me, Honey," Babe said dolefully. "I called my mother while you were upstairs. She says I can't stay for dinner because I was granted permission only to come over after school, and that now I was trying to take advantage. That if staying for dinner was what I had in mind all along, I should have said so but now it's too late."

"Couldn't you get her to change her mind?"

"Oh, no! My place is already set at the table," Babe said, as if *that* were an irreversible situation.

"How about you, Sam? You can stay, can't you?"

"Sure. Is your mother coming for you, Babe?"

"Oh, darn, we didn't discuss it. I guess she assumed one of Honey's parents would drive me home—"

"*One of my parents?* You didn't tell her that I lived just with my father?"

"Frankly, I didn't. I didn't say *anything*. I just let her assume whatever she assumed. I never told her your mother is that French actress who made all those sexy pictures either. All I said was that your father was a writer and that he went to Princeton; that was enough for her to overlook his major shortcoming—"

"What shortcoming?" Honey's voice shook. *That he drank?*

"That his name is Rosen," Babe said, ducking her head in embarrassment. "It's not that she *hates* Jews, exactly. She says that they have their place in the scheme of things, only their place isn't in her living room. I'm sorry."

"*You* don't have to be sorry. I understand. Neither of us exactly picked our mothers," Honey said softly.

Actually, she was relieved. If she had to choose between the two, she preferred that her father was scorned as a Jew rather than as a man who drank. Teddy had taught her to take pride in her Jewish heritage, and it mattered not at all how other people felt about that. But she couldn't bear for her wonderful father to be known as a man who had to find his solace in a bottle.

"But what am I going to do now? If I call her back and tell her I don't have a ride, she's going to make me give her all kinds of explanations and— Do you think that your father could possibly tear himself away for a few minutes to drive me home? It wouldn't take more than twenty minutes or so."

Honey was stricken. How could she explain that Teddy wasn't in condition to drive anyone?

Sam looked between Babe and Honey's equally agonized faces. "Oh, damn!" she said. "I just remembered. Daddy's bringing home someone for dinner—an actor who's in that new soap they're shooting in Palm Springs. He's thinking of casting him in a picture and he wants to know what I think of him—you know, his teenage sex-appeal quotient. So I have to go, after all. So I'll just call and have Nora send Olaf to pick me up, and then he can drop you off too, Babe."

"You know, Sam, if you weren't so snotty, I'd kiss you," Babe said, relieved.

"And if you weren't so snobby, Babe, I'd kiss you back."

Honey was so happy the problem was solved, she kissed them both.

# FORTY-FIVE

———— •••• ————

Babe shoved her Beasley Chicken Supreme aside.

"It *does* look gross," Sam agreed, nibbling at a spoonful of peach yogurt. "You really should know better. They dump chicken à la king straight out of the can, plunk a canned peach half on top, and present it as gourmet cooking à la Beasley. You should have stuck to your usual cheeseburger. There's not much they can do to ruin a thin slice of cheese on top of a skinny beef patty garnished with two limp slices of pickle, all slapped together on a soggy, stale bun."

"I didn't want to become a slave to habit. But it doesn't matter. In fact, I may never eat again."

"Okay, what's bothering you?" Sam demanded.

"Okay, I might as well get it over with. We *have* to go to my house after school today. I've delayed as long as possible, but Catherine insists on meeting *my little friends* and she's rearranging her schedule so she'll be free. So for once, Sam, don't give me a hard time and just say you'll go."

"I wouldn't dream of giving you a hard time. Specially since I've been *dying* to meet your mummy from the first day we met. I'll just let Olaf know he doesn't have to pick us up."

"Why do we have to go on the school bus? Olaf always picks us up when we go to your house."

"That's because I *never* take the school bus. The driver on the Bel-Air run wouldn't even recognize me. What diff does it make who drives us?"

"The diff is that it will impress Catherine if we arrive in a chauffeured Rolls, and we need all the help we can get with the impressions. When I told her who your father was she was not what you'd call thrilled. And she's *not crazy* about Nora already—they bumped into each other at some civic function, and she *knows* Nora's an active Democrat. If there's anyone she frowns on more than a *Jewish person* or a *movie person*, it's a *Democrat!*"

"Okay, if you think it makes me more acceptable to be the stepdaughter of a Democrat if I ride in a chauffeured Rolls, we'll go with the Rolls. And if you like, I'll personally disavow the whole Democratic party. Will that help?"

"Oh, stop being such a smart-ass. This isn't funny. If she gets a bug up her butt about you two, that's it. Finis!"

"I see." Sam sighed heavily. "Do you think it would help if I told her how many Oscars Daddy's flicks have won?"

"Uh-uh. The movie business, you know. Déclassé."

"And it won't help that my mother was a real, live—well once she *was* alive—debutante from Pasadena?"

"No, we've already discussed that, remember? Passé."

"Well, in that case I'll just have to fall back on being my natural self and hope that she'll be impressed by my charm, intelligence, and good breeding."

"No! The *last* thing you want to do is act your natural self. Are you trying to sabotage the effort? Seriously, you know what I think you should emphasize? Grantwood Manor. Talk about how grand it is, how large a property, how Nora imported most of the antiques from England, and how you have that golf course and the reproduction of the pro shop at St. Andrew's. Anything that even *smells* of being landed gentry or of riding to the hounds, of being to the manor born. Oh, before I forget!" she cried. "Try not to say anything about either your mother or the divorce, Honey. And don't call me Babe in front of her. Try to remember my name is Babette!"

"We'll do our best," Honey vowed, and Sam said, "Try and relax. If it gets too bad we *do* have an out—we can always kill ourselves, right?"

Babe nodded in relief. "Right. You're absolutely right."

*  *  *

"You know, I think your mother got her states mixed up," Sam crowed as they walked up the driveway.

"What are you driveling about now?" Babe asked nervously.

"This house is Tara personified and Tara was in Georgia, and I thought you Lees were supposed to be from Virgin-i-ay."

"Really, you're *so* ignorant, Sam. If you *must* know, the style of this house is Late Georgian, an architectural statement that's found throughout the *entire* Southeast. And I wish you'd watch what you say. She might hear you."

"From out here?"

"She's probably listening at the window."

Sam looked up at all the windows. "I don't see anybody."

"That goes to show what you know. Catherine is *always* watching and listening, even when she isn't. . . ."

A maid answered the door since Babe, not deemed responsible enough for the privilege, didn't own a house key. "Your mother's waiting in the morning room," she told Babe.

"Don't get uptight that we're on the way to the morning room. It's spelled like the first part of the day, not like the state you're in when someone dies. All it really is is the same room other people call a sunroom or maybe the den. You know, the room where you entertain guests you don't want to bother messing up the living room for."

"I guess that tells us how we rate with quality folk like your mom," Sam said. "It also reinforces what I've always known about Nora—that she really *is* riffraff. She'd mess up our living room for just about anybody, whether it's the president—well, probably not Nixon—or the Mexican gardener if he has something he wants to talk over."

"Do you realize that you just said something *nice* about Nora?" Honey laughed.

Sam was stunned. "I guess I did at that. Well, I'll just have to watch my step so that I don't do *that* again!"

"Sh!" Babe shushed her abruptly. "We're here," and she ushered them into a room conventionally attractive in pastels.

Then a surprisingly young, pretty, and incredibly slender (as Babe had told them, her mother *was* a disciplined size four, which meant a willingness to embrace starvation) Catherine Tracy rose to greet them, and she was smiling though Babe had given the impression that that was something she never did.

"How nice, finally, to meet Babette's new friends." Her dark, bright eyes moved from Sam to Honey and back again, giving the impression of a high-powered, double-lensed, fast-speed camera recording pictures meant to last a lifetime.

"It's a pleasure to meet *you*," Honey said.

"Oh, yes," Sam said quickly, "a real pleasure." She was determined to be as sweet as Honey.

"Well, Babette? We're waiting—" Catherine smiled.

Sam and Honey looked quickly at Babe, who seemed to have lost a couple of inches from her original five feet nothing. But Babe was at a loss. "Waiting for what?"

"Perhaps if you think about it, it will come to you." Catherine was still smiling, but there was steel in her voice.

"Oh, Christ!" Sam muttered under her breath, and Catherine turned the burning spotlight of her eyes directly on her.

"Did you say something?"

"Oh, no, something's caught in my throat." She made a big show of trying to clear it.

Catherine's eyes turned back to Babe and, laughing sourly, she said: "I suppose I must tell you, then, Babette, if you have so forgotten your manners. We were waiting for a proper introduction, isn't that so, girls?"

Sam and Honey kind of smiled while Babe mumbled, "But you said you were glad to meet them and they said they were glad to meet you. Isn't that an introduction?"

Catherine shook her head in dismay. "My, my, what will your friends think? That Judge Tracy's daughter doesn't know that a proper introduction means an exchange of *names?*"

"But they *know* your name. They know you're my mother and that my name is Tracy and so is yours. And you know *their* names because I told you about them—"

The smile was gone. "I think that it's time for you to make a decision, Babette. Do you wish to *argue* or do you wish to

make the proper introductions? We're waiting for your decision. . . ." She began to tap her foot.

Honey silently prayed that Babe would comply and get it
over with and Sam silently prayed that Babe would tell Catherine to go fuck herself. After a few more moments, Honey's
prayer was answered as Babe mumbled: "Sam, Honey, I'd like
you to meet my mother, Mrs. Tracy."

Honey immediately stuck out her hand, then Sam followed
suit. But Catherine did not extend hers. "That's not *quite* right.
You gave no indication which young lady is Sam and which is
Honey, and one always introduces a person by using their family
name as well as their Christian. And the same rule applies to me.
It should have been: 'I'd like you to meet my mother, *Catherine
Tracy*,' relying on their judgment to address me as *Mrs.* Tracy."

"I don't *believe* this—" Sam burst out.

Catherine's gaze focused in on Sam. "Can't believe what, my
dear?" Her tone was icy enough to freeze the blood, and Sam
looked at Honey, whose eyes pled with hers to be *good*, and then
at Babe, whose eyes just begged . . . *period.*

"I can't believe that Babe—I mean Babette—doesn't know
how to make an introduction properly. But I really don't think
it's her fault, Mrs. Tracy. I believe that the responsibility lies
with the schools we've attended."

It was a quick recovery, but now Sam was warmed to her
task. "I know that *my* parents—my father, T. S. Grant, and, of
more recent date, my stepmother, Nora Grant—my poor
mother who made her debut at the Pasadena Grand Assembly
having passed away when I was only a baby—have always sent
me to the best of schools. Before Beasley, I went to a fine school
in the East, you know, and they relied on these schools to teach
me at least the *basics* of proper etiquette, but unhappily"—
she threw her hands up— "they've failed us all."

Towering over the tiny Catherine, Sam reflected how she
could probably floor the bitch with one left hook. But she
smiled ingratiatingly. "It's really too bad that we don't have
women like yourself working in the private-school system. I'm
sure if we did, girls like us would surely know more about
proper social techniques and—"

"Quite . . ." Catherine cut her off frigidly, dispelling any notion Sam might have had that she was successfully snowing her. "Now shall we sit and have some refreshments? I know how ravenous teenagers are when they come home from school. Babette, will you please advise Hilda that she may serve?"

"On the intercom?" Babe asked, frightened now of committing another *faux pas*. Even in her wildest imagination she hadn't visualized this nightmare.

"Of course, on the intercom! What did you think I had in mind? For you to go into the hall and *bellow* like a foghorn?"

"No, I—" She buzzed the kitchen, and when the cook answered, she said, "May I speak to Hilda, please?"

"For heaven's sake, Babette! '*May I speak to Hilda, please?*'" Catherine imitated her cruelly. "Will you just tell her to tell Hilda to bring in the tray?"

"Yes, ma'am," Babe said quickly, then corrected herself. "I mean, yes, Mother." But it was too late and Catherine turned to Honey and Sam. "I have told Babette that only servants and tradespeople use the term *ma'am* as a form of address, unless, of course, one is addressing the queen."

Out of nervousness Honey almost said, "Yes, ma'am," but she was cut off in the nick of time by Sam, who gave a little cry of discovery. "Oh, my! It just came to me who you look exactly like, Mrs. Tracy! Nancy! Nancy Reagan!"

"You mean the governor's wife?"

*Who do you think I mean—the fat lady in the circus?* "You could be her twin, but, of course, you're much younger."

"Well, as a matter of fact, I am," Catherine beamed. "By several years—at least ten. But I'm flattered. She's actually a great friend. We often have lunch when she flies down from Sacramento for her weekly appointment with her manicurist here in Beverly Hills. Poor thing! She says it's impossible to get a decent manicure in our state capital, which is a sorry state of affairs. Oh, yes, we've been friends for years. Actually, the Judge and I had a lot to do with Ronnie being elected governor. We worked hard to help get him there. How astute of you to notice the resemblance."

"And that dress you're wearing. It's so much Mrs. Reagan's

style. I bet it was you who advised her what to wear when she was hitting the campaign trail."

"Well, yes, I must admit I did, Sa-man-tha," Catherine admitted. "Such a pretty name. I can't imagine what your stepmother is thinking of allowing you to be called Sam."

Here we go again, Sam thought. Was there no end to the toadying necessary to satisfy this bitch? Then she remembered what Babe had told her to say about Nora.

"Well, Nora's British, you know. And she *was* married to landed gentry who rode to the hounds and always lived in very grand houses, as grand as Grantwood Manor, which, while Nora may have some weird political beliefs, she has decorated very tastefully with fine English antiques. But you know how it is— these old landed gentry think differently than we, the descendants of fine old *American* families, do. Personally speaking, I myself am fourth-generation native Californian, and when I say native, I *don't* mean native *Indians*. And Babette has told us how you're descended from General Lee! Wow, I can't tell you how much that impresses me. And I can't tell you how I cried at the sight of all those gallant Confederate boys lying on the ground by the thousands in that railroad-depot scene in *Gone With the Wind*. Really, I cried at that even more than I did when Rhett told Scarlett that frankly, he didn't give a—well, you know— damn."

When Catherine's laugh tinkled out pleasantly, Sam leaned back, satisfied that she had won not only the day but the war.

\* \* \*

"Did you ever?" Sam gasped once she and Honey were on their way home in the Rolls in a state of hysterical laughter.

"I could have *died* when you said we'd stay for dinner."

"Did you think I was going to leave without seeing the Judge? But I thought I'd pee in my pants when you addressed him as 'Your Honor, the Judge, sir.' "

"I almost threw in 'Your Highness' for good measure."

"Well, now that we've met Catherine and His Honor the Pompous Bore, all that remains is to meet *your* father, Honey."

"I know. He was so sorry that he wasn't able to at least say hello when you were over, but he promised that next time he's not only going to spend a lot of time with us but he'll prepare his specialty—*Biftek hache à la Lyonnaise.*"

"It sounds wonderfully French."

Honey laughed. "It's only ground beef with onions and herbs. Teddy says it's the herbs that make the difference."

"Do you think we'll ever get to meet your mother?"

Honey sat very still. "It's not likely."

"I know! When we graduate the three of us will take a trip to Europe—a continental adventure where we'll each have sex with at least one man from each country! But first stop, Paris and Mimi L'Heureux!" She gripped Honey's hand. "At the least she deserves to see what she's been missing, and she's going to be one miserable lady when she does!"

"How do you know she'll be miserable?"

"Oh, Honey, how can she help it? You're the sweetest, and isn't that exactly what I told Catherine the Asshole when she inquired why you're called Honey when your name is Honoria? Because you're as sweet as bee's honey, and don't you ever forget it no matter who else does. . . ."

# FORTY-SIX

———— ◦•◦• ————

S am had been talking about the Grants' Christmas Eve party for weeks, and now that it was only a few days away, she was more excited about it than ever, going nonstop:

"Even I must admit Nora really knows how to throw a groovy party. She says it all starts with the guest list. First you invite a few brilliant people, but only a few because if you have too many geniuses the other guests feel like dorks and get uptight and tight people make for a dull evening. Besides, geniuses are mostly egotists who monopolize the conversation. But once you have your Einsteins, you invite *tons* of famous people because the guests who aren't famous only know they're at a great party if they can tell other people they rubbed kneesies with Mick Jagger."

"Who wants to rub *kneesies* with Mick?" Babe giggled. "I can think of better things to rub and it rhymes with *Mick*. But are you absolutely *positive* he's coming?"

"Not *positive*. I was just using him as an example. Nora says the idea in inviting a load of celebs is that out of all the ones you *do*, only half accept because the other half won't admit they're free—they'd rather stay home playing with themselves than let on they're not busy jet-setting around. And then, out of the ones who accept, only half actually show because it's a power trip not to. But *all* of Hollywood's 'A' list is coming, including Liz Taylor. She adores Nora for reasons I cannot fathom. Maybe it's because they're both English and/or have been married a zillion times. And Nora's hired completely outside help for the night so that all our regular staff can enjoy the party as guests."

"Oh, that's really nice of her—" Honey interrupted.

"But she's *not* doing it out of *kindness*—it's because that's how things are done in merry old England. She says that everyone who lives and works on the estate comes to the manor house for a big party on Christmas Eve with presents for everyone. And there *will* be presents for everyone, but what does she care how she spends my father's money as long as it's not her own? And who would she be in this town without him? A nobody! And where would she *throw* her parties if she didn't have *our* house to throw them in?

"But wait till you hear what's on the menu—oysters on the half-shell plus those big, fat oysters from Oregon that they dip in batter and fry. Lushy. And since everyone loves *smoked* salmon so much—you know, *lox*, the kind you get at Nate 'n' Al's—there's going to be pounds of that too. And tons of caviar. The caterers are going to set up a station where they're going to make blinis right on the spot, but that's only the beginning. There's going to be roast beef and turkey plus roast goose since, I suppose, that's Englishy for Christmas and Nora makes sure to always remind everyone how English she is. I guess that's why she invited the whole colony of Brits—Roger Moore and Sean Connery—"

"Yikes!" Babe practically swooned. "I *adore* Sean Connery! He's the sexiest! But I still don't understand why you're so excited about this party. Sure, it sounds great, but you're always having big parties at Grantwood."

"Because it's *Christmas Eve*! Every year, as long as I can remember, I've been away at school or other girls' homes. This is the first time I've been home for Christmas in years."

She burst into tears and Honey was shocked. Sam just wasn't the crying kind. "Oh, Sam, what is it?"

"It's just that sometimes I miss my mother so!"

Honey was silent—she knew what Sam meant. But Babe said, "How can you miss a mother you never knew?"

"I always miss *not* knowing her, but especially at Christmas. All those Christmases I wasn't even home. If my mother had been alive, I would have been." Then she burst out in a fresh torrent of weeping, gasping, "Hubie . . ."

"What about him?" Babe asked.

"I'll tell you what about him! I begged Nora to let him come home for Christmas, but she won't even talk about it."

"She must have her reasons," Honey offered. "Besides, it's not like he's a child. He's a grown man."

"So what?" Sam sniffled. "He's still *her* child."

*   *   *

The party was only hours away, but Honey was still trying to talk Teddy into going to the party with her instead of just dropping her off and going back home to be alone.

"No, sweetheart, you go and have a wonderful time and don't worry about me. I'll be just fine."

"But *why* won't you go? You're invited."

"Yes, and it was very nice of the Grants to include me in their invitation, but they're your friends, baby, not mine."

"But they all want you to come. Sam says she adores you and that after her father, you're the sweetest man she knows. And Nora said she's dying to meet you, that she read *In Celebration of Longing* and loved it so much that even after she finished reading it, she couldn't get it out of her mind."

He smiled his gently ironic smile. "And did she say that she read *Night's End* too and couldn't get *it* out of her mind?"

"No," Honey admitted reluctantly. "If she did read it, she didn't mention it. . . ." She dropped her eyes, unable to bear the pain she saw in his. She knew that, even now, years after, he still mourned the publication of his second novel, which had died at the hands of the critics. Possibly he mourned its demise as much as he mourned the loss of Mimi.

"But what's the real reason you won't go? Is it because you're afraid you won't know anyone there? You don't have to worry—there's going to be over five hundred guests, most of them movie people. And Nora's invited some literary people from the East, and there's going to be guests from Europe, maybe from Paris. You're *bound* to know *some* people there!"

"Maybe that's the problem, too many people I've known too well." He smiled sadly. "People who'd rather run from me than talk to me. They're afraid that what ails me is contagious and maybe they're right—maybe failure *is* catching." Then he obviously regretted his words, knowing that they hurt her. He tried to laugh it off. "Just a poor joke."

But it was he who had told her that words, once spoken, were irretrievable. "When you put them down on a page, they can be crossed out, erased, eradicated with that little bottle of white stuff, but when you speak the words *out loud* to someone else—someone you care about very much—you can't take them back no matter what. No matter how sorry you are, no matter how hard you ask to be forgiven, no matter how strongly the other person says they've already forgotten them, they're indelibly there, imprinted on the brain forever. . . ."

She had wondered at the time whose words he was thinking of—his or Mimi's—or even if his theory was sound. Now she knew it was because she doubted that she would ever forget what he had just said or the pictures he'd conjured up . . . people running from him in horror.

She certainly couldn't continue to urge him to go to the party, where he might be shunned. Now it would be hard enough for *her* to go to the party and not look at each guest and wonder if he or she were one of the people who would dodge Teddy as if he were the bearer of a killing disease—her sweet father, who was their better by far, every last one of them.

\*   \*   \*

When she came downstairs in a black off-the-shoulder jersey, Honey thought Teddy might say that she was exposing too much shoulder, but all he said was that she looked very beautiful, though he did have a question: "Aren't you a bit young to be wearing black to a party?"

"Sam said my best colors are black and white. But for real glamour and sophistication, I should wear black, especially for a party, when I want to look my most dangerous."

"And tonight you want to look your most dangerous? I don't think I like the sound of that."

Though she knew he was joking, she also knew he dreaded the time she would start dating. *Because it would mean that she was growing up, or did it have to do with Mimi?* Was he afraid that she would be like her mother, a hot number, a woman men took one look at and, as Sam said, immediately took dick in hand?

But if that were the case, he had nothing to worry about. The last thing she wanted was to be a woman who provoked sexy images and leery jokes. She wasn't even eager to date. For that matter, neither was Sam, even though she talked about sex a lot, as if she were an expert on the subject. Actually, only Babe was eager to date and really interested in sex, which was ironic considering that Catherine was, as Babe proclaimed, not only the original ice cube to come out of a freezer but the original virgin they'd named the state after.

"I don't think I'll be in any danger tonight. Most of the men there will be too old for me to even talk to—I wouldn't even know what to say to them."

"Well, good. There's only one thing you *should* say to them—*no!* If you remember that, you'll do just fine."

She knew he was just teasing, but she laughed tearfully, feeling suddenly emotional and strange—as if she were swelling up with the love she felt for him. "I'll remember, Teddy. I'll never do anything that will make you unhappy."

"No, don't promise me that, Honey. Promise me only that you'll never do anything that will make *you* unhappy. . . ."

"But they're one and the same."

He smoothed the silky hair that fell to her waist. "You think so now, but you won't always."

"What am I to do, then?" she asked mournfully.

"You must follow your heart."

"But what if I follow *my* heart and break yours?"

He thought about it. *Is he thinking about Mimi?* "You'll still have to follow your heart wherever it leads you."

*But he had done that, and look where it had led him. . . .*

"Well, ready to go?" he asked, suddenly edgy.

"I'll call Babe to be ready. We're picking her up."

"Hop to it, then, while I get the car out of the garage."

She wondered why his mood had changed. Because their conversation had made him melancholy? She knew he hadn't had a drink all day so that he would be sure to be in condition to drive her, just as—except for that first time—he made sure to be in perfect condition to talk to her friends on the days they came over, and to drive them home if necessary. She guessed now that he was in a hurry so that once he dropped her off, he could rush back to start his own private celebration. . . .

\* \* \*

When Babe answered the door, she whispered urgently, *"They* want to meet your father. Can you ask him to come in?"

Honey looked anxiously at her father sitting in the car. To ask him to meet the Tracys with his nerves already jangly was really a bit much. "But we'll be late."

"It'll just take a minute. Honey, please! It's bad enough I can only stay at the party for a couple of hours, and she's *insisting!* She'll be offended if he doesn't and—"

"Oh, let her be offended. I'm sick— Oh, God, Babe, he's not even dressed. He's not wearing a jacket—just jeans and a sweat-shirt, and then she'll say something about that too."

"Please, Honey!" Babe was practically jumping up and down in her anxiety.

But then Teddy was standing in the doorway. "Is there a problem, ladies?"

"Well, yes, there is, Mr. Rosen. My mother and father are *dying* to meet you, but Honey says there's no time. But my mother will be *so* disappointed and—please, Mr. Rosen!"

Teddy put his arm around Honey. "It will be all right, sweet-heart. It won't make a bit of difference if you get to the party a few minutes late. At these big parties people come and go at all hours and no one knows the difference."

His chin was set resolutely—heroically, she thought—and his soft brown eyes reassured her.

\* \* \*

A half hour later both Tracys saw them to the door. Catherine said, "I'm so glad that we had this occasion to chat," and the Judge harrumphed, "Indeed," and Teddy said, "It's been my pleasure," managing to sound as if he meant it.

Then Catherine said, "I'll remind you again, Babette, that you're not to drink any wine or eggnog with spirits in it and that the cab I'm sending for you will be at the door at ten sharp, so you just make sure you're there, ready and waiting."

Once they were in the car, Babe said, "You were *so* super, Mr. Rosen, thank you!"

Teddy laughed. "That's a dubious compliment. Did you think I *wouldn't* be, and what did I do that was *so* super?"

"Well, my mother does have that way of interrogating people, sort of like in this movie I saw on TV with the gestapo asking these frightened Jews a lot of questions."

Honey could see Teddy's hands tighten on the wheel. Still, he said, "It's okay. Parents *should* be concerned about the people whose homes their kids visit. It only shows how precious they think you are and I can understand that."

"You always put things so beautifully, Mr. Rosen. I just wish—" She sighed heavily.

But it wasn't the questions about Teddy's Jewishness that had set Honey's heart to racing but those about his career. What right did the nosy Catherine and the Judge think they had to do *that?* They really were insufferable. Teddy would have been right if he had just told them both to go to hell.

But he hadn't. He hadn't even accepted the Judge's offer of a drink. All he'd done was answer all their questions in his soft and sincere way, a complete gentleman, which should have shamed them both but didn't, since the Judge wasn't a gentleman and Catherine was no gentlewoman.

"You know, I could just kill myself that I can only stay at this party till ten. Sam says Mick Jagger's coming, and Paul Newman! Do you believe that, Mr. Rosen? That they're *really* coming to the party?"

Though Honey laughed, Teddy didn't. "I'm sorry, Babe, but I can't answer that one. It's been my experience that you can never tell about these things . . . about who will and who won't . . . really come to the party. . . ."

\* \* \*

Sam, in bright-green taffeta, came running over the minute they stepped into the hall, which had the biggest Christmas tree they'd ever seen, its branches hung with gold balls and silver stars reaching to the vaulted ceiling.

"Where have you two been?" Sam accused. "The party began almost an hour ago and I hate to tell you this, Babe, but Mick Jagger has already come and gone. . . ."

"Oh, no!" Then, "Are you telling the truth, Sam, or are you just being mean?"

"Of course I'm telling the truth! Do you think I would tell a lie or be mean on Christmas Eve? Really!"

"I think I'm going to kill myself right now!"

"Well, don't do it here. People are coming and going and we don't want them to get the wrong idea. If you want to kill yourself, you'd better go upstairs."

"Look," Babe said, squirming out of her coat and handing it to the waiting maid. "I've only got two hours so let's get rolling. I can talk to you two any old time. Where do I stick these presents and where's the food and where's the dancing, and, above all, where's all the hot celebs?"

"You put the presents under the Christmas tree in the living room," Sam said as if she were talking to a small child. "And you'll find the buffet in the dining room, where you'd *expect* to, with several bars set up throughout the house just in case it's of interest." She rolled her eyes. "And the dancing is in the conservatory, where the two bands are alternating. As for stars, you'll just have to take your chances going from room to room. They're all over. And if you're lucky, maybe you'll even find a couple of them upstairs making out." She giggled. "Oh, and in case it turns you on, I just saw Henry Kissinger in the library."

"Kissinger? Catherine will never believe this! Maybe I should call her and let her know and then maybe she'll let me stay an extra hour." She thought it over. "No, I guess not, so I might as well not waste what little time I do have."

"Also, there's mistletoe hanging over every doorway. As a matter of fact, I kissed Mick under the mistletoe right there!" Sam gloated, pointing to an archway.

Babe went pale. "But why didn't you tell us right away, the minute we walked in?"

"I didn't want to break your heart."

"Did you take him by surprise?"

"Kinda."

"So, what did he do?"

"He kissed me back."

Then Babe was off and running, with Sam and Honey frantically running after her, trying to keep up, pushing through the assorted groups, dodging waiters balancing silver trays of champagne and waitresses offering canapés.

"Babe, you maniac, what do you think you're doing?" Sam shouted at her back.

"Trying to make up for lost time!"

When Babe grabbed a glass of champagne off a waiter's tray as it crossed her path on her way to the dining room, Honey blanched. "Oh, God, what will Catherine say? She forbade her to even taste eggnog."

"She can't say *anything* if she doesn't know, silly, and who's going to tell her?"

"She's sure to have one of those machines that test your breath at the front door. We have to make sure she doesn't take another glass!"

Then Honey was stopped by a couple conversing in a mixture of French and English who demanded to know if she was related to the French actress Mimi L'Heureux. When Honey admitted it, they practically detained her by force and called over some of their friends to take a look at Mimi's *baby*.

"*Some* baby!" seemed to be the consensus.

By the time Honey got away, she'd lost sight of Sam and Babe. But then she was stopped again. This time it was Sam's father who drew her into an animated group, introducing her as Teddy Rosen's beautiful daughter. One man, looking pointedly at her breasts, said she was indeed a beauty. A woman thin to the point of emaciation snickered and another man smirked. "I know old Teddy. What's he up to these days, Honeychile?''

When Honey replied that he was working on both a screen-play *and* a new novel, the man snickered and the woman smirked. Honey could feel her face glowing with heat. She wanted to toss off a clever retort that would wipe the smirks off their faces, but she couldn't think of anything. She looked to T.S. to say *something. Even though he doesn't actually know Teddy, couldn't he say, "He's a brilliant writer," or words to that effect?* But he kept silent, chewing on a cigar.

Then Nora came rushing up to give Honey a big hug. She took a quick look at Honey's flushed face and another at the faces surrounding them and chirped, "Has everyone met our Honey? You all must have heard of her father, F. Theodore Rosen, the novelist? He writes such beautiful books. And why wouldn't he? He's an absolutely beautiful man."

Honey wanted to kiss her. *How did she do it?* Sam was right—she *was* a witch . . . but one of the good kind.

"Run along now, Honey, and have some *real* fun instead of hanging around these fuddy-duddies," Nora suggested. "I saw Babe and Sam boogieing up a storm in the conservatory."

Honey flashed her an appreciative look and mumbled a "Nice to meet you" to the others, unable to suppress her instinct to say the well-bred thing even though she wanted to. Then she spent most of the next two hours trying to keep track of the time for Babe, who seemed to have forgotten it completely.

\*   \*   \*

After a couple of turns around the floor slow-dancing with a tall, dark, and suave older man who held her very tightly—so tightly she could feel his *thing* pounding away at her belly, she being that much shorter—Babe wasn't much turned on. All that was going to happen was that he was going to come in his BVDs, and she would be left no better off than she'd been before. Besides, he wasn't really the type she liked. She liked them more muscular and more hip, and younger, rougher, and tougher for sure—like the bartender who had told her that if she weren't underage, he would make her a drink that would send her into the next world. Maybe she would go back and try to convince him that she was older than she looked. . . .

\* \* \*

Honey went in search of Sam, whom she found in the library delivering a heated monologue about the sorry state of the art of filmmaking in the Soviet Union to a middle-aged man who seemed more interested in trailing his fingers across her nearly bare back than in Soviet films.

"I can't find Babe," Honey wailed, "and the cab her mother's sending for her will be here soon!"

"Oh, shoot! I think I saw her go to the powder room about twenty minutes ago. Do you think she's still there throwing up or something? She did have an awful lot of lobster thermidor when I talked to her last, and she had *two* more glasses of champagne."

"Why did you let her?"

"What did you expect me to do, wrestle her to the ground? We'd better go check on her." Slapping the man's hand away, she jumped to her feet and snapped, "Dirty old man," and he muttered, "Cock-teasing bitch!"

\* \* \*

Sam pounded on the locked door while Honey called, "Babe, are you in there? Your taxi is going to be here any second!"

They heard Babe muttering and mumbling.

"Babe, what's going on in there?" Honey asked, and Sam commanded, "Unlock this door this minute!"

"Who do you think you are giving orders around here—my mother?" Babe yelled back. Then there was complete silence.

"Babe, you'd better come out this minute or your mother's going to kill you!" Honey implored, and Sam threatened, "If you don't open this door, I'm calling somebody to break it down!"

"Oh, all right!" There were a few seconds more of silence

and then sounds of someone fumbling around with the lock, and then they were astonished to hear a distinctly male voice cursing under his breath.

*   *   *

"I could understand if it was Warren Beatty, but one of the guys from behind the bar? That has to be the tackiest thing I ever heard of; you deserve any punishment the Judge doles out," Sam lectured as she and Honey buttoned Babe into her coat. "Would you tell me *what* you were doing in there?"

"That's for me to know and you to find out," Babe said with a smirk just before she threw up.

Honey moaned and Sam said, "I'd better go get Nora to clean up this mess one way or another."

*   *   *

Nora explained to Catherine that there seemed to be something wrong with the lobster thermidor—several people had been taken ill. They'd put Babette to bed in Sam's room and called the doctor, who said she would be fine by morning. "So I thought that if it's agreeable with you, we could just let her sleep and take her home first thing tomorrow."

Catherine could hardly say no.

Nora suggested that Honey sleep over too, so Honey called Teddy, but when, after seven or eight rings, he still didn't pick up, she knew she *had* to go home to see if he was okay.

"No answer. I guess he went out. He told me he might and told me to take a cab in case I didn't get him in."

"So you'll call him later and tell him you're sleeping over. He won't mind, right?" Sam said matter-of-factly.

"No, I think I'd better go home now. He'll worry if he walks in and doesn't find me there. So I'll just call a cab like he told me to."

"No," Nora said. "I don't want you taking a cab to an empty house at this hour. It's not a good idea."

"But I don't want to bother Olaf. He's a guest tonight."

"We're not going to bother Olaf. I'll drive you home."

"But you can't leave your party."

"I won't be gone long, and this party will get along fine without me for a while. Besides, I can use the fresh air. And I'll let you in on a little secret. The real fun of a party is *before* the party—in the anticipation. . . ."

"Always?" Honey asked, disappointed.

"Of course not *always*. Sometimes you get lucky and the party is even better."

\* \* \*

"Thanks so much for the ride." Honey was ready to bolt out the car door, her house key already gripped in her hand, but Nora said, "Wait, I'll go in with you in case your father's not home yet so that you don't walk in alone."

"Oh, there's no need," Honey said hurriedly. "See, some of the lights are on. He must be home now."

"But doesn't he leave a few lights on when he goes out?" Nora got out of the car. "I'll just check. It will only take a second and *I'll* feel much better."

Honey opened the door and called out, "Daddy?" Oh, if he would only answer, she prayed. Then Nora would be satisfied and leave without coming in. But there was no answer.

"Maybe he's home and just fell asleep in the library, reading or something. . . ." She could only hope that if Teddy had passed out, it was in some noncompromising position.

But just as she was reaching for the knob, the library door opened and Teddy blinked to see them standing there. "I thought I heard you come in," he said, appearing only a *little* confused. "And this must be the wonderful Nora of whom an angel sings."

"Daddy!" Honey protested, embarrassed.

"But you have *not* damned her with faint praise, Honey."

Nora laughed, offering her hand. "Yes, I'm Nora Grant. I'm pleased to meet you, Mr. Rosen."

Teddy smiled his sweet smile, the smile that could break your heart, Honey thought, when he looked so young and boy-

ish. "You must call me Teddy. And you shouldn't have bothered Mrs. Grant, Honey, to drive you home. You should have
called—"

"Oh, no bother," Nora said. "I was glad to get away for a bit
and I'm glad we had this opportunity to meet. But now I'd best
be getting back. I hope we get to know you better, Teddy. Will
you come to dinner with Honey sometime soon?"

"I'd be delighted," he said, and she said, "Good. I'll ring
you, then. Good night."

Teddy made a sweeping bow. "Good night, fair lady, and a
Merry Christmas to one and all. . . ."

# FORTY-SEVEN

———— •▪•◂ ————

When Honey and Babe stepped off the school bus, Sam was eagerly waiting for them in the parking lot. "Guess what *I* have? A half-lid of the *really* good stuff," she whispered.

"What good stuff?" Honey asked before turning away to talk with a girl from her French class, but Babe chirped, "A half-lid! Wow! How good is this good stuff?"

"Keep it down! *Acapulco Gold!* I got it from Roberto. He's one of the tree cutters that's working at the manor this week. He said it's every bit as good as *Panama Red!*"

"*Panama Red!* I guarantee you this tree snipper never *saw* Panama Red much less smoked it," Babe scoffed loudly.

"Sh! How do you know he never smoked it?"

"Because there's no such thing. Kids rap about it as if it were a mythical experience, but when you pin them down, it's never *they* who smoked it but somebody else. It's a fantasy potheads dream about. But Acapulco Gold's great. Where's it stashed?"

"In my purse."

"Oh, my God! You're carrying the dope in your purse? Are you crazy?" Babe screeched. "Suppose it *falls out?* They'll throw *you* out of school and Catherine would never let me talk to you again. You should have left it at home. We could have smoked it after school. But since you *didn't* and you *do* have it with you, when do we go for it?"

\* \* \*

"Okay, Sam, let's see the color of your grass," Babe demanded as they hunkered down on the cement floor in back of the furnace in the utility room, which was safe—the janitorial staff took their lunch break at noon too. "Since we're short on time you'd better roll just one joint."

"Yes, one will be plenty." Honey was as nervous about smoking dope for the first time as she was about being caught.

"Of course we're going to roll only one joint! Did you think we were going to blow the whole bag in one sitting?" Sam sputtered, taking out a packet of rolling paper, a plastic sack, and a small box of wooden matches. "This shit didn't come cheap. You have no idea what I had to do to get it."

"Oh?" Babe smirked. "You mean no cash changed hands?"

"No, but then, there is *no* such thing as a free lunch."

"Oh, Sam, you didn't—" Honey began, but Sam said, "You don't want to know, Honey. Suffice to say that Roberto has this nasty-looking wart on the tip of his—"

Honey covered her ears. "I *don't* want to know."

"I was going to say—*nose*. Okay, who's rolling?"

"I've *never* rolled a joint," Honey said in a rush.

"Didn't they teach you anything at that school you went to? At Devon's they had a course in the refinements of modern living, and the first refinement was how to do drugs with panache. But here—" She shoved the bag and papers at Babe. "Since you're the eager beaver, you do the honors."

"That's okay." Babe pushed them back. "The honor should be yours since you earned it by doing things that would turn a weaker sister queasy and *you* know how to do it with panache."

"Well, to tell the truth, I never *did* get the hang of it," Sam confessed. "I always bought my dope by the stick. Loose joints, as they say in the East."

"Or is it that you're really chicken, Sa-*man*-tha?"

"Me? I'm the one who sacrificed my all to get it!"

"If we postpone it we'll still have time to go have some yogurt or something," Honey urged hopefully.

"No," Babe said resolutely, "we're going to do it *now* even if Sam won't admit that she never rolled a joint in her entire life and probably never smoked one, either."

Sam made a halfhearted protest while Babe shook out a little of the pot on a sheet of paper, then recklessly dumped the entire contents of the bag. "Will you look at *that?*"

Sam stared at the marijuana. "What about it?"

"Take a look at this shit. Obviously you never saw any before. *Shit* is what it is! It's at least *half* seed and stems! Whatever you did to get it, you grossly overpaid."

"No, I didn't! Mostly I just let that crud touch me but no place important, and when he took his own cruddy joint out of his cruddy jeans I insisted he put it back immediately."

"Well, let's just hope that out of this mess we'll be able to make a few cruddy joints of our own," Babe said as she quickly rolled one, lit up, took a deep drag, and inhaled sharply before passing it to Sam, who did exactly what Babe did before passing it to Honey, who gingerly took a puff, then inhaled for so long she grew dizzy and thought that she might pass out.

"Easy does it," Babe said, and they repeated the process until they were down to a tiny, sticky roach, which Babe wrapped in a tissue. "We'll save it for another time when we have a toothpick handy," she said, and began to roll a fresh joint, murmuring, "Nice and fat this time," though Sam, more *numb* than high, said, "Why don't we save some thrills for another day?" and Honey, feeling extremely nauseated, agreed.

"Don't be silly. You two are just green but you'll see! The more you smoke the better it gets."

*   *   *

"We only smoked three joints between us, which comes down to only one a piece, so if we share one more that's only one and a third each." Babe merrily began to roll a fourth when the bell rang, signaling that lunch hour was over.

"Oh, damn, isn't that inopportune?" Sam greeted the bell with relief as Honey staggered to her feet.

But more inopportune was the appearance of Dean Perkins, who was escorting several members of Beasley's board of directors to see for themselves how seriously antiquated the furnace was and how desperately the school needed a new one.

\*     \*     \*

Even before the dean dismissed them pending a decision on whether they were going to be expelled or merely suspended—certainly the next infraction of the rules would bring *instant* expulsion—letters were on their way to their parents via the Hollywood Star Messenger Service.

"God, if this had happened at any other school I would have had at least a day before Catherine got the fucking letter," Babe moaned. "Maybe I should just kill myself now."

"You can come home with me," Honey offered. "Teddy probably won't even answer the door when they deliver the letter, then the messenger will slip the letter through the slot and I'll probably see it before Teddy does. I'll be able to prepare him for the shock before I give it to him to read."

"You'll get it before he does and you'll *still* let him read it?" Babe demanded. "Are you crazy?"

"I *have* to let him see it. Otherwise, it would be like cheating. But it'll be all right even if he reads it before we get there. He won't yell. The most he'll do is tell us a story that has a moral to it."

"Better still, come home with me," Sam urged. "Nora's in New York doing an interview with Gloria Steinem for this new magazine called M*s*. For some dumb reason they think Nora's some kind of positive feminist figure because of her causes and her politics and stuff, which is ridiculous. She's done nothing but live off men her whole life. And my father won't even bother to open the stupid letter. He didn't get to own a major studio by wasting his valuable time."

"No, I better go home and face the music. I only hope the music that's playing isn't 'She's a Lady.' Catherine gets really worked up about me *not* being a lady, and she's not going to look on this as very ladylike behavior. But just in case dear old Dad decides to send me to a home for delinquent girls, you'll be sure to visit, won't you?"

Honey and Sam promised that they would, though they doubted things would go that far. Then they offered to go home with her to be there when Catherine confronted her, but Babe shook her head. "It would only make things worse. . . ."

*　*　*

The next morning Sam was waiting in the parking lot to catch Honey and Babe as they got off the bus, but only Honey was on it. "Where's Babe?" she demanded, frightened.

"I don't know. She didn't get on at her stop. And last night I kept calling but the maid kept saying she wasn't home. I kept calling you too, but your line was always busy."

"I kept calling Babe too, that's why. And I got the same rap with the maid until finally I got the *Judge*. He said that Babe was *incommunicado* and I wasn't to call again."

"Incommunicado? But what does that mean?"

"It means you can't communicate with a person."

"I *know* the word. I mean, what do you think it means as far as Babe's concerned?"

"I don't know. You don't think they *already* sent her to that home for delinquents, do you?"

"I don't think so. Even *they* wouldn't be *that* mean. . . . *Would* they? Besides, it wouldn't happen that fast, *would* it?"

"I guess it's possible," Sam said dolefully. "Who knows what that woman's capable of. Even Nora, who bumps into her now and then, thinks she's a woman of mystery. You know that bull she feeds Babe about her being one of the aristocratic Lees of Virginia? It just ain't so. She doesn't come from Virginia at all. She actually comes from Memphis, Tennessee."

"Nora told you that?" Honey was astonished.

"No, but I overheard her telling it to one of her friends from some committee or other. I forgot to tell you."

"How could you forget a thing like that?"

"It slipped my mind, all right? But do you believe it?"

"Nora wouldn't say it unless it was true."

"I guess this time you're right. Anyway, Nora told this woman that the info was to be considered confidential—if Catherine chose to be a Lee from Virginia, that was her biz."

"But why would Catherine *tell* a lie like that?"

"If you wanted to cover your tracks, would you go around advertising where you're really from?"

"I guess not. But why did she pick Virginia?"

"Well, if you're a Southerner making up a place you're from and you wanted to present yourself in a fancy light, why *not* a Lee from Virginia? And give poor Babe just one more thing she has to live up to. . . ."

"I guess. But I don't think we should say anything to Babe about this. She'll be upset. I know I'd be to find out that my father lied to me about something, wouldn't you?"

"I sure would. Okay, we won't say anything. But wouldn't you die to know Catherine's *real* story? I wonder how much *more* Nora knows about her. Actually, I wouldn't put it past her to keep a complete dossier on Catherine."

"A dossier—a *file?* On Babe's mother? You've said a lot of crazy things about Nora but that's the craziest yet."

"It's *not.* Both Nora and the Tracys are involved in politics but on opposite sides. Why, the Tracys are practically Birchers and Nora's very big with the Democrats. And that's how politics work—each side tries to get dirt on the other. Besides, judges *always* know where the bodies are buried, so Judge Tracy probably has his share of dossiers too. I wouldn't be the least surprised if he has one on Nora. . . ."

\*   \*   \*

At lunchtime they weren't hungry and sat dispiritedly on the front steps of the school wondering what to do about Babe when suddenly Honey jumped to her feet. "Look! At the curb! It's Catherine's Mercedes and Babe's getting out!"

She started down the steps, but Sam pulled her back. "Wait until Catherine leaves." But Catherine got out of the car too and Sam muttered, "Arrogant bitch. She's leaving her car in the street instead of in the lot like everyone else.''

"I guess she's going to see Dean Perkins. Poor Babe! Do you think we should say hello to Catherine as if everything was normal before we speak to Babe?'' Honey whispered.

But before they could utter a word, Catherine, wearing a muted-gray suit and matching inch-heeled pumps, sailed right past them with Babe silently shuffling behind her, eyes glued to the ground, while Sam inaudibly mumbled, "Catch you later.''

\* \* \*

Babe looked nervously around the locker room as if there were spies everywhere. When a door banged shut, she jumped as if she'd been shot. "I'm not supposed to talk to you two at all,'' she whispered. "Catherine told Dean Perkins that you're both a bad influence, that you've been raised in a permissive environment which she and the Judge disavow, and that she expects the school to enforce her no-speaking rule during school hours, including lunch hour, even if Dean Perkins has to assign a teacher to do nothing else but watch us.''

Honey's eyes filled but Sam was enraged. "What is this? The Russian Secret Police? And you're going to submit?''

"Oh, Sam, get real, it's that or getting transferred to another school or some kind of place for bad girls.''

"But you're *not* a bad girl,'' Honey cried.

Babe smiled grimly. "Tell it to the Judge.''

\* \* \*

Honey and Sam sat on the floor in Sam's room seeking consolation in barely unfrozen Sara Lee fudge brownies. "So, what *did* your father say when you showed him the letter?''

"He said exactly what I expected,'' Honey sighed. "Or rather, he told me a story with a moral to it.''

"What was the story?'' Sam asked through a mouthful of brownie so cold it hurt her teeth.

"He told me how his mother caught him smoking when he was fourteen—he was in a playground with a bunch of friends.

She yelled at him right there in front of them, which humiliated him, then dragged him to the grocery store and bought him a box of Marlboros and made him smoke over half the pack until he was sick. Then she tossed him the rest, telling him to let her know when 'the big smoker' needed more so that she could buy them for him just like she bought him milk or orange juice. She thought that by shaming him and letting him get sick, he'd never smoke again. But he kept on smoking and never stopped, even though it makes him cough. He says it doesn't even taste good anymore."

"That's the *whole* story? What was its point?"

"It's pretty clear. That once you have an addiction it's stronger than almost anything and it doesn't matter what other people do or say or even what you tell yourself. If you don't *want* to have an addiction, don't acquire the taste. I'm sure he wasn't only talking about smoking cigarettes or even dope, but all drugs and whatever else is bad for you."

*Like alcohol and women like Mimi . . . They're his addictions worse than any tobacco habit could ever be. . . .*

"That's pretty neat, that all you got was a story."

"But he has to meet with Dean Perkins and, you know, make it okay with her, and I feel bad that I've placed him in that position. But I wish someone could talk to Catherine and make it okay with her so Babe can be friends with us again. But what happened with you? Did your father say anything?"

"No. He never read the letter. It was with the rest of the mail and he never looked at it. But Nora's coming home from New York late this afternoon and she'll read it and I'm sure she'll be delighted to make a big deal out of it just for the pleasure of it. And my father isn't coming home to dinner and that means it will be just the two of us unless you stay. You will, won't you? In the meantime, should I go down and get another cake out of the freezer? I think I saw a Sara Lee cherry-cheese hiding out beneath a box of cauliflower. . . ."

\* \* \*

Nora sat them both down in the library. "Before we sit down to dinner there's something I want to get out of the way. I read the letter from Dean Perkins but I'm not going to lecture you. Besides, I'm sure your father has already discussed it with you, Honey. As for you, Sam, if I tell you that smoking pot is *not* a good idea and *not* to do it again, you're not going to listen to me anyway, so I won't bother. But I will say that smoking it at school was an incredibly *stupid* thing to do and if you're smart, you won't do that again. At least that's what I will tell Dean Perkins. And now that I've had my say and *not* that I think you girls really deserve a present, as I've already dragged them back from New York I might as well hand them out. Since the women at *Ms.* told me that no matter how liberated a girl might be, she still loves gorgeous undies that come in a Bloomie's shopping bag, that's what I've brought—teddies for the three of you. By the way, where *is* Babe? No, don't tell me. Her mother has grounded her. I really can't say as I blame her."

With that, Honey burst into tears.

"Now, come on, it can't be all that bad."

"But it is! Babe can't *ever* speak to us again!"

*　*　*

Babe bit into her cheeseburger with great gusto. "I don't know what Nora said or how she did it, but after she left our house last night they called me down and told me that after much thought and soul-searching they decided that their previous decision was a bit harsh and so they were going to give me, as well as you two, a second chance to demonstrate that our friendship is not detrimental to my character, health, and general well-being."

"It's a miracle!" Honey declared. "And you don't know what Nora said to make them change their mind?"

"No, but I thought maybe you two might."

Honey shook her head, but Sam looked like the cat that had swallowed the canary and Babe asked: "Do *you* know, Sam?"

"No, she didn't tell me anything and I don't know *what* she said. But I think I know *how* she did it. Blackmail."

Babe started to choke on her hamburger. "Blackmail? My mother and father, of all people?"

Sam looked smug. "Laugh if you like, but remember what we talked about yesterday, Honey?"

"What did you two talk about yesterday?"

"Dossiers," Honey said. "Sam said that probably Nora has a dossier on your mother."

Babe whooped. "That's the funniest thing I ever heard! But if it's true, I'd *kill* to see it."

# FORTY-EIGHT

———— ••• ————

Two weeks before the annual fall mixer—an event at which the Downey School's boys joined Beasley's girls for dancing and punch—the girls were hanging out in Sam's room listening to Janis Joplin when Babe suddenly jumped up to turn off the record player. "I have an announcement to make. My parents have been asked to chaperone at the dance."

"And they accepted?" Sam asked incredulously.

"Of course! They love a chance to supervise other people, and when it's slow-dancing time they'll probably walk around with rulers measuring the distance between bellies."

"Well, if Catherine's going, I'm not," Sam said flatly. "But I wasn't crazy to go anyway. Who really wants to mix it up with that bunch of doofuses? Between the zits and the sweaty palms, who needs those dwarfs and gooks? What about you, Honey? Are you going to submit to this *added* torture?"

"I don't care either way. I'll do whatever you two do."

"Wait a minute," Babe cried. "If my parents are going, I don't have a choice, and if I have to go and you two *won't*, then you really suck and I'll—"

"What?" Sam scoffed. "Kill yourself?"

"No, that wouldn't be punishment enough to pay you back. But I very well might consider resigning from the GAMS."

"Oh, no, say it isn't true," Honey begged, and Sam said, "If you promise not to resign I'll do *anything*. I'll kiss Catherine's you-know-what and even dance with the Judge."

Babe smiled smugly. "I knew you'd both go."

"How come?"

"Because that's what being a best friend means. Doing the best for your friend even if it means doing the worst thing you can think of. . . . And when you have two best friends, well—doubles on the worst!"

But the night before the mixer, Babe called Sam to scream, "There's good news tonight! My mother has the flu. She can't go tomorrow night."

"That *is* good news. I can think of only one thing bet—"

"I hope you weren't going to say that the only thing better would be if she never recovered. She *is* my mother."

"Really, Babe, I wouldn't *say* it. I *was* going to say that the only thing better would be if your father wasn't going either."

"He *isn't*! He said it was clear where his duty lay—home with Mother."

"What dedication! And to Catherine of all people!"

"Well, I better go now and see if she wants a cup of tea since my father fired the maid for insubordination and the cook is acting up. She says she's tired of doing all the fucking work around here. Now, if the czarina was on her feet she'd give that serf a taste of the whip, but in the meantime Father says we must do our part to keep Mother comfortable."

"Did you stop to think, Babe, that this might be your big chance? Now that Catherine is at her weakest, you *could* take advantage. You could hose her down with ice water or take away her blankets and tell her as she's shivering that you're only doing it for her own good—to lower her temperature."

"I *have* thought of torturing her a little, but then I thought about what would happen once she got better. Oops, I think I hear her calling in that weak little voice. Hold on one minute while I check." She held the phone a few inches from her mouth: "Yas'm, Miz Tracy, ah's acomin' and ma head is bended low. You heard it, Sam, and away I go."

An hour later, Sam called Babe back. "I thought you'd want to know. The school called to ask if Nora and Daddy would chaperone tomorrow night."

"That would be cool. At least they're lots of fun."

"So Nora is, but Daddy can't. He's going out of town."

* * *

Teddy hung up the phone to tell Honey, "That was Nora."

"Oh? Did she invite you to dinner again? I hope this time you accepted. The Grants don't bite, you know."

Teddy laughed. "I didn't think they did. At least, I didn't think *Nora* did," and Honey wondered if that meant he thought that T.S. did. Then she wondered if T.S. was the reason he never accepted Nora's invitations to dinner.

"But no, she *didn't* invite me to dinner but she did ask me to be her fellow chaperone at the big shindig tonight."

"And you said yes?" She was surprised. "How come?"

"Because she presented her offer in terms I couldn't refuse. She asked me to come as a special favor to her, to keep her company as she faces a 'fate worse than death'—a roomful of rocking teenagers and the Beasley faculty. Only I promised not to quote her on that so you can't repeat it."

"I won't. And I think it was really nice of you, Teddy, to go just to help her out." She also thought it was nice of Nora to ask him, suspecting it was a ploy on Nora's part to try to draw him out of the house . . . out of himself.

* * *

Sitting on one of the gold leatherette chairs lining the walls of the gym, Sam refused all offers to dance. Honey, sitting next to her, also said, "No, thank you," to all comers, thinking she should keep Sam company since Babe, the most popular girl there, hadn't missed a dance all night.

"It's not hard to figure out Babe's popularity with the boys," Sam said. "She's the only girl here who's shorter than they are."

"She's also the best dancer. And you didn't *have* to wear those high heels. You did it to make *sure* you'd be taller than every boy here so you'd have an excuse not to dance."

"So what's *your* excuse?"

"I'm sitting here to keep you company."

"No, Honey, that's only what you're telling yourself. I think the truth is that we *both* don't fit in. Me because I'm too mature, and you because you're afraid.''

"Afraid of *these* boys?''

"No, you're afraid of being popular. Any other girl with your looks would be setting all these little boys on fire just for the fun of it, but you hang back. You always hang back when a boy so much as looks at you. Look how you acted last week in the Hamlet when those boys from UCLA tried to pick us up. Babe was practically ready to crawl under the table with any one of them, but you acted like you had turned to stone.''

"And what about you?'' Honey was defensive. "You weren't exactly friendly. You were definitely snotty.''

"But I *reacted*. I was being *provocative* and I got off some really fabulous cracks and I threw my hair around a lot.''

"Okay, Ms. Psychologist, why do you think I'm afraid to be popular?'' While Honey was annoyed, she was also piqued.

"I'd say you're afraid to turn out like your mother.''

Honey was upset but she said, "I'll have to think about that. And you—do *you* want to be like *your* mother?''

"We were talking about *you*, not me.'' Sam was visibly agitated and Honey was sorry she'd asked. The only comment Sam ever made about her mother was to say she was a debutante from Pasadena every once in a while—the remark that was guaranteed to drive Babe crazy.

But now Sam said, "No, I don't want to be like my mother. Why would I? She died practically before she ever lived.''

Honey asked softly, "What did she die of? You never said.''

"What do you think she died of? From being seriously ill. She certainly didn't die from old age. But my father's the one who really suffered. It took him a long time to get over it. He didn't marry for a long time until he let the ex-countess get her claws into him, and just look at her now.'' She pointed to Nora dancing by with Teddy, she animatedly talking as he smiled down at her. "Looks like she's charming him completely, doesn't it? Even though she's *years* older than he is. She's utterly shameless.''

"Sam! All she did was ask my father to come tonight since he's a parent too, and she's not *that* much older.''

She'd been feeling so happy that her father had come and that he was looking so beautiful in his dark suit and white shirt with his longish yellow hair curling down over his collar. He hadn't taken one drink today—not so you could tell anyway—which proved that he really didn't have to. And no matter what Sam said, she wasn't going to let it spoil her pleasure that he was here.

"Of course," Sam said, "it doesn't hurt any that he's so good-looking and brainy too, does it? But not to worry, Honey. He's not rich enough for her to make him number five, or is it six? I never know whether to count Hubie's father."

Honey stared at her in disbelief. "You really are out of your skull. And now, if you don't want to dance and you refuse to even talk to anyone, let's at least get some punch."

Sam made a face. "Why? It's only unspiked pink piss straight out of the can, and if we turn it down all week long at school, why should we drink it tonight?"

Honey thought about it for a while. "Maybe because it's the only drink in town and we're thirsty?"

*   *   *

When they were ready to leave they couldn't find Babe. Both Teddy and Nora were upset, feeling that somehow they'd been derelict in their duty.

"Don't worry," Sam said, rolling her eyes. "We'll find her, won't we, Honey? We know just where to look."

After they pounded on the door of the girls' room in the basement for nearly five minutes, Babe finally emerged with a boy shorter than she by at least two inches and Sam drawled, "Really, Babe! You're going to have to curb yourself of this fixation for males and bathrooms before it becomes an addiction—one you'll never be able to break. *Then* what will you do for the rest of your life?"

# FORTY-NINE

———— ◦•◦ ————

As soon as the date for the Beasley Spring Follies was announced—an event in which every sophomore was expected to take part as a performer or in some facet of production—Sam volunteered to be its executive producer and appointed Babe and Honey her associate producers.

Babe immediately wanted to know if the term *associate* was movie-talk for assistant to the big cheese, and Sam told her that she was quite willing for her to pick her own title. "But it's multiple choice—choose one: subordinate, junior, gofer, or stooge."

Sam then talked a reluctant Honey into doing a dramatic presentation from Shakespeare since Honey *was* considering pursuing a career as a serious actress. "How are you ever going to perform on the legitimate stage if you don't get over this shyness of yours?"

"And what's the big-cheese producer going to do by way of entertaining us?" Babe asked good-naturedly enough.

"Really, Babe, as *executive* producer I can't possibly be expected do anything else. After all, does my father act in his own movies? But I do have the most terrific idea for how we can best utilize *your* talents for singing and dancing. I'm thinking of a big musical number as a finale—the kind of number they used to do in the forties' movies à la Garland and Rooney. You know the kind of act I mean, like when all the kids in the neighborhood get together and someone shouts, 'Come on, gang, let's put on a show!' and suddenly there's swing music playing and everyone starts jumping and singing and dancing. It could be a really big production number with the whole cast jitterbugging! What do you think?"

"I think it's not *le idea hot*, or, if you prefer, I think the idea sucks," Babe stated unenthusiastically.

"Well, I think *your* reaction sucks, especially since I only thought up the idea to showcase *your* talent."

Babe was contrite. "I appreciate that. But this is only a crummy school show and you're talking *Garland* and *Rooney* and *finale* and *showcase*. The trouble with you is that you think of everything in terms of movies. Can't you think of anything else? Like boys, for instance. Here my mother's given me permission to start dating if the boys are the right kind, and you two won't cooperate by triple-dating with me."

"No, I *don't* have boys on my mind, Miss Teenybopper of 1972," Sam huffed wearily. "*I'm* not boy crazy."

"Let's get back to the Follies," Honey said quickly before things really heated up. "Babe's right about the big production numbers, Sam. It's way beyond us. It would take hours of rehearsal, coordinating costumes, choreographing. We should just have solo numbers, and if you like we can have a simple finale with everyone in the show onstage singing a tune that everyone can carry without a problem and without a million rehearsals."

"Very well," Sam said coldly, "I'll accede to the majority opinion. And since you have no interest in being a real star, Babe, what *do* you want to do by way of an act? Will you do one of your silly tap dances and *call* it modern jazz or do you want to do a gymnastic routine?"

"Neither and I don't want to sing either. I want to do a comedy routine. You know, stand up and tell jokes. . . ."

\* \* \*

It was the girls' obligatory once-a-week afternoon at the Tracys, which Catherine insisted on so that she could "touch base" with the girls and know "where their heads were at." But they were dedicated to keeping their heads inviolate, and usually they made sure to cover every surface with textbooks and loose-leafs so that no matter how often she popped in on them they were ready to cease all normal conversation to be found immersed in their schoolwork. But today they didn't bother with the usual subterfuge since they were working on a legitimate school project—the Follies.

First, they had a run-through of Honey's Portia from *The Merchant of Venice*, which left her friends fairly speechless: "God, you're a natural!"

Honey, pleased but blushing, sat down on the floor next to Sam. "Are you sure you don't have *any* suggestions? Do you think I should use my hands more?"

"We'll see, but now I think we'd better check out Babe's routine, see if she's come up with some material that's more original than what we heard before."

"Excuse me," Babe said, getting to her feet, "but *I'm* the original, the one and only—Babe Lee Tracy!" She took a few steps to simulate running out onstage and rubbed her hands together. "Good evening, ladies and germs—"

"Babe, that's *lame!* Now, start over and why are you rubbing your hands together?"

"I've been watching the comics on Johnny Carson. They *all* rub their hands together."

"But what does it *mean?* Every gesture is supposed to *mean* something."

"Who says? This is comedy I'm doing, not method acting."

"Good. In that case, why don't you try being funny?"

"Oh, *that's* very funny." She started over. "Good evening, ladies and gentlemen *and* members of the faculty—"

This time Sam giggled. "I like *that!*"

"A funny thing happened to me on the way here tonight. A guy came up to me and said, 'I haven't had a bite in three days,' so I bit him! Then he said, 'Will you give me ten dollars for a cup of coffee?' so I said, 'But a cup of coffee is only fifty cents,' and he said, 'I know, but I need nine-fifty for the valet parking.'"

Encouraged by Sam and Honey's laughing, Babe really warmed up: "I have an aunt who got a phone call from her husband, which isn't unusual except that he died a few months ago. She said, 'Edgar, I can't believe it's you,' and he said, 'It's true, Harriet. I've come back!' And she asked, 'You mean you've been reincarnated?' and he said, 'Yes, and I'm in a real nice place with a lot of cows. One of them is really lovely!' Then she asked, '*Where* is this nice place?' and he said, 'I don't know, but this cow—*she's gorgeous!*' Exasperated, she said, 'But Edgar, why do you keep on talking about a dumb cow?' and he said, 'I don't think you understand, Harriet. I've come back as a *bull!*' "

The three of them were convulsed with laughter until they heard: "What, may I ask, is going on here?" They snapped to attention to see Catherine standing in the doorway, eyes boring, lips compressed.

"We're wor—working on the Follies," Babe stammered.

"If you're working on the Follies, why were you telling that disgustingly vulgar story?"

Babe looked to Sam and Honey for help and Honey quickly said, "Oh, that was just a— We weren't really going to *use* it. Were we, Sam?"

"No. We wouldn't dream of using it. Someone told Babette that dumb joke and she just wanted us to hear it—she had no intention of using it in her comedy routine. I mean, she wouldn't tell a vulgar joke like that. . . ."

"*What* routine?"

"The routine I'm doing for the Follies," Babe blurted.

"I'm just going to pretend you never said that, Babette. Young ladies of good breeding do *not* do comedy routines for school productions and that's my final word on the subject."

Sam recognized a final word when she heard one, and she threw an apologetic look at Babe before saying, "Those are my sentiments exactly, Mrs. Tracy, especially since Babe . . . Babette . . . is such a great dancer and terrific at gymnastics. No one else in school is the whiz she is at gymnastics—"

"Yes, she could do gymnastics or dance," Honey said quickly. "Or she could sing . . . something uh . . . classical."

"No!" Babe said between clenched teeth. "I don't sing *classical.* I've never sung classical in my life. And if—"

"That will do, Babette. And watch your tone of voice. If you're to perform at all in what appears to be turning into a circus, you will play the piano since your father has provided you with lessons for some eight years from which he's never derived one moment's pleasure."

"I'm *not* going to play the piano! I hate playing the piano and you can't make me!"

Honey gasped and Sam opened her mouth to say something, then shut it again.

"Oh, I think you will, because you will either play the piano or you will not take part in the Follies *at all*, which also means no behind-the-scenes participation. But don't make a hasty decision. Talk it over with your friends by all means. You can let me know what you decide by this evening."

She left the room, and once she was gone, Babe put her ear to the door to hear if she was truly walking away before she turned back to Sam and Honey. "I'm going to say this only once—I am *not* going to play the piano, and if you're my friends you won't say *one* word urging me to. And you *won't* quit the show as a gesture of support either. Gestures suck!"

*   *   *

Honey and Sam were deeply depressed—it was their first rehearsal in the school auditorium without Babe.

"Did you speak to Nora about her talking to Catherine?" Honey asked.

"Yeah, but she said she couldn't *meddle* in a matter like this. She said it was *absurd*."

"But she made Catherine change her mind about letting Babe be friends with us again."

"Don't you think I reminded her? But all I got was a lecture. She said being involved in politics had taught her a lesson—that sometimes you pushed and sometimes you held back. That not everything was worth pushing for because if you pushed too often, you had nothing left to push with for the bigger battles. And she said that since Babe was making an issue of choosing *not* to be in the show as a matter of principle—taking a stand— no one had a right to mix in."

"I guess that makes sense," Honey said thoughtfully.

"Maybe it *would* if Babe could keep on doing it—standing up for herself—but she can't. Catherine and the Judge are just too strong for her and she's too scared of them. You know that. Still, I *did* learn something from my chat with Nora even if I didn't get anywhere with her. Remember when I said that Nora must have a dossier on Catherine or at least have the goods on her? Well, now I know it! After our talk was over and I was already walking away, she said something that convinced me I was right. She said, 'Anyway, you don't use a cannon to squash a mosquito.' Now, think about what *that* must mean. *That she's got a cannon.*"

* * *

It was an hour before showtime, but Honey was already anxiously peeking from behind the stage curtain at the empty auditorium while Sam stood behind her. "Nobody's here yet."

"It's too early. Besides, who cares? Once Babe wasn't in on it, it stopped being fun."

"I know, but you've done a wonderful job, Sam. Everyone says so. Even Dean Perkins."

"Well, who cares what *she* thinks? I only care what my father thinks and he isn't even going to be here! I just found out this morning. He had to fly to Yugoslavia—one of his dumb prima donnas is acting up and slowing up production."

"I guess that has to come first. You always say that, Sam—that making movies is *important* and always comes first. What about Nora? Will she be back in time to come tonight?"

"Who cares if *she* comes? Besides, she won't. She's too busy stomping for McGovern's nomination to be bothered with a school production. With Nora, *politics* come first."

"Well, no matter who comes you did a great job and you should be proud of yourself. I know *I'm* proud of you."

"You ain't doing so bad yourself, kid. You're going to knock them right out of their socks. And you look mighty fetching in that white chiffon dress. Where'd you get it?"

"It's my . . . my mother's. There's a trunk of stuff she left behind. It was always padlocked, so I never saw what was inside.

But when I told Teddy that I was going to do Portia, he . . . well, he went and took this dress out of the trunk. He said I would be as beautiful as my mother—"

"I've got news for you, Honey Bunch. You've already left your mother in the dust. Sure, she's sexy, but you're sexy too, and in addition, you have something even better."

"Yes?" Honey was sure Sam was going to say something like inner beauty, a special radiance, or even just a great personality. "What do I have that's better?"

"*Me* as a best friend!"

\* \* \*

A half hour before curtain time the auditorium was filling up and there was no sign of Teddy, and Honey was almost in tears. She'd asked him to come early so that he would be sure to get a good seat up front, but now she wondered if he was going to show up at all.

Sam, frantically rushing about and issuing orders, caught her peering out into the audience again. "Look, Honey, don't I have enough to worry about without you popping up at that damn curtain every two minutes? He'll be here! Would *your* father miss your first public appearance?"

*He might if all the memories became too much for him.*

"Now, will you get back to business? You *are* supposed to be my assistant and Pam Folstein has misplaced the bow from her dumb violin. Do you think you could help her find it?"

\* \* \*

Honey walked out onstage heartsick. She just *knew* she was going to be awful. But it didn't matter. Of the three people she was really eager to see her perform tonight, one was absent by default, immersed in the misery of his past; a second was at home with her mother, quite miserable in the present; and the third was backstage, giving everyone holy hell. There was no one out there watching her to tell her later, "Oh, Honey, you were really *good!* You made me proud."

Before she began, her eyes swept the audience—from left to right and from front to rear, the way both her father and Sam had told her it was done. Mostly the faces were a blur, and she didn't know if this was because of the lights or the tears in her eyes. But there was a frantic waving down in the front row so that she couldn't miss it even if she tried. It was her friend Sam out in the audience, just making sure that there was someone out there who loved her, who *knew* she was going to knock them out of their socks. . . .

\* \* \*

After the grand finale the cast took bow after bow—the audience composed mainly of enthusiastic friends and family insisting on it with their thunderous applause. Then the girls onstage, following Honey's lead, chanted, "Producer! Producer!" until Sam, snappy in the forbidden strapless green mini she had changed to, came running out to take her bow.

\* \* \*

"I guess I'd better call Olaf to come pick us up," Sam told Honey backstage as the small space was overrun by proud parents and general well-wishers. "We *could* ask someone for a ride home but I'd rather not, if you know what I mean."

Honey nodded. She knew exactly what Sam meant. It was as embarrassing as it was depressing that neither one of them had a single person in the auditorium ready to claim them.

"What the hell, Honey, it doesn't matter. What matters is that we did good, you and me both. And we didn't do it for the old Gipper either," Sam laughed. "We did it for the GAMS and we did the GAMS proud even if Babe wasn't here. Right?"

"Right," Honey agreed after she recalled that the line "Win just one for the Gipper" was from an old black-and-white movie with Ronald Reagan that they had recently watched on television. Babe was right about Sam—she *did* think only in terms of movies. But tonight it was just as well. There were so many things it was better *not* to think about, she as well as Sam—that

Teddy hadn't made it there tonight, and that in a weak moment she had actually written her mother a note telling her all about the Follies and that she was going to do the monologue from *The Merchant of Venice*. She didn't even know what she'd expected in return. A note of encouragement? A word or two dashed off about how she was proud of her daughter? Or even a postcard from someplace glamorous that said, "Wish you were here," and was signed, "Love, Mother."

*   *   *

"Where have you two been hiding? We've been looking all over for our stars!" Sam and Honey couldn't believe their eyes. It was Nora and behind her was Teddy, both of them smiling and exuberant. *Where had they come from?*

"Oh, Daddy." Honey flew into his arms. "Where *were* you?"

"Right here, sweetheart, bursting with pride."

"But I looked and looked for you. I couldn't find you!"

"We were seated way in the back. Nora called me from the airport. She said she wouldn't be arriving until the very last minute and that she hated going places alone and would I wait for her so that we could go together. So I did. How could I not after she took about a half dozen different planes and traveled all day just to get back here in time for what she called a very special night?"

Honey whirled around to tell Nora how glad she was that she had made it only to see Sam and Nora sort of waltzing around one another, taking each other's measure the way she'd seen prizefighters on television doing just before they came out slugging.

"What are *you* doing here?" Sam demanded. "I thought you had a rendezvous with destiny or something at that rally for McGovern in Minneapolis, or was it Duluth? I hope you didn't let old George down just for little old me. . . ."

"No, certainly not. You know I don't believe in letting anyone down, not even my worst enemy."

"So, what happened with the rally? Did you miss it?"

"Oh, that. No, I didn't miss a thing. The rally was called off—we were rained out."

"Oh? Of course. I bet you were disappointed."

"At the rally being called off?"

"No, disappointed that you came to see the show that I produced and that I didn't fall flat on my face."

"Quite the contrary. I wasn't disappointed at all. Rather, I'm pleased that I can report to your father about what an extraordinary job you did. You see, I wouldn't want *him* to be disappointed—he thinks his daughter can do just about anything better than anyone else."

"Really?"

"Yes, of course, really," Nora said crisply before turning to Honey. "And you, love, you were *so* beautiful!"

And Honey was gratified, knowing that Nora was talking about her performance and not just how she looked in her mother's lovely white dress.

# FIFTY

———◆•◆———

**B**abe had to go home—her mother's orders—and she asked Honey if she wanted a lift. "But we have to leave in ten minutes. She's picking me up at eight-thirty."

Sam urged Honey to sleep over. "M*A*S*H is on tonight. We'll watch it together."

But when Honey called to tell Teddy that she was sleeping over, there was no answer. She tried calling several more times—maybe she'd dialed the wrong number or Teddy was in the shower or had gone to the store. Finally she stopped dialing.

She knew he'd been dejected lately, ever since he had signed to rewrite a screenplay, and then, after he'd worked on it for weeks, been replaced by another screenwriter. He'd tried to console *her*. "It happens all the time. *They* don't know what *they* really want or they change *their* minds and tell you it's not what they'd been looking for. You can't take it to heart," he'd said, though she knew *he* did.

"But it's so hard *not* to—I don't see how you can't."

"When I first came to Hollywood a very clever man gave me some advice. He said, 'You have to go with the flow or you might as well put a gun to your head. . . .' "

"Who was the man?"

He smiled enigmatically. "T. S. Grant."

"You *do* know him, then?" Honey asked. She'd sensed that he did. And now she instinctively knew that she was also right about something else—the reason Teddy never accepted any of Nora's invitations *was* because he was avoiding T.S.

"Not *know*. *Knew* is a better word. It was a long time ago and I haven't spoken to him in years."

"Did you have a fight with him? An argument?"

"Let's just call it a parting of the ways."

"Did he know Mimi too?"

"Yes." And then that haunted look she knew so well crossed Teddy's face and she couldn't ask any more questions.

Still, he hadn't honored his own advice to her not to take the rejection to heart and he hadn't followed T.S.'s advice either— to just go with the flow. Rather, he'd sunk into a depression that grew deeper with each passing day, and started drinking more heavily just when she thought he had begun to drink less. . . .

"I have to go," she told Sam urgently. "I can't reach Teddy and I can't stay if I can't tell him that I'm staying."

"Okay, but since you've already missed your big chance to ride with Catherine, I'll get Olaf to do the honors since he's still around, waiting to pick up my father later on. And I'll go along to keep you company. Then I can go in and say hello to your father. I haven't seen him in a while and I love talking to him. He's so soothing."

The last thing Honey wanted was for Sam to come in. "But my father might not be home. I mean, if the phone is working and he's not answering, then he went out. And even if he is home, he's probably busy. Besides, I think I'll survive the ride without you, fascinating as your company is."

"Okay, so I'll go along just to keep Olaf company on the ride back. He loves my company."

"But you'll miss M*A*S*H."

"So, who cares? I'll see it on the reruns. I just feel like going for the ride. Do you mind? God!"

But Honey was saved. When Sam told Nora that she was going along with Olaf to take Honey home and that maybe she would stay awhile, Nora said she'd better think again. "It's too late for you to first start visiting." She suggested that instead Sam go upstairs to check out her homework.

Honey was worried that Sam would argue with Nora, but this time Sam just made a face, kissed Honey good night and went trudging up the stairs muttering, "I might as well be in prison, or even living with Catherine and the Judge," which

ordinarily would have made Honey laugh, but not tonight. Tonight, she was too worried about Teddy.

\* \* \*

Honey fumbled around in her bag filled with just about anything
any teenager could possibly need, but what she really needed—
her key—she couldn't find. She waved at Olaf, waiting in the
Rolls as per his orders, to signify that she had everything under
control and he didn't have to get out of the car. Then she tipped
the urn of geraniums to get the spare key, but it wasn't there!
Teddy must have used it and not put it back. In a panic she
alternated between pressing the buzzer and pounding on the
door furiously.

Olaf got out of the car to see what the problem was, which
was exactly what Honey was praying wouldn't happen. "The
spare key isn't here and my father must have gone to bed and
doesn't hear the bell," she explained, trying to appear calm,
wanting desperately for him to leave. "But I can climb in a
window on the back patio. I'll be fine. You can go."

"I don't think I can. Mrs. Grant wouldn't want me to. Now,
let's go find that window."

\* \* \*

When they found Teddy lying unconscious in a puddle of blood
in the library, Honey didn't utter a sound but sank to the floor
to pillow his head in her lap, to kiss his still-bleeding forehead.
Then she saw Olaf at the telephone and whispered hoarsely,
"Are you calling nine-one-one?"

"No, I'm calling Mrs. Grant. She knows how to get things
done and fast. The ambulance will be here before I hang up."

Honey nodded, then, remembering, looked around the
room frantically for incriminating evidence. She saw the empty
liquor bottle on the coffee table but realized she couldn't do
anything about it. Teddy's head was in her lap, slowly staining
her gray skirt a bright red, and she couldn't do anything but

wiggle out of her jacket to take off her white shirt to try to staunch the determined flow of blood.

She had to fight not to pass out. She never realized how nauseating the smell of fresh blood could be, especially mixed with the stink of alcohol. It seemed to be exuding through her father's pores, even as his head was exuding his life's blood.

*　*　*

The ambulance took Teddy to the emergency room at Cedars, where they treated a cut so deep it required many stitches. (The police, who had arrived at about the same time as the ambulance, had ascertained that he had fallen, and in falling had struck his head on the sharp edge of a table. As bad luck would have it, it was the French campaign table fashioned out of steel.)

"He lost a lot of blood," the doctors told Nora, assuming that she was in charge, while Honey listened more scared than she'd ever been. "Lucky you found him when you did. He could have bled to death without ever gaining consciousness. It's happened before."

Two hours later, conscious and bandaged, after it was determined that he'd suffered only a minor concussion, Teddy insisted he wanted to go home, but the doctors insisted that he stay overnight so that they could properly check him out.

"I don't think you have much choice, Teddy," Nora said, smiling cheerfully, "but to listen to these doctors." She put her arm around Honey, who was still wearing her blood-stained clothes. "Come on, love, you're coming home with me."

"But I want to stay here with Teddy. Can't you ask them if I can stay overnight with him? He *needs* me."

"Not tonight, Honey. Your father's getting all the care he needs and I'll bring you back first thing in the morning."

"You go with Nora, Honey. I'm fine. And thank you, Nora, for everything, but most of all for looking after my girl."

Then Nora said something Honey thought odd. She said, "That's the easy part."

* * *

When they were in the car, Nora took her eyes off the road for a moment to look at Honey, who sat with her head buried in her hands. "You know, Honey, you can love your father very much but you can't really help him. Not alone."

"But when he comes home from the hospital, all he'll have to do is rest. I'll be able to take care of him myself."

"That's not what I'm talking about. I'm talking about your father's drinking," Nora said as kindly as she could.

At first Honey only thought of denying that Teddy drank. *If only I'd managed to hide that bottle before Nora arrived.* "Oh, you saw that bottle," she said, as if to dismiss it with a shrug. "Sure, he has a drink once in a while, like maybe once a week. But don't most people? Don't you and Mr. Grant?"

"I learned a long time ago, Honey, that it doesn't help to deny the truth either. The truth is funny that way . . . and stubborn—it refuses to go away. And no matter what you do or say, you really can't protect your father from the world."

Honey began to cry. "It's not his fault," she sobbed. "He's a wonderful man. It's *her* fault. She left him."

"Your mother? Nothing's ever *all* one person's fault, and you don't know all the facts. Perhaps she *had* to leave him."

"But she left him *and* me!"

"Sometimes that's all people *can* do. Leave . . . cut themselves free . . . to save themselves."

"*You* wouldn't. You'd never do that."

Nora's mouth curved into a sad smile. "Sometimes one *can't* stay, no matter what. And as far as helping someone—well, the person has to *want* to be helped. Mostly, the only one who can really help anyone is the person himself."

"But can't we try to help someone help himself?" Honey asked in a small voice. "Do you think—?" she faltered, not knowing exactly how to put it. "Do you think that maybe *you* could try to help me help my father help himself?"

Nora burst out laughing. "You don't give up, do you?" But then she stopped laughing and said soberly, "The problem with never giving up is that *sometimes* you win, but many times all you end up with is what the French call *chagrin d'amour*, which loosely translates to a broken heart. But I'll think about it."

Having no choice but to be satisfied with that, Honey sat back in her seat and thought about the phrase *chagrin d'amour*. It was deceiving. It sounded so romantic and at the same time it was deadly. Then a thought occurred to her. "Sam said you were living here at the same time that my mother and father were in Malibu . . . when you were married to an English actor."

"I wasn't really *living* here. I was just visiting, you might say—two or three months." She sensed the question that was coming.

"Did you ever meet my mother?" Honey whispered.

"Well, yes, once. Briefly. For a few minutes only."

"And what did you think of her?"

"That she was the most smashing woman I'd ever seen."

Then they were zipping up Grantwood Manor's driveway and there was no more time for any more questions or answers. . . .

Sam was waiting at the door in her long Lanz nightgown. She threw her arms around Honey and turned to Nora accusingly. "When Olaf came back and said Mr. Rosen went to the hospital, I thought for sure you'd call to let me know how he was!"

Nora apologized. "You're right. I should have realized that you'd be waiting to hear. But he's going to be fine. So now you can run along to bed with a clear mind."

"But isn't Honey coming up with me?"

"In a while. First we have to get her cleaned up and then I'm taking her into the kitchen to have a cup of tea. My mother always said that a drop of whiskey was fine, but for a bit of real comfort there was nothing like a nice cup of tea."

"Well, can't I have a nice cup of tea too?" Sam asked piteously. "I'm very upset about Mr. Rosen too."

"Of course you are," Nora said quickly. "And yes, you certainly can have a nice cup of tea."

\* \* \*

As Nora, Sam, and Honey, now wearing a nightgown too, sat at the long table in the kitchen working on a second pot of tea along with a platter of assorted biscuits, T.S. appeared in the doorway wearing an old, homely bathrobe. "I thought I heard a big commotion down here. It's a strange time of day to be having a tea party," he said, grinning at the trio.

"Oh, Daddy," Sam cried, "It's Honey's dad. He fell and hurt his head and they had to take him to the hospital."

"Olaf told me all about it and that you went to take care of things, Nora. I knew then that everything was going to be fine. It *is*, isn't it?" he asked, and Nora nodded.

"Good. Keep smiling, Honey. Now I'll say good night."

"Don't you want to sit down with us, Daddy, and have a nice cup of tea too? It's very comforting."

"I'd love to but I've got a heap of work still waiting for me. Be sure and say hello to Teddy for me, Honey. Tell him I sent my regards."

But Honey knew she wouldn't tell her father anything like that. Though she didn't know what had happened between T.S. and Teddy and Mimi, she trusted what she felt in her heart and she certainly trusted her father. Whatever happened was bad and T.S. had been the perpetrator. . . .

# FIFTY-ONE

———◦•◦———

When T.S. offered to give Sam a party at the restaurant of her choice, the girls decided it would be fun to celebrate their sixteenth birthdays at the same time, though Honey's wasn't until July and Babe's not until September. Sam chose Ma Maison since it was also the restaurant of choice for many of her film favorites, like Steve McQueen and Ali McGraw. Too, Ma Maison's Patrick Terrail always kissed her hand on those occasions when Nora took her to lunch there to stargaze under the patio's infamously hot plastic flowered canopy, and that made her feel special—as if she were really part of the movie scene.

"It's going to be fabulous! Daddy's going to invite a bunch of movie people," Sam enthused.

"But won't that cut down on the number of guests *we* can invite?" Babe asked, worried.

"What are you afraid of? That we won't have room for the tons of boys you want to ask?"

"Well, it *is* supposed to be my and Honey's party too. And what's a Sweet Sixteen without boys?"

"You know, Babe, there *is* another life out there without boys. And some girls actually have *all-girl* Sweet Sixteens."

"Yeah, but there's also a life out there that doesn't center around movies, movies, movies. What would you have done if you grew up in Sioux City or someplace like that?"

"But I wouldn't have been T.S. Grant's daughter and movie-making wouldn't run in my blood, so I wouldn't have the same interests."

"Since Nora said we could each invite twenty guests and I

don't have any boys to invite and we all have the same list of girls, I'm officially donating nineteen of my invitations to you, Babe," Honey said.

"You know what she'll do?" Sam sighed. "She'll post them on the bulletin boards of every boys' locker room in town."

"I couldn't," Babe giggled. "If my mother found out she'd skin me alive. But why are you offering me only nineteen invitations, Honey? Who are you saving that last one for? Some mysterious stranger?"

"Yes, very mysterious. My father. Do you mind?"

"Do you *have* to invite him?"

"Yes, I *have* to!" Honey was exasperated.

"Don't take it personally. It's not that I don't want your father there, but if my mother finds out you've invited *your* father, she'll want to know why I didn't invite her and my father, and they're the last people I want there."

"I can well imagine," Sam drawled. "But if you don't want them there you'd better tell Nora because she says Honey's father and your parents are getting *official* invitations. She says that since she and my father are going to be present, then your parents and Honey's father have to be there too, and you know that old saying—'I can't do a thing with my hair'? Well, I can't do a thing with my steppie."

\* \* \*

"I knew it was a mistake to invite my mother and father. Now Catherine says that if it's *my* Sweet Sixteen as well as yours and Honey's, she'd like to invite some of *her* friends."

Sam was furious. "But she can't! I refuse to have my party ruined!"

"She did say that she'd be more than willing to pay whatever extra it costs," Babe offered miserably.

"Oh! I think I'm going to throw up! If that isn't the tackiest thing I ever heard of—to bring money into it!"

"Well, don't blame me. I don't even want to go to this party myself anymore. I think I'll just kill myself. How many ludes do you think it would take to overdose?"

"I don't know, but if you find out, let me know. Maybe I'll join you. How about you, Honey? Care to join us?"

Honey forced a smile. She no longer was thrilled about this party herself. She was sure that at the last minute Teddy would find some excuse for not going, that he would *never* go to a party at which T.S. was playing the host.

"Well, let's wait to hear what Nora has to say about your mother's latest demand, Babe," Sam chuckled. "She thinks she's so smart, let's see how she gets out of this one."

But Honey could see that even Nora didn't know how to deal with Catherine other than to let her have her way after she offered to pay for the extra guests. Once Nora dealt with the money part by saying, "Don't be absurd," it gave Catherine permission by default to ask anybody she pleased.

Suddenly Honey realized how this party was going to turn out—a disaster! Catherine and the Judge would come with their friends and Babe would have a miserable time. And she herself would be miserable because her father hadn't come because he knew T.S. would be there. But then T.S. himself wouldn't show up because some business thing came up, and Sam would be miserable.

Nora must have been thinking these same thoughts because suddenly she said, "You know, I've been thinking that instead of having this party—for the next couple of months you girls are going to go to Sweet Sixteens till they're coming out of your ears—we should call it off and do something more original to honor the occasion."

Sparks glinted from Sam's eyes. "Like what?"

"Like, I'd take you girls on a trip instead."

"Wow!" Babe said, but Sam demanded, "Where to? Disneyland?" thinking this the height of sarcastic repartee.

"No, what I had in mind was flying to Washington, D.C., to see the sights the first week school is out."

"First-class?" Sam asked immediately.

"Of course, first-class. Would I expect a first-class girl like you to travel any other way?" Nora asked dryly.

"And we'd stay in a hotel? Which one?"

"I haven't planned an itinerary yet, but I assure you the

accommodations will be all that you desire, if not deserve."

"All right," Sam agreed. "If Babe and Honey want to go, I'll sacrifice the party."

"But I don't know if I'll be *able* to go," Honey said. "I don't know if I can leave my father for a whole week."

"Try it. You might be surprised to find out that he can get along without you very well," Nora said with a smile.

"Well, I know for sure my parents will never let me go," Babe said dolefully. "They'll be afraid you'll take me to some kind of a demonstration or even a McGovern rally."

"Oh, my, that *would* be awful!" Nora laughed. "But don't worry. I'll speak to your parents. I'm sure I'll be able to persuade them to let you go by promising them you'll attend nary a rally nor a demonstration and that I'll get invitations to all the right places. Even to the White House."

"How can you? The Nixons are in the White House!"

"Yes, they are, but I lived in Washington for a long time and I have wonderful friends there on both sides of the aisle. Even, would you believe, old Dicky?"

"*I'd* believe it," Sam said, unrelenting even though now she was excited about the trip. "I'd believe that there isn't a man you ever met that *isn't* your friend one way or another. Except for Hubie, of course. I bet he doesn't feel so friendly toward you now, does he?"

When Sam saw how decisively she'd scored with that one as Nora's face darkened, she felt a little twinge—didn't know if she were glad or not. For one thing, it certainly put a damper on everyone's upbeat mood.

# FIFTY-TWO

Just as Honey and Babe had celebrated their birthdays early so that they could share Sam's birthday with her, Sam and Honey waited until September, when Babe turned sixteen, so that they all could get their driver's licenses together.

"But Olaf can't take us down to Motor Vehicles for our test," Sam said, "even if he's the one who took us out practice-driving. Can you imagine what would happen if a chauffeur drove us there for our road test in a *Rolls?* They'd fail us out of sheer class resentment. And my father will be sure to be out of town, and even if Olaf took us in the Ferrari it would be even worse. All the guys who take you out for the test drive would probably *kill* for a Ferrari."

"What about Nora?" Babe asked.

"We can't count on Nora to be in town. This close to the election, she has *her* priorities and *I'm* not one of them."

"I bet she'd still let Olaf take us in her Jag."

"Yes," Sam said. "But I doubt that the class resentment would be any less if we took the test in the Jag. A Jag's probably worse than a Mercedes. They see lots of *them*."

Babe turned pale. "If you're thinking what I *think* you're thinking—of my mother taking us in her *Mercedes*—don't! She doesn't even think sixteen-year-olds should *have* licenses—that it's giving them a license to kill."

"She's right," Sam said cheerfully. "The first thing I intend to do when I get my license is drive over to your house, call Catherine outside, and plow into her. Then, when she's lying in the driveway bleeding, I'm going to put the car in reverse and run her over again. But actually, I was thinking along the lines of your *father* taking us in his car."

"My *father?*" Babe screeched. "Are you out of your glue-sniffing mind? With him watching me drive away in his Lincoln, I'd probably drive straight into a wall and then the inspector would fail me for sure. Why would you even *want* my father?"

"For his registration, fool, what do you think? Before you take the test they check the registration of the car you're driving, and when they see the name *Judge* Terrence Tracy on the old reg, who would *dare* fail us?"

"But why do you have this obsession with us failing?" Babe complained. "Why *should* we fail? Nobody could possibly *not* pass us, unless, of course, you start driving like a cowboy on wheels as usual. Besides, Vanessa Casey said all the inspectors are guys, so all you have to do is wear a short, tight skirt, and if he puts his hand on your thigh you just moan as if he's getting you so hot it's hard to keep your mind on your driving. Or you accidentally put your hand on his weenie until *he* moans, at which time you know you're doing fine because, what with his hard-on, it's difficult for him to concentrate on your driving.

"Then there are other alternatives. Cambria Shoemaker claims she knows a girl who was such a lousy driver that the only thing she could do to get her license was get down and give the creep a blow job."

"And you *believe* that story?" Sam scoffed. "How could she drive a car and give head at the same time?"

"I figured out exactly how she did it. He told her where to drive—which road and all—which is what they do, right? And as soon as they passed an alley or some deserted place, he told her to cut a right and pull over because he wanted to check her right-hand turns and how well she pulled over. Then he told her to turn off the ignition and put on the emergency—he had to check her out on *those* little items too—and then, before she could say, 'Oh, my, you don't mean—?' she was down on the floor and—"

"That's disgusting!" Sam cried. "You know, I think that after everything your poor mother's done to make a lady out of you, she's failed, after all. I mean, sometimes I'm forced to think that you've just got no class."

"Oh, ho ho, listen to you! Don't you think it's rather déclassé of you to try and use my father's judgeship to intimidate a poor inspector into passing you when your driving really *sucks*? Besides which, my father won't do it. Actually, he and Catherine are working to have the driving age *raised* from sixteen to *eighteen*, forget seventeen completely. I'm just lucky she's letting me get my license altogether."

Finally, Honey, who'd been silent through Babe and Sam's entire conversation, spoke up, her voice clipped and distant. "I'm sure my father will be willing to take us."

"But why didn't you say so in the first place and spare us all this discussion?" Sam demanded.

Honey didn't answer. Maybe it was because once Sam said that both Nora and her father would be too busy to take them, she'd been reluctant to admit that Teddy was available because *he* had nothing else to do that couldn't wait until the next day or the day after, except maybe to stay sober enough to take them. Or maybe it was that magazine article she'd read last night about people who abused alcohol, which stated that unless a person was willing to say "I'm an alcoholic," he couldn't ever recover. And how could *she* ask *him* to say it when she herself couldn't say it except for that one time with Nora, when she'd been forced to.

"Anyhow, Sam," she said in a frigid voice, "since all *we* have is our old Ford, you won't have to worry about being failed due to class resentment. As for what you're willing to wear and what you're willing to *do* to ensure passing, Babe, that's entirely up to you. Personally, I'm going to wear jeans and keep my hands on the wheel and my eyes on the road at all times since I'm satisfied that all it takes to get a license is to drive a car *adequately*, and I hope *you* won't do anything to embarrass me or my father."

"Oh, come on, Honey, don't be such a doofus," Babe said sulkily. "Can't a girl have a little fun?"

"Really, Honey, you *are* in a snit. What did we do or say to bring this on?" Sam was upset and sat down on the bed to try to put her arm around her. "What's the problem?"

Honey shook her arm off brusquely and then Sam was hurt. "All right, if that's the way you want it—"

"Okay, if you really want to know what my problem is I'll tell you!" Honey sat up straight. "My father is an alcoholic! There, I've said it, and I hope you're satisfied. . . ." There was a stunned silence before Honey began to cry.

"Oh, Honey, Honey." Sam threw her arms around her. "Don't cry. It'll be all right."

"No, it won't," Honey said. "It never will be!"

"Of course it will," Babe said, hugging her too.

"There's hope for him," Sam insisted. "He's so sweet and *alive*. And I never told you how my mother died, did I?"

Honey's sobs abated somewhat. "No . . ."

"She was in a sanitorium for the mentally disturbed—" Sam made circles with a finger and pointed to her head. "And then one night she got hold of a razor—" She drew a line across her neck and made a funny croaking noise in her throat. "She bled to death and she was only twenty-three."

"But who told you that?" Honey asked, horrified, not crying anymore.

"My grandparents did when I was around five. *They* were the ones who were really sick to do that to me even though I didn't know it at the time. How could I? I was only a little girl. I think they were just trying to punish me."

"But why would they want to punish you with such a terrible story?" Honey asked, the tears flowing again.

"I guess they didn't like me because they were mad at my mother for what she did. And they couldn't punish her, so they punished me instead." Then Sam burst into tears and Honey put her arms around her while Babe got to her feet.

"Okay, since this is show-and-tell, or at least *tell*, I've got an announcement to make too."

Honey was wary. "Babe, if this is going to be something really terrible, tell me now so I can prepare myself."

Sam, wiping at her eyes with her hands, looked nervous but she said, "Don't let her fool you. She can't bear not to be in the spotlight, so she's going to make something up just so she isn't left out. Go ahead, Babe, let's hear what you have to say, but try not to make it too big a whopper, okay?"

"No whopper," Babe said. "My mother's been married before and I think the Judge *adopted* me."

This time, nobody cried. Rather, there was a stunned silence until Sam, not doubting Babe's sincerity after all, asked shakily, "What makes you think so?"

"Because last week after my date with Evan Layton, and I came home just a *few* minutes late and just a *tiny* bit rumpled, the Judge took one look at me and said to Catherine, 'This is what comes of my taking in another man's trash when I married you!'"

Sam was aghast. "But how could you keep that to yourself? Why didn't you tell us before?"

"If you were called another man's trash, would you go around bragging about it?" Babe laughed.

No, you didn't brag, Honey thought. *You just cried yourself to sleep until you told your friends about it and laughed so that it didn't hurt so much.*

But Sam said, "You have to look on the bright side of things, Babe. If you're some *other* man's trash, then at least you're not *his*. Did you ask Catherine what he meant?"

"I tried to, but all she'd say was I was never to mention the subject again but that I should get down on my knees every night in thanks for having a man like him for a father."

"Do you think that's what *she* does?" Sam asked. "Gets down on her knees every night to give . . . um . . . *thanks?*"

\* \* \*

Teddy, sober as a judge, made cheerful chitchat to relax the girls as they drove down to the Motor Vehicles Bureau in the old blue Ford. Still, they were nervous and they argued over who should go first.

As it worked out, Honey, in jeans and a denim workshirt, went out with a middle-aged inspector and came back smiling widely. Sam, in a long denim skirt that topped her cowboy boots, went out next with a young and good-looking inspector to return giving them all the thumbs-up sign.

Then it was Babe's turn. In a tight and very short jeans skirt and wearing high heels Sam and Honey had never seen before (where *had* she dug them up?), Babe wobbled over to the Ford to await the official who was going to take her out for her spin. And in a couple of minutes the inspector appeared, a snappy-looking woman (Babe's eyes popped) who took one look at Babe's towering high heels and sneered, "One . . . just *one* false move, kid, and you're dead in the water. . . ."

# FIFTY-THREE

———— •◦• ————

"What are you doing up so early?" Honey demanded when Sam called her at six-thirty in the morning.

"I'm just calling to tell you not to get on the bus today. Just wait for me and don't ask any questions."

At ten to eight there was a great blasting of horn coming from the usually quiet street—it sounded like someone was in trouble—and Honey ran to the door, Teddy right behind her. But when she threw the door open, all she saw was Sam madly waving from a bright-green Alfa Romeo!

"Meet the new Beasley Express!" Sam yelled, getting out and running up the path. "Isn't she gorgeous? Did you ever see anything so beautiful, Mr. Rosen?"

Teddy laughed, but Honey, ever sensitive to his every expression, observed that it wasn't his best laugh. What was wrong? Was he worried about her riding with Sam? Sam did have a tendency to speed, but she'd been riding around for months with Sam at the wheel of her parents' cars, just as she'd driven Sam and Babe in the Ford. Was it any different now that Sam had her own set of wheels? Then, with a pang, she realized what the problem was—Teddy was jealous that Sam had a shiny new Alfa Romeo while his Honey didn't! She wished she could tell him that having him for her father was worth a million new cars, and that Sam having the Romeo was almost as good as she herself having it. But that would be acknowledging that it was painful for him. . . .

"Ready? Then, let's boogie!" Sam said, pulling on a pair of racing driver's gloves.

"In a sec." She dashed back into the house to grab her bag

and books and dashed out to find Sam and Teddy at the curb for a close-up inspection of the car.

"It's truly a marvel," Teddy said, kissing Sam on the forehead. "And as my mother would have said, 'Drive it in good health.'"

"Oh, that's cute!" Sam giggled. "Most adults would say, 'Be sure to drive carefully.' I like your advice better. Ready, Honey? We're late and we have to pick up Babe!"

As they tore away from the curb, Honey blew a kiss to Teddy as he stooped to pick up the newspaper, a disconsolate droop to his shoulders. He blew a kiss back, but she knew he wasn't going to have the best of days.

"I'd have called you last night to tell you about the car," Sam bubbled, "but I didn't get it until almost midnight, when Daddy got home. He was so funny. He said, 'It's all yours but don't do anything in it I wouldn't do.' But do you know what Nora said? That even though it's April, the car's my seventeenth-birthday present, so I should try not to total it before my birthday in June. Did you ever hear anything so mean? But you should have seen it! Daddy had it all tied up in pink plastic wrap and all these purple balloons!"

"Purple balloons hardly sounds like your father."

Sam laughed. "I guess you're right. It does sound more like Nora, but why not? What else does she have to do?"

"Still, it *was* a nice thing to do," Honey said wistfully, thinking of the last gift that had arrived from Paris—a tall, white chef's hat and an apron that said, *"Bon Appétit!"*

Sometimes she wondered about Mimi's weird gifts, that maybe it really *wasn't* that her mother didn't give a damn. Maybe it was more that she was *on something*—stoned out of her mind for the duration of her daughter's lifetime.

\* \* \*

When Babe, waiting in the driveway, saw the car heading for her as if with intent to kill, coming to a stop only inches from her, she let out a shriek, but it was one of pure joy. "Do I see what I think I see or am I dreaming?"

"Climb in quick, short person. We're already late and I'm going to have to do eighty to make it to school on time."

"Where am I going to sit?"

"Don't be dumb. You sit sort of scrunched on top of the seats. Haven't you ever ridden in a sports car before?"

"*I'm dumb?* There are three of us and you get a car that seats only two?"

"What kind of car did you think I'd get? A station wagon? The *cool* cars all seat only two. Half the fun of riding in this car is scrunching up. And when you're scrunching you can sort of hang out the window and yell out insults to other drivers. Climb in. You know how it's done."

"Oh, all right. Get out, Honey, and let me go scrunch. Better still, how would *you* like to scrunch since it's half the fun, and I'll just sit in front like a plain person who's not having any."

"I don't think so," Honey said, laughing. "Since you're the shorty, it's better for you to do it because that way you'll be higher than us and we'll all kind of come out even."

Without waiting for Honey to get out, Babe proceeded to climb over her to get to her perch as Sam helped with a shove, and the three of them screamed with laughter until the front door opened and there was Catherine in a pale-blue satin robe demanding to know what was going on.

"Oh, shit!" Babe hissed. "We woke her up!"

Sam waved to Catherine. "Hi, Mrs. Tracy. How are you this great morning? The sun's shining and—"

"The sun's usually shining," Catherine said sourly. "Now, will you tell me what's going on here and why you're not on the school bus, Babette?"

"Oh, I just got my new car last night, Mrs. Tracy, and I wanted to pick up Honey and Babette this— Well, I know we're a tiny bit late but—" She gave Honey an elbow in the ribs.

"But we'll make up the time," Honey blurted. "We'll be at school in ten . . . fifteen minutes at the most, right, Sam?"

Sam gave her a withering glance. "No, *twenty* minutes is more like it. I wouldn't dream of going over twenty-five miles an hour and I also believe in defensive driving."

Catherine gave Sam a withering look and fixed her daughter

with an eaglelike eye as Babe tried to appear to be sitting nor-
mally. "I have always trusted you to get on the school bus every
morning without supervision. Do I have to stand out here and
see that you get on the bus as you're supposed to?"

"I'm sorry," Babe whined. "I thought that this once it would
be all right since Sam just got her car and I didn't want to wake
you just to ask you if it would be all right. And now I've already
missed the bus—"

"Do I have your word that this won't happen again without
your asking permission?"

"Oh, definitely, Mother. I swear."

"Very well. I'll let it go this time since it's not my intention
to keep you girls from having *fun*," she said, as if *fun* were a dirty
word. "But as you're already late and I don't want you speeding,
if you'll get down from that ridiculous perch, Babette, and come
back in the house, I'll write a note for the three of you asking
that your tardiness be excused." But just before Catherine disappeared through the doorway, she turned and smiled tightly.
"Good luck with your new car, Samantha, and be sure to drive
carefully."

Sam groaned. "I was hoping she wouldn't say that."

In a couple of minutes Babe smilingly emerged to report that
Catherine had insisted she and Honey exchange places. When
Honey groaned, she said, "You better. Her eyes are upon us."

Conscious of those eyes, Sam eased the car into the street as
if it were made of eggshells, then slowly inched to the corner
before exploding into a burst of speed after she took her left
onto Sunset. "I can't believe she let you go."

"I knew she would the moment I saw her in the doorway."

"But how could you?"

"Because I remembered why she was up so early. It's Friday
and she's got a standing ten o'clock at Elizabeth Arden's, and
since I had already missed the bus, if I didn't take the ride with
you, *she'd* have to drive me, which would make her late for her
appointment. By the by, when you come to our turn for school
don't make it. Just keep on Sunset until you hit the old PCH,
then hang a right!"

"The Pacific Coast Highway? Are you crazy or what?"

"Crazy like a fox. This is the first day you have your car and you have to do *something* special to break her in. Well, what's so special about driving to school? But if we go up the coast to the Malibu pier— Well, the surf's up and there's going to be a lot of action at Surfrider's Beach."

"But what about school?" Honey protested. "Tomorrow's Saturday. We can go to the beach tomorrow."

"But then it's not special anymore. *Anybody* can go to the beach on a Saturday," Babe said reasonably.

"But they'll call home if we don't show up. Your mother's note only excuses us from being a little late, doesn't it? What does it say, exactly?"

"There is *no* note," Babe said smugly. "Knowing that my mother was anxious about *her* time—she needs at least an hour to put on her face *before* she goes to Arden's to have them remove the face before they work to improve the face—I suggested that she just *call*, which she did, telling the office clerk that we were going to be late, but she didn't specify *how* late. Get it? We can show up at two o'clock and still be in the clear and have about five hours to catch some rays and check out the action. The surfers always have such cute little butts in those rubber tights. Now do you see why I'm crazy like a fox?"

"Crazy!" Sam agreed, whizzing past the turn for school.

"But if we get caught you're the one who's most vulnerable, Babe," Honey pointed out. "Your mother won't let you out of the house for a month! Maybe a year!"

Babe sighed breezily, turning on the radio. "Sometimes you just have to go for it," she said, bopping to the strains of "Aquarius." "This really *is* the age of Aquarius, you know."

"How are we going to go on the beach in our uniforms?"

"We don't, Honey, you worrywart. We take them *off*."

"To put on what, or do we go on the beach bare-assed naked? Then we'd be *sure* to get all the surfers' attention."

"I don't believe in being *that* obvious. We put on our bikinis, which we buy at that little shop right near the pier."

"With what, or are we just grabbing them and running?"

"We use the credit card Nora gave Sam."

"Hold on! Anything I buy that Nora hasn't authorized

comes out of future allowances. She's chintzy that way."

"Well, don't *you* be so chintzy. Oh, all right, we'll pay you back out of *our* future allowances."

"But isn't the water going to be awfully cold this early in the season?"

"Really, Honey, who said we have to go in it? All we have to do is lie in the nice, warm eighty-degree sun working on our tans while the boys check out our bods. Now, will you relax? I swear, sometimes you sound just like my mother. . . ."

As Sam made her right turn onto the PCH, Babe pointed at the Pacific sparkling in the sun. "Now, I ask you, aren't you glad we're here instead of in American Lit?" She turned up the volume on the radio to let "California Dreamin' " blare through the air to mix with "Me and Julio Down by the Schoolyard," which was blaring from the MG in the right-hand lane cruising in tandem. Its driver, a surfer type with bleached white hair, wearing black Ray-Bans and a T with the sleeves cut off at the shoulders, yelled, "Where you headed, doll?"

"Surfrider's," Babe yelled back. "You?"

"Zuma," he said, "but maybe we can negotiate."

But just as she opened her mouth to answer, Sam stepped on the gas to zoom ahead, leaving the MG in the distance, and Babe, outraged, demanded: "Are you insane? He was *cute!*"

"Come on, Babe, he has Valley Boy written all over him."

"What are you, some kind of a West Side snob?"

"I was just acting in *your* best interest. I didn't want to see you waste your valuable time because he'd never pass muster with Catherine and the Judge."

"What did you think I was looking for?" Babe asked in disgust. "A lifelong commitment?"

\* \* \*

When Sam and Honey awoke after dozing off in the sun, they looked around for Babe. "Where do you think she is? It's time we headed back," Honey said nervously.

"Let's check down by the water and up by the wall where those kids are hanging out."

When their search proved futile, Honey said, "Let's go back to the car. Maybe she's waiting for us there."

As they neared the car, Sam let out an eardrum-breaking screech. "Do you see what I see?"

"If you mean Babe and that guy from the MG getting out of your car, then I see exactly what you see."

*   *   *

No one said anything until they were heading back, a subdued Babe in the scrunch seat. Finally Sam said coldly, "May I ask what you were doing in my car with that creep?"

"What do you *think* I was doing, playing Scrabble?"

"Oh, stop trying to imply that—"

"But I'm not just *implying.* I—" Babe sounded as if she might cry. "I mean—*all* the way."

"Oh, my God! You mean you did *it* in my new car?" Sam screamed, her eyes darting frantically around the car while Babe, frightened, asked: "What are you looking for?"

"Semen, if you must know! But there isn't any! Did you *swallow* it all?"

Honey gasped, then whispered to Sam, "Don't," while Babe uttered, "I might never forgive you for that!"

"*You* defile my car and you won't forgive *me?*"

"Damn you, Sam, why are you acting like this? And you, Honey, Miss Goody-two-shoes, why don't you say something? I thought the least the two of you would do was ask me how it was and you're both acting like my mother!" She began to cry.

"Well, who did you expect me to act like—Nora?" Sam demanded, suddenly remembering *her* first and only time and how Nora had reacted. But hers had been a beautiful experience and Babe— Poor Babe! Her first time seemed to have been a bummer. . . . "Okay," she said, trying to make up. "I apologize for acting like Catherine, but only if you tell us all about it. Everything he said . . . and *did.* Every last detail."

"I accept your apology," Babe said, only sniffling now.

Now Honey knew she had to say *something,* anything that would show Babe she wasn't being judgmental. And she wasn't.

It was only that she would have wished for something more meaningful for Babe her first time—as she would wish it for herself. That surfer had just walked off when she and Sam showed up, without so much as an "I'll see ya" or a good-bye hug. Not even so much as a wave or a smile.

"I'd like to take this opportunity to congratulate you, Babe," she said finally, "and wish you many happy returns of the day . . . *I think.*"

"Okay." Babe tried to smile. "That's better. As for details, Sam, I want you to know one thing about your new car—it's *awfully* hard to do *it* in a car that has no backseat and bucket seats in the front. It's just lucky I'm so good at gymnastics or it might never have happened at all!"

"Well, I'm *so* glad that you managed to manage and my first question is: Did the earth move for you?"

"So *that's* what that was! At first I thought we were having an earthquake . . . but then it turned out to be only a tiny tremor. . . ."

# FIFTY-FOUR

————•◦•————

It was understood that once the fall term started for a Beasley
senior, everything else took a backseat to her college applica-
tions. It was also understood that it was incumbent upon a
girl to attend the finest school she could get into—she owed it
to her school and to the Beasley girls who came after her. Accordingly, each student was encouraged to apply to at least three
of the most prestigious schools in the country, with an emphasis
on the seven sister schools in the East and Stanford to the north,
regardless of her SAT scores and academic standing. Beasley
subscribed to the theory that character was as important as
scholastic achievement, as were social standing, prominent
ancestors, and the willingness of parents to make a donation to
the school in question. In addition, it was mandatory that at
least three additional colleges, slightly less desirable, be applied
to as "safety schools." Accordingly, letters were sent out to set
up appointments with parents so that they could be in on these
strategy-planning sessions along with the students and guidance
counselors.

When Honey found the letter to Teddy in the pile of un-
opened mail, she threw it in the trash. There was no need for
Teddy to meet with her guidance counselor since she already
knew which school *he* wanted her to attend—his own alma
mater, Princeton, a top choice that her counselor would heartily
approve. Beasley had had many of its girls go on to the sister
schools, but not one had gone on to what some viewed as the
most elite of the elitist schools, which had only recently elected
to take in women.

The only hitch with Princeton as the school of choice was

she herself—much like the girl in the nursery rhyme who couldn't leave her mother, she'd decided she couldn't leave her father. *Who would watch over him?*

\* \* \*

Nora brought the letter from the school to the breakfast table— the one time of day the three of them were sure to be together— so that T.S. could be consulted as to what time would be best for meeting with the counselor. She knew that Sam not only would want her father there but that she would be crushed if he weren't.

It was a surprise to her when Sam didn't object when T.S. said it was impossible for him to commit to an appointment— *Gone Yesterday* was weeks behind schedule and millions over budget and he had no idea when he would be free. But she did object when he told Nora, "You and Sam can take this meeting without me. Just get Sam set up at Vassar or Radcliffe. Smith wouldn't be a bad choice, either."

"But I don't want to go to Vassar or Radcliffe, Daddy."

T.S. picked up a piece of toast to lay it down. "Nora, the toast is cold. You know how I hate cold toast," he said, sticking his bottom lip out like an aggrieved little boy.

Nora smiled and rang for the maid.

"Didn't you hear what I said, Daddy? I said I have no intention of going to Smith, Vassar, or Radcliffe."

"That's fine. You and Nora decide where you want to go, then Nora can tell them at school what we all want."

The maid appeared, but then T.S. said to forget the toast, he was running late. He scraped back his chair to rise, picking up his cup to grab a last gulp of coffee. "Coffee's cold too. What's going on around here, Nora?" he said, grinning. "What's happening to my perfectly run household?"

"Oh? I didn't think you noticed." She went to the sideboard to fetch him a fresh cup.

"Daddy, we haven't finished discussing my plans!" Sam cried petulantly.

"I told you. You and Nora work it out. And whatever you decide, tell that school that if *they* can't get you in, *Nora* will. She has all kinds of fancy connections and lots of negotiating skills. That's what comes from marrying an earl, a highfalutin' diplomat, and being a big shot in the Democratic party. Ain't that right, Nora?"

He smiled at her in that devilish way of his, and Nora felt herself, as always, responding to it, though she knew that she shouldn't . . . couldn't.

"But nobody's listening to *me*," Sam shrieked. "I'm not going to college at all!"

T.S. was mildly surprised. "What will you do with yourself? You have to do *something* to keep busy. Oh, I know what it is you want to do." His face creased into a grin and Sam relaxed. *Of course he knew!*

"You want to disco the nights away, right? Then sleep in the next morning and maybe around eleven get dressed to bomb around town or maybe get in some shopping on Rodeo. Get your hair done at Jose Eber's. Then zip over to the Ivy for lunch, after which you'll just have time enough to get your nails done—" He shrugged. "Well, why not? That's fine for killing time until you grab yourself a husband. It sure beats the hell out of being one of those hippies with dirty feet who go around protesting every damn thing."

If it were anyone else who'd said what T.S. had, Sam would have torn his head off, but she couldn't be angry with her father. Besides, he was probably just teasing her.

"Daddy, maybe getting a husband was all Nora had on her mind when she was a girl way back when"—she cast a sly look in Nora's direction but Nora merely sipped her tea and smiled— "but it couldn't be further away from what's on *my* mind, or Honey's, or even Babe's. Women want to do something on their own these days and—" She laughed. "Look how Billy Jean King whipped Bobby Riggs's little old ass."

"Oh, well," T.S. said, "he was a fool. An old man challenging a woman half his age to a tennis game. But what do I know about these things?" He drained his coffee cup. "Why don't you tell Nora all about it? She knows and understands *everything* and she won't steer you wrong."

Then he was gone, leaving Nora and Sam silent until Nora

said, "If you don't want to go to college, what is it you *do* want, Sam?"

"If you know so much, why don't you tell me?" Then, in a burst, she cried, "You *know* what I want! That I want to work at the studio! Making movies runs in my blood!"

"When you graduate, Sam, you'll only be eighteen, and when a girl's eighteen, no matter *what* runs in her blood she really has no idea of what she wants her life to be."

Sam looked at her with narrowed green eyes and said, with what she perceived as great shrewdness: "I bet I know what ran in *your* blood when you were eighteen and that you knew exactly what you wanted. Shall I tell you?"

Nora thought of the young and, in her way, innocent girl who had gone to London town with her blood running hot, dreaming of all the men who would love her and make her laugh . . . the girl who had never thought of her future. It had never occurred to her to think about what she wanted her life to be.

"No, Sam, *don't* tell me. You'd only be guessing, so it doesn't make any difference what you think. And this way, I can fantasize that you were going to say only the nicest things. But what I *will* tell you is that I *wasn't* prepared for the future, which is always a mistake for anyone."

"You mean like Hubie, for instance?"

Nora looked down for a few seconds so that Sam wouldn't know that she had scored with that one.

"The only future you need to concern yourself about, Sam, is your own. And you'd be wise to prepare for it. It's not enough these days to go into the movie business and think you're going to make it big because you're the boss's daughter. Just suppose this scenario: For some reason your father is *out* of Grantwood Studio soon after you begin. Then *you're* out of there too and you still don't know a bloody thing. But if you learn the craft of making movies first, then you have a basis from which to proceed. Gain experience, and after that, who can stop you from being anything you want to or can be?"

"You think I should go to college to learn the basics?"

"That's the gist of it."

"Would you consider making a deal with me?"

"I might . . . if your terms are reasonable."

"Since my father listens to you and he doesn't take anything I say seriously, would you talk him into giving me a job at the studio next summer after I graduate, and then in the fall when I'm in film school at UCLA or USC, I can work at the studio part-time. Now, that's reasonable, isn't it?"

"Perhaps . . . It all depends on where you're willing to start—at the bottom so you can learn the business?"

"If those are *your* terms."

"Those would certainly be my terms. But we're talking deal here and, so far, we know what *you* want to get out of it, but you still haven't told me what *I'm* going to get."

"Well, I know what you want in general. You want to do a great job on me in order to show Daddy how great you are. Isn't that how it works? In return for everything you're getting out of this marriage—his love and devotion and all the advantages of being Mrs. T.S. Grant—you run a great household, make great parties, and give great—" She smiled slyly and said, "Oops! I mean—raise his daughter to be a credit to her father or something like that."

Nora smiled coolly. "Something like that. . . . So, what are you offering in return?"

"I'm offering to be a really good girl, not to give you a bit of trouble and no back lip, either."

"Well, *that* would be a pleasant change. How could I possibly turn down a deal like that?"

"So we *have* a deal?"

"Done."

"Done," Sam repeated, giddy with pleasure. "If I wanted to risk melting that icicle of a heart of yours I could almost forget myself enough to give you a big hug. But I dasn't. I mean, then what would you do for a heart?"

"Fortunately, we'll never have to find out."

* * *

"Are you sure your father couldn't come to this meeting, Honey? Perhaps we should postpone it until I have a chance to talk to him," the guidance counselor asked.

"Oh, no, Mrs. Durand. He's immersed in his new novel and you know how writers are. Their muse is all! He doesn't even stop to eat or sleep." She thought that Mrs. Durand would be impressed with that line. Most people were. "Besides, there's nothing to discuss. I'm going to UCLA—they have a very fine school of drama and there's no reason for me not to go there since drama is what I want to study and I can still live at home."

"But *we* were counting on you going to Princeton. And that *is* what your father told us when he enrolled you—that he wanted you at Princeton. You're letting all of us down."

Honey felt the need to apologize. "Our plans have changed and— Besides, we don't know if I could have gotten into Princeton." She stood up, thinking that if she did so, Mrs. Durand would dismiss her. "Probably, I wouldn't have—"

"Of course you would have! You scored almost perfectly in the SATs and you're a Beasley girl who is number one in her class, one we *hoped* would be our valedictorian. And your father's a Pulitzer Prize–winner who himself went to Princeton. They never would have turned you down except maybe for— Well, there is one thing they might have turned you down for," she said, smiling meanly in her frustration.

"Because I'm half Jewish?" Honey suggested softly.

"Of course not," Mrs. Durand said. "They took your father, didn't they? And that was over twenty years ago. If they turned you down it would have been only for your *looks.*"

"My looks?" Honey asked, bewildered.

"Yes. It's hard to take a girl as pretty as you seriously, you know. But I suppose that won't hurt you if all you want to be is an actress."

"But I want to be a *serious* actress."

Mrs. Durand smiled cynically. "In that case, you may have a problem and I can only wish you luck."

"I do have one more question. You said something about me possibly being valedictorian. Since I'm not applying to Princeton, does that mean I'm out of the running?"

"I didn't say that," the counselor said defensively. "But what does it matter anyway? What does it mean on an actress's resume to say she was valedictorian of her class?''

"It's an honor, and if I earned it fair and square, then I want it! I want it for my father. It will make him glad.''

*　　*　　*

When she came home Teddy was waiting for her. "Mrs. Durand called.''

Honey sighed. "I thought she would.''

"Don't you think you should have talked this over with me before you came to your decision?''

"But I've made up my mind and there's no use talking about it. Are you terribly disappointed?''

He shook his head.

"Are you mad?''

He shook his head.

"Then, what are you?''

"Glad. I would have missed you so.'' He opened up his arms and she ran into them.

"But they may not let me be the valedictorian now, Daddy, and there was a good chance I might have been. I wanted you to be proud of me.''

"Then, it doesn't matter. I couldn't be prouder of you than I already am. But that doesn't matter so much either.''

"Oh, Daddy, you're not making any sense. Of course it matters if you're proud of me. What could matter more?''

"Your being proud of yourself . . .''

*　　*　　*

Babe was torn between wanting to go away to school and wanting to stay in Los Angeles with Sam and Honey. Going to school on the East Coast and living away from her mother and father would be liberation at last. Of course, if she could have gone off to school *with* Honey and Sam, that would've been heavenly liberation. But it wouldn't be *her* decision anyway. It would only be Catherine and the Judge's. She wouldn't even be asked what she wanted or where she wanted to go. Still, it was one of the few times that even they didn't make an instant decision. Rather, Babe overheard them toss it back and forth for a while, and it sounded like a two-character play:

SHE (wistfully): It would be nice if we could say that our daughter was going to Radcliffe. Janet Rush is always bragging that *her* daughter goes to Radcliffe. It means that a girl is intellectually superior and will get a fine academic education. It was my father's dream that I'd go to Radcliffe. . . . (voice trailing off)

HE (severely): We agreed a long time ago that we would not talk about your father just as we agreed that we didn't want Babette to go to Radcliffe, isn't that so? All she would meet at Radcliffe would be boys from Harvard, which is a hotbed of radical professors, drugs, and Jews. Besides, Babette is *not* intellectually superior and has no need of a fine academic education since she's never going to be a scholar. Most likely she will never practice a profession no matter what she majors in.

SHE (subdued): Well, Alicia Madison went to Smith and she married a lawyer who graduated from Harvard who isn't Jewish. Kevin O'Keefe. He's practicing in Boston.

HE (scoffing): Boston Irish! Catholics! And we know what we want, don't we?

SHE (sighing): Yes . . .

HE (sternly): And considering everything, I don't have to remind you that Babette needs constant supervision.

SHE (tremulous): Yes, of course.

HE: And we don't want her traipsing off to the East to find herself a husband and stay there after all our work. We want her right here, don't we? Isn't that what we agreed on?

SHE (sighing): Yes, Terrence, of course.

To Babe it sounded as if there had been no need of a discussion—as if everything had been decided a long time ago. And she didn't need a superior intellect to gather that, many years before, some kind of a deal had been struck between her mother and father and that a big part of the deal had to do with her—she whom the Judge had referred to that one time as another man's trash.

But one thing *was* a big surprise. She had always thought that Catherine ruled their roost, leaving only the courtroom for the Judge to strut his stuff. Now she wasn't so sure. The conversation she had just overheard almost sounded as if her mother were the defendant who had already copped a plea.

\*   \*   \*

"We've decided that you're going to the University of Southern California, Babette."

"But both Honey and Sam are going to UCLA. I'd really rather go there too. Can't I, please? Since both are really good schools, what difference does it make?"

"The difference is that UCLA's part of the state university and USC is private, and we feel that it's to your advantage to go to a private university. And as far as Honey and Sam going to UCLA, it's time to broaden your horizons. We can't have the same friends for the rest of our lives."

"But I thought you *liked* them. You've always said that no matter what else, Honey *was* a lady and very bright. And you said that in spite of everything, Sam had a certain style. You *did* say that, Mother, you *did!*"

"Yes, but what of it? We have to move on in life. We must grow! And I never said you still can't be friends with them just because you're going to different universities."

"They'll develop different interests—"

"Let's hope so, since Samantha is going to be in film school and Honey is taking drama, and *you're* going to major in political science."

"That's another thing. *Why* am I going to major in political science? I don't even like it."

Catherine indulged in that laugh Babe hated. "More reason you should study it. We must extend our interests. That's the reason we educate ourselves. Now, just suppose you meet and marry a man who's interested in a political career. You'll be all prepared to make him a wonderful wife—"

"But what about what *I'm* really interested in?"

Catherine smiled at her in that annoying way. "You mean, there *is* something besides boys?"

"It's possible," Babe snapped. But could she tell Catherine that she wanted to be a stand-up comic? She would go straight to the phone and call the Judge and they would discuss whether they should have her committed. "What would you say if I told you I was interested in becoming a brain surgeon?"

"I'd say you were making a joke. . . ."

# FIFTY-FIVE

———•—••—————

For months the puzzle of which came first—the chicken or the egg—had plagued Honey. Did Teddy drink because he couldn't write a novel to equal the genius of his first, or was he unable to write it because he drank? Did he drink because Mimi had left him, or had he lost her because of the drinking? The failure? Which addiction had come first—the failure, the bottle, or Mimi? Could he recover from one without being cured of the others? Maybe the only way to find out for sure was if they saw each other again. Anything could happen, even a reconciliation.

Then, when it was announced that she was to be valedictorian, she thought that this was her big chance. She would write a letter *begging* Mimi to come to her commencement to hear her deliver the valediction. She would *swear* that if Mimi would come, she would love her forever. What mother, even an alley cat, could resist an offer like that?

\* \* \*

Having left Teddy downstairs in the library watching a movie on television—one he himself had written that had never made it into the theaters—with a bottle of vodka close at hand, she sat down to compose the letter. The last thing she expected was to have Teddy walk in on her as she was nearly through writing it. Quickly she covered the letter with an open copy of *Cosmopolitan.* "Movie over already?"

"No, but I saw enough—I already know how it all comes

out." He smiled, his speech a tiny bit slurred. "I thought I'd see what you were up to."

"Just reading this magazine Sam gave me."

"Come on." He grinned. "I saw you cover up something you didn't want me to see. You were working on your speech, right? But you don't have to worry about *me* seeing it before it's finished. Let's take a look." Before she could stop him he uncovered the letter and began to read and she was terrified at his expression. Never had he looked at her this way—with such cold rage!

"How *could* you write that *ugly* woman *begging* her to come to your graduation? After how she's treated you!"

*But she's not ugly! Everyone knows she's beautiful!*

"Where's your pride? She's never asked to see you. All she's ever done is send you those stupid gifts! I didn't say anything—I didn't want to fill you with my poison. I kept hoping she'd do better. But she never has. And now, this—"

"Daddy, please!" She tried to put her arms around him but he pushed her away and she was stricken.

*It has to be that he's even drunker than he appears.*

"You're not a little girl anymore. I thought by now you'd have figured out for yourself what she is, but you haven't or you wouldn't be begging her to *love you*. I was so proud of you. I thought you were the one thing I'd done right! Now I see I've failed again. By writing this letter you not only shame yourself, you shame me!"

"No, don't say that!" she screamed. "I did it for you! I only wanted her to come to my graduation on the chance that you two could reconcile—because you love her so much!"

He stared, the soft eyes wild. "Love her? I *hate* her! I've hated her practically from the moment I married her!"

*     *     *

After she cried and he cried and they apologized to each other over and over, they talked over hot chocolate and cookies. "But, Daddy, why didn't you tell me you hated her? You'd never talk about her, you were always so sad when I brought up her name.''

"I thought only a bad father would tell his daughter that he hated her mother—he'd have to tell her *why* and I couldn't do that to you.''

"But when you married her you loved her?''

"I was bedazzled, spellbound. I remember the first time I saw her. I still can't imagine any young man *not* falling in love with Mimi L'Heureux.''

"But how could you love her so and end up hating her so?''

"Disillusionment. There is no one who hates so much as he who's disillusioned.''

"But how were you disillusioned?''

"By betrayal. There is no one quite so disillusioned as one who's been betrayed. Think of a very young man, starry-eyed in love with an irresistible woman—a woman most men would die for, who made you think that out of a world of men she loved and desired only you. What kind of betrayal do you think would practically destroy such a besotted fool?''

There was only one answer. "Sexual betrayal.''

"Yes.''

"But *not* right away?'' she begged.

"Right away. At first, I couldn't believe it. I thought I had married a goddess, but all I'd married was a whore.''

The word sent a shiver through Honey. "But why did she marry you only to betray you like that?''

"Because I believed in her . . . in the golden myth of her. Because she thought that with my help she could transcend what *she* was—a face and body with a golden tarnish—to become a great actress who could transcend time. She married me so she'd have her very own writer to help her make the big leap. But it didn't work out that way. In the end we both turned out to be what we were intended to be all along—I the failed writer and she the eternal slut!''

"Oh, Daddy! But once you found out what she was and you no longer loved her, why didn't you leave her?''

"I couldn't.''

"But why not? If you hated her—''

"Because by the time I was ready to admit that my marriage was a failure she told me that she was pregnant."

"You mean *me?*"

"Yes. She said that if I left her she'd have an abortion and she knew how much I wanted a child."

"And *she* didn't?"

"Women like Mimi don't really ever *want* children. Pregnancy puts one out of commission and it's a worry about what it will do to the figure. Then, once a child is born, one has to do *something* with it—if not a responsibility, it's a burden. Worse, it's always a reminder of one's age both to the public and to one's self. And if one is a sex goddess—well, age *is* a consideration as much as the figure."

Everything he said made sense but for one thing. "But if she never loved you and she didn't really *want* a child, why was she willing to have a child just to keep you?"

"Ego and greed. The ego couldn't bear that there was a man who didn't love her . . . want her . . . and the greed wouldn't allow her to give up anything she already possessed."

"So you had me. And after I was born you and she left France and came here to Los Angeles. . . ."

"Yes . . . for the money. I told you, Mimi was greedy."

"But that didn't work out either?"

"It didn't. Not for either of us. And then she wanted to go back to France, where she was still the sex goddess."

"And by then she was through with both of us—you and me? She didn't want us anymore."

"Oh, no, she wanted us. By then we were part of the total baggage she toted around—all the Vuitton suitcases and trunks and jewelry boxes and makeup cases—and she never wanted to give up anything that was hers. Who knows? Maybe she thought she could make use of us someday—her faithful husband, the beautiful little girl that looked just like her. If nothing else, it *was* a great publicity shot."

"She wanted us and yet we *didn't* go with her?"

"I refused for both of us. By then I knew you were better off without a mother who didn't love you. It's a terrible thing to love and not be loved in return."

"Yes, and you loved me enough for two," Honey said, and even though it wasn't a question, he whispered, "Yes."

Still, there *was* one question that remained since Mimi L'Heureux was a woman who slept around so widely. *Was she, Honey L'Heureux Rosen, really Teddy's daughter?*

\*    \*    \*

She studied her face in the long mirror before she went to bed—the golden hair, the topaz-colored eyes, the cheekbones, the dazzling white smile. Then she stepped back to better examine her body—the full breasts, the narrow waist, the round swell of hips. Oh, she was Mimi L'Heureux's daughter for sure, but there had never been a doubt about that.

Oh, God, if only there was something as positive to prove that she was Teddy's!

*But if I wonder, then he must too.*

*But is it really important to either one of us*—the daughter he loves completely . . . the father she loved without equal. And he was *such* a lovely man who had been no less than that for as long as she could remember. Oh, no, proof was immaterial. . . .

Still, the dirty word *betrayal* crept into bed with her as she switched off the light. *Who were the men Mimi had betrayed Teddy with? Was one of them anyone she knew? . . .*

# FIFTY-SIX

"Since we'll be graduating soon I have an idea that will ensure us a place in Beasley history," Sam said over lunch in the cafeteria. "We're all familiar with the saying 'All a Beasley girl has to do to get a higher education is walk down the street to the Playboy Mansion and jump the fence.' But no one ever *has* . . . until today, that is!"

"You mean *us?*" Babe asked, her eyes shining.

"Do we have to?" Honey asked. "I don't see the point."

"There *is* no point and that's the point," Sam said, sighing. "We do it just to do it. To become part of the legend."

"Let's plot the action!" Babe enthused. "Do we go over the fence at the main entrance or over the back wall?"

"We can't go over the back wall. That's where the sentry house with the guards are—we'd be spotted in a second."

"So, then, we *have* to go over on Charing Cross. The electric gate is too high, but the wall's low, even with the iron spikes mounted on top and the chicken wire in back. That whole business can't be more than four feet tall. I can hop it easy and so can you two if you're careful not to get one of those spikes up your ass," Babe chortled.

"But it can't be *that* easy," Honey said. "If it were, they'd have a mob climbing it every day. It must be wired to give electric shocks."

Babe howled. "They can't do that! If they were allowed to do that, it would be like giving them a license to electrocute and the lawn would be littered with fried bodies."

"True," Sam agreed. "At the same time, the wall *has* to be wired to an alarm system. The minute you start to climb an

413

alarm must go off. They couldn't have such a low wall if it's not wired for security. It'd be an open invitation for all the weirdos who want to see the girls walking around with bare boobs and those bedrooms with the mirrored ceilings."

"*Those* rooms are in a separate building apart from the main mansion," Babe said with authority, and when Honey and Sam stared at her, she rolled her eyes. "No, I'm *not* speaking from personal experience, I'm quoting from an article I read."

"What we have to do is get around that security system," Sam said, thinking hard. "The important thing is not *how long we last* once we're inside, but only that we *get* inside so we know we've done it and can describe it all to the rest of the girls and become part of the Beasley lore. And I think I know how we can do that without any bodily risk:

"We just saunter up to the *rear* entrance, where the guard-house is, and Honey, bold as brass and shaking her ass, says, 'Hi, I'm Mimi L'Heureux's daughter and Mommy said I should drop by and say hello to old Heff for her.' Then the guard takes one look at the body and the mop of hair and says to his buddy, 'Hey, man, this is the real stuff!' and they call up to Heffie, who says, '*Mimi's daughter?* By all means send her and her friends ahead!' Then we're *in*, and I wouldn't be at all surprised if, besides meeting Hughie in his silk pajamas, we get a guided tour—mansion, grotto, pool, sex rooms!"

"Great scenario, Sam," Honey said. "Only there's a hitch. I refuse to announce myself as Mimi L'Heureux's daughter. As far as I know, there *is* no such person. She doesn't exist."

\* \* \*

"Okay, this is the plan." Babe gave Honey and Sam last-minute instructions as they stood in front of the mansion's grounds on Charing Cross with not a security guard in sight. "When I say, 'Go,' it's over the wall. It should take three or four seconds at most before we land on the other side and the security alarm starts blasting. But don't stop for a second—just keep running to where all the shrubbery is. It will probably take them at least a minute or two to get here from the guardhouse, and by that time we should be able to hide, so they'll have to hunt us down. By the time they catch up with us, we'll at least have gotten an eyeful."

"If they don't cart us off to jail," Honey said, "and then we'll have to call the Judge."

"Don't say that even in jest. You *know* all they'll do is show us *out* the gate. Isn't that right, Sam?"

"I suppose . . . if they don't shoot first."

"Okay, but if they do, just remember that this was your idea, not mine. Okay, I'm going to count. At three, we go."

At three they went, but only Babe managed to make it over the wall before she was immediately surrounded by plainclothes guards with walkie-talkies transmitting the message: "We got a live one."

"Yikes, there must be twenty of you good-looking guys!" Babe giggled. "But I'm sure we can work something out." She smiled at the men suggestively, winking at Honey and Sam watching goggle-eyed from the other side of the fence.

"I don't think I like that wink," Sam whispered. "You stay here and talk to them too. Stall for time while I try to reach Nora just in case they *don't* just show her the gate."

"But what will I talk about?"

"Anything! It' an emergency! Tell them you're Mimi L'Heureux's daughter."

But before Honey could even retort to that, the guards were showing Babe through the gates with a "Come back in a couple of years, kid, and we'll give you an escorted tour."

# FIFTY-SEVEN

———•••——

When Honey didn't feel well during rehearsal and it was discovered she was running a fever, Sam wanted to drive her home, but the nurse said that she would— school policy.

"My father's going to be surprised to see me," Honey told the nurse, but when they pulled up to the curb and she spotted the Jaguar behind their Ford in the driveway, *she* was the one who was surprised. And glad that Sam hadn't been the one who'd driven her home since it was *Nora's* Jaguar, and when it came to Nora, Sam had a very active imagination. And then she realized that her own wasn't doing badly, either.

*What is Nora doing here at eleven in the morning?* She was hardly in the habit of dropping in at their house, had never even made a formal visit. Then she found herself wishing that she wasn't thinking what she was thinking.

"I'll walk you to the door, Honey. And I *should* speak with your father," Nurse Laughlin said.

"Oh, I'm not *that* sick—I probably just have that flu that's going around. And I see my father has a visitor, a business appointment probably. We'd better not disturb him."

"But it's my responsibility to—"

Honey laughed. "You really don't have to bother. I'm not *that* sick. I *can* get to the door on my own and I know how to get into bed, turn on the television, and drink lots of fluids. I'll probably be back in school tomorrow."

"Okay, Honey, I guess it'll be all right. But I'll sit here until you're inside just the same."

Honey walked up the path slowly. If the nurse weren't

watching, she wouldn't even walk into the house. She would just hide out until she saw Nora leave, just to be sure she wasn't walking in on something . . . something she didn't want to see.

*But I'm being silly. Nora's probably here to ask Teddy to be on a committee or something, or maybe they're planning some kind of a surprise for me and Sam—a graduation party.*

Still, if she tiptoed into the house and they *weren't* downstairs having coffee in the kitchen or a conversation in the living room, she wouldn't go upstairs at all. She would just keep on tiptoeing until she was out the back door.

Soundlessly as possible she turned her key in the lock, tiptoed in, and her heart sank. It was as silent as a graveyard . . . which meant that they *were* upstairs!

*Oh, Teddy, how could you? With Sam's father's wife! And Nora! Sam had been right about her after all. . . .*

Well, she would do what she had planned—keep on going through the house and out the back door. She would go for a walk, come back in a couple of hours when Nora's car was bound to be gone, and she would pretend she'd just come home, didn't know a thing.

*But nothing will ever be the same again.* She wouldn't be able to look her father in the eye for a long time to come, and she wasn't sure she could ever act normal around Nora again.

Then she saw that the door to the library was closed. *They were in there!* Though she'd always thought eavesdropping was despicable, she tiptoed to the door to listen. When she heard the low hum of conversation, she was relieved that at least they weren't moaning and groaning. But she couldn't make out what they were saying. Maybe it was the conversation of sated lovers caught up in the afterglow. . . .

She went outside again to cross the street to wait and watch, and before long they came out together. *He was walking her to her car.* Well, Teddy would do that. Didn't a gentleman always walk the lady to her car afterward? And even if he *were* having an affair with Sam's father's wife, wasn't her father always the gentleman? she thought bitterly.

But Teddy wasn't as much to blame as Nora. *He* wasn't the one who was married. And maybe it was that he was so vulnerable, Nora was just one more person or thing he couldn't resist becoming addicted to. . . .

After Nora's car pulled away, she walked back to the house and let herself in, calling out, "Teddy, it's me!"

When he came rushing out to ask, alarmed, "What are you doing home so early? Is something wrong?" she shrugged.

"Not really. I wasn't feeling so good, so the nurse drove me home. She says I have a little fever. But it's nothing. I'll just go to bed for a while." She started for the stairs, eager to go to her room so that she wouldn't have to talk to him.

"All right, you get into bed and I'll bring you up some soup. Or would you like scrambled eggs and toast?"

"No, thank you. I don't want anything. I'm not hungry."

She was halfway up the stairs when he said, "It's too bad you didn't get here a few minutes ago. You just missed Nora."

He was actually telling her that Nora had been there, so maybe it wasn't what— She turned around, trying to sound casual. "Nora? What was *she* doing here?"

"Bringing me news so good she had to come tell me herself." His voice was full of excitement. "Some friends of hers are doing a special for CBS and Nora suggested me as the writer. I had a meeting with them but I didn't want to say anything to you until it was definite. But today she came over to tell me I got it! *I'm* going to write the special!"

"A *television* show? *Not* a screenplay?"

"Yes, a television show, but don't sound so disappointed. It's going to be a Thanksgiving story—a two-hour drama about a sick man who's made a mess of his life, coming home for Thanksgiving after being gone for twenty years. This is a great opportunity. When I get an assignment to do a screenplay it's just hack stuff. They won't take a chance on me for a quality movie. But this is something I can sink my teeth into—this is very possibly Emmy-winning material."

"Oh, Daddy, that *is* good news!" How could she have suspected that he would fool around with another man's wife?

*And Nora . . . How could I have doubted her? She was helping Teddy help himself. . . .*

"I'm very grateful to Nora," he said as if reading her mind.

"I think she did a lot of fancy talking and fast footwork to persuade them into giving me this chance."

"I'm sure they're giving you this chance because they *know* you're the best writer in Hollywood. Probably all Nora had to do was tell them that you're a genius."

He laughed. "I think you and Nora are a bit prejudiced. But I'm going to have to work very hard not to let her down."

"Yes," she agreed, "you can't let her down. But to tell the truth, all along I've been disappointed that— I was always hoping that—" She caught herself. She'd almost said that she was always hoping that Nora would help him help himself, but she couldn't say *that*. She amended it to: "I always wondered why she didn't get T.S. to give you a wonderful assign—" Her voice trailed off. *Now, why did I say that? The worst thing I could have said . . .*

Teddy looked at her sharply and said stiffly, "I guess because she knows what you and I both know—that I would never work for T.S. no matter how much I needed the work."

She could have asked him then how Nora would have known that, but she didn't want to spoil the day.

"You know, Daddy, I feel so much better now, I don't even have to go to bed. And I'm starving. Why don't we go in the kitchen and celebrate by sharing some scrambled eggs? If you'll scramble, I'll toast. Deal?"

"Deal."

He put his arm around her as they walked into the kitchen, and she saw the two *empty* liquor bottles on the counter next to the sink and could still smell the alcoholic fumes coming up from the drain. And when Teddy turned to the refrigerator to get out the eggs, she quickly snatched the bottles and threw them in the trash on her way to the bread box. Some things you just didn't talk about—you just kept your fingers crossed and whistled a lot.

# FIFTY-EIGHT

―――――・―・――――――

"Where's Daddy?" Sam asked, sitting down to breakfast.

"He had an early meeting."

"It's only seven o'clock. How much earlier does it get and where does he eat at that hour?"

"Mmm . . . a twenty-four-hour coffee shop?" *And hospital testing rooms that served up nasty things and stuff—hold the toast!* "Did you want to speak to him about something?"

"Not him. You. I was thinking it'd be nice if we had a party the night of graduation."

"No, I'm afraid not. Perhaps we can go out to dinner that night with Babe and Honey, someplace you like—"

"You're saying that you *refuse* to make me a party?"

"It's just not a good time, Sam."

"But you're always giving parties for everybody. Just last month you gave that party for that senator from Colorado. And when I ask you for one little party, you say no?"

"But that was last month. *This* month's not a good time. You're not a baby. It can't be so hard for you to understand that I might not have the time or—to make a big party now."

Sam's eyes narrowed. "Well, I guess it's a matter of priorities. You haven't found it difficult to find the time to spend visiting with Teddy Rosen lately."

Nora tried to ignore Sam's innuendo. "True. I believe that helping out a friend who needs a favor does take priority over making a party for a *mature* young woman who's going to a ton of graduation parties this month anyway."

"I'll accept that helping out a friend is a priority, but could you explain to me of what possible assistance *you* could be to

Teddy Rosen? Do you do windows, or is it only that you give good—'' She broke off grinning slyly.

For a moment Nora considered giving her a good crack, but she forced herself to smile. "What I do is give good *ear* since Teddy asked me to listen to him read his teleplay so that he could get some feedback."

"Oh? Is that what they call it these days? *Feedback?* Maybe you ought to tell Daddy about it. Maybe he could use some of that feedback stuff at the studio, you know?"

Again Nora was sorely tempted to slap the insolent face, but again she resisted. It wouldn't do any good. Sam was going to need a lot more than that to get her through the next few months.

# FIFTY-NINE

———— •••• ————

"Look how they're wasting our time!" Babe groaned. It was graduation practice, but mostly they'd been sitting around doing nothing for what seemed like hours. "We could be out shopping for our formals for the prom. Have you decided yet if you're going to wear one of your mother's dresses, Honey?"

"I've decided and I'm not."

"How do you feel about *me* wearing one of them?" Sam asked. "There must be a gown in there that would fit me. *All* of them are so spectacular. It's a shame for them to go to waste no matter how you feel about your mother."

"They're not going to waste. Last week we donated the trunk complete with contents to the Salvation Army."

"*All* those beautiful dresses," Sam mourned. "Why?"

"We just decided we didn't want them around anymore."

*Just like we don't keep bottles of vodka around anymore either.*

"But you know what they say, 'Dresses don't kill people, people kill people,'" Babe said, cracking up at her own joke.

But Honey didn't laugh and Sam just shook her head in disgust.

"All I meant was that keeping those dresses couldn't really hurt you or your father," Babe explained.

"It's not that. It's more that they had become . . . well, superfluous. Teddy always thought he owed it to me to keep them just in case when I grew up I'd want them, like a legacy. And I always dreamed that when I grew up, I'd want to wear my mother's dresses, the way boys sometimes want to step into their father's shoes. But now that I'm *pretty* much grown up—'a young lady stepping into adulthood,' as they keep reminding us—I've outgrown the dream. I know I'll *never* want to wear her dresses. And so giving them away is sort of another kind of graduation, if you follow me."

"I guess I see what you mean," Sam acknowledged.

"But why did you pick the Salvation Army?" Babe asked. "You should have picked a more upscale charity. I don't mean to sound snobby, but the people who shop at the Salvation Army stores aren't exactly in need of a gold lamé evening gown."

Honey smiled. "But I think that some of these people may be very much in need of a glamorous evening gown . . . more so even than someone who can afford to shop in an *upscale* resale store. Just suppose some girl from a poor home is shopping for a dress for *her* prom and, like a dream come true, she finds a movie star's evening gown she can buy for a few dollars. After all, you know what they say," she said, giving Babe a poke in the ribs, " 'One girl's nightmare can be another girl's dream.' . . ."

# SIXTY

———— •• ••• ————

Babe relished the game of pulling the wool over her mother's eyes, and more so every day.

"Why is Sam picking you up instead of your date?"

"It's easier this way. The party's at a frat house and our dates are on the hosting committee."

"But I never met this boy."

"Neither did I—he's a blind date."

"You know I don't like you dating men I haven't met."

"Well, look at it this way, Mother. If I like him, you'll meet him, and if I don't, you didn't waste your time."

"What's his name?

"I told you, I don't know. I'm just doing Sam a favor by going since she's dating his buddy."

"Well, you must know the name of the fraternity?"

"Uh-uh. All I know is that the frat house is on Hilgard. You know, UCLA's Greek Row."

"Is Honey going to this party too?"

"No, she has to stay home to practice her valedictory."

"What a pity *you* couldn't say that."

*Okay, score one for you, but she who laughs last laughs best, and if you knew who I was really dating, you'd croak.*

\*    \*    \*

"You have to cover for me in case my mother calls, Honey. She might get it into her pointed head to check out my story with you, which is that I'm double-dating with Sam and we're going to a frat party. She thinks *you* don't lie even if you are part Jewish and part French Catholic."

Honey sighed. She hated lying for Babe and she worried about the boys Babe went out with on the sly. Now she had a new boyfriend she wouldn't even tell her and Sam about. He really had to be *bad* medicine!

"Isn't she more likely to call Sam's house?"

"I'm covered there because Sam's picking me up. Then she's dropping me off to meet my date, but don't bother asking who he is because I'm not telling. All you have to do is corroborate my story, and you don't have to get in a sweat about lying—you're not testifying in court. She probably won't call anyway—either I'm getting better at my stories or she's getting older and slipping. Bye, gotta go!"

Honey dialed Sam's number. "I was hoping I'd catch you before you left to pick up Babe."

"I was just about to leave, so talk fast."

"Babe said you were going to drop her to meet her date and I was wondering if you could sort of hang around until you saw who he is. She's acting so mysterious—I'm worried. Why won't she tell us who he is? She always has before."

"I'll try. But if it means hanging around for a long time, I *can't*. Not tonight. I just don't have the time."

"Why? What do *you* have to do?"

"I gotta go. Talk to you later, okay?"

The phone went dead, leaving Honey more upset than ever. What was going on? First Babe, now Sam was being mysterious. What did Sam *have* to do tonight that was so urgent?

When Teddy walked into her room an hour later, he found her still mulling gloomily. "Something wrong, sweetheart? You look like you lost your best friend. Is it that bad?"

She smiled, shaking her head. For a brief second she considered telling him her problem, but it would sound so ridiculously trivial and Teddy had enough to deal with—writing his teleplay and at the same time staying sober. That was enough for *any* man without having the added concern of not knowing with whom Babe was possibly exchanging bodily fluids.

She noticed then that Teddy was wearing his dark-gray suit—the one he wore for really serious occasions—for the second time that week, the suit he'd already worn at least four or five times that month. "You're going out?"

"Yes."

She tried to sound casual. "Heavy date?"

"*Heavy*, but I don't know if you'd call it a date," he said as if he were about to say more but then didn't.

*Now* he's *acting mysterious!* "What would *you* call it?"

"More like a meeting." Again he acted like he might say more, but there was a horn honking out front and he said, "I have to go. See you later." He kissed her and was gone.

She went to the top of the stairs to see him race out the door, slamming it shut behind him. She ran down the stairs, meaning only to yell after him, "Have a good time," but it was too late—the dark-green Jaguar was already pulling away from the curb. *Nora!* And then she saw a bright-green Alfa Romeo shooting past as if in hot pursuit. *Sam!*

*Teddy was going somewhere with Nora and Sam was tailing them!* And Sam thought playing detective with Nora was more important than playing detective with Babe since she had had to race back from dropping Babe off to pick up Nora's scent. *Why?* Did she *know* that Nora was picking up Teddy? What did she suspect? *Clandestine meetings? Meeting* was the word Teddy had used. Why *was* he having *evening* meetings with Nora? It was one thing to see her during the day since she *was* helping him with his teleplay—acting as his sounding board—and everyone knew about *those* meetings. But evening meetings were another thing, especially if no one else knew about them. That did make it all sound less than innocent, and though it wasn't unusual for Nora and T.S. to go out in the evenings separately—he on studio business and she busy with her political things—*something* had aroused Sam's sleuthing instincts.

Suddenly, a bolt of relief shot through her. Teddy had used the word *meeting* and Nora was forever going off to political meetings. Since Nora was helping *him*, it made sense that he would try to help *her* with her activities in any way he could. And he hadn't mentioned it to *her* because she always teased him about being a totally apolitical animal.

Now she felt ashamed that she had doubted him and Nora but had to laugh, thinking of Sam following them to what she presumed was a *clandestine* rendezvous. Was she going to feel silly! But then the thought of the word *clandestine* brought Babe back to mind and again she was plunged into gloom.

*   *   *

Anxious not to lose sight of the Jag, Sam made a left onto Pico on red without bothering to check the stream of traffic coming at her. *But talk about your déjà vu!* This was the same trip she'd taken only a short while ago when she'd dropped Babe off at that slimy joint in Hollywood down the street from that fleabag motel with the neon light flashing its name, STARDUST HEAVEN, along with its main attraction—adult movies. But she reminded herself that Pico ran for miles. It would be *too* much of a coincidence if Nora and Teddy were headed for the same bedbug heaven as Babe.

Still, it would be a howl if Nora and Teddy and Babe and her sleaze-squeeze met in the parking lot when the two couples were leaving. So much to talk about! If nothing else, they could exchange critiques about the adult movie they'd all just seen. Maybe the four of them would even go out for coffee.

But then, as she saw Stardust Heaven's neon light flashing, she said a silent prayer that the Jag *wouldn't* make a left into the motel's lot, and it *didn't*! But just as she was saying, "Thank you, God," the Jag made a right into the parking lot of a small, shabby church right across the street!

*You have to hand it to Nora—she's smart as a fox.* Why park a distinctive-looking car in Trash Heaven's lot where anyone might spot it when all you had to do was first park, then cross the street to heaven. Who would even notice a car parked by a little shabby church you could easily overlook?

\*   \*   \*

Honey jumped when the phone rang, not knowing what she expected to hear—a report of a car accident or Sam telling her she'd discovered Teddy and Nora doing unmentionable things to each other. She breathed a tentative "Yes?" to hear Babe breathe raggedly, "Honey, I need you to come pick me up. Please, Honey, come fast before I do something terrible. . . ."

\*   \*   \*

Sam waited several minutes for them to come out from the church's parking lot and cross the street to the motel. When they didn't, she was puzzled. What had happened to them? Was there another exit in back? Leaving her own car in the street, she went to investigate. No, there was no other exit, and *yes*, there was the Jag, parked next to a pickup.

*Crazy!* Had they driven to Hollywood only to desecrate a church with their unholy screwing? Then she saw an elderly couple get out of a Buick to enter the church through a side entrance. Quickly she followed them in, to find herself in the back of an auditorium in which some kind of a meeting was going on. Then she spotted them up front, Nora sitting, Teddy standing, and then she heard Teddy's resonant voice: "My name is Teddy and I'm an alcoholic. . . ."

She ran out, desperate to leave before they spotted her. She would die of shame if Teddy found out that she'd been spying on him or what she'd suspected him of . . . or even that she'd heard him declare himself. He was such a fine, sensitive man, he was sure to consider her conduct repugnant and unforgivable, and when he told Honey what she'd done, Honey would never forgive her either.

She jumped into her car, but when she turned the ignition key the engine coughed then died. *God!* Was she going to be stuck here to be discovered when the meeting let out? She thought about abandoning the car when the motor caught. *Thank you, God!* Then, to make a fast U-turn in the middle of the street, she took a reckless left into the flow of traffic without looking, not even noticing that she barely missed being slammed into by an old blue Ford making its own left into the driveway of the motel across the street.

*　*　*

Honey's eyes searched the lot frantically. Babe had sounded so desperate, had threatened to do something terrible. *Like what?* But she didn't see her anywhere. She parked to circle the lot on foot. Maybe Babe was hiding between cars, not wanting to be seen. *Oh, God, where is she? Did she go back into one of those rooms? Had someone dragged her back?*

Then she prayed that she wouldn't have to go knocking on the doors of all those sordid rooms to find Babe. But even worse would be to look beyond those doors and still not find her. Then she would have to call somebody to help her search, and whom could she call? *Oh, God—not the police!* And not Catherine and the Judge! That would be betraying Babe so badly she might never recover. And she couldn't turn to her father or Nora. She didn't even know where to reach them. But maybe Sam would be home by now. Having discovered that Teddy and Nora were engaged in some innocent activity after all, she might have raced home to nurse her embarrassment. Yes, if she didn't find Babe on her own she would call Sam, and maybe between them they would figure out what to do short of calling the cops.

*　*　*

Driving home, Sam found herself wishing that she could find the courage to confess to Honey what she'd done, taking her chances that Honey would forgive her. It would make *her* feel better not to have any secrets between them. But would it make Honey feel better or would it just make her worry? And what about Teddy? If he wanted Honey to know that he was going to AA, wouldn't he have told her himself?

*Whatever, it's not my secret to reveal. . . .*

As for Nora, tonight she'd been innocent, but that didn't

mean she wasn't guilty of being unfaithful on numerous other occasions with someone other than Teddy Rosen. For days now her father had had the look of a haunted man—something very serious had to be worrying him. And it couldn't be the studio that was worrying him since they had a terrific smash on their hands—*Dead on Target* had been number one at the box office for weeks already. It had to be something else, and what else could gnaw at a man as trusting and good-natured as T.S. than being betrayed by the woman he adored?

*   *   *

There was only one more thing for her to do before she started knocking on doors, Honey thought, sick to her stomach. She would check in the office to see if the desk clerk, or whatever they called the person who gave out keys in places like this, had seen Babe. But just before she entered the office, she saw a car partially hidden behind a clump of shrubs alongside the structure and walked around to take a look. But it couldn't be! Her heart pounded violently. Not *his* Ferrari! But then she saw the vanity license plate and knew that there was no way she was ever going to be able to call Sam—the vanity plate read STUDIO 1. There was nothing like advertising, but really not the thing to do if one wanted to make Stardust Heaven one's home away from home. . . .

*Oh, Babe!*

"Honey . . ."

She spun around to see Babe, seemingly tinier than ever, with her cheeks tear-stained and her eyes smeary with mascara, her bright-yellow party dress an incongruous note in the dimly lit lot. At first, Honey shuddered with relief. At least Babe was safe. Then she was overcome with rage, shaking Babe like a rag doll. "Where were you?"

"I was walking. I was thinking of just disappearing."

"I thought you were dead!"

"I thought of that too. Just killing myself."

Honey looked at the Ferrari and back at Babe. "Maybe you should have at that," she said furiously.

Then they both burst into tears before she hustled Babe to her car. "Let's get away from this place before he comes out. It's bad enough looking at you. I don't think I could *bear* looking at him!"

Actually, it had been quite a while since she was able to bear looking at T.S. as it was, thinking of the possibilities . . . of all the reasons that Teddy might have for not being able to bear looking at him too. If what she thought might be true, then it had to be very hard for Teddy . . . hard for the betrayed to look into the face of one who was instrumental in the betrayal without wanting to kill him. And it would be especially hard for Teddy—he was such a gentle man.

They drove for several blocks, silent except for Babe's soft weeping, until Honey said, "You'd better stop crying before you get that mascara on your dress. It's going to be hard enough to get you cleaned up in a hurry so I can take you home to your mother."

"Honey, are you ever going to forgive me?" Babe asked in a small, piteous voice.

"It's not I who has to forgive you," Honey said in despair. "It's Nora! And Sam! Oh, Babe, how *could* you?"

"You don't understand. When he first asked me to meet him I thought he was kidding. And then, when I realized he *wasn't*—that the great T. S. Grant, who could have his pick of beautiful women, of practically every sexy wanna-be in Hollywood, wanted to fuck *me*, well . . . I was flattered. I mean, if he picked *you*, I could understand it. Or even Sam, if she weren't his daughter. *But me?* It was like suddenly I was special and no one ever thought I was special before—certainly not my mother or the Judge."

"Oh, Babe, but you *are* special—you always have been."

Babe shook her head. "No. Well, anyway, that was the first time and it was over so fast—he said he had an appointment—it was like I didn't get enough. I wanted to hear him tell me he loved me. And then, after the second time I realized that he was never going to say it because he *didn't* love me. He was just another Hollywood letch with the hots for anything *young*, like it would rub off on him, and the only reason he picked me was because he *knew* I was an easy lay. As if it were written all over me.

"But then I met him a third time because, if nothing else, I was putting it over on everybody, especially my parents. I thought that was really cool and I didn't even *think* about Nora or Sam. But tonight, when I started to take off my dress and he told me to hurry—he had another appointment in an hour—I realized that it *wasn't* cool and that the only person I was really putting anything over on was . . . me. I did think of Nora then, and of Sam. How heartbroken she'd be, and I felt really scuzzy. So I never took off the dress and I told him I was leaving. And do you know what he called me? A cunt! But that was okay—that's what I am."

"No, Babe, you just made a mistake! And what he saw written all over you was that you were vulnerable. And that's probably who he always searches out—the vulnerable. He's a . . . a *spoiler*. But his car's still there. How come?"

"I can't figure it out. After he called me a cunt he just buried his face in the pillow and started to cry."

"*Cry?* But that doesn't sound like him."

"He *cried*. But somehow I *knew* that it had nothing to do with me, that it really didn't matter to him if I stayed or went, that he was crying only for himself."

They were silent then, thinking about why T. S. Grant would cry—the man who always smiled, no matter what.

"Honey, do you think I *have* to tell Nora and Sam?"

"No. What you have to do is *never* tell them. I'm not sure about Nora, but I am about Sam. She adores T.S.—this would break her heart. It has to be our secret forever."

"What about T.S.?"

"*He's* not about to tell anybody."

"But how will I ever look at him again? I can't."

"Well, maybe we'll both get lucky and we won't have to."

\* \* \*

Honey had barely crawled into bed after taking Babe home when she heard Teddy coming up the stairs. Busy with Babe, she hadn't thought about him and Nora and Sam in hours. She clicked on the light and called out, "Teddy, I'm awake."

"Good," he said, coming in and sitting down on her bed. "There was something I wanted to tell you. I hesitated to before . . . well, I didn't want you to be disappointed in case I slipped. But I don't want there to be any secrets between us so I want you to know that I've been going to AA."

*Oh, God!* "And *that's* where you were tonight?"

"Yes," he said with eloquent satisfaction. "And Nora's been going with me for backup."

She threw her arms around his neck, crying, "Oh, Daddy, I'm so proud. . . ." Then she *hoped* that Sam had found out where he and Nora had gone, because she couldn't tell her—it wasn't her secret to reveal. "I'm so glad you told me! I'm so glad you're going! And I *know* you won't slip. . . ."

"That's what Nora said. It was she who urged me to go, and I don't know if I would have ever had the guts to do it if she didn't offer to go to be my own private cheering section. I'd hate to let her down."

"You won't. You're not a man to let anyone down, and I think Nora is wise enough to know that."

*And probably a whole lot more . . .*

# SIXTY-ONE

---

"You *have* to go to commencement tomorrow, T.S., if it's the last thing you ever do!"

"You're *something*, Nora," he said admiringly. "You don't give up. Going to that graduation before I check into the hospital might well *be* the last thing I'll ever do, but you're *still* determined to get me to that damn commencement."

"I shouldn't have phrased it that way. It was stupid of me, but you *are* only checking in for an exploratory."

"Checking in only to be told I'm checking out?" he laughed. "Sure sounds like a hell of a waste of time."

"I won't listen to this, T.S. Even if the news isn't, well—*good*, it doesn't mean that it's all over, that—"

"Still playing the cheerful optimist? But that's one of the reasons I married you. Your optimism. I know you think it was only the money, but your other fine qualities counted for a lot too. For one, I've always admired your guts."

"And I yours, which is why I won't tolerate all this whining." Her tone was chipper, but it was painful to see in the too-bright glare of the setting sun streaming in through the window how pale he was—his year-round L.A. tan all but gone—and how worn, the creases of his craggy face having deepened to that point well past the image of one who has only laughed too well and looked too often into a noonday sun.

She went to the windows to draw the draperies, musing on the perversity of nature—how in these minutes before it disappeared into the horizon, when all too soon it would be twilight, the sun seemed to be at its most brilliant.

"But what I've *most* admired about you, Nora, is your

honesty. How you don't hold back. It's disappointing that you're holding back on me now."

Smiling, she sat down next to him on the chintz-covered couch. "I don't know what you're talking about, T.S."

"Yes, you do," he said, kissing her brow tenderly.

*Don't tempt me now with tenderness. Tenderness was never your thing and it's too late for tenderness anyway.*

"Let's lay our cards on the table and get on with it."

He's only asking me not to demean him by being less than honest. But did she owe him honesty? Much easier to gloss it over with optimistic phrases and glib assurances right up till the end rather than help him accept the relentless inevitable.

*What do I owe him? Count up the score, Nora.* Yes, he *had* deceived her when he married her and it *had* been a devastating blow to discover that he loved her money more than he loved her. But they'd made their peace, she realizing that if he didn't love her as she loved him it was because he was incapable of that kind of love. And she knew that he not only admired and respected her, he *liked* her thoroughly, probably more than he had ever liked anyone, and that wasn't nothing. True, they'd often been adversaries, but they'd never been enemies. Rather, they'd been partners in a manner of speaking, and even intimate friends. . . .

And even after they had sat down to deal and her terms had emerged far tougher than he had imagined, he'd been a good sport. He had never held it against her that she had held him up, and ever since then they'd both been as honest as they could and had kept scrupulously to the terms of their agreement.

The truth of it was that at this moment she loved him no less than she had ever loved him . . . when she had married him for the best of everything. And God help her, she had never ceased to yearn for him even as she was forced to deny them both the comfort and the joy of physical love. No, it hadn't been what most would call a brilliant marriage, but if she had come up short on one end, in many ways she had gotten far more than she'd bargained for. . . .

Yes, she owed it to him to lay the cards on the table honestly—no matter the pain.

He kept smiling, didn't even flinch. But what she wasn't prepared for was *his* honesty at this moment, at *his* laying out his really wild cards to reveal more than she could bear.

"It was an act of unfaithfulness," he began.

"But confessions aren't necessary," she broke in. "Our agreement never specified fidelity, only discretion."

"But I committed an *indiscretion* and a pretty lousy one at that. And while I might not have violated the letter of our contract, I violated its spirit."

"Please, don't do this, T.S. Whatever it was—well, it doesn't matter anymore."

"But it does, and since we're spelling it all out it's the only honest thing to do. If nothing else, won't you indulge a dying man by letting him confess his sins?"

She didn't answer, but then she was sorry she'd given him permission by default when he said in a flat monotone, "I screwed Babe."

Then she could only whisper, "*Our* little Babe? Oh, damn you, you son of a bitch, why *her?*"

"My only excuse is that I was depressed about my condition and was reaching out. . . ."

"But that doesn't explain choosing *Babe*," she cried in despair. "She's so young and so vulnerable. You took advantage of her desperate need for a father's love. You could have had your pick of hundreds of women!"

"But I thought only sweet and tender flesh could save me. I thought, how can I die if this sweet young woman loves me? I thought there was a magic to it—some kind of strength, some kind of redemption. Can you understand?"

*This is what he calls being honest? Laying this grotesque aberration on me? How dare he talk of redemption? How dare he ask for my understanding now?*

What she understood was that, while she'd been bending over backward to rationalize everything he did and didn't do and didn't feel . . . had spent tortuous hours trying to *understand* and forgive him for making it impossible for her to lie in his arms, he—when looking into the face of death—remained as selfish as ever with his usual disregard for every other member of the human race.

"So Babe was your choice of victim. But why not Honey?" she demanded. "She's as young as Babe and much more beautiful . . . easily as desirable as her mother, whom you didn't hesitate to fuck when it suited your purposes. . . ."

"I *never* considered Honey."

"Why? Because she wasn't an easy mark like Babe? That you knew she'd reject you? That she has your number and shies away from you? Don't deny it. I've seen her do it."

"It's true she avoids me, just like her father avoids me. Maybe it's because she's figured out—as Teddy Rosen has—that it's possible *I could be her father.* . . ."

*Of course.* She could not deny that she hadn't thought of that herself a long time ago. *He and Mimi in Cannes at the right possible time.*

"And that's why you didn't try with her? How admirable! How noble! You didn't try to fuck the girl who was possibly your daughter! And Sam? You knew *she* wasn't your daughter and she would never have resisted you! Oh, no, never." Her voice was low now, ragged with her bitterness. "She's always been so hungry for your love, she would have done anything you asked of her, and with a passion. Tell me, why not Sam?"

She didn't know what she hoped to hear in answer. Maybe that he'd say, "Because even though *I* knew she wasn't my daughter, *she didn't,* and that made it impossible—that the idea of sex with her own father would, in the end, prove too damaging for her to live with." But he didn't say that or anything that she could in some way find redeeming. Rather he said, "It never even occurred to me. Frankly, I never found Sam sexually appealing."

With that, such an uncontrollable rage swept through her that her hand whipped out involuntarily to slap him, but he didn't even blink; he only smiled that little ironic smile and then she ached to spit into the smile.

"But you didn't let me finish. I was going to say that the reason I never found Sam appealing or wanted to be around her is that the sight of her makes me feel guilty as hell."

Did this guilt, then, constitute a measure of redemption? She was too heartsick to care. Still, he insisted on telling her about the affair, which soon proved to be unsatisfactory to both Babe and him and had ended with her walking out on him, leaving him to weep into the motel's moldy pillow.

"So, why did you weep? Because Babe came to her senses and was rejecting you or because you were being denied the magic you hoped would save you while you knew *nothing* could?"

"Wrong on all counts. I wept because of the realization that I had *had* the magic that would have saved me right in the palm of my hand"—he cupped her face in the heel of his palm—"and I didn't know it and bargained it away."

She went to the windows to open the draperies now, to let in the last light of day, and buried her face in the curtains to weep because it was so late . . . too late for everything . . . even for the magic potion called love.

*    *    *

"All right, Nora, I'll go to the commencement to please you, but it will have to be a trade-off."

"What do you want in exchange?"

"I don't know how long this damn business will take, but however long, I'm prepared to play out my losing hand with as much grace as I can muster. But the one thing I refuse to put up with is having Sam sitting by my bedside fussing over me, moaning and whining and carrying on, begging her daddy not to leave her. You'll have to spare me that, Nora. Send her away someplace . . . as far away as possible."

She agreed for Sam's sake, if not for his. Sam had to be spared the pain of watching the man she believed to be her father die, and now that she knew that T.S. had acquired this penchant for revelation, she also had to protect Sam from a possible deathbed confession that would reveal that she wasn't his daughter. It was a truth that could destroy her.

He took her hand. "But you'll be there? Till the end for as

long as it takes? I know I don't have the right to ask, it was never part of the deal, but what the hell—a dying man deserves a little something extra, and you've always been a damn good winner."

"Win or lose, I'll be there."

And then it was inevitable—as inevitable as the violet twilight deepening into a velvety darkness—that he would take her in his arms. There was a fitness to it and a timeliness, she thought, that she would go into them as passionately as that first night they had met. . . .

# PART EIGHT

# COMMENCEMENT

————•••————

## Los Angeles, 1974–1975

# SIXTY-TWO

————— •• •• —————

S
he called Mick, waking him. "In case you're too sleepy to recognize the voice, old chum, this is Nora Grant."

"I'm not too sleepy to know that when you start calling me 'old chum,' it's a favor you're after and not a marriage proposal."

"Neither. I have a business proposition for you."

"But I'm an actor, remember, not a businessman."

"But I'm offering you an opportunity to be both. Also something you always said you were dying to be—a producer."

"Am I dreaming or are you trying to pull a fast one?"

"Trying to pull a fast one, as in *tomorrow*, first thing."

"As you well know, Nora, there's only *one* thing I'm good at this early in the morning, so if it's speedy action you're after, maybe you'd better spell it all out for me fast."

After she did, he moaned, "I *knew* I'd be sorry it wasn't a marriage proposal. All I can say is I hope I won't let you down. The first time around I didn't hold on to *you*, and the second time around I didn't manage to hold on to *Hubie*."

"That's what's wonderful about life. Each time around it's a new deal. But please, don't let this one get away."

\*   \*   \*

Teddy woke Honey at seven-thirty and she complained, "But I don't have to get up yet—graduation's at two."

"I couldn't wait any longer. I have a surprise."

"Belgian waffles with strawberries or blueberry muffins?"

"Just put on your robe and slippers and come downstairs."

He made her close her eyes before he threw open the front door. When she opened them and saw the white Thunderbird in the driveway, she screamed, "A T-bird!" and burst into tears.

"I hope those aren't tears of disappointment. You weren't by chance expecting a Maserati—?" But they both knew she was crying tears of joy, and it wasn't because the T-bird was far beyond her expectations, but that it meant *they* had accepted the teleplay and paid out the final check.

"Oh, Daddy, did they *really, really* like it?"

"Did you say *like* it, kid? They *loved* it!"

"Oh!" She gave him another hug. "Does Nora know?"

"Well, *she* helped me pick out the car, and she said *white*. She said beautiful blondes should always drive white."

"But the question now is, what *are* we going to have for breakfast? Belgian waffles or blueberry muffins?"

*   *   *

"I think *you* should tell her when she comes down to breakfast, which should be any moment now, T.S. She's getting up early so she can allow two hours for makeup and hair."

"But why do I have to be the one to tell her?" T.S. demanded. "All you said I had to do was go to graduation. Why can't *you* tell her about London and the movie?"

Nora took a sip of tea to wash down a second aspirin. "Because it's her graduation present and it will mean a lot more to her if *you* tell her. If I do she'll only get suspicious that I'm trying to get rid of her."

"But she'll carry on so! All those tears and kisses and general hysteria. You know how I hate hysterics. That's what I like about you, Nora—you take things in stride."

"She *is* only eighteen, she's entitled to make a fuss. Especially about such an exciting offer! To fly off to London to work on a film! I remember when I was eighteen and going to London. I didn't take it in stride. I was *so* excited."

Her eyes shone with the memory and T.S. looked at her

longingly. "I wish I had known you then," he said finally.

"Oh, you wouldn't have liked me," she laughed. "I was hardly your film-star type. I was so—well, *unformed,* like a lump of unmolded clay, and very unsophisticated."

"I still think *you* should be the one to give her the news. After all, Mick was *your* idea and *your* husband." He cracked his soft-boiled egg. "Nora! This egg's *not* right and you *know* how I count on you to see that things are just so."

*  *  *

Babe called Honey at ten. "Only got a minute. We're going for breakfast at the Hotel Bel-Air in honor of the big day. I just called to see what kind of car you got."

"You're amazing! How did you know I got a car?"

"Easy. Half the girls at Beasley already have a car, like Sam, and the other half are getting them today since it's the practical gift that serves a twofold purpose—graduation present *and* necessity. So, what kind of a car *did* you get?"

"A white T-bird! I love it! You *did* get a car?"

"Yeah," Babe said without enthusiasm. "A Mustang."

"But a Mustang's super. Don't you like it?"

"A *brown* car is super? *You* get a white car, *Sam* has a bright-green one, and I get asshole-brown. Well, it figures. I always get the shitty end of the stick."

"Really, Babe, you should be ashamed. How many girls graduating all over America are getting brand-new Mustangs?"

"But do you know what the Judge said when he handed me the keys to the *refined*—that's how Catherine describes the color—shit-brown car? He said he hoped that I appreciated it, while Mrs. Ice Cube stood there and nodded. Well, at least he never sexually abused me—at least not that I can remember. And *she* never beat me except for those few times she lost it and cracked my face with a hairbrush. But I must go—our refined breakfast awaits and I wouldn't be surprised if *the* graduation special is shit-brown scrambled eggs. I hear it's the last word in refined dining."

\* \* \*

"Honey, where have you been? I've been calling you for the last half hour every minute on the minute."

"If you really want to know, Sam, I was taking Teddy for a spin in my beautiful white Thunderbird!"

"A T-bird? That's *neat*. Happy graduation, Honey Funny!"

"The same to you, Sammy. But why were you calling me every minute on the minute? Did you get another *new* car?"

"No, not a car. I'm going to England! Daddy told me this morning. Grantwood Studio is making a movie there and *I'm* going to London to work on it! And guess who's going to be the executive producer and the star? This will *really* blow you away. Nora's ex, Mick Nash! I bet it must be *killing* her because the whole time Daddy was giving me the details she kept interrupting to remind me that while she *hoped* I'd enjoy the experience, the purpose of my going was to *learn*, and she hoped I would take proper advantage of the opportunity and not forget why I was there. Honey, why don't you *say* something?"

"I'm recovering from shock. How long will you be away?"

"As long as it takes to make the flick, I guess. Maybe a whole year. I don't think they have a shooting script or anything yet, but Daddy says it will be the best training if I'm right there from the *very* beginning of the project."

"That means you won't be starting UCLA with me in the fall," Honey said forlornly.

"No, but I'm going to have my very own flat, so you and Babe can come visit as soon as you get your first school break and we'll really have a blast! I'm leaving tomorrow!"

"*Tomorrow?* How can you leave so fast? And why? It's not like it's an emergency, is it?"

"Well, you know what Daddy always says: 'It's *always* an emergency in the movie business.' Anyhow, Nora made the reservation and that's the flight she booked me on, tomorrow at the crack of dawn. I don't know why she made it *that* early, but I suppose she figured if I was leaving, the sooner the better. Honey, you haven't told me that you're happy for me."

"Of course I am, but it's all so sudden. Oh, Sam, I'm going to miss you so. . . ."

"Me too you, but I'll be back, Honey Bunny, and you'll be coming over to visit. Now I have to call Babe and tell her. See you soon, Honey Moon, at the grad, with your dad."

\* \* \*

Even before they were out the driveway, the Judge—sitting next to Babe at the wheel of the Mustang—began his critique of her driving until she was ready to jump out at the next red light, or maybe even while the car was still in motion. Finally she asked him if he would be happier if *he* took the wheel and he took the question in the sarcastic spirit it was intended. "Since you haven't a trace of appreciation in you and don't even know how to keep your fresh mouth shut, I'm more inclined to take back *the car* than the wheel."

She was dying to snap back, "Why don't you, and then I won't have to hear about how ungrateful I am, which is getting boring but not *as* boring as *you* are to start with." But she didn't say it because then he might do just that—take back the car— and she would really be stuck for the summer without wheels of her own. And in the fall she would have to rely on *them* even for transportation to school, and the whole point of going to college was to get away from the two of them for a while.

But Catherine still demanded she apologize for having been fresh as well as unappreciative, threatening to forget about the breakfast *and* the graduation exercises as well.

Still, Babe was tempted *not* to apologize, even if it meant missing graduation, but the idea of spending the rest of the day locked up in the house with the two of them was too dismal to contemplate, and she mumbled the required words. But when she brought the car to a halt in front of the hotel's entrance, she hit the brake so hard that if it hadn't been for his safety belt, the Judge would have gone through the windshield.

She winked at the parking attendant, smiled sweetly at the Judge, and, once seated in the elegant dining room—with Catherine looking around to see if there was anyone worth noticing and the Judge intent on studying the menu—got their full attention when she said with wide-eyed innocence, "While you have been a really wonderful father to me, I *know* you adopted me and I thought that now that I'm graduating you might want to tell me who my real father is."

They answered simultaneously. Catherine, pale with either shock or anger blurted, "*Was*, not is, and that finishes this discussion," while the Judge sneered, "You wouldn't want to know, and believe me, if you did, you'd understand why you have so much difficulty being a lady."

\* \* \*

"So what happened then?" Sam demanded, her blood boiling.

"She ordered eggs Benedict, he ordered apple pancakes, and, since I wasn't very hungry, I only had a glass of hemlock."

"I wasn't asking for a rundown of the menu," Sam barked. "What did you say after he said you wouldn't want to know who your father was or that you had a problem being a lady?"

"I didn't say anything," Babe said miserably.

"Why not? You have every right to know the facts—who your father was and why your mother refuses to talk about it!"

"No! I *have* no rights. All I have is *them*, and if I don't let them call the shots and behave myself, I won't even have *them*. And who cares who my father was if he's dead—where was he when I needed him?

"Besides, from what the Judge implied, he must have been a murderer or a rapist or— Anyhow, it's the Judge who counts because he's the one who married her and adopted me, forgiving me my bad blood. So I guess Catherine's right—I *should* be grateful he gave me his name and all—and it's no wonder she wants to keep it all a big, dark secret. Anyway, I don't care about the Judge or what he says. It's *her*—she's my *real mother* and she's *supposed* to love me. But she's *ashamed* of me, and that's what hurts."

"Did you ever stop to think that maybe she's really ashamed of *herself*?"

Babe had to laugh. "That's a hot one! Catherine the Great

ashamed of herself? Why would she be—she's not only a Lee from Virginia but a perfect size four and a perfect lady who's married to a judge! But tell me more about *your* news. Oh, God, what I wouldn't give to be on my own in London!"

"And what about working with Mick Nash? I saw his picture in a magazine. He's still devastatingly good-looking even though he must be really old considering he was married to Nora. Though I don't plan on holding that against him," she giggled. "Wouldn't it be a howl if I had an affair with Nora's ex? Besides getting *her* where it really hurts, I've always had a thing for older men."

"Yeah," Babe offered dully. "I know." The last thing she needed or wanted was to discuss having an affair with an older man, *especially* with Sam. "I better go. Though I already took a shower this morning, Catherine suggested I take another. I guess she thinks I really stink!"

* * *

Nora found Sam in the library, lost in thought. "We have to leave soon. Hadn't you better shower and dress?"

Sam looked up. "Do you think I *need* a shower?"

"*Need?* Don't you usually shower before you dress?"

"Usually. But Babe just said her mother told her to take a shower though she'd just taken one a couple of hours before. Babe thinks it's because Catherine thinks she stinks."

"That's silly. If Catherine suggested she take a second shower, so what? Why is Babe making a fuss over nothing?"

"But it isn't *nothing* to Babe. It's her state of mind. She really believes that she stinks as a person. And it's Catherine the bitch and the asshole, the Judge, who've talked her into it. And I think *you* should talk to *them* about it."

Nora stiffened. "Even if what you say is true, what makes you think I'm the one to talk to them?"

"Remember that time we got caught smoking pot and Catherine said Babe couldn't be friends with us anymore? You talked her into changing her mind. I'm convinced she caved in because *you* know where some of her bodies are buried."

"That's nonsense."

"Is it? Babe guessed that the Judge adopted her and now he's admitted it, but they still won't tell her *who* her real father is. All they said was that he was someone really bad, which makes Babe think she's bad too. And I overheard you tell someone that Catherine wasn't from Virginia at all but from Memphis, Tennessee, and that her maiden name wasn't really Lee. *Why* did she lie? And if you tell me you don't know I won't believe you. I'm convinced that you do!"

"In that case, I won't bother affirming or denying. But even if I knew the answers, what makes you think *I* have the right to divulge another woman's secrets or interfere—tell her what she should tell her own child? And if you have it in mind to tell Babe that her mother wasn't really a Lee from Virginia, you'd better be sure that this is what she's *ready* to hear and will be the better off for knowing."

"But everyone's better off knowing the truth!" Sam cried.

"No, not *always*. As for Babe finding out that she *doesn't* stink—that has to come from self-discovery. Now, if you don't get ready, we'll be late and your father's dressed and waiting—impatiently, I might add. And since we're pressed for time, why don't *you* skip the shower? You already smell sweet as a rose, even a rose by any other name."

"Now, how am I supposed to take that?" Sam said in exasperation. "That you're serious or making fun of me?"

"You're eighteen, graduating, and are supposedly mature, so why don't you figure it out for yourself?"

\*   \*   \*

It's a beautiful day for an outdoor graduation, Nora thought, much like the day an eager bride might choose for her wedding day. *Happy is the graduate the sun shines on today.*

Even the setting was perfect—Beasley's Shakespeare Rose Garden, in which every Beasley girl took pride since all its varied specimens had been raised in their own hothouse of roses (symbolic of the young women entrusted into its nurturing care) before they were transplanted to the outdoor beds, each named after a fair maiden from one of the Bard's works (a scholarly reference to its hallowed soil).

They were a little late, which meant that Sam, in her robe and tasseled hat, hair streaming behind her, had to run to join her classmates lining up for the procession while Nora and T.S. took the first two small white chairs they spotted. Looking around, she saw the Tracys to the left of them in the next row forward and Teddy sitting in the front and to the right, head turned, eyes searching the rows, and she thought: *He's looking for me to make sure I'm here.*

Then he spotted her and waved and she waved back as T.S. watched with a little smile and enigmatic eyes. He was about to say something, but just then the band struck up and the girls, lined up by size—Babe first, Sam last, and Honey somewhere in the middle—began their march up the aisle.

"Sort of like a wedding but without any bridegrooms," T.S. whispered to Nora dryly.

"Oh, the grooms will come along soon enough. After all, this is commencement and that means it's all just beginning."

Each girl took part in the program. When Sam joined with three other girls in song, Nora heard only her sweet voice above the others; saw only her tall, graceful figure and her fine uplifted head; and felt her heart beat with love, pride, and prayer. She glanced quickly at T.S. to see if there was *something* showing in his eyes, but he was studying his hands. Who knew what he was thinking or if he was even listening?

*But it doesn't really matter except that Sam* thinks *he heard her. All the good qualities are there just bursting to get out and it has nothing to do with whose daughter she is—she's Sam, and, with lots of love, she'll do just fine. She'll even find out who she is and who she's capable of being.*

Then, as always, her thoughts leaped to Hubie, from whom she only occasionally received a card. She'd done what she could—she'd loved him and provided him with the right name and protected him with secrecy. Now she could only hope he would find the maturity to know for himself who he truly was.

* * *

Babe took her place at the white Steinway (Beasley prided itself on having only the finest in the way of equipment) to offer up a piece by Chopin, and again Nora glanced at T.S. to see what emotion played on his face—shame, regret, even some small trace of affection? But he was studying his shoes now as if admiring their high polish.

Then, with Babe's adequate if not brilliant rendering floating on the balmy air, Nora looked over toward the Tracys to catch their faces in profile. The Judge's face was devoid of expression, his head moving from side to side like a metronome. But Catherine's head was tilted back high as if she were holding it proud, her eyes shut closed all the better to hear, and, while she wasn't smiling, her determined chin nodded as if in approval.

Then the realization hit Nora that, while Catherine *wasn't* a nice person, the truth was that she probably did love Babe! And the bottom line was that Catherine had done no more than she herself had—woven a swaddling cloth out of secrets and lies to secure a name and a future for her child and to give that child a good life according to her lights. How dared she, Natalie Nora Hall Hartiscor Nash Cantington Grant, presume to sit sanctimonious judgment on pretty Katya Marcus?

What was her crime, after all? That she'd fled her Russian-Jewish immigrant father's dry-goods store in Memphis to marry comic Jackie White, who had changed *his* name from Jacob Weiss? And who could blame her that she had fled that life too when instead of being exciting and fun, it turned out to be a series of dismal one-night stands in dreary clubs, the newlyweds holed up in even drearier rooming houses?

Perhaps it was Babe's birth that had moved her to leave Jackie behind to find safe haven with the Judge, who offered her and her daughter his name, prestige, and Protestant heritage, asking in return only that Katya Marcus Weiss be obliterated, that she take on *his* coloring and be what he wanted her to be.

*Have I done any less? Does she love Babe any less than I love*

*Hubie or Sam? Who's to say what form love may take—what path it makes you walk? Have I lied that much less or do I keep fewer secrets? How can I condemn her or dream of divulging her secrets when I'm not prepared to divulge my own? And, like Hubie and like Sam, Babe has to find out for herself who she is or it won't count for much.*

\* \* \*

After the presentation of the diplomas, it was time for Honey's valediction. Honey, with her usual grace and self-assurance—*oh, she knows who she is, F. Theodore Rosen's proud daughter, and let no one dare tell her differently*—favored them with her fabulous smile and began to speak. . . .

Without looking at him, Nora could *feel* T.S. squirming. Was he bored or only uncomfortable sitting so long on the small chair not built to accommodate a man of his frame? Was he in physical pain or only mental? "It won't be long now," she whispered. "After Honey, it's all over."

"But it's not over until the fat lady sings."

\* \* \*

"Finally, here at last!" Honey spread her arms in an encompassing gesture. "Our commencement! Now it all begins—life! And we greet it with open arms for we, Beasley's class of '74, so beautifully endowed with the love and learning bestowed upon us by all of you, our friends and teachers, our mentors and parents"—she blew a kiss to Teddy—"are ready to go out into the world prepared to embrace it in love and in truth and in celebration. . . ."

Her voice was clear and rang out with a sincerity no one could deny and an enthusiasm that was contagious, and when she finished there was thundering applause as once again the band struck up and the new graduates, diplomas in hand, rose to their feet to march back down the aisle triumphant.

"Great delivery. Our Honey is going to make a hell of an actress," T.S. commented in an aside to Nora as Teddy, on his feet and applauding wildly, turned to wave again at Nora, reveling in *his* triumph. And Nora waved back just as enthusiastically with tears of shared pleasure in her eyes.

"You *really* like him," T.S. observed, and though it was a statement rather than a question, Nora answered, "Of course I do. How not? He's such a lovely man."

Now T.S. shook his head to say, bemused, "And I always figured him for a loser, which just goes to prove that I wasn't as good at casting as I thought I was." He laughed. "No wonder I find myself in this lousy predicament."

*No, Teddy wasn't a loser. And if one were casting a movie, one might even cast him in the role of hero.*

*        *        *

The graduates broke formation to rush to their parents and friends to kiss and hug. Sam rushed to her father to throw her arms around him so violently, he thought she would solve his problem by strangling him. "Oh, Daddy, isn't this a wonderful day? I'm so happy I could die!"

"In that case, before you do," T.S. said, disengaging himself from her embrace, "maybe you'd better give Nora a hug too since she's the one who decided you should go to Beasley."

"Of course," Sam agreed, now that he had made a point of it. And it was true enough that Nora *had* made a wonderful choice—without Beasley there would have been no Honey or Babe in her life. But she made a quick job of it before she dashed off to join Babe and Honey in hugging Teddy to pieces.

It was out of the question that she and T.S. would remain for the reception, Nora decided. For one, T.S. was champing at the bit, and for another, it would be awkward with Babe and Honey, each for her own reason, trying to avoid him. Any minute now Sam would try to drag the girls over to T.S. to be congratulated, and they would surely resist, and then Sam would be puzzled and hurt.

"Why don't you sit here, T.S., while I pay some respects and tell Sam we're leaving, and then we can go." She made the rounds—the graduates whom she knew, the Beasley people, the

Tracys and some of the other parents—and girded herself to tell Sam that she and T.S. were not staying for the reception.

"You stay here with your friends."

"But why can't Daddy stay just an hour or so?"

"He wants to write a few memos to Mick so that you can take them with you tomorrow morning."

"But what about our graduation dinner? I thought we'd be going out with Honey and Babe and their parents. It's the last time I'll be seeing them for a long time."

"But you have to pack yet and I thought you'd want to spend this last evening alone with your father."

"I didn't think of that. Of course I do."

"Good. Now, before I leave, I must congratulate Babe and Honey." It would be the last time she would be seeing them for a while too. She doubted very much that they would be coming to visit at Grantwood again until Sam came home . . . after T.S. was gone.

\* \* \*

Teddy caught up with her just as she was about to claim T.S. and leave. "You didn't say good-bye to me."

"Did I ever tell you I sang songs in a cabaret filled with soldiers and sailors during the war? Well, I did, and one of the songs I sang was 'I'll be seeing you, always . . .' "

"I know the song you're thinking of, but I'm afraid you're a little mixed up," he said teasingly. "There's no *always* in there. 'Always' is a separate song. A very lovely song, if I recall."

"You're right," she said, blushing, remembering that "Always" was as frankly a love song as it could get. "I guess I got my titles muddled. It *was* thirty years ago and you know how it is. . . ."

"Yes, I think I know exactly how it is."

# SIXTY-THREE

<hr>

When the doctors suggested and Nora insisted that T.S. undergo radiation and chemotherapy, he demanded, "What for? The reviews are in and it's a dog, and when the movie's a dog, there are two ways to go. You can prolong the torture by waiting for the box-office receipts to kill the dog off, or you can get it over with by pulling it out of the theaters immediately. I always believed in the fast kill."

"But life isn't a movie."

"No, it's a magazine. When I was a kid that was a joke. Someone said, 'What's life?' and the answer was: 'Life's a magazine.' And what's there to do with an old magazine that's already been read but get rid of it?"

"No, T.S.! Do the radiation and chemotherapy for me."

"I would if I thought I'd be doing it for you, but you want me to do it for *Sam* so that after I'm gone you can tell her, 'He tried against all odds . . . he fought valiantly so that he could be here for you.' Deny that if you can."

She didn't. She couldn't. She said nothing.

"Well, since it's my show I'm going to do it my way. I'm going to go to the studio every day until I can't go anymore. Then I'm going to sit by that damn pool that I never had time to use until I can't sit up anymore. Then I'm going to lie down in my own bed in my own house and wait for them to carry me off to the cemetery. And that's what you can do for me—*let me*. Promise me there'll be no treatments, no hospitals, and that you'll let me go out in my own style."

She nodded. He hadn't made a brilliant husband and had

456

certainly been a lackluster father, but at least she would be able to tell Sam that her dad had been a stylish kind of guy.

*   *   *

Nora knew T.S. wasn't planning on going to the studio again when he came home and asked if the pool was still heated now that it was fall.

"It is. Are you taking a swim before dinner?"

He laughed. "You know that joke about the guy who gets his finger chopped off and they sew it back on and the doctor says, 'There you are—good as new. Now you can sit down at the old piano and bang out Mozart.' And the guy says, 'Gee, medical science sure is great these days. I didn't even know how to play the piano before.' The point of which is I never swam before, so why the hell should I start now?"

No, the point was *not* that he had never swum before but that he was telling her not to get her hopes up by expecting him to die a better man than he had lived.

"And I never said I planned on *swimming*. All I said was that I was going to *sit* by the pool, in peace, I hope."

"Well, if you're not interested in swimming, what about a relaxing Jacuzzi? All you have to do is *sit* and let the jets do the work. The night air's cool but the water's hot. . . ." she said provocatively.

"Sounds good, but only if you'll join me."

"That's what I'm here for," she said, slowly starting to disrobe. . . .

The next morning T.S. was already sitting poolside when she awoke. "What are you doing here even before breakfast?"

"What does it look like I'm doing? I'm reading scripts since your cute ex and clever stepdaughter still haven't come up with a worthy project and I hate to see all that money you gave them go down the drain. Maybe you ought to call up your winner-friend, Teddy, and see if *he* has any bright ideas."

"I just might at that," she said, going back into the house to get him a breakfast tray, wondering if T.S., so close to the end, was just teasing her, exhibiting jealousy, or simply trying to mend his fences. . . .

*　*　*

When Teddy answered the door to find Nora, he was surprised and then elated. He hadn't seen or even spoken with her on the phone since the girls' graduation. But he drew her into the house and closed the door behind her before he said, "Long time, no see. Dare I ask to what I owe this pleasure?"

"You may dare, but I'm not sure you'll think it quite so pleasureful when I tell you—"

"Is anything wrong? Is it Sam?"

"Partially, but not entirely." Then, after she finished explaining, she asked, "So, will you help me out? As you see, I'm in a race against the clock. For both their sakes I'd like to see a film in the can before—well, the end."

"But why *me?* With all the hungry and gifted screenwriters loose in Hollywood and London, *why me?* Even with the Thanksgiving special showing this month, I'm not out of the woods yet. How do you know I can come up with something good enough in so short a time?" He looked at her suspiciously. "Are you sure you're leveling with me? That this isn't another one of your projects to help the needy and, just incidentally, make nice-nice all around? Because I personally have no *need* to make nice with T. S. Grant, no matter what."

"I know that, Teddy. But I think *he* does."

At first he was disappointed to learn why she had shown up on his doorstep, but then he grew angry. "You want me to write this damn screenplay just so he and I can kiss and make up before he meets his maker, not because you *need* me or even *think* I can come up with a great screenplay in a race against time. I *thought* it strange that in all this time Mick couldn't find a decent screenplay to go into production with."

"You're only partially right about the making-up part. I *do* need you and it's not so strange, really, that Mick can't get it together to find the right screenplay. That was a miscalculation on my part. You see, I needed a friend to do me a favor—an old, loving friend I could trust—but while Mick *is* an *old* friend, it seems I sent a boy to do a *man's* job and now I'm trying to rectify that error. Understand?"

He sat down beside her to look into her eyes and traced each eyebrow with the tip of a finger, which was as close to a caress as he dared allow himself. Then he smiled and said, "I understand that you make it difficult for a *man* to refuse."

"I must confess—I was *sure* you wouldn't refuse me though I knew I was asking a lot. Probably more than I have any right to considering your and T.S.'s history."

"How could you be so sure I wouldn't refuse?"

She laughed. "Because I'm Nora Hartiscor Nash Cantington Grant, and that means I know my men." *It means that by now I can tell the men from the boys, the losers from the winners—can even pick out the few heroes from a field of winners. . . .*

"It's almost lunchtime," he said. "Let me make you lunch. We can eat by the window overlooking the garden."

She gazed around the living room ablaze with sunlight. "I think not. It's too bright in here. One sees too clearly and too much. Sometimes it's better not to see *everything.*"

"We don't *have* to eat in here," Teddy said, studying her face. "There's the library—it's very dark in there." But before she could answer he shook his head. "No, that won't do either. In the dark you can't tell one thing from another—can't even see what you might be stumbling into. Besides, it's too early in the day to go into such a dark room. . . . Maybe the best thing would be if I took you *out* to lunch."

"No, the best thing would be if I went home to have lunch with my husband. He gets lonely and restless when I'm not there. He depends on me."

"Yes, I'm sure."

But she wasn't sure just *what* he was sure of—that she should go home and have lunch with T.S. or that T.S. depended on her. There was a big difference.

She asked about Honey before she left. "How's she doing at UCLA? Is she enjoying her classes?"

"She's in seventh heaven. Her drama class is doing *Romeo and Juliet* and guess who's Juliet?"

"The starring role? How wonderful! Honey is a natural."

"Honey's a honey," he agreed. "And how's Sam doing, movie-producing efforts aside?"

"Oh, she's having a marvelous time, seeing the sights, driving here, jetting there. Between you and me, I don't think she gives a damn whether they ever get started on the film at all. One thing I must say about Mick. He might not be a great producer, but he knows how to show a girl a good time."

Teddy smiled rather wistfully. "That's a talent too." And she could not disagree.

She found T.S. in a petulant mood when she returned, demanding to know where she'd been. But she understood—it was hard to sit by the side of a pool while life went on around you.

"Where were you?" he asked again, and when she said, "At Teddy Rosen's," he said, "Of course."

"It was *your* idea for me to ask Teddy to come up with a screenplay," she reminded him. "And he said yes."

"Hah! I bet he *leaped* at the chance!"

"Not really. I had to talk him into it. He definitely held back." *In more ways than one . . .*

# SIXTY-FOUR

————— •·•·•· —————

am called to wish her father a happy Thanksgiving, but T.S., who had insisted on eating his turkey dinner in the library and washing it down with bourbon while he watched Astaire and Crosby cavorting in the old classic *Holiday Inn*, wouldn't pick up the phone. "I can't now. I'm up to the part where Bing's singing about being thankful and I'm dying to hear every word."

"Your father can't come to the phone right now but he says, 'Happy Thanksgiving to you,' " Nora said, noting that there was a lot of merry noise in the background. "It sounds very festive there. Did some Americans take pity on you and invite you to Thanksgiving dinner?"

"Not exactly," Sam giggled. "I'm on this darling Greek island and all that noise you hear are Mick's friends celebrating something or other. I haven't the slightest idea what but it's so much fun. We're dancing and drinking wine and breaking dishes. This is the most fun Thanksgiving ever!"

"I can just imagine."

Yes, she had sent a boy to do a man's job and now she was beginning to wonder what else the old boy was up to.

After *Holiday Inn* they watched Teddy's Thanksgiving Day special, and when it was over, there were tears in her eyes and another shot of freshly poured bourbon in T.S.'s hand. "I have to hand it to you, Nora," he said, his speech a little slurred. "You sure know how to pick those winners. Is he going to be number five? Or is it number six?"

She struggled with her temper, reminding herself that T.S. was a dying man and quite drunk, for which she couldn't blame

461

him. *What does he have to gain by staying sober?*

"Oh, I don't know. I think it might be time to call it quits," she drawled.

"But you can't quit yet," T.S. said slyly, and she was fool enough to respond, "Oh? Why can't I?"

"Because after I go you have to try and even out the score. If you count Hubert Hartiscor, you've been widowed three times but only twice divorced. You're entitled to one more divorce." He raised his glass in salute. "Better the gay divorcee than the merry widow!" Then he shook his head. "No, I should drink to the *real* winner—Mr. Next. After all, better gaily divorced than unmerrily dead."

# SIXTY-FIVE

 ◆●◆ 

When it became necessary to increase T.S.'s pain medication and he said that the days were growing too cool to sit by the pool, Nora decided she would make a Christmas Eve party after all—cheer things up. But T.S. said, "Christmas is almost here—it's too late to plan. We can't have people saying that the latest Grant party fizzled at the box office."

The next day he refused to get out of bed and insisted that, instead of cluttering up his space with hospital equipment, his projection equipment be brought up along with stacks and stacks of film reels. And Nora had to agree—she could see that there wouldn't be room for medical monitors and machines, all those wires that would only get in the way.

When Teddy called during the second week of the month to tell her that he had a first draft of a romantic comedy he had tentatively titled *In the Name of Love*, she asked him to bring it over immediately. While she had no hope of T.S. seeing the film in the can, it would be something if production could at least get under way in his lifetime, and Sam would be able to take some small comfort in that.

"I was thinking of sending it over via messenger."

"No, I want you to take it up to T.S. *personally*. That's part of our deal. You're not going to welch on me, are you?"

"I can think of many things I might do to you but welching is not one of them."

"Good. I'll be expecting you."

But when Teddy arrived, T.S. said he had no time to see him or any scripts. "I like the old ones better and I'm right in the middle of a great little oldie. *The Man Who Wouldn't Die*. I have to see how it comes out. Then I'm going to watch *The Thing That Couldn't Die*. But my last selection for the afternoon sounds the most intriguing. It's got a catchy title: *Wives and Lovers*. I hope you'll watch it with me, Nora. It's not the same without you."

She went downstairs to tell Teddy that since T.S. was only into black humor that afternoon and *In the Name of Love* was a romantic comedy, he wouldn't be able to evaluate it properly. "I think I'll just send it off to London so they can get started and we won't waste any more time. And since time *is* of the essence, you'll forgive me if I don't ask you to stay for tea. We have a lot of films to get through before . . . before we're through. Hundreds and hundreds of titles."

"I understand, but speaking of titles, remember when we were talking about song titles at graduation? At first you said the title of a song you used to sing was 'I'll Be Seeing You Always,' and I corrected you. I said that 'Always' was a separate song and then you agreed . . ."

"And—?" she said warily, looking down at the floor.

"I was thinking about it and the lyrics of 'Always' came back to me. Would you like to hear me sing them to you to refresh your memory?"

But her memory needed no refreshing. The lyrics were overwhelmingly about love.

She raised her eyes to gaze steadily into his. "I'm afraid I don't have the time to listen. T.S. is waiting for me to watch a movie with him and he has first call on my time."

\*   \*   \*

As Christmas grew nearer she couldn't help but think about Sam and Hubie so far away. This Christmas was going to be the saddest and loneliest she'd ever known, and it didn't help that T.S. insisted on viewing all the old Christmas classics, one after the other, beginning several days before the twenty-fifth and going at it for punishing hours at a time. It was as if he were trying to go through those towering stacks of film reels with an urgency and a vengeance.

But there were two pleasant surprises on the twenty-third. One was a Christmas card from Hubie from some illegible place in Africa postmarked a month before. The other was a brief visit from Honey and Babe, who came bearing gifts. Honey had two—one from her and one from Teddy. "Daddy said he wouldn't get a chance to bring this over. . . ."

No, he wouldn't want to come himself, she thought. "I know how it is," she said. "The holiday season's so hectic, but now that you're here I can save a trip. I was planning on dropping these off tomorrow." She handed Babe one gold-foil-wrapped box and Honey two. "Will you please give this one to your father for me with my very best wishes?"

"I will," Honey promised, "and if you'll give me a hug, I'll pass it along too." Babe got into the act, demanding a hug, one that she would keep just for herself. The three of them laughed then and Nora was relieved. She'd been afraid that the girls wouldn't feel comfortable at the manor with T.S. permanently at home, but she supposed that what made the difference was that now T.S. was permanently upstairs.

"And now I want to hear what's going on with you two. Your father told me that you're going to play Juliet, Honey."

"It's only a class production, but it would mean a lot to me if you'd come see it. It's going on in the spring."

"I'll try to make it. And what are you up to, Babe?"

"Well, my classes don't exactly thrill me but I'm having fun. At least I'm meeting lots of boys and going to lots of parties." They all laughed at that. "But—well, I wanted you to know, Nora, that I'm getting along a lot better with my parents. My mother and I had a long talk and she told me that she realized she was being unfair not to tell me anything about my *real* father. She said she never wanted to talk about it before because it was so painful—she and my father had been so much in love and he died in a boating accident not long after I was born. And she said I had nothing to worry about when it came to bloodlines because he came from a fine, old Southern family. That the only reason the Judge sometimes made disparaging remarks about him was because he was jealous of him since *he'd* been first and I was really *his* daughter and all. So I can understand why he'd be jealous. I even kind of feel sorry for him, you know."

"Yes," Nora said, glancing at Honey. Her face was inscrutable but her hands were clenched tightly. *She knows what's what without knowing the facts, but she, like me, knows that sometimes people had to be protected from too much truth.*

"Mother even told me his name. William Butler Cranford of the Charleston Cranfords. Isn't that a beautiful name?"

"Beautiful," Nora agreed. The important thing was that Babe was happy and that, for the time being anyway, she and her mother were friends. *Making up was a healing process and life meant healing the breach.* . . .

She asked the girls then if they would go up and wish T.S. a Merry Christmas before they left. "It will mean so much to him to see a young face around here since Sam isn't at home and—well, it *is* the season when all good men and women should come together in peace and goodwill."

She knew she was putting them on the spot—they could hardly refuse her without making a clean breast of things and they were hardly about to do that. After they agreed, she asked them to wait while she checked to see whether T.S. was napping. But he was watching a movie. "Babe and Honey are downstairs. They'd like to wish you a Merry Christmas."

He didn't remove his eyes from the screen. "I'm sure they're just dying to," he laughed. "I can see you're still up to your old tricks, Nora, healing those breaches. But we agreed that I was going to go out in my own style. Tell the girls that I wish them the best of the season but I can't be disturbed. I'm watching *Christmas in Connecticut* and Babs Stanwyck is having the boss over for Christmas dinner. I gotta see if everything turns out okay."

After Honey and Babe left she opened Teddy's present. It was a little gold charm—a replica of a musical note. Her present to him was the same musical note fashioned into a tie pin. They seemed to be two people with a single thought. Or was it the same sweet song of love?

\*   \*   \*

Sam called on Christmas Eve. "I'm at the Ritz Hotel in Paris! Mick thought Paris would make a great background for one of the scenes in *In the Name of Love,* so we hopped over to check it out. Wasn't that a great idea?"

Nora thought it would be a great idea to wring Mick's neck but then thought better of it. If Babs Stanwyck could spend Christmas in Connecticut, why couldn't Sam and Mick spend Christmas in Paris? As a matter of fact, maybe they ought to retitle *In the Name of Love.* Make it *Christmas in Paris* instead. . . .

# SIXTY-SIX

———— ••·•• ————

When T.S. could no longer keep down the meat-and-potatoes kind of food he liked and she couldn't interest him in custards or gelatin surprises, they struck a deal: For every custard he ate she would give him an ounce of bourbon. But when even the custard didn't go down easily, she let him cheat. It was barely possible that he could get through all his reels of movies before the end, but the supply of bourbon was something she could count on—there was no way they would run out. All she had to do was call the nearest liquor store.

Still, she was running out of a commodity she'd been counting on to see them through—her good cheer. She'd promised T.S. she would keep smiling, but it was getting harder every day to deliver. And it didn't help that it began to rain endlessly. While it was welcome—there'd been a drought—it was also depressing to those used to sunnier days. But then, during the last week of January, out of the rain came a miracle when Elena, the new maid, told her there was a man downstairs waiting to see her. "What's his name?" But Elena lifted her shoulders and threw out her arms. *Who's to know?*

"Did he tell you what he wanted?"

Elena repeated the gestures. *Who's to say?*

His back was to her but she would know that back anywhere. Then he turned, smiling, and it was as if the sun had come out. Nobody had a more beautiful smile than Hubie, who was as handsome as ever despite the differences the years had made. He was brawnier, his hair was sun-bleached almost white, and he now had a mustache and a beard that were the color his hair used to be. And there was something else that was indefinable and she struggled to think what it was.

"I missed you so, Mum, and it was different, somehow, than how I missed you when I was in Nam."

"Oh, Hubie, how many different ways are there to miss a mother?" she laughed through tears.

"Well, when I was in Vietnam I used to get scared sometimes and wished that you were there to make things all right. But this time, in the Legion, I'd wish you were there just so I could hear you talk and make things fun. It was as if I missed you as a person more than I missed you as a mother. Does that sound screwy?"

"No, it sounds wonderful." What it sounded like was that he hadn't missed her as a boy might but the way a grown man would. Was this the indefinable difference, then—that the boy had finally grown into a man? Then she realized that he was still in his dripping raincoat and they were standing in the middle of a puddle. "Let's get you out of these wet things. And it's almost dinnertime. Are you hungry?"

"Starved. I could eat a horse," he said, and she laughed. There were some things a boy never grew out of, there were some things that never changed, and then there were all kinds of things you wouldn't want to change even if you could. . . .

\* \* \*

Though T.S. had forbidden anyone besides Nora and, over protests, Dr. Ross, entrance to his room, including a nurse, any member of the staff other than Olaf to load the projector, or the maid to change the linen when Nora was not available, he gave Hubie frequent access. "Hubie's got a big smile, which I don't see too much around here anymore. I gotta tell you, Nora, you're kind of losing it lately. And Hubie doesn't tense up even when I'm spitting up blood. That's my kind of man. You know how I believe in people going with the flow. Besides, Hubie was always good company, like his mother used to be before she started losing her sense of humor. And now that he's been around the world, he's got some great stories to tell and a lot of what you might call he-man jokes. And you know what I always said—always leave 'em laughing."

But then, though he tried to laugh, he couldn't quite make it and she called in Hubie to give him an injection, since she'd about lost the energy it took to administer the needle, and the stomach for it, and Hubie had both energy and a good stomach as well as a gentle hand. It seemed as if he had shown up in the nick of time, as he had when Martin was dying. It was good to have a son she could lean on and she wondered if Hubie was at last ready to assume the responsibility of his legacy now that it was nearly time to do so.

\* \* \*

Perhaps she wouldn't have been so furious with Hubie when he told her that he would be taking off soon if she hadn't been counting on him to help T.S. "leave 'em laughing." This time, she felt his behavior was more than irresponsible—it was the height of insensitivity, so unfeeling as to be bordering on the cruel. If this was Hubie the man, she would gladly take back the immature but warm and loving boy he had once been.

"Where will you be off to this time—to join up with the circus?" she asked bitterly. "Or maybe some hippie commune? Aren't you getting a bit old for this sort of thing? And is this need to run away so strong that you can't put it off for a few weeks? At least until it's spring?"

"You don't understand. I'm *not* running away. It's that I have a commitment, one that commands a higher priority."

"Commitment . . . higher priority? Such high-sounding words. Tell me, what *is* this noble commitment?"

"I've joined the Peace Corps."

"You *what?* You must be joking!" But Hubie wasn't smiling. "You're serious! But what will you *do* in the Peace Corps?" she asked, perplexed, all anger gone. "You never really went to college, you have no profession or training other than that of being a soldier and making war." But even as she spoke the words it struck her how incongruous they sounded—loving, gentle Hubie making war. Still, the big question remained: Of what possible use could he be in the Peace Corps?

"When I was serving in Nam, Mum, I learned a few things other than just combat. There was always a guy who needed a letter written or help filling out forms, or someone just to read to him so he could hear a human voice. And there was always a poor chap who needed his hand held or a few sympathetic words, and it was you who taught me about that. Sometimes all it'd take to cheer up a bloke would be a joke, and I tried to remember all the jokes Mick told me when I got into trouble so I'd laugh instead of feeling sorry for myself.

"But even more important were the things I had to learn under fire. You learned fast how to use equipment you hadn't been trained in, or even how to give last rites if pressed, or give emergency medical treatment. Once I had to cut off a buddy's smashed leg to free him so that we could carry him to safety. I know all this sounds as corny as hell, but the point is that what I had to offer without training was better than *nothing*. And that's how it is in some of these Third World places—*something* is better than nothing, which is what they have now. And who taught me that if not you and Martin? So you see, I'm better-trained than you think."

"So I see," she said, ashamed now, and so choked up it was an effort to get the words out.

"Too, the man you see before you *is* a man with a craft."

*A craft? What kind of craft can he possibly have?*

"A couple of years ago I was stationed in this tiny village in Africa and we legionnaires had nothing to do except hang around, swat flies, and play cards. Then one day I saw some natives struggling to put together a kind of primitive structure with almost no materials, no machinery, and no know-how, so I pitched in to try and help. To be honest, I wasn't doing it for any other reason than that I was bored out of my skull. But we got it built even if it was pretty shabby, and it struck me—if I had had the least bit of training, I could have done it better and faster. And the fact was, I *loved* doing it—working with my hands to build something. So I took a correspondence course in carpentry and then another in basic construction. And you know what? I found out I had a real knack! So I do have a trade,

and I can *do* and *teach* wherever they don't have something or
someone better." He laughed joyously, the way he had when he
was so young and so foolhardy as to jump recklessly into puddles. "Next, I'm going to take a course in plumbing. I figure
wherever I go it will come in handy. At worst, it can't hurt."

*Oh, no, Hubie, it can't hurt! And it can't hurt to jump into a few
more puddles—each bigger and more beautiful than the last—before
you're too grown up for that kind of thing.*

But even as she hugged him, she thought of the people whom
he said he'd learned from—herself, Martin, Mick. But there
were the others—the substitute fathers who surely had left their
mark no matter what. Dear Hubert, whose sweetness and loving
nature had probably influenced Hubie whether or not he had
memory of him, and Jeffrey, who, no matter what, had had
many fine qualities. And T.S.? They hardly knew each other and
she was sorry. How wonderful it would have been if he could
have learned something from him too.

But this skill . . . this love Hubie said he had for working
with his hands, this knack that obviously had been there all
along, unplumbed and undiscovered, had to come from somewhere, from someone. And who else could it be but the Duke
of Butte, Montana . . . Johnny Wayne?

For a brief second it occurred to her that all she had to do
was make one call and in a matter of days she could know
everything there was to know about the Duke. But no, she
didn't have to. In the final analysis, Hubie was his own man and
that was enough for her to know.

"When do you leave?"

"In a few days. I thought I'd be able to stay till spring but I
can't."

"That's all right. I have a feeling that spring will come early
this year."

"But, Mum, you really have to let him go to the hospital.
You can't keep this up. There's nothing left of him—he's just
skin and bones and you're not far from that yourself."

"I *can't!* I promised him he'd die in his own bed and that's
the way it has to be. You didn't fail your friend when he needed

you to remove his leg so he could live, did you? Well, I can't
desert my friend when he needs me to help him die the way he
wants to."

"What can I say, then, except that I'm proud of you, Mum?
It takes courage to do what you're doing. And T.S. too. I've seen
a lot of men die bravely in the field, but T.S. has shown me a
man can die bravely in his own bed, laughing even when the
laughing hurts as much as the thing that's killing him."

Despite her own pain, something inside her rejoiced. T.S.,
never a father to Hubie in the remotest sense of the word, *had*
left his mark on her son after all in a positive way. And that
would be something to tell Sam too—how valiantly her father
had faced death.

"Oh, Hubie, I'm glad that you learned that from T.S. If
someone teaches you a valuable lesson about dying, it's the same
as if he'd taught you something about living. It's like a legacy.
And speaking of legacies, I think it's time we talked about the
money you inherited from Martin."

"What's there to talk about? Dad, being the wise man he
was, left it to you to keep in trust for me for a very good
reason—because he knew it was better entrusted to you than to
me. He knew you'd keep it safe for me until I was ready."

"I think you are ready. At least ready enough to know what
I've done with it."

"Right now it's enough for me to know that I'm earning my
own keep. As for what you've done with it—whatever it is I
know that it was the right thing. There is just one thing that
worries me. Or I should say one person. Sam."

"Oh, Hubie, there's no sense talking about what happened.
It was terribly wrong, but you were really only a boy, and now
that you're a man, well, it really doesn't matter anymore."

"It isn't that. I was wondering how she's going to take her
father's death when she doesn't even know he's dying. It's
going to be a terrible shock. Don't you think you should prepare her?"

"I thought it was more important to spare her."

"You know, you really can't spare anyone anything." And

she wondered if Hubie, in his newfound maturity, was right.

And then Hubie was gone and it still wasn't spring.

\* \* \*

She couldn't tell whether Dr. Ross was angrier with himself or with her. "I can't do it anymore, Nora! I won't give you any more morphine! I was crazy to let you talk me into the morphine injections without a registered nurse here to administer them. Don't you realize the untenable position you've put me in, not to mention yourself? It was irresponsible, unethical, and danger-ous! The day he couldn't keep the Dilaudid down was the day I should have either insisted you send him to the hospital or withdrawn from the case."

"But you couldn't have withdrawn. You're my friend."

"Friend!" he said in despair. "What friend puts a loaded gun into a friend's hand when that person isn't even thinking ration-ally? Who would believe, if it came down to it, that you didn't give him an overdose intentionally to end his suffering, or screw up the injection by mistake?"

*Sam's the only one who might question my motivation. . . .*

"On top of that, you've been giving him whiskey along with the morphine! Don't you know that's like playing Russian rou-lette?"

"I never gave him whiskey at the same time and never a *lot*. Besides, if you had put him in the hospital, you would have given him glucose—sugar. At this stage, the whiskey isn't much more than that; it's probably what's keeping him alive since he can't keep anything else down. But why are we arguing about this? It's all immaterial, isn't it?"

"Let me at least bring in a nurse."

"No, I promised and I don't break promises. And if you won't give me the morphine, then I'll get it someplace else. I'll go buy it out on the street myself if I have to."

"You wouldn't?"

"Don't try me."

But soon after, she knew that spring had come when she gave

T.S. his last needle and he opened his eyes wide and gave her what passed for a smile. "You'd better get married again, Nora. You're too good at it to give up the habit."

And that was it. All that was left was to arrange for a cremation, set a date for a memorial service, and call Sam. . . .

# SIXTY-SEVEN

————— •••• —————

Nora anticipated that Sam, crazy with grief, would turn on her with a litany of accusations. Probably Sam even had a mental picture of her withholding an agonized T.S.'s pain-killer, threatening to flush it down the toilet unless he signed over everything. She was even prepared for the accusation that she'd been so greedy for an ill-gotten inheritance, she'd hastened her father's death by murderous means. But what she wasn't prepared for was to have Sam get off the plane with Mick, announcing: "Meet my husband!"

"Oh, no!" she cried out, only to have Sam snap back, "Oh, yes," while Mick looked sheepish and moved forward to kiss her. But she aborted the act by recoiling from him.

As he usually did when faced with an uncomfortable situation, Mick reacted with a joke: "May I call you Mummy?"

"Only if I can call you Sonny," she cracked back, forcing herself to smile, unwilling to let Sam see her anguish. What Sam obviously wanted was to see her out of her mind with jealousy, and if she showed any signs of being wounded, Sam would only assume that she'd achieved her goal.

When she saw the copious amount of luggage the newlyweds had brought, she was more reflective than surprised. It would seem that Sam at least was planning on digging in for a long stay and expected to do her digging in at the manor. What better place to flaunt the joys of her marriage, intent as she was on sticking her knife into what she perceived as her stepmother's jealous heart?

Once they were in the car Nora asked, "When were you married?" and Sam answered, "The *same* day you called to let

me know Daddy was dead, which was probably the same day
you had him burned into a pile of ashes. If one was of a suspicious nature one might wonder at this haste to get rid of the
body."

*Yes, the inevitable litany of accusations . . .*

\* \* \*

"We must have some champagne so we can properly toast your
marriage," Nora said when they arrived at Grantwood. "But
first I'd like to speak to you *alone*, Mick."

Sam voiced immediate objection. "Anything you have to say
to my husband you can say in front of me."

"But Mick and I have *business* to discuss, Sam, so why don't
you take a stroll around the garden until we're through? Spring
came early this year and everything's in bloom."

"What business do you have with Mick that you can't discuss in front of me?"

*We might as well get this over with once and for all.* "Studio
business—between the boss and the man who works for her.
How many employees do you think drag the little wife along
when they're talking business, even when she's as cute as you,
and the boss's stepdaughter besides?"

It took a few shocked seconds for Nora's words to sink in,
then Sam shrieked, "So it's true! First you got rid of me, then
you kept my father from getting proper treatment, then you
tricked him into leaving you his studio, *my* studio!"

*Yes, we might as well get it over with, with the usual formula of
one part truth, one part white lies, one part secrets kept, and one part
love. Mix well, hope for the best.*

"Don't be a little fool. You're letting your imagination run
away with you. But I suppose that's natural considering that
you're only a teenager and immature despite your marriage to a
man—what is it?—*almost three times your age?*" She paused to
glance at a shamefaced Mick and shook her head. "My good-
ness, I never stopped to consider, but you *are* getting rather long
in the tooth, Mick." She turned back to Sam. "Now, let's get a
few facts straight before you make a complete ass of yourself.

First of all, I didn't *have* to get rid of you—your father did that when *he* decided to send you away because he wanted to spare you the pain of watching him endure his own. And I didn't *have* to keep him from getting treatment because that was *his* decision—he's the one who wanted to go out in style, *his* style, which was, incidentally, a very courageous act. And I certainly didn't *have* to kill him, the cancer did. As for tricking him into leaving me the studio, why would I have to do that when I *already* owned it?"

Mick tried to wrap his arms around her, but Sam pushed him away. "What do you mean—you *already* owned it?"

"I owned it almost from the beginning. You've heard of prenuptial agreements? Well, ours was what you might call a postnuptial—your father signed it in the spring of 1970."

"He signed the studio over to you just like *that*? I don't believe you!"

"But you don't have to believe *me*. I'll show you the signed agreement, all very legal. And if you don't believe the rest of it, all you have to do is check the records—the lawyers', the doctors', the death certificate. As for who sent you away, I'll show you a studio check signed by CEO *T. S. Grant* made out to producer Mick Nash to finance a Grantwood production to the tune of several million dollars, which, not incidentally, I, as the owner of record and present CEO, am demanding the return of immediately. That's what I wanted to talk to you alone about, Mick, since I didn't want to embarrass you in front of your wife. But the fact is that I regard what you did as close to fraudulent. You were entrusted with that money to produce a film . . . *not* to marry the boss's daughter."

While Sam shrieked in rage that Nora was just jealous, a crushed Mick mumbled, "That's not fair, Nora."

"*Why* isn't it fair? Do you have a single foot of film? Do you have *anything* to show me—a scrap of paper, a memo? Anything at all besides your marriage certificate?"

Mick was silent.

"I didn't think so," she said sadly, and turned to Sam. "As for your accusation that I'm jealous, why would I be? I *chose* to be divorced from Mick; I *didn't* choose to be the widow of the remarkable man who was your father.''

At these words Sam began to howl and Mick, disgruntled, dismayed, and depressed over what a mess things had turned out to be, sought to comfort her but without success. He had anticipated some bad blood when they arrived, but he had never suspected it would be *his*. He certainly hadn't expected Nora to make such a stink about the film or to pull the rug out from under him so quickly. He would have gotten around to doing something about the picture sooner or later. He *had* counted on her understanding about the marriage as he had on her knack for smoothing things over, and he certainly would never have believed that she was capable of being so snide about his age.

Actually, Nora felt sorry for Mick, watching him fuss over Sam without effect. And most likely much of this was her own fault rather than Mick's. She'd sent a boy to do a man's job and the boy simply hadn't been up to it, and thus she was to blame for Mick's present fix—married to a woman who didn't love him. Poor Mick. He was in for a severe jolt when he realized that Sam had married him only to spite his ex-wife.

But there were other matters still to be resolved and questions Sam had yet to ask that were as inevitable as the rest of it, so they might as well get on with it.

"Well, what's done is done, and since you're my stepson-in-law, and since you and Sam are *so* much in love, we won't allow *In the Name of Love* to stand between us and a harmonious family relationship. Just return the advance money and we'll forget all about your participation in the film. The studio will make the film here with a Hollywood producer since it's too wonderful a script *not* to be made, and you and Sam will be free to return to London to get on with your married life.

"Ah, how well I remember the thrill of starting a new marriage. Now, when do you plan to return to England? The same day as the memorial service or the day after? Seeing as it's so soon, you may want to make your plane reservations early . . . like today."

Sam stopped crying to sit straight up. "Wait a minute—"

"In the meantime," Nora went on, "I'll call the Beverly Hills Hotel to reserve a bungalow for you two lovebirds."

"Hold your horses!" Sam snapped. "Why should we go to the Beverly Hills Hotel when there's a zillion bedrooms right here? As a matter of fact, what's wrong with my old room? It has the king-sized bed and closet space enough for six."

"Oh?" Nora said in surprise. "I hardly thought you and Mick would want to spend your honeymoon in *my* house—"

"What do you mean, *your* house? For your information, I was *born* in this house!"

"Yes, and I don't mean to be unkind, but being born in a house doesn't give you squatter's rights. There are legal considerations, like who presently owns it. Besides," she giggled, "a bungalow at the Beverly Hills Hotel is perfect for newlyweds. Remember, Mick? Didn't we have a time of it?"

Mick grinned foolishly, but Sam didn't notice. "So you ended up with both *my* house and *my* studio! I can't believe Daddy didn't leave me *anything*! I'm his blood . . . his child!"

Nora ached now to take Sam into her arms, but she couldn't, not if she was to do what had to be done. "Of course you are, and he *was* thinking of you to the very end, and there is a *kind* of trust fund—"

"A trust fund!" Sam uttered, and Nora could see a wave of relief lighting up the green eyes. "Then, he *did* leave me something! But what do you mean by a *kind* of trust fund?"

"Well, he didn't specify when you're to get it or even an amount. He left everything to me and told me—practically his very last words—that he trusted me to disburse it when I thought you were mature enough to handle it."

"But that means I'm at your fucking mercy! That's totally unacceptable!"

"I'm sorry you feel that way," Nora said regretfully, "but I don't think you have any choice but to accept it. But your father *did* leave you something outright. His library of films. It takes up practically a whole room—stacks and stacks of reels. T.S. said you *had* to have them because you and he felt the same way about films—that the love of movies ran in your blood. We'll have to ship them to you in London. And now I'll call the hotel to make the reservation. You'll be my guests—my wedding present. Then I'll tell Edmund to bring out the champagne and Olaf to stand by to drive you over. Oh, dear, what a shame we had all that luggage carried into the house only to have it all dragged out again. Oh, well''—she smiled her brightest smile. ''That's life. . . .''

*　*　*

After the first shock wore off, Nora wondered if she'd been wrong about the union. God knew she'd been wrong about marriages before (quite a few of them, actually), and maybe Sam and Mick would help each other grow up. Did it really matter that Mick was so much older than Sam if they were at the same level of maturity? And while Sam *had* married for the wrong reason, maybe she'd come to discover something she didn't yet know—that she really loved Mick. Well, she would hope for the best even though reason told her not to be surprised if the marriage didn't last the year.

But then she *was* surprised when a woebegone Mick came over only a few days later—the morning after the memorial service. ''Mick! You *are* an early bird today! I was just having my breakfast. You must join me.''

''I'm not hungry.''

''Sit down anyway and have a cup of coffee? Tea?''

''Tea, please. I was brought up on tea for breakfast and it's too late for this old dog to learn new tricks.''

She gave him a look. Was he trying to tell her something? ''Tea it is, then,'' she said. ''You're the boss.''

''But that's it. Maybe I *should* be the boss but I'm not.''

''Maybe you'd better start from the beginning, Mick, so I know what you're talking about.''

''I told Sam that now that the memorial service was over we should think about going back to England, but she refuses to consider it. I told her that I can't sit around the Beverly Hills Hotel forever doing nothing.''

"Well, if you want to stay on in L.A. and you don't like living at a hotel, you *could* rent a house—"

"No, England is my home."

"Look, Mick, while I think that essentially I was fair in my assessment of our movie deal, perhaps I was too hasty and even a little mean. Would it help solve your and Sam's problem if you got involved in the production here?"

"No. The idea of working in Hollywood was fun when you and I were married, Nora, but the fact is, as you reminded me, I was twenty years younger then and, well . . . I'm too *old* to learn to be an expatriate."

"I see." What she saw was that Mick was starting to grow up, however late, and now he would leave Sam behind in more ways than one.

"I know you'll think I'm running out on my responsibility to Sam, but if she refuses to go back with me, what can I do? The whole damn thing was a mistake. She doesn't love me. She's not ready to love any man. Since we've been here she's spent more time with Babe and Honey than she has with me. I don't even know why she was so hell-bent on us getting married except maybe that she'd just lost her father and was looking to replace him—saw me as a father figure."

Not wanting to hurt his feelings, she suppressed a smile. Even Sam wasn't immature enough to see Mick Nash as a father figure. And he still hadn't figured out that Sam had married him only to spite her. But did it matter *why* Sam had married him? It still added up to the wrong reason for getting married. "Tell me, Mick, why did *you* marry Sam?"

"Because at the moment it seemed the right thing to do. She was so disconsolate at losing her father, I didn't know what she might do, and I remembered how her mother had died and I was afraid. At the time you put Sam in my care you specifically told me, 'Mick, don't let *this* one get away.' And I knew that I owed that to you—not to let Sam get away. Don't you know, Nora, that I married Sam for you?"

"Oh, Mick!" she wailed. He *had* married Sam out of love, but love of the wrong woman.

\*   \*   \*

She drove Mick to the airport herself, and when she returned
home she found Sam being helped out of a limousine by a
uniformed chauffeur, who then proceeded to unload her many
pieces of luggage. Seeing Nora, all she said was, "Good. Now
that you're here, you can pay the driver."

"Lucky me," Nora chuckled, taking out her billfold. "You
didn't care for the accommodations at the hotel?"

"Well, how could I stay there? Once Mick left, I knew the
honeymoon was over and you wouldn't go on paying the bills
there and I don't have any money. I'm a penniless orphan. Mick
was so sweet—he offered me all kinds of money, but—"

"You didn't take it?"

"Of course not. *I* didn't marry him for his money, even if
some other people did."

"That's commendable. You wouldn't want to be a cheat."

"I suppose there's a point to that remark?"

"Well, if you *had* married Mick for money, he hardly got
*his* money's worth, did he? But it's over with. Let's talk about
your plans instead. I take it you came to pick up your car? Well,
why wouldn't you? It's yours. Shall we have Olaf load it with all
that luggage . . . if it fits, that is. Well, we can always send it on
to you when you're relocated."

Sam's eyes opened wide as her mouth fell open. "You mean
you're actually throwing me out of my own home?"

"We've already established that this house is *my* home, and
since you're over eighteen I'm under no obligation to provide
you with shelter even if you were my own flesh and blood."

"But you know I have no place to go," she cried. "I never
thought you'd be mean enough to throw me out in the street. I
thought that at least you'd be fair."

"But are *you* being fair in your expectations? You expect me
to give you a home, but what are you offering in return? Friendship, good company, good cheer? No, hardly. But I'm willing to
give you a chance. You'll always have a home here if you're

prepared to do your share, and I don't think I have to spell out what that means as I did when you were thirteen. You should be able to figure it out for yourself by now."

Sam stuck out her hand, smiling politely, if falsely. "It's a deal. But there *is* one more thing. I *will* need some spending money. Do you want to give me an advance on that trust-fund money? A few thousand, say?"

Nora laughed. "Don't push it, kid. But, of course, you *will* need money. And the way to get money is to do what most people do—work for it. So, you can start at the studio next Monday if you like—"

"As what? A glorified gofer?"

"Yes, at the bottom, if that's what you mean. But you can get your own job if you prefer. I'm sure there are plenty of jobs for a girl as clever and attractive as you. There is one other alternative. A schoolgirl is entitled to an allowance, and I'm willing to go for that if you want to start college."

Sam sighed in grand affectation. "You certainly know how to drive a hard bargain, Nora. That's one thing I can definitely learn from you. I'll have to think about that. Job or school. But in the meantime I'll need an advance either on my salary, my allowance, *or* my trust-fund money."

Nora shook her head admiringly. "When it comes to driving a hard bargain, you're no slouch yourself."

Smiling smugly, Sam picked up a piece of luggage and headed for the stairs. "Oh, it *is* good to be home again."

Nora, watching her go up the stairs, reflected that Sam was most likely using all this game-playing and talk of money as a way of suppressing—or perhaps, dealing *with*—her grief over her father's death. In any case, there probably would be a lot of moving in and moving out before she and Sam were through. Maybe even a few more husbands. As a matter of fact, she wouldn't be surprised if one of these days Sam up and married a diplomat or even a duke.

# SIXTY-EIGHT

One of the good things about Sam being back, Nora reflected, was having Honey and Babe around again, swimming in the pool, playing tennis, filling the house with their laughter. Still, it was different than before—the three young women had more purpose to their lives and less free time for play, while she had more free time and less purpose since she'd dropped all her outside activities so that she could give T.S. 100 percent. Now there was a huge void in her life, which for the first time that she could remember she had no inclination to fill—not with politics and not with the studio, which was being run ably enough without her. Was it that she wasn't quite ready to let go of T.S.? *Or was it that she was waiting for Teddy Rosen to call?*

They hadn't really spoken since the day he'd brought over the script. He'd come to the memorial service with Honey and shaken her hand, murmuring all the right words. He was too much the gentleman not to do that and too much the gentleman to look too lingeringly into her eyes. . . .

Then she realized he *wasn't* going to call. He was waiting for *her* to call *him* so that he would be sure he wasn't trespassing on another man's marriage even though that man had passed on. And while she yearned to make that call, she couldn't. Not yet. A call to Teddy at this point wouldn't be just a call—it would be a commitment, and she didn't know if she was ready for *that.* It was possible that she would never be . . . that she'd had enough commitments to last her a lifetime.

Still, as he had come to pay his respects to her and Sam at T.S.'s memorial service, she would go to see Honey play Juliet in the same spirit—out of respect and friendship for the father as well as affection for the daughter. But she would only shake his hand as she offered him her congratulations and she would not look too long into his eyes. . . .

\* \* \*

"I want you to go to the phone this minute, Babette, and invite Greg to go with you to the play tomorrow night."

"But I've been out with him two times this week and it's not like I wasn't inviting him to a big event. It's only Honey's class production. Greg won't even want to go. A drama class production's not *his* idea of a big time." *He'll only sit there and make snide, superior little cracks the whole time and spoil the whole damn thing for me.*

"That's not the point. You want to invite him so he'll know you're not excluding him from any part of your life. You're going to be sorry if you do anything to spoil *this* relationship. Greg's a young man with a brilliant future. He's going places, and if you had half a brain you'd make sure that you're right there by his side. For once in your life, can't you try and please your father? Is that asking too much after all he's done for you?"

"Oh, all right! I'll ask Greg to go if it will make both of you so goddamn happy!"

"Good. But try to refrain from using swear words. At least in Greg's company. Anyone can see he's a young man with old-fashioned values who wouldn't dream of marrying a woman who might embarrass him by presenting a bad public image."

"*Marrying?* Give me a break, I'm only *dating* him—not getting ready to march down the aisle!"

"You could do a lot worse and probably *will* if you're fool enough to let this one get away."

Well, she had no one to blame but herself, she thought. If only she'd run the other way the day she literally bumped into Greg. Instead she'd brought him home to show *them* that she could attract an "acceptable" man, not guessing then that it would be love at first sight, that they wouldn't see the ambitious third-year law student as just another date but as their White

Hope who, with a bit of a financial push, a dash of influence, and the right wife, could go the distance. And how could she have known right off that Greg—interested in a career in politics— would fall like a ton of bricks for her father, the powerful judge; her mother, the savvy socialite; and *all* their paraphernalia—the Beverly Hills house, the membership in the L.A. Country Club, the correct dinner parties, and the right connections?

Looking back, she realized he'd never really been all *that* enthralled with *her*, but at the time she'd been too pleased with herself to notice. For the first time she was basking in her parents' approval, pretty heady stuff. It even made her feel that at last she was worthy of their love.

Then she began to see the cracks in his façade, defects her parents failed to see or were determined not to. They found him so genial, but she had seen him angry and an angry Greg wasn't a pretty sight. But when she said as much to the Judge, all he had said was that any man who didn't react with anger once in a while was a man without backbone, and after a little reflection, she'd regarded that as a reasonable statement and decided to give him another chance. But when Greg drank too much at a party, she recalled what she'd once heard Nora Grant say: "Anybody can drink too much on occasion. The test of a man is not whether he can hold his liquor but how he *behaves* once he's drunk." And Greg had turned *nasty*, had accused her of trying to upstage him by getting bigger laughs with her jokes than he had with his, which was absurd. But try telling that to Catherine and the Judge! When she did, they missed the point and told her that they too found a young woman telling jokes unfeminine.

"He's going to go to the play with me," she told Catherine after she made her call. "Are you satisfied?"

"But I'm not the one who has to be satisfied. *You* are, and you *should* be delighted that out of all the young women Greg Ryan could be going out with, he's chosen you."

*And that's how a girl gets herself into this kind of a predicament—by going out with a guy whom her parents adore but whom she doesn't even like. And how was she going to get out of this predicament now? . . .*

*    *    *

Sam hung up the phone angrily and turned to Nora. "That was Babe. She's going to the play with Greg tomorrow night instead of me."

"Why can't the three of you go together?"

"Because *I* would rather not. He's a total dork. An egomaniac! A few minutes with him and I discovered homicidal instincts I never knew I possessed."

Nora, grateful for this girl-on-girl conversation, laughed. "He can't be all that bad if Babe likes him."

"She *doesn't*! It's the Tracys who are mad about him."

"Then Babe has to point out the error of their ways. In the meantime, why don't we go to the play together, with you in the driver's seat?"

"Are you *sure* you're not already spoken for?" Sam asked.

"Who'd offer me a ride to see a play at UCLA?"

"Teddy Rosen, maybe? You and he were always tight."

Sam's tone was casual and Nora made sure hers was too. "Tight? We're friends, but I've seen him only twice since your commencement, and one of those times was at the memorial service. How tight is that?"

"But we're only talking about going to see a school play, not a commitment. And I *know* you'd never make a commitment to Teddy Rosen," Sam laughed.

"How did we get from going to a play to making a commitment? And just as a matter of curiosity, how do you *know* I'd never make a commitment to him?"

"With your record, that's easy," Sam drawled. "He doesn't have enough money for you."

Nora sighed. *First she dazzles you with fancy footwork—some friendly conversation—but then, when your guard is down, she clobbers you with a left-right combination to the heart. . . .*

# SIXTY-NINE

— ◦•◦• —

"**Y**ou're going to be wonderful so there's no reason for you to be nervous," Teddy reassured Honey as they walked into the as yet empty theater.

"I wouldn't be, but Professor Beaumond has invited some *real* professionals and that makes me a *little* nervous. Even Joshua Prince, the head of Royal Productions, is coming."

"*Even!* Well, I *am* impressed," Teddy teased.

"Really, Daddy, looking down your nose at TV now that you're writing a big movie? You didn't mind accepting that Emmy for the Thanksgiving show, did you?" she teased back.

"I beg your pardon, Ms. Honey. Do you really want to compare *my* show with one of Prince's T and A series, or one of his shoot-em-up and car-chase fantasies?"

"Well, Professor Beaumond says Josh Prince's company is providing more prime-time hours for television than any company in TV history and has consistently boasted more top-rated shows. Now, that's *something*, isn't it, even if it's only what you snob types consider entertainment fluff?"

"Touché," he laughed. "But I wasn't downgrading Mr. Prince's achievements. I only wanted to impress upon you that you don't have to be nervous over the likes of him. You're a *serious* actress and he probably couldn't tell a real actress from a bimbo if she hit him in the eye. But it sounds like your Professor Beaumond is really tooting Mr. Prince's horn."

"They're friends, so naturally he'd say nice things about him. Besides, I think Professor Beaumond's eager to direct a few episodes of Mr. Prince's entertainment fluff. He says a dramatic-arts professor does not live by Shakespeare alone—he needs some *real* bread too," she giggled.

"He's right." Still, he wondered why Beaumond, who'd been around Hollywood for ages and was a friend of Prince's to boot, would drag the producer down to a class play just to see how well he directed. Surely by now Prince knew his work.

"I'd better go backstage now, Daddy. They're probably worrying where I am. Why don't you sit down in front and save a couple of seats for Babe and Sam? Oh, I forgot. Do you know who else is coming tonight? That Italian director, Vittorio Conti. He's here making a movie for Columbia. He's a friend of Professor Beaumond's too."

\* \* \*

"Look, Nora, there's Teddy in the front row with two empty seats next to him. He must be saving them for me and Babe, so we might as well take them." Sam started down the aisle before Nora could protest and she had no choice but to follow.

Teddy stood up. "Sam . . ." He gave her a hug. "Nora, it's so good to see you. I had no idea you were coming."

"Oh, I wouldn't miss Honey's first dramatic appearance for anything," she said quickly.

"Please sit down. I was saving these two seats for Babe and Sam, but Im sure that they won't—"

"Not to worry. Babe's coming with her boyfriend and they can find their own seats. Whoops, speak of the devils, there they are! You two sit while I zip on up to say hello. Oh, and you know how you were going to take Honey, Babe and me out afterwards, Teddy? Since Babe's with her beau, you think you might want to take Nora instead?" she asked ingenuously.

"Sam, really!" Nora wanted to throttle her.

Teddy laughed. "I'd be honored if Nora will join us. But I think it would be nice if we still included Babe, along with her boyfriend. Invite them both on my behalf, Sam."

"Are you sure you really want *him?* He's a drag. Then again, if you want Babe, I don't know if you have much choice. What say you, Nora? You always know the right thing to do. If Teddy's taking Honey, Babe, and me and now *you* out for a celebration, does he have to include Greg too?"

Then, without waiting for an answer, she was off and Teddy appealed to Nora, "You *will* come, won't you? I have a feeling I'm going to need some help."

"Yes, of course, I'd love to. Besides, I owe you one. I still remember how you came to my rescue when I was serving as chaperone at the Beasley mixer. Recall?" She was careful not to meet his eyes, which led her to look at his tie to see that he was wearing the tiepin she had given him for Christmas.

"Oh," she said, and he said, "I recall," while looking at her hair to avoid looking into her eyes, thinking: *It really is the color of gold.*

Then she flushed and fumbled for the little gold musical note that she wore suspended on a chain that reposed inside the V of her dress to finger it as if it were a good luck charm. Still, they avoided each other's eyes.

Sam came back to take the seat on the aisle and report: "The happy couple can't make our party after all—they have to go back to the Tracys. It seems the Judge has offered Greg a clerkship or something and tonight the four of them are going to hold their own private celebration. Poor Babe . . . What about you, Nora? Are you coming along?"

"Yes, thank you for thinking of me."

"Super! And guess who I saw sitting in the back of the theater? Josh Prince . . ."

"Where's he sitting?" Teddy asked, and when Sam pointed Prince out to him, he asked, "Where did you meet him?"

"Oh, I never met him. I recognized him from his picture. There just was an article about him in the paper. He's casting a new series called *Three Wise Gals.* It's about three investigative reporters with lots of jiggle and it seems he's looking for fresh faces," she laughed. "Aren't they always? And what's more, it seems he's searching for one sexy, gorgeous blonde; one sexy but classy redhead; and a sexy, perky brunette. Now, what three wise young women with fresh faces and jiggle does that bring to mind? It's too bad that I'm only interested in *making* movies and Babe's parents would rather see her dead than performing, and Honey's only desire is to be a serious actress. But what a team we would have made!"

Neither Teddy nor Nora made comment.

"And did you see who's sitting next to the Prince? The Italian director, Vic Conti. Now, there's a man whose talent you have to really respect—it's awesome!"

"So is his ego and his talent for manipulation," Nora commented dryly.

"You know him?" Sam sat up straight.

"I met him years ago in Europe when—well, believe me, the man is bad news."

"Really?" Sam's eyes lit up and she smiled slyly. "Maybe you just didn't press the right buttons."

Nora was sorry then that she'd opened her mouth, realizing she had just pressed the worst button possible as far as Sam was concerned—the button marked "challenge," or was it simply the button marked "Nora"?

Then the lights dimmed and the house went quiet as the curtain started to rise.

*   *   *

When the curtain came down on the final curtain call, Teddy, on his feet applauding, turned to take another look at Joshua Prince to see how enthusiastically *he* was applauding. But both Prince's and Vic Conti's seats were empty and he guessed that they had already gone backstage. To do exactly what?—that was the question.

"I'm going backstage," he told Sam and Nora. "Do you two want to wait here for us or—?"

"I should say not," Sam said. "We can't wait to tell Honey how proud we are too. Right, Nora? Oh, look, here come Greg and Babe. I guess they want to congratulate Honey too before they go home to Mammy and Pappy."

\* \* \*

Teddy saw that he had guessed correctly. It was a scene right out of a movie: Conti, the prestigious director, standing to one side viewing the proceedings with a jaded eye while Beaumond, the professorial director, draped a proprietary arm about his protégée—a radiant Honey, virginal in her Juliet dress, her hair a golden halo framing a flushed face, locking enthralled topaz eyes with the admiring brown eyes of a seemingly equally bedazzled Joshua Prince.

Reluctantly Honey tore her eyes away to greet her father and her friends and to excitedly introduce everyone to everyone else. Then Teddy could not help but admire how silkily Prince managed his part of the introductions:

"Ah, the legendary Nora Grant," he said, and while he didn't actually kiss Nora's hand it felt as if he had, and he followed up by offering her his sympathy on the recent death of her husband. Next he proclaimed what an honor it was to meet the fortunate man who possessed such treasures—the remarkable Honey, a Pulitzer, and an Emmy—which showed Teddy that Joshua Prince was a man who did his homework. Undoubtedly he also knew that Honey's mother was the legendary French sex kitten—a bit of information that wouldn't hurt a campaign to publicize a potential sex kitten of the American television screen. Then Prince politely acknowledged Greg's existence, but when he got to Babe and Sam, he laughed with pleasure. "The beauty in this room is blinding!"

Then Teddy saw that Sam was a fine prophet when Prince said, "And what's amazing is that I have a series coming up— *Three Wise Gals*—that I could cast right here and now if I could talk three lovely young women into a great career move. Isn't that so, Vic?"

But Vic Conti didn't hear, nor did an entranced Sam. They were already deep into an intense discussion of the artistic superiority of European films over American. But Babe heard and said wistfully, "You could talk *me* into this great career move but I doubt you could talk my mother into it."

Then Greg abruptly prodded her, "Speaking of your mother, Babette, we'd better get moving. Your parents are waiting."

Once Babe and Greg left, Teddy suggested that Honey change so they wouldn't be late for their reservation, and Honey enthused, "Oh, Daddy, can you call and tell them that there will be three more? I've asked Mr. Prince, Mr. Conti, and Professor Beaumond to join us and they'd love to."

Prince told Honey to call him Joshua before Teddy spoke, about to say it was too late to change the reservation. But Nora placed a staying hand on his arm. "In the end it won't matter," she whispered. "It's part of the growing-up process."

*  *  *

There was a scramble for transportation to The Scene, the newest and hottest place in West Hollywood, which Teddy had chosen thinking the girls would enjoy it. Since Vic Conti had come with Josh, who asked Honey to ride with him in his Lamborghini, which seated only two—an offer she accepted enthusiastically—Vic was left without a ride, a void Sam quickly offered to fill, but since her car was also a two-seater, this left Nora without a ride.

"I'm afraid you're stuck with me," Nora told Teddy, who said, "I can think of worse predicaments. Being stuck with Jacques Beaumond, for instance," and they both laughed because they *were* both stuck with Beaumond since Teddy's was the only car that accommodated more than two.

*  *  *

The Scene was noisy and the music hot though the food was bad and the drinks watered, which really didn't matter to anyone but Jacques, since he was the only one who sat continuously downing margaritas and stuffing his face.

Teddy and Nora, sitting at the table with him, ate little and drank only Perrier as they watched the others dance. Sam and Vic, preoccupied with rubbing bodies and ceaseless conversation, were too busy to eat while Josh and Honey, without saying much at all, kept a couple of inches between them as they danced, more into staring into each other's eyes than making direct physical contact.

\*   \*   \*

"Vic and I are leaving," Sam said, picking up her purse.

"But why?" Nora asked, startled. "Where are you—?"

"If you must know, we're going back to the house to screen *Citizen Kane* and Bertolucci's *1900* to compare their relative artistic merits. That's okay, isn't it, since Daddy did leave *me* his library of films?"

Teddy watched Nora watch Vic and Sam make their exit, anxiety written all over her face. He reached across the table to take her hand. "You can't stop her even if you know she's going to get hurt. You just told me that that's part of the growing-up process."

"I know, but I can't help wishing she could grow up in a hurry without so much trouble and pain."

"At least you don't have to worry about her getting into trouble tonight," he offered wryly, trying to get her to smile. "Even without *Citizen Kane*, the cut version of *1900* runs at least four hours. Which version do you have?"

She laughed. "The original—six hours."

"There you go. That will take them through the night."

But then, when Honey came running over in a flurry of excitement to tell him that she and Joshua were leaving—"Josh wants to take me on a tour of Royal Productions!"—Teddy stood up to protest the lateness of the hour.

"It's okay, Daddy. I don't have any classes tomorrow," she said, and Prince reassured him, "She'll be fine, Mr. Rosen. I promise to take good care of our Honey Rose and not bring her home too late. And thank you for a wonderful evening."

He then thanked Nora for the pleasure of her company, ignoring Beaumond, who was busy working on yet another margarita, while Honey threw her arms around her father to thank him for everything, and then they were gone.

Dazed, Teddy sank down into his chair to ask Nora: "Is this it? After all these years? One evening and I have to let her go? Is it over that fast?"

Now she reached across the table to take his hand. "But it's not over . . . for either of you. For her, it's just the beginning, and for you—it's the beginning of another time . . . a new time . . . a different time. Like with me and Sam."

"But Honey isn't *like* Sam. Honey doesn't have Sam's defenses. Sam's tough and worldly-wise and Honey's still an innocent . . . vulnerable."

"It's possible, you know, that it's the other way around. That Honey's really the tough one with more inner resources to fall back on and Sam's the vulnerable one. Who's to say, really? Only time will tell . . ."

"But how can I trust that man with my daughter? He's way too old for her."

"He's not *that* much older. Thirteen . . . fourteen years at most. Honey probably wants . . . *needs* an older man because she looks up to *you* so much."

"But you saw him . . . heard him. He's *too* smooth. His manners are *too* good to be sincere."

She smiled faintly. "Your manners are very good too, but you're sincere. That's probably one of the reasons Honey's attracted to him. She'd never like a man with bad manners."

"But I'm sure he only wants to use her."

"He *may* want to cast her in that series of his, but that's not to say he can't or won't love her. Only Honey can determine that."

"But you heard him—he called her Honey Rose. He just met her and already he's trying to change her name. . . ."

"That's silly. Think about it. All he did was leave the *n* off the Rosen—he didn't call her Honey Prince."

"Yet . . ."

"Yet . . . But I don't think we have any choice but to let go of our girls and let them grow up in their own time."

He nodded. "I suppose you're right. Aren't you *always* right? Isn't that what everyone *always* says about you?"

"I think you're teasing me and it's time for us to go."

"No, not yet. Have some caviar."

"But I'm not hungry."

"You don't have to be hungry to eat caviar. Have some anyway. I'd like you to."

She laughed. "Why?"

"I want you to have something rich and wonderful."

"Then give me a twenty-dollar bill."

As Jacques Beaumond said plaintively and drunkenly, "*I'd like something rich and wonderful*," Teddy handed Nora a twenty. She rose to go over to the band leader, and by the time she made her way back to the table the band had switched from boogie to the strains of an old melody and she held out her arms to Teddy and he got up to clasp her in his.

"*Always*" . . .

As they danced—her arms around his neck, his arms encircling her waist—they looked directly into each other's eyes to see the same, raw compulsion there—a compulsion that could no longer be denied, and her trembling body confirmed it. It was time, she thought, the right time. And then *he* confirmed it by demanding of her, "Where?"

Not her place. Not this first time. Sam was there and so was T.S.'s ghost. And not his place either—his house had its ghosts as well. It had to be someplace neutral, and not the Beverly Hills Hotel with its ghost of Mick Nash. It had to be someplace *new* for them both . . . a beginning.

"Why don't you let me make the arrangements?" She threw her head back so his lips could find her throat. "You know what they always say about me?"

"What do they always say?" he murmured.

"That I'm really terrific at planning a great party. Trust me—it's what I do best."

He laughed heartily, trusting her completely. "But what do we do about *him*?" He indicated Beaumond with his head.

"Sometimes a person *has* choices, after all. We can just leave him here, crying into his margarita, and stick him with the bill, which is no more than he deserves. Or, we can be nice and pour him into a cab."

"This is our time so we want to be nice," he whispered urgently. "But the hour is late so let's do it quickly."

# SEVENTY

———— •••• ————

**B**abe knew it was an unusual evening as soon as she and Greg walked into the house, and it wasn't because they were having this celebration. Over the years they'd had quite a few of these private parties to mark a special occasion— when her father had been named man of the year by his fraternal order, when her mother had been elected president of her women's club, and when she herself had performed well at a piano recital. Her parents had toasted her at their own little party and she could still remember how special she had felt and how proud—how she'd thought she would give anything to recapture the moment.

Catherine had always considered these small celebrations an ode to family solidarity, the Tracy brand of "togetherness," and never once had there been a fourth person present. Also, they'd never celebrated in the drawing room, which was reserved for those social occasions which truly merited its use. But tonight, though it was still considered a family affair, they were honoring a fourth person—Greg—and they were celebrating in the drawing room! And there was a lavish spread, the kind of delicacies usually served only to her parents' most august guests: gravlax, Beluga caviar, *Foie Gras Truffle de Strasbourg*, tiny sautéed lobster tails, escargots Bourguignonne, and, because Greg was so fond of it, even sushi. There was also a pitcher of martinis that the Judge had mixed himself in addition to the Cristal champagne reposing in the silver cooler. It was assuredly a *special* celebration, and for what, she wondered—a crummy job down at the courthouse when Greg had yet to pass the bar?

Then, suddenly, she found herself all alone on one of the

twin sofas upholstered in palest peach, facing the three of them on the matching sofa. And as if it were a dream running in slow motion, she saw the Judge pouring the Cristal into four flutes, Greg reaching into his breast pocket, and heard Catherine's voice: "When we told Greg that we were making this party for him he was so *dear*—he said that he wanted to make it all *really* special by sharing *this* moment with us."

Then, amazed, she saw the three of them raise their champagne glasses high. *They were toasting her!* Her mother was smiling tremulously and the Judge was looking proud while Greg leaped forward to thrust this *thing* at her—a diamond ring winking up from a little blue velvet box. Then Catherine said, "Quickly, darling, pick up your glass so that we can all take the first sip together!"

\* \* \*

The room was dark except for the light emanating from the projector to illuminate Robert De Niro grappling with Dominique Sanda, with the sexual electricity practically leaping out from the screen. But Sam and Vic Conti, bare to the waist and grappling on the projection room's red carpet, were totally oblivious to any other sexual electricity but their own.

Sweating profusely, his breath coming fast and labored, Vic lay under her, his hands reaching up to fondle the breasts hanging suspended as she sat astride him. But she wouldn't permit the contact. Rather, she grazed his face with the tips of her dark-pink nipples, teased his lips with them, moved them down to taunt his swollen bulge. Then, as his hands attempted to pull down his zipper, she pushed them aside to do that herself, to draw out his engorged penis, to stroke it slowly with her hands while the master director grunted and groaned and begged for her lips. But she sat up straight and moved her own body down in order to pull his trousers free, and then, when he was completely nude, she parted his thighs to run her tongue lightly over the tautened skin.

Cursing her now, the director supreme attempted to take charge of the production—to maul her breasts, to bite her lips and shoulder, to tear away her skirt and panties until, finally, they were both completely nude, their bodies heaving and glistening in the semidarkness. Moving swiftly then, taking him by surprise, she rose to move to the door as he staggered to his feet to come after her, but she taunted him with a laugh before proclaiming, "Not here . . ."

"Where?" It was an animal cry.

"Upstairs . . ."

Then she was out of the projection room, out into the hall and starting up the stairs with him hot after her. She had to run faster, she knew, because if the great director caught her on the stairs, he would take her then and there in a violent rage and she wouldn't be able to stop him. And she was determined that the only damn place Nora's "bad news" was going to fuck her was in Nora's bed, where once Nora had fucked T.S. And after that, well—who knew? Maybe she would even marry the bastard. There was a lot she could learn from him about making movies.

*   *   *

Royal Productions' lot was an eerie place at night, full of shadow and half-light, but it was a beautiful, romantic place too, Honey thought as Joshua proudly walked her around the sound stages, showing her where they produced his different series—the cop show, *Hollywood Beat*; the fantasy, *Enchanted Isle*; and *Heartland*, which was about a family in Wichita, Kansas—something for everyone. It was a beautiful, romantic place because it was both a dream factory and the place where Joshua Prince's personal dream had come true.

Entranced, Honey watched his face as he told her how he'd come to Hollywood with nothing but his vision and his belief in himself that he could make his vision a reality—producing entertainment not for the elite group who had access to legitimate theater or for the millions who went to movie theaters, but for the *many* millions who relied only on their television sets to enrich their lives and make them happier. Then she was sure his dream was as noble as it was inspired.

Suddenly, it came to her that Joshua reminded her of Teddy,

but how he must have been before he'd been derailed, youthfully exuberant and confident in his own abilities and in the rightness of his dream. And there was that same soft voice and gentle manner, even a slight physical resemblance—the same velvety eyes, the same fine, clean line of feature.

Joshua took her next to his private domain, an elegant room where he lit a fire in the large fireplace though it was late spring. Then, sitting on the sofa in front of the fire, he showed her all the planning materials for the projected series, which was only awaiting its star before going into production to become a reality.

"Star? You mean stars, don't you? Three of them?" she asked, herself starry-eyed.

"No, now that I've met you, I realize that the other two 'wise gals' can only be supporting players. Only the Honey Rose can wear the princess's crown because she's the ultimate American dream girl come true."

"The Honey Rose, the American dream girl," she repeated after him. Oh, it *did* have a lovely ring to it, and she knew for certain that she wanted to be part of Joshua Prince's vision—his princess come true. And when he put his arms around her, bent his head to kiss first her eyelids, then her lips, then her throat . . . to bury his face in her breasts before he undressed her slowly and tenderly to kiss each and every part of her, she was ready at last to embrace love and lovemaking, with *all* of her—mind, body, and soul. And when he entered her she knew that she was ready to be anything Joshua Prince wanted her to be.

\* \* \*

A bemused Teddy pulled up in front of the canopied entrance to the Hotel Bel-Air. This was a new experience for him—he was forty-eight years old and had in his time checked into many hotels, but never before had he checked into a fine hotel at two o'clock in the morning. But obviously this was possible and in no way extraordinary since a parking attendant leaped to open his door and inquire after the luggage, while another ran to open the car door for Nora.

"Did we remember to bring the luggage, dear?" he asked Nora since she was the one who had made the arrangements.

"Of course we brought the luggage," she said huffily, walking around to the trunk to tell the attendant which pieces were to be carried in. "Mmm . . ." she murmured as she surveyed the trunk's contents. "That—" she pointed to a battered typewriter case, "and that—" a bruised attaché case, "and of course, that—" she indicated a new burnished-leather briefcase. "And this—" *This* was a tennis racket in sore need of restringing. Then she smiled brightly and led the way down the canopied stretch to the lobby and up to the front desk, where she stepped aside to allow Teddy to claim his reservation and register.

"My name?" he murmured in an aside.

"Of course *your* name, my darling, though a Rosen by any other name would smell as sweet. . . ."

Then, when they followed the bellman to a bungalow in the rear of the hotel, he whispered, "You give good arrangements," and she whispered back, "You ain't seen nothing yet."

Still, when the bellman opened the door, he was amazed to see a living room with a fire blazing in the hearth and a midnight supper laid out on a table set with roses and candles, flowered china and sparkling crystal, and with a magnum of champagne cooling in a silver bucket. His mouth dry with a growing urgency, impatient for the bellman carrying the typewriter, tennis racket, briefcase, and attaché into the bedroom to be gone, Teddy managed to mutter, "You sure know how to throw a party."

She lit the candles and blew him a kiss. "As with all good parties, the best is yet to come."

With those words hanging in the air, he sprang like a tiger to wrap his arms around her from behind, cupping each breast with a hand and pressing himself against her. But he jumped away when the bellman reappeared from the bedroom to collect his tip and ask if they would like a maid summoned to do the unpacking. At this, Teddy almost laughed, though his body throbbed with its unbearable ache. Still he played the game, aware that every party had to follow its own schedule. "What do you think, Nora? Do we want the maid?" But if she said yes, he was prepared to throw her to the floor and take her right there by force. She must have known this, for, eyes laughing into his, she demurred. *No maid.* Still, she teased, "The waiter, then, to serve our supper?"

Then he knew it was clearly time to assert himself—she was the partygiver of all time, but he had his rights too since he was the man who had been so beautifully invited to come to this party. He dismissed the waiter and blew out the candles, then slowly bent to kiss her upturned lips. "Everything in its time. And now, at last, I think *our* time has come and we can't delay any longer."

He stood on one side of the room, she on the other. First, he watched her undress, then she stood perfectly still while he undressed. When he was nude she came to him and he picked her up and carried her into the bedroom and placed her on the satin spread to make love to her body with his lips, and it was so sweet she suddenly couldn't remember that there had ever been anyone else.

She felt the years slipping away and it was all new again as if it were the first time. And then she made love to him in the same way, sweetly and slowly so that *his* ghosts would dissolve into nothingness and it would be all new for him . . . as if it were his first time too. Then, lying side by side, she feeling his body against her feverishly demanding, he feeling her breath upon his flesh hot and ragged, they both knew it was time for the future to begin.

\*   \*   \*

It was dawn when he asked her how, when, and where they would be married since she was the expert on this sort of thing.

*Married? Of course he would want to marry. I should have known that he was the marrying kind. . . .*

She recalled what T.S. had said about her marital record— thrice widowed if one counted Hubert and twice divorced—and if she were to marry again, she still had one divorce coming to even the score. And while she knew it was foolish to give any credence to this sort of nonsense, she could not help but wonder: Had this just been one more of T.S.'s cynical remarks tossed off for effect or was it based on firmer ground—one of T.S.'s frequently *shrewd* observations?

*Was* she being silly regarding it as a possible curse . . . a kind of hex, a prediction foredooming the marriage to failure? She didn't believe in superstition. Still, why endanger something as precious as their love by marrying? Why tempt some evil, jealous, wrathful god by flaunting her good fortune? Better to savor its sweetness in secret and guard it well. One more secret couldn't hurt.

Besides, she had married different men for a variety of reasons with mixed results. Maybe she wasn't a woman made for marriage. Maybe it was high time she stopped marrying but took herself a lover. It would be fun . . . maybe it would even be good luck. Maybe it would turn out to be the most brilliant union of all. . . .

One thing she did know—it was going to be wonderful finding out.

# PART NINE

# AFTER THE PARTY

Los Angeles, June 1990

# SEVENTY-ONE

———— •••• ————

Though it had been some fifteen years since that first time with Teddy at the Hotel Bel-Air and she had been a widow for even longer—hardly accountable to anyone—Nora still felt like a sneaky teenager who'd stayed out all night, and let herself into the house as quietly as possible so that the women asleep upstairs wouldn't hear her. She wasn't quite ready to reveal *where* she'd been, though if the day went as she hoped, she might do even that. God knew, Teddy had been after her for years to dignify their affair with the shining light of truth since she wouldn't legitimize it with marriage. But, then, Teddy was given to absolute truth much as she'd become addicted to secrets.

Well, today was the day she was ready at last to tell a few truths, and the chips would just have to fall where they might. If the girls weren't ready by now, they would never be, and she and Teddy deserved more of her undivided attention.

It wasn't yet six o'clock. Still time to shower, put on makeup, and pull herself together to face the girls and what promised to be a long day. But a bedraggled Honey emerged into the hall before she made it to her bedroom. "What are you doing up so early?" she asked, grateful that Honey was too much of a lady to ask her what *she* was doing up so early with a coat thrown over her nightgown and negligee.

Honey smiled forlornly. "I'm due in court at eleven, so I thought I'd go home and change and generally prepare myself."

Nora smiled sympathetically. "I know how hard all this must be on you even if you do walk out of that courtroom with a quarter of a billion dollars. It isn't easy to destroy a man you

507

once loved even though you might hate him now."

"But I don't *hate* him! I could *never* hate Josh. I just want a different life for myself than the one he wants for me. And you used the word *destroy*. I don't want to destroy him! All I want is what's rightfully mine, what I'm entitled to, morally and legally."

"Oh, my dear, I know you don't *want* to destroy him. Still, that's what you're doing, isn't it? How do you think he's going to raise a quarter of a billion dollars? He's going to have to liquidate—sell off a great deal of Royal Productions: its assets, its real property, its contracts, the different divisions. And once you start to tear at its foundation, the whole thing will crumble. I know something about these things and I know that the whole is usually worth a lot more than the sum of its parts.

"Oh, yes, you're going to destroy Royal Productions, and if you destroy his company, you will, in effect, be destroying the man. But that's not *your* concern. As you say, you're entitled to whatever is legally and morally yours, even if it is Josh's blood money. And you're your father's daughter, Honey—you'd never do what wasn't right. But since it's still early, why don't you stop off and have breakfast with your father? He'll cheer you up. And be sure to let us all know how things turn out in court."

"Oh, I'll be back the moment it's over. Sam and Babe are counting on me to do that." *Especially Sam. She's waiting for me to return so we can take my money . . . Josh's blood money . . . and make an offer for Grantwood Studio. . . .*

*       *       *

"Cheer up," Teddy said as Honey made only a few forlorn stabs at her pancakes. "This is the day you've been waiting for. D day. That's what they used to call a big day in my youth. The reference then, of course, was to the big war. I guess the contemporary reference would be the divorce wars."

"Really, Daddy, is that supposed to be a joke?" she said miserably. "If it is, I don't find it very amusing."

"No, it wasn't a joke. It was more of a wry observation. But this *is* the day you've been waiting for so you can get on with your life. So, why *are* you so down in the dumps?"

She told him what Nora had said—that the settlement she'd been fighting for would destroy Royal Productions and, ultimately, Josh himself. "I'm so confused."

"I see. Then that *D* in D day doesn't stand for divorce but destruction? Is that it?"

"Daddy!" She stood up so abruptly she knocked over her coffee cup, and they both watched the brown liquid drip to the floor until Teddy wiped at the mess with paper towels and she said, "I'm sorry, but I was startled to hear *you* of all people say that to me. Were you *deliberately* trying to be cruel?"

"I think you know better than that just as I know you better than to think you'd ever *intend* to be destructive."

"Then, you think Nora is right?"

"Much as I respect Nora's wisdom, I think that as far as you and Joshua are concerned, only you know the true answer."

"But I *don't!* I don't have *any* answers. How can I when I don't even know who I am anymore—Joshua's wind-up doll, Mimi's sexpot clone, or Teddy Rosen's impossibly idealistic daughter? I thought life would be so simple. That all you had to do was love someone and you lived happily ever after."

"I think you know very well who you are. Remember when you and I acknowledged between us that it was possible I wasn't your natural father since your mother was sleeping around with several men, including T.S., at the time of your conception? You knew in your heart that it didn't matter. We *both* knew in our hearts that you were truly my daughter. And the truth is that you're not Josh's Honey Rose any more than you're Mimi's sexy look-alike or even Teddy Rosen's disillusioned daughter— you're Honey Rosen Prince, your own person, and a special one at that. And all you have to do is look inside your heart and you'll find her there and you'll know exactly what to do—what's right."

She went home to Crown House to get ready for court, no less confused. What her father had given her was a vote of confidence, not any easy answers.

*   *   *

No sooner had Nora sat down to the breakfast table than Sam
made her appearance wearing a green kimono with a Chinese
dragon emblazoned on its back and dark circles under her eyes.
"Babe had a terrible night but she's sleeping now."

"Good. But if you don't mind my saying so, you look as if
you could have used a little more sleep yourself."

Sam looked at Nora warily. She had to weigh every word she
said to her this morning since she was about to present her
proposition that Nora sell the studio to her and Honey, but she
couldn't just blurt it out. She had to feel her way.

"Why should I mind? It's not the worst thing you've ever
said to me. The worst thing you ever said to me was what you
said last night—that you were selling the studio out from under
me, which is why I never fell asleep at all."

"Too bad. I saw Honey this morning before she left and she
didn't look as if she'd slept much either, poor thing."

"She's *not* a poor thing. Naturally she's nervous about how
much money she's going to get, but this is the day she's going to
begin getting on with her life. That's what we *were* celebrating at
the divorce shower yesterday, wasn't it?"

"That was the idea, but I don't know if Honey was really in
the mood. I think she's taking her divorce harder than we realize. She was married to Josh for almost fifteen years and I never
saw a girl so in love. It's not like *your* two marriages. You were
married to Mick for about fifteen minutes and your marriage to
Vic Conti lasted what—?"

"You know very well that the marriage lasted six months,
the separation a few months more, but the divorce lasted for
years. It really took." She smiled bitterly. "But I can't say you
didn't warn me—what a bastard he was and how he'd try to
exploit me. Sometimes I wonder about that. Like you *knew* all
you had to do was say something bad about him and that'd be
enough to send me rushing into his arms."

Nora poured Sam a cup of coffee. "That's saying I manipulated you into that marriage, and I always gave you more credit

than that. You're too clever to be manipulated into *anything*, especially into marrying the likes of Vic Conti. And, *of course* I warned you against him. I swore to your father on his deathbed that I'd watch out for you." She sighed. "I guess that was a no-win situation for me. I was damned if I warned you against him and damned if I didn't. Still, *children* blame others for their failures—not mature women in their thirties."

Sam bit her lip. "Yeah, you covered all that last night among a lot of other things—how immature I am."

"Well, perhaps I said *too* much. With the studio being sold off, it doesn't really make much difference how we feel about each other anymore, does it? So, I apologize for hurting your feelings and now we can forget about it all."

"Wait a minute!" Sam cried. "I have to talk to you about the studio. Honey and I want to make you an offer!"

*Of course. We're right on schedule.* "You're going to make me an offer with Honey's settlement money, I presume?"

"Yes, and if it's not enough to satisfy you, I thought you could add my trust-fund money to—"

"Don't start that trust-fund business again. I've told you— that's yours only when I decide you're ready and I'm hardly satisfied that you are. So, until that time, what's your and Honey's offer? I'm waiting to hear."

"What are the other people offering?" Sam asked cagily.

"I'd be a bad negotiator if I revealed my bottom line."

"Is that all that's important to you—those dollar signs all in a row?"

"I didn't say that. You did, and I'm still waiting."

"But I won't know that until we hear what Honey's getting," Sam anguished, forgetting about being cool. "They might not give her the full quarter of a billion dollars—"

Nora looked at her without emotion. "I'm sure she'll get something close to it since she's been responsible for generating the larger part of Royal Production's income for years and never actually received a share of what, I suppose, was simply shoveled back into the company. In any case, I'm sure there'll be enough for us to at least discuss it."

Sam stared at Nora, unable to believe that it had been this

easy after she had anticipated that Nora would set up all kinds of stumbling blocks. "And your other buyer?"

"I suppose I *owe* it to you and Honey to at least listen to your offer first. But we can't talk until we hear from Honey, poor baby. Either way, she's going to end up a loser."

Sam's eyes narrowed. "Why do you say that?"

"Because I know Honey has no interest in owning a studio. All she wants is to be a serious actress, to study and try for the legitimate theater. That's been her dream all along."

"But she said she doesn't care about it anymore. She said she *wants* to own the studio with me . . . wants me to run it while she does the acting, has her pick of the best roles."

Nora smiled sadly. "You *are* a lucky girl, Sam, to have a friend like Honey—willing to give up her dream for yours. And you know Honey—how sensitive she is and how guilty she's going to feel about destroying the man she once loved no matter that she's divorcing him. What she didn't stop to realize is that Josh is going to have to liquidate so much of Royal Productions to raise that settlement money that the company won't be much more than a skeleton when it's all over. That will be a terrible burden for Honey to bear."

"But she herself says that she's morally *entitled* to that money, as well as legally. She earned it!"

"I know. But that will be cold comfort when she sees Josh and the company so shattered. And I feel sorry for you."

"Why should you feel sorry for me all of a sudden?"

"Because it's going to be a terrible burden on you too—an awesome responsibility to make good so that both Honey's dream and Joshua's life's blood aren't sacrificed in vain. For your sake and Honey's, I hope you're up to it."

# SEVENTY–TWO

— ••• —

oney felt that no matter what happened today, she still owed it to her public to look her best. She spun around in front of the mirrored wall of her dressing room to check out the total effect—face, hair, the Zandra Rhodes suit a modest but modish two inches above the knee. Then she sat down at the dressing table for a close-up shot of her lids to consider if she'd applied too much or too little shadow, but she was unable to concentrate—the only thing she could think of was the four *R*'s: ratings, reruns, residuals, revenues. Fifteen years of them. She picked up the silver-framed picture standing on the dressing table—their wedding picture, which had appeared on *People*'s cover.

He wore Armani gray and a satisfied smile. She wore Saint Laurent and her trademark smile. The dress was white satin and lace with a traditional fourteen-foot-long train but an untraditional mini in front as Josh had insisted, unwilling to forgo a photo opportunity to display his star's legs. There had also been tears of joy that the camera hadn't caught.

*Dissolve to shot in courtroom where the brilliant Hollywood marriage is dissolving into the brilliant divorce, Hollywood-style.*

\* \* \*

Sam sat down at her dressing table to apply concealer to the dark circles under her eyes, but when she peered into the mirror she wished only that she could see some answers there.

*"For your sake and Honey's, I hope you're up to it!"* Oh, damn *you, Nora, for making me doubt myself!*

513

But the truth was that she'd been doubting herself even before Nora spoke the words. Last night after Honey had made the offer of her settlement money, she'd asked herself if she were really up to running the studio, had even told Honey it was possible that she was just full of hot air. Oh, God, if only she'd stuck to those crummy jobs she'd had in the Industry for more than a couple of months at a time, maybe she would know more . . . would be surer about her abilities.

And was Honey sure that this was what she really wanted, or would she regret this decision for the rest of her life? And how would she herself be able to deal with that, knowing that she'd caused Honey so much pain? Oh, damn that stupid voice in her head that kept saying that Nora was right . . . that Honey really wasn't cut out for divorces and settlements—it was too hard for her to go for the jugular.

She sighed, hearing Babe calling from the bedroom, and rose to go to her. Babe looked god-awful. The circles under her eyes were darker even than her own. "How do you feel?"

"Terrible, thank you. What time is it, Sam?"

"Almost ten."

"Has *anybody* called? You know—to see if I'm here?"

"No, I don't think so, Babe."

"Do you think I have to get up yet?"

"I don't know. I'll go ask Nora if she thinks you should get up after I take an aspirin. Would you like one?"

"Oh, Sam, I just don't know. I don't know anything."

*Fine. That makes two of us.*

*　*　*

"Mr. Rudman is downstairs, Mrs. Prince. He said to tell you that you have to leave right now, that the traffic will—"

"Thank you, Gladys," Honey said, fastening pearl earrings in place. "Please tell Mr. Rudman I'll be right down." Suddenly she pulled off her pear-shaped diamond engagement ring and tossed it into the jewelry case. She'd discarded her wedding band months ago and today was the day to let go once and for all. Besides, Babe, who kept up on this sort of thing, had told her a few months ago that Tiffany pear-shaped solitaires were out and Cartier emerald-cut solitaires were in, so how could a today's woman wear the former?

*And that's who I am now, aren't I? A today's woman? . . .*

She thought about selecting another ring from what Josh called "the collection," but she was unable to make a decision, which was frequently the case now. Josh had always made all decisions for her, however trivial. Divorcing him was practically the *only* decision she'd made for herself since the day they met. He had even ordered for her in restaurants without consulting her, without taking into consideration what she might be yearning for just once.

*Caviar?* "Too salty. You'll retain water."

*French fries?* So obvious a no-no it wasn't even worthy of comment.

*Chocolate mousse?* "You know chocolate's bad for the complexion, and it's not even your birthday."

A hamburger was too greasy and a *feuillete de poisson* in a wine butter sauce, which she adored, had too many calories. "You're the Honey Rose, not the fat lady in the circus."

As for babies, there was no place for them on the Honey Rose's personal menu this year or next. *Maybe a few years down the road . . .*

Finally she decided to go with naked fingers embellished only with her French manicure à la Jessica's, currently Hollywood's manicure and manicurist of choice. And in case anyone noticed, her bare fingers *were* a statement of choice.

But then, suddenly, she picked up a diamond tennis bracelet and fastened it around her wrist. She'd bought it for herself by herself only months before she and Josh parted—the only piece of jewelry she'd bought on her own. It was almost as if she'd taken the step not of her own volition. She'd been strolling down Rodeo, passing Van Cleef and Arpels, and suddenly it was as if some invisible force propelled her into the store, made her ask to see the entire collection of tennis bracelets—a style Josh had ruled out as too pedestrian for her regal wrist. Then she'd paid for it with a scarcely used credit card instead of making it a house charge, which would have been sent on to Josh's business manager, in itself a departure from the norm.

That probably *was* the moment she'd decided to re-create Honey Rosen, and the decision to buy the bracelet had nothing to do with tennis bracelets at all. But that wasn't so strange since the wrangling over money that had pervaded the decline and fall of their marriage hadn't been about money any more than it had been about Joshua's destruction. *So, what am I to do about that destruction?* She had given Sam her word and she was never going to divorce her friend Sam. . . .

* * *

"You're going to have to get dressed, Babe," Nora said, sitting down on the edge of the bed.

"But I feel terrible." She pulled the comforter higher about her shoulders. "They haven't called, have they?"

"No," Nora said, and Babe sighed in relief before Nora added, "but I called them."

"But you said you wouldn't!" Babe cried. "You promised."

"I said that I wouldn't call your parents last night . . . that we'd sleep on it."

"But why did you have to do it at all?"

"Because if I didn't it would have only delayed the inevitable. You can't just run away and hide out. That's what a child does . . . runs away so that she gets everyone's attention and gets everyone upset so that when they catch up with her, they say, 'Poor baby,' and forgive her instead of punishing her for being naughty. But you're not a naughty child. You're a grown woman who hasn't sinned against anyone but herself, and one with a problem that has to be settled decisively so you don't have to keep running away. . . ."

"But I'm so afraid to face them," Babe moaned. "When are they coming?"

"In a couple of hours. That's why you must get dressed."

"But can't I stay here in bed while I talk to them?"

"So that you can lie there cowering under the covers like a frightened child? That puts you at a psychological disadvantage. You should be dressed and meet them downstairs. Show them that you're strong and in fighting condition."

Babe moaned again. "Will you at least stay with me, Nora? Please," she begged.

"No, I can't, Babe. This is something you must do for yourself by yourself. Otherwise, your parents will think that without me standing by you're going to fall apart and revert back to a little crybaby."

"But they'll only say what they always say—that if I try to divorce Greg, they'll support him by saying I'm just a sick, confused girl who—"

"Not this time they won't. They're going to back off and they'll make Greg back off too. While I can't be at your side, I *am* going to give you some ammunition to do your fighting for yourself."

Babe's eyes opened wide. "What's the ammunition?"

"A small synopsis of your mother's life and a bit of information about your real father. . . ."

*Sometimes you tried to keep other people's secrets as you hoped they might keep yours. But sometimes those same people made it impossible and sometimes only the truth could set people free and set things right. . . .*

# SEVENTY-THREE

———◆•◆———

Press Rudman took his eyes off the road for a second to smile reassuringly at Honey as he ducked in and out of the clogged lanes of Los Angeles's morning traffic, and she smiled back. Known as the best *women's* lawyer in town, as opposed to "a man's attorney," whose specialty it was to defend a male clientele against greedy wives or live-in lovers, Press had consistently acted the good friend rather than the divorce lawyer. Still, she couldn't bring herself to tell him what was troubling her at this late hour—*Joshua's destruction.*

"You've been wonderful, Press, and no matter what happens I'm satisfied you've done everything you could."

"I tried, and I tried to spare you all this crap in court, and I would have if Josh hadn't fought us every inch of the way. If he had even tried to meet us halfway—"

But, of course, Josh hadn't. He was furious with her and still didn't really understand *why* she wanted a divorce, and his lack of cooperation in reaching an equitable settlement was the least of it. He had given out interviews that were a quiet and sorrowful indictment: "It's an old Hollywood story—I made her a star and she turned on me."

"We have only five minutes to run for it," Press said, maneuvering the Porsche into a space on the street two blocks from the courthouse in the hopes of arriving without fanfare. But the plan didn't work.

He'd figured on entering the courthouse through a back door, giving the slip to the crowd mobilized in front. But then, finding the door locked, he was forced to hustle Honey around to the front after all, cursing himself for not hiring a couple of muscle men to keep the mob at bay.

As they fought their way through the onslaught that greeted them, the clamoring mob's attention was partially diverted by Josh's arrival in a white, gold-flashed limousine with his flamboyant lawyer, Cassius Bushkin, in a ten-gallon Stetson, plus Bushkin's assistant and a publicist. Then, just for a moment, as Press shoved a photographer out of their way, her eyes met Josh's and she saw a look she'd never before seen on his face—total *desolation*, and it was no wonder. His destruction was imminent!

\* \* \*

"So, now you know as much as I know," Nora said.

Babe's face was as white as the lacy pillow slip. "I can't believe it! My mother, Catherine Tracy, was Katya Marcus, married to Jacob Weiss who was Jackie White! A stand-up comic! But why did she do it? Lie to me all these years?"

*Who knew if she'd lied for her own sake or for Babe's or for both their sakes?* "She probably believed she was doing it for you—to give you a proper background, a good life."

"No, don't defend her! She probably did it to hide being Jewish and because she was ashamed of marrying a comic named Jacob Weiss! And she did it for the Judge! But, Nora, I trusted you. Why didn't you ever tell me this before?"

Nora understood what Babe was going through—to have her true identity revealed in a few brief minutes after a lifetime of thinking she was someone entirely different *had* to be shattering. It would take her a while just to absorb the shock before she began to pick up the pieces, and the accusations and the anger were probably a necessary phase.

"Why didn't I tell you before? I'm afraid there's no one answer. I didn't believe it was my place—your mother had her own dream for you and I didn't think I had the right to interfere. Play God. I wasn't even sure it would serve any good purpose to tell you—that maybe you didn't *have* to know or wouldn't *want* to know. And I thought it possible that when you were ready, *you* might search out the answers yourself."

"Then, why did you tell me now?"

"I told you—I felt that I no longer had a choice but to give you the ammunition you needed to fight with. But *you* do have a choice, you know."

"Me?" Babe asked bitterly. "I never had a choice before, so what kind of a choice do I have now?"

"You *can* choose to fire your ammunition in the form of blackmail and your problem will be solved. I'm sure your mother and the Judge will back down rather than have the true story made public, or—" she paused for a second, "you can do it all yourself *without* using blackmail because you *know* who you are: a strong woman who's not afraid to stand up for what you believe in—*yourself*. And, you know, I have the feeling you might even fall in love with that woman. But it's a *choice* and only you can make it. Now, get dressed and put on your face. This is your big moment of truth and I always say a woman must look her best for life's big moments."

\* \* \*

From the vantage of the conservatory, Nora watched Sam and Babe sitting by the pool, each of them waiting—Sam for Honey's return, Babe for her parents' arrival. As always they made an incongruous pair—Sam so tall in jeans and tennies, and Babe so tiny, dressed in the Chanel suit and towering high heels she'd arrived in for yesterday's party. They alternately spoke and fell silent, each staring into the blue of the pool as if to find some answers there. Sam appeared somewhat calmer than Babe, staying put in her chaise, while Babe jumped up to pace every few minutes before throwing herself down again. Still, Sam kept running her fingers through her hair, which she always did when she was anxious.

No, she wouldn't go out to them. She'd done what she could, said as much as she could, now it was up to them. Perhaps the two friends talking things over might be able to help each other come to the right decisions.

The phone rang and she rushed to answer, thinking it might be Honey calling from the courthouse. But it was Teddy. "Did the Tracys get there yet?"

"No. Did you hear anything from Honey?"

"No, but I think I'll come over there to wait with you."

"I don't know if you should."

"I'm coming," he said resolutely. "What's wrong with a friend coming over to wait with a friend? What are you so afraid of? That—" And he started to hum a melody she recognized at once. It was *"People will say we're in love."*

\* \* \*

Leaving the courthouse was even more difficult than entering had been, the hordes hungrier than ever for quotes from the principals since Josh's publicist had just announced that the final settlement had been worked out in the privacy of the judge's quarters but gave no figures. And then, as the mob followed them all the way to his car, Press cursed himself for having parked the Porsche so far away. Some days you couldn't win, he thought as he hit out, sending a photographer sprawling. Then he had to restrain Honey from going to the asshole's aid. "Let him sue!" he growled.

He stole a glance at her as he guided the car into the stream of traffic, wondering what she was thinking about—the *settlement* that had been hammered out at the last moment? Or was she thinking only about Prince? What the future held in store for them both? A good divorce lawyer had to be part psychiatrist, and usually he knew what a client was about, but, in her guileless way, Honey was as much an enigma to him now as ever. He'd never been sure whether she was still in love with Prince and he still wasn't. And he'd never been sure if she knew exactly what it was she wanted any more than he knew now if what she'd gotten was what she truly desired.

He'd often felt as if he were picking his way through yards of pink gauze to get her to see the necessity of certain moves—to make her realize that a few foul blows to the kidneys were obligatory for a successful divorce. It had taken *him* a while to realize that she had no killer instinct at all. Then he'd regretted that it had fallen to *him* to try to instill one in her—he, who had fallen in love with her just as she was. How could Prince have been such a fool?

He glanced at her again as he took the Sunset Boulevard exit off the freeway. She was still deep in thought and he guessed that it was the divorce itself she was thinking about, and *not* the settlement. He took his one hand off the wheel to take hers. "Believe me, it only hurts for a little while."

But he was wrong. It was very much the settlement Honey was thinking about and what she was going to tell Sam. . . .

\* \* \*

Nora and Sam sat in the conservatory waiting while Babe was behind the library's closed doors with the Tracys. Watching Sam biting at her nails, Nora was tempted to put her arms around her, to croon, "There, there, everything will be fine." But she couldn't. For one, it would be a violation of the rules of their game, and for another, she still didn't know for sure that things would indeed be fine.

"Poor Babe," Sam said, and Nora was pleasantly surprised. She'd assumed that Sam was thinking only about herself, and it seemed she was agonizing over Babe more than her own situation. "Do you think Babe's going to be able to stand up to them? That she won't fall apart even armed with that stuff you told her about Catherine and her real father?"

"I'm hoping she'll stand up to them *without* that stuff."

Sam shook her head. "I guess that's the difference between you and me *and* the problem we have with one another. *I'm* willing to settle for small miracles but *you* want it all! You always did. The big, splashy *miracle*, and you want it overnight! You not only want it or expect it—you *demand* it!" Sam's voice was slowly rising. "And you demand too damn much! Don't you understand that?" And then her voice broke and the tears began to flow down her cheeks.

*Oh, dear God, is it possible? Are we getting so close to an understanding, to that big, splashy miracle?* Still, she risked blowing it

all to say, "Don't be an ass, Sam. Twenty years is hardly overnight. . . ."

But that only made Sam cry even harder, and she didn't
stop, not even when Teddy walked in singing. Then, seeing Sam
in tears, he ignored Nora, who was looking at him in exasperation, and sat down next to Sam to console her. "Don't cry. I
have a feeling everything's going to be fine."

"But how do you know?"

"Because I have faith."

"In miracles?" Sam sniffled, looking at Nora.

"In miracle-workers . . ."

Then Sam looked from Nora to Teddy, a question on her
lips, but before she could ask it, they heard the library door
opening and shutting and then the front door *slamming*, and she
leaped to her feet. "They're leaving! It's over!"

Nora got to her feet too, remembering what T.S. always said:
"It's not over until the fat lady sings." And neither size-four
Catherine nor little Babe exactly qualified.

But then a tiny woman in a yellow suit and high heels stood
in the doorway grinning with her arms spread wide and she was
singing. The tune was "My Way," but she paraphrased the last
line so that it came out, "I did it *your* way . . ."

*      *      *

Press had to swerve to avoid a head-on collision with the Lincoln tearing down the driveway as they drove up. "It's the
Tracys—my friend Babe's parents," Honey said morosely. "She
was terrified about having a showdown with them about divorcing her husband and I was supposed to be here to lend her moral
support. But it appears that I'm too late."

"Well, don't feel bad," Press consoled her. "She's a big girl,
old enough to do for herself."

*Maybe. But Sam can't, not this time, not without me. . . .*

"Sure you won't have lunch? Actually, it's *de rigueur* for the
divorcee to do lunch with her lawyer after the fact."

"No, they're all waiting for me. But thanks for everything,
Press. You've been a good friend."

"Well, feel free to call *anytime*—for lunch, dinner, or . . . *whatever*. And if your friend Babe needs a divorce lawyer, send her along. Any friend of yours is a friend of mine."

She watched the Porsche vanish down the driveway, sighed, and slowly approached the door when Babe flung it open, waving her right hand in the air, *thumb up.*

"Oh, Babe! I guess I don't have to ask how *you* made out!"

"Honeychile, you can say that again! And I did it *all by myself* after being pointed in the right direction by my good friend Nora. But I'll tell you all the details later along with the rest of my news—stuff Nora told me about Catherine and my father . . . my *real* father. But right now everyone's waiting for you, dying to hear all *your* details. In the meantime all I'll say is this: When Catherine and the Judge started reading me the riot act, I kept in mind the famous words of *their* favorite heroine, Nancy Reagan: "Just say no!""

Honey would have liked to laugh, but how could she? That's what she was going to have to say to her friend Sam—*no.* . . .

# SEVENTY-FOUR

W hen Nora and Teddy hugged Honey, she knew it was
their way of saying that she was their honey no matter
what, but all she could think of was, would she still be
Sam's honey once Sam heard her news. But before she could
speak Sam announced, "I want you to know, Honey, that after
I asked a certain widow if she'd entertain an offer from you and
me to buy her studio and she agreed to at least listen to our
offer—"

"Sam, I have something I must tell you—"

"No. Let me finish. As I was saying, after Nora agreed to
listen to our offer, *I changed my mind!* I decided I didn't want to
be your partner because you'd make a really crummy one.
You'd grab all the best roles, and frankly, I don't think you're
quite up to movies and we'd end up with a bunch of bombs and
a fine studio would be down the toilet. I'm afraid that at this
stage you're strictly TV material and you should do what you
planned on doing originally—go to New York, study drama,
and, when you're ready, shoot for the stage. The theater's good
training for actresses who want to *eventually* act in movies. Unless, of course, you don't plan to go to New York anymore
anyway and intend to stay in TV."

Honey didn't believe a word of it. Sam was letting her off the
hook so that she would be free to do whatever it was she wanted.
She looked from Sam to Teddy to Nora to Babe. They were *all*
looking at her expectantly, yet no one had asked her the big
question: Had she gotten her quarter of a billion dollars? And
the reason they weren't asking was that they all assumed she'd
backed down at the last minute and relinquished what was

rightfully hers and/or agreed to do another series for Josh. *Or even that she'd reconciled with him because she was still in love with him.* . . .

"Well, why doesn't somebody ask me what happened? I know what *you're* thinking, Sam. That even if I *did* get what I asked for, I'm too *chickenhearted* to take it—that I want to give it right back to Josh. That's why you said what you did. You were giving me room so I wouldn't feel guilty about letting you down, and you're even giving me room to change my mind about studying for the theater, just in case I intend to let Josh talk me into another series."

"Not too chickenhearted, Honey, too *sweethearted.*"

"Well, thank you, Samantha." Suddenly it dawned on her that there *was* something she *could* do for Sam, after all! But she would get to that later.

"What about you, Daddy? Don't *you* want to know what happened—how much money I got?"

"It doesn't matter. More money, less money. The only thing that matters is whether you can live with it, be happy with it. And I already *know* that you can."

"I think that means that *you* think I let Josh settle for a lot less than I originally demanded." When he didn't answer, she turned to Nora. "You gave me something to think about. Don't *you* want to know the result of my thinking?"

"I don't have to know. I'm sure whatever you did, it's the right thing."

"Then I'll take a guess at what you're *thinking.* Since you're basically a romantic at heart no matter what you want us all to think, I think you think that I'm still in love with Josh and acted accordingly—like a woman in love."

Nora only smiled enigmatically, but Babe threw her arms around her. "Oh, Honey, it's *okay* to admit that you still love Josh. After all, you loved him so much and I never even *liked* Greg. And I think I speak for all of us when I say we *understand* if you wanted to marry him again."

"Well, thank you, Babette, for your understanding."

Actually, she knew that she didn't have to offer explanations or make excuses—these were her friends, her family, her loved ones. All she had to do was *tell*. But she couldn't resist teasing, "Well, since no one has the guts to ask what happened, I think I'll let you all wait to hear it on the five o'clock news." But when they began to advance on her, she laughed: "Oh, all right! As they say, at the last minute we settled out of court, and you're now looking at the half owner of Royal Productions."

They were all stunned, except perhaps for Nora.

"Are you sure this is what you want, Honey?" Teddy asked.

"*Sure.* I get everything I deserve—morally, legally, financially—and I don't destroy the company or Josh."

"And that's it—just a business relationship?" Nora asked, and Honey said, "Yes, I can see I was right about you—you *are* a romantic, and all I have to say is yes, for now that's all it is—a business relationship."

"I caught that 'for now,'" Babe said. "Are you leaving a door open there for some future adjustments, and if not, are you slamming it shut with a bang?" and everyone laughed.

"But I *was* right about one thing," Sam said. "The Honey Rose who owns half of Royal Productions *will* be staying here in Hollywood and working in TV, after all."

"Wrong. I'm going to be only a *quarter* owner of Royal Productions. You see, since I *am* going to New York to study, I want to make sure I'm leaving people I can trust to take care of my interests, even if they are only *TV* interests and not movie interests," she teased. "But be that as it may, I think with my friend as well as my ex running things, I have nothing to worry about. And you won't mind *too* much being only a *quarter* owner of a mere TV company, will you, Sam?"

Sam was shocked. It took her a few seconds to recover before she said, "No, Honey. I can't accept it."

"But why not? I know it's not your dream—your studio— but isn't it the next best thing?"

"But that's it. No one can hand anyone else a dream. Like with Babe. She had to tell Catherine and the Judge to fuck off herself. No one could do it for her. And that's how it is with dreams. You have to chase them yourself, and then, if you catch them, you really have *something*." She lowered her voice confidentially though the others were standing right there. "And between you and me, kid, I'm not ready to take charge of a newsstand, much less the biggest TV company in the world or Grantwood Studio. That was only a pipe dream, not a real one." She turned to Nora. "So, what do you think?"

"About what? Your very mature decision?"

*Did she use the word* mature? *I must be dreaming!*

"Actually, I was referring to something else, Nora. . . . Wondering, that is, if you could put in a good word for me with those other buyers for the studio, ask them if they can use a smart *if* inexperienced person who has a *feel* for films. You can even tell them that moviemaking runs in my blood."

"I *could* do that. Or maybe, since you're now big on people doing for themselves, you can ask for yourself."

"Well, it *would* be better if you did it. After all, it's you who's famous for your charm and I only for my arrogance."

"Let's not get *too* humble, Sam. Besides, you don't have to worry about this person not finding you charming. You and he have met, you see, and his view of you is most positive."

"Nora, will you stop playing games and tell me who—?"

"It's Hubie. He's coming home and he's *already* one of the two future owners of the studio. At least he will be once I transfer that which I've been holding in trust for him."

Sam sank down on the sofa. "I can't believe it! Hubie's finally coming home and he's going to own half the studio? You've been holding it in trust for *him*?"

Honey and Babe ran to sit on either side of Sam, not knowing if she could really handle this. Then Teddy gently pushed Nora down on the sofa facing them. "Nora, I think everyone's waited long enough for an explanation. . . ."

*Yes, the time has come for some truth and only a few white lies. . . .*

"It's not all that complicated. When Martin Cantington, Hubie's adoptive father, died, he left Hubie a share in his estate equal to that of his four natural sons. But he realized that Hubie was not mature enough to cope with the responsibility of his legacy and so he left Hubie's share in my care, trusting that when

Hubie was ready, I'd turn it over to him. Well, that time is at hand."

"But the studio—?" Sam cried, still bewildered.

"I'm getting to that. Soon after I married T.S. he told me that he was in financial difficulty and needed a great deal of money to save Grantwood Studio from the banks. Actually, I think what he was trying to do was to somehow save the studio for you, Sam, since he always regarded it as your rightful heritage. He always said, 'Movies are in that girl's blood as much as they are in mine.' "

She paused as Sam moaned. "Did he really say that?"

"Yes, he did," she lied easily. "So I did the only thing I could do—I gave him Hubie's money, but I was honorbound to do it legally and we made a fair trade since Hubie's legacy was more or less equal to half the worth of the studio."

"But what about *your* legacy from Martin Cantington? Surely he left you as much as he left Hubie and his other sons?" Sam asked. "Why didn't you use *your* money instead of Hubie's?"

A natural enough question, Nora thought. But in answer should she reveal that she'd bought the studio outright using *both* her and Hubie's money or should she lie again? *I tell half a lie.* "Because my money was tied up at the time."

Sam nodded, accepting the explanation, then, choked up, she said, "I'm glad that you did what you did, Nora . . . that at least my father was able to keep and run the studio until he died and that Hubie will now own part of it—he is my stepbrother and it's like keeping the studio in the family."

She awaited Sam's next question: *Who was the prospective buyer of the remaining half interest in the studio?* When it wasn't forthcoming—perhaps with her newfound humility, Sam didn't think she had the right to ask—Nora stood up. "Now that that's settled and it's much too late for lunch, why don't we have an early dinner?"

Teddy stood up too. "But don't we have a few more matters to be settled?" He both smiled and winked.

"All in good time," she said, leading the way to the dining room, and when she opened the door they saw a roomful of balloons crisscrossed with streamers, and a table set not for dinner but for a party. Laughing at the look of surprise on their faces, she shrugged. "You all know how much I like celebrations, and I thought it would be lovely to end the day with a commencement party since no matter how things went today, we'd all want to make a toast to new beginnings. . . ."

# SEVENTY-FIVE

———— •••• ————

"There are envelopes with your names on them so you'll know where to sit," Nora directed. "But they're not place cards but party favors. What's a party without favors?"

"I know you won't mind, girls, if I open my favor first," Teddy said. "Ever since I first met Nora I've been dying to get a favor out of her."

Giggling, they watched him open his envelope to find a shiny gold key along with a note. He read it aloud: "This key to my heart is the key to my house since my house is your house," he read, and Honey said, "Oh!" and Babe sighed at the romance of it all, while Sam just looked wise.

"My turn," Babe said, tearing her envelope open to find a key too. She read before she wept: "If you need a place to hang your hat till you find a home where your heart is, use my house. Nora Grant signing for F. Theodore Rosen."

Teddy, as surprised as Babe, reassured her, "No need for tears. It's not all *that* touching."

"But I'm not crying because I'm *touched* but because your key looks like real gold and mine is just plain brass."

They all laughed and Nora said, "Sorry about that. But since I didn't know until last night that you might need a temporary home, I didn't have a chance to have one made up in gold. That's the key to his house that's been hanging on *my* key chain."

Though she couldn't have spelled things out any clearer, she flushed when Sam said, "I guess if Babe's getting the key to *his* house and *he's* getting the key to *your* house, I guess *his* heart has found a home."

"And though no one's *asking*, I heartily approve," Honey

531

said, opening her envelope. "I can't wait till I get *my* key."

But no metal key fell out of her envelope, only a cutout replica of a key, an airplane ticket, and a note: "The realty agent in New York will give you the real key to the apartment of your choice paid for six months in advance, no questions asked, and the ticket is for a one-way trip *from* New York back to L.A. so that you can fly on the wings of love to those who love you best when and if the spirit moves you."

For a moment, Honey sat mute, then she rose and walked around the table to hug Nora. "No mother could have given me a lovelier gift." They all applauded, Teddy the hardest.

"This is better than the Oscars and now it's my turn," Sam said, ripping her envelope open. "I think I already know what door *my* key is going to unlock—my own apartment. I think the mamma bird is finally pushing the baby bird out of the nest so that the lovebirds can have the joint to themselves and I guess it's only fair." But an oversized key fell out—a fake one with a tag affixed—and there was another envelope inside the larger envelope. "I'll do the tag first," she said and read: "The key to the magic kingdom." She laughed uncertainly. "Is this some kind of joke?"

"Read what it says on the envelope," Honey urged.

Haltingly Sam read, "Certificate of Maturity," then asked huskily, "But what does that mean?"

"Just what it says," Nora said. "Why don't you open it?"

Sam did, but by now she had an inkling of what was inside. She took out the certificate to see that it was a transfer of property, and there at the bottom was Nora's signature. Silently she passed it around for Babe, Honey, and Teddy to see that she was now the legal owner of 50 percent of Grantwood Studio. But she had to say *something*, so finally, smiling at Nora through her tears, she said, "All I can say is it's about time you handed my trust fund over. . . ." to which Nora responded, "And all I can say is it's about time you grew up."

She *could* have kissed me, Nora thought. She could even have said, "Thanks, Mom." But for now, it's enough that she *thinks* that T.S. willed her half the studio and that she knows I'm on her side. She smiled at Teddy. "I think we're ready for the champagne."

"Wait a minute," Sam said. "There's something else we have to discuss, Nora. I've grown up enough to realize that I don't know enough to run the studio, and while I know Hubie's matured into a competent person and has done wonderful things in the Peace Corps, what does he know about running a studio or making movies? He knows less than I do. I'm afraid that between the two of us we'll run the studio into the ground."

"That statement shows how mature you really are, Sam, but there's no problem. Just because you and Hubie own the studio doesn't mean you have to run it yourselves right off without experienced hands to guide you. Those people are there, many of them the same people your father relied on. So, all you two have to do is go with the flow, as T.S. himself always said."

Then Babe piped up. "I just realized. With all the excitement about finding out about who I really am, I never asked if my father's alive, and if he is, *where* is he?"

"I'm sorry, Babe, but I don't know," Nora said. "But there's no reason *you* can't find out. You might even begin by asking your mother and the Judge what they know."

"No, I don't want to talk to them."

"But you must *sometime*, Babe. You can't really face the future until you come to terms with the past, and that means reconciling your differences with your mother and the Judge for all your sakes."

"And you also have to think about what you're going to do with yourself now that you're out of a job as a wife," Sam added. "How'd you like to come to work at the studio? I'm sure we can find something that interests you, keeping in mind, of course, that we don't need any tap dancers. They're not making those kinds of movies anymore."

"*Très amusant*, Sam, but from now on leave the jokes to me. You know how I always wanted to be a stand-up comic and now I know why—because my father was a comic and it runs in my blood! And now that I don't have to ask anybody's permission, that's exactly what I'm going to be! Anyway, I'll give it a shot.

And maybe I'll find my dad and he'll teach me a few tricks of the trade, and don't anyone dare laugh!"

No one did except Honey, who tried to explain that she was laughing only because she was recalling one of Babe's more memorable jokes. "You were talking about—"

"Don't bother to explain. I *know* your kind."

"*My kind?*" Honey half-smiled. "What does that mean?"

"*Your* kind—the ones that are only *half* Jewish," she said smugly. "I just realized that I'm *all* Jewish! Like you, Teddy. You're going to have to tell me all about it. I might even go to Hebrew school to study up." She sighed happily. "Wow! I'm really going to be busy. . . ."

"On that note I think it's time we made our toasts or we're never going to have any dinner tonight," Teddy said, reaching for the champagne standing in its silver cooler just as Edmund appeared to announce that Mr. Prince was on the phone and wished to speak to Honey.

"I'll take it in the library—I'll be just a minute."

\*　\*　\*

"Okay, what did the big man talk you into this time?" Sam demanded when Honey returned.

"He only wanted to have dinner with me tomorrow so that we could discuss putting Crown House on the market."

"And what did *you* say to that?"

"I said I'd take care of it before I left for New York, but it really wasn't necessary for us to meet for dinner. Then he asked if he could come visit me in New York sometime once I'm settled in and I said that would be very nice."

"*I* wouldn't trust him. He'll try to get you pregnant just to get you back."

Honey giggled. "I don't think that's a very nice topic to bring up in front of my father. Besides, getting pregnant still takes two consenting adults. End of discussion."

"Let's hope so," Teddy said. "And if everyone is quite finished, I will now open the champagne. But before I do—"

But then Edmund came in to announce that there was another call for Honey, and once again she left the room.

"Wow!" Babe said. "For a lady who just got divorced she's sure scoring a lot of action."

"Okay, who was it *this* time?" Babe demanded when she returned. "Warren Beatty maybe, or Jack Nicholson?"

"Sorry, but it was only my lawyer, Press Rudman."

"What did *he* want?"

"For me to have dinner with him tomorrow night."

"To discuss divorce business, of course," Sam said.

"Well, no, just to have dinner. And I said great, but that I was going to bring my friend Babe along because *she* needed to discuss divorce business."

"Great!" Babe said. "Is he cute?"

"He's no Warren Beatty, but *you* might find him sexy."

"That really does sound great!" Babe enthused, at which the three friends dissolved into a gaggle of juvenile giggling until Teddy demanded, "Nora, will you *please* do something about the level of maturity at this table?"

Giggling herself—it reminded her of the old days twenty years before—Nora countered, "Why don't you? Aren't you the master of the house now?"

"No, as a matter of fact I'm not. In this house I've only been assigned the role of live-in lover, and as yet I haven't even decided whether to take on that role. . . ."

The giggling petered out as Nora asked, "What is this? Have you just been leading me on?"

"You say *that* to me when all you've ever been since the day we met was manipulative?"

"Me, manipulative? Girls, defend me!"

"Sorry, Nora." Sam shrugged. "You *are* manipulative. What about when you lied—"

"Don't be absurd. When have I ever lied to you?"

"Just last night when you said you had received an offer for the studio . . . that you had buyers all lined up?"

"Oh, that!" Nora said in relief. She'd been afraid for a moment that Sam hadn't been kidding about the lying. "I had to do *something* to get you moving on the road to maturity. That's what's called a little white lie."

"No, I'm afraid not—that's more manipulation than a little white lie. And isn't that what I told you girls right along—that my old steppie was the master manipulator?"

"She did, Nora, and I'm afraid she's right," Honey said, sighing dramatically. "I think we've all been the victims of your fine manipulative hand. Especially today. In evidence, I point to the fact that even *before* any of us knew what was going to happen—before we had completely made up our minds what *we* were going to do—*you* were all prepared with your party favors. That means you had to arrange everything at least very *early* this morning. And Sam's certificate of ownership in the studio—you probably had to have that drawn up days ago. So, what can the answer be but that you manipulated us into doing exactly what you wanted us to do? As for Daddy's key, that was really cold-blooded manipulation. Knowing what a perfect gentleman he is, you knew he would never embarrass you by refusing to accept that beautiful gold key."

"Well, as far as I'm concerned, she can manipulate me any time she wants. I'm perfectly satisfied," Babe said.

"But," Teddy declared, "I am *not*. Actually, I'm dissatisfied on the quality of the manipulation."

"Oh? Let's hear the source of your dissatisfaction," Nora asked. "You know I'm not one to turn down a challenge."

"I thought by this time you'd have manipulated me into winning the Nobel, or, if not that, at least into marriage."

"Well, let's put it this way. I'm still working on the former, and as for the latter, if you're willing to be my *live-in significant other*—I've never had one of *those*—I'll take the matter under advisement. What do you say?"

"I say," Teddy said, popping the cork, "we'll drink to that. And while we're at it, we might as well drink to the *last* of the brilliant divorces. . . ."

# A YEAR AFTER THE PARTY

## Los Angeles, June 1991

———••——

Nora stands at her bedroom window gazing down at the panorama that was Grantwood Manor as she did every morning when she awoke, and once again thinks of that first day she had seen it, already T. S. Grant's so-happy bride. Today—a very special day—it's impossible not to think of all her weddings: the one with Hubert that had never taken place, the one at Hartiscor House that *had*, the quickie ceremony on the Las Vegas Strip, the grand celebration in Palm Beach, and, last, the elopement in Maryland. And she thinks of all the parties she's given here at Grantwood through the years though there'd never been a wedding. It seems only fitting that the last party she is throwing at the manor *is* one, and that it be the most brilliant party of all—a wedding made in heaven . . . a wedding impervious to the jealous gods of separation and divorce.

Everything is almost ready. The dance floor is in place, the north lawn canopied over in pink and white chintz roses, the south lawn set with rows of small gold chairs facing the rose-covered gazebo, where the ceremony will take place. The musicians are already tuning up their instruments and the day is as perfect as a day would ever be.

She looks up at the cloudless blue sky, the sun still well in the east—the wedding scheduled for high noon. Time enough to put on the deep-pink gown laid out on the bed, to add a last-minute touch of rosy blush, a few minutes yet to spare for remembering—putting the past into perspective—before she moves on. . . .

*The past!* T.S.'s robust presence filling the house even when he wasn't at home . . . the three young girls planning a shared

537

teenage birthday party . . . an exuberant Hubie running across the grounds as if chasing moonbeams, the sun turning his yellow hair to pure gold. Now it is Teddy's more gentle aura that permeates the manor's rooms, the young women have just celebrated their shared birthday with a bridal shower instead of a birthday party this year, and Hubie is forty-five, too old at last to be chasing moonbeams.

But then her heart jumps as she sees a man in a white cutaway *running* across the lawn to approach the bandleader, but his hair shines *silver* in the sun. No, it isn't Hubie but *Teddy,* already dressed for the wedding only two hours away.

There is a knock on her door and she turns to see Sam in one of her ubiquitous green robes. Sam had even wanted to wear green for the wedding, but she had forbidden it. "We must keep to the color scheme—all the women in the wedding party will wear shades of pink and all the men pure white," and Sam, muttering under her breath about manipulative stepmothers who always insisted on having their way, had given in.

"But Nora, you're not dressed yet," Sam says now, and Nora points out that neither is she.

"I know. I haven't been able to get off the phone. I've been trying to locate Honey. When she said she couldn't get here until this morning, I just knew that she'd be late. And Josh is already downstairs, driving everyone crazy. I thought maybe you could think of something we could do to find her."

"Yes, I can. Since Josh is the only one around with nothing to do, why don't we let *him* locate Honey?"

"Good idea. I knew the great machinator would think of something. By the way, I spoke to Babe. She's coming with Press Rudman, but she wanted to know if it was okay to bring two extra people. I said fine, but I bet those two people are the Tracys and who really needs them here today?"

"But it would be wonderful if she brought them, Sam! That's what I've been hoping for, that she'd make up with them. You know what they say—a girl's best friend is her mother."

"So they tell me. Well, are you going to spring any surprises today? I hope it isn't *Honey's* mother. That *would* kind of spoil the day for Teddy."

"I wouldn't dream of spoiling the day for Teddy," Nora laughs. "But maybe we *should* get to work on that little reconciliation. At least, let's think about it for sometime in the future. In the meantime, don't you think you should get dressed?"

But Sam looks as if there is something more she has to say. "What is it, Sam?"

To her amazement, Sam's eyes fill up and she runs out of the room. An old picture flashes through her mind: a red-haired girl and a golden-haired boy-man making love on the floor in a Malibu beachhouse. She wonders if what Sam had been about to say had anything to do with that by-now faded image. . . .

The house phone rings and she picks up to hear *that* voice singing to her again.

She laughs, "Really, Teddy, you are impossible!"

"But I didn't call up just to sing to you, Nora mine, but to let you know that your and Sam's ex, dashing Micky Nash, has arrived, looking a bit worn around the edges."

"Ah, Teddy, but don't we all?"

"But some of us more than others. So, what shall I do with him? Shall I send him up to you or across the hall to Sam?"

"Neither. We're both getting dressed. But I understand Josh is here making a bloody nuisance of himself, so let them entertain each other. They can start a club—the Mexes, which is what you get when you put male and exes together."

"You *are* bright, Nora. No wonder I've been after you to marry me. When are you coming down? I miss you."

As soon as she puts the phone down it rings again. "Sorry to disturb you again," Teddy says, "but Babe's just arrived with her petunia-pink dress already on, and she insists on going up to see you with this couple she has in tow. Unfortunately, she's leaving Press Rudman down here and Josh looks like he'd like to kill him and Rudman looks like he might be handy with his dukes. But not to worry. I'm going to leave dashing Nash to act as a buffer."

"But where are *you* going?"

"Well, Hubie has just come down, and since the bar's open for business I thought I'd buy him a drink. But not to worry— I'm saving my one glass of champagne to toast the bride."

Teddy hangs up before she can ask if the couple with Babe are the Tracys, but then Babe is pounding on her door before bursting in, her arms spread wide: "Ta-da! Here she is, folks! The ex–Mrs. Ryan with her pop—the all-time greatest comic in the world, Jackie White—and his lady, Blanche Weiss, who you better watch out for, Nora—she's about to give you some real competition in the great-stepmother department."

"Oh, Babe, I'm so happy for—" Nora begins, but stops because Jackie White is hugging her for dear life and she can only hug him back while Babe cries and Blanche Weiss—calling Babe darling—cautions her stepdaughter not to stain her pretty pink dress with her tears.

It is all so lovely, Nora thinks, and she is only sorry that Babe hasn't brought the Tracys too. *I guess some things just take more time.*

Seconds after they leave, Honey comes tearing up the hall, clutching her baby-pink dress to her breast. She waves at Nora through the open door before disappearing into Sam's room. Ten minutes later she emerges picture-perfect and ready for a wedding, and races back down toward the stairs.

Nora runs out into the hall to call after her, "Where are you going in such a hurry, Honey? You didn't even say hello!"

"I'm sorry, Nora. I love you very much but I have to find Teddy. There's something I must tell him right away!"

"Something wrong?" What's so urgent? she wonders and worries. Does it have something to do with Josh or their company? Sam had told her that Josh had been flying back and forth between the coasts at least once a month ever since Honey moved to New York. *Is it that she's pregnant?*

"Oh, I might as well tell *you*, Nora, you witch. You always know everything before anyone else does anyway. No, nothing is wrong! Something is wonderful!" She breaks into her dazzling smile. "I think I've landed a part in an off-Broadway production, and guess what—the former Honey Rose is going to play all three acts without a drop of makeup!"

"Oh, that's smashing, Honey! Your father will be so proud."

\* \* \*

It is almost time to begin. The pianist is playing songs of love as a prelude to the wedding march as the guests take their seats, and Nora isn't at all surprised to hear the strains of "People Will Say We're in Love" floating up. The phone rings. Teddy again. "The members of the wedding party are all assembled in the conservatory except for you and Sam."

"Coming, my love."

There is a knock on her door and she assumes it is Sam checking to see if she is ready to go down. But when she says, "Come in," she is surprised to see Hubie.

He rushes in to give her a tight hug. "I had to come up. I just had to tell you how much I love you, Mum."

She reaches up to touch his sweet face. "Oh, Hubie darling, I *know*, and I love *you* so much. And I was hoping you *would* come up because I have something for you."

"But you've already given me so much, and I'm only beginning to realize *how* much in the terms of a lifetime."

"But this really isn't a gift. It's to replace something I denied you a long time ago—your ancestral home. You could have been a lord and lived in a castle. Well, now I'm giving you this in exchange." She hands him a sheaf of papers. "Your heritage."

He doesn't understand what she is talking about until he glances down at the papers. "But this is the title to Grantwood Manor. But I can't accept it! It's not *my* heritage. If it's anyone's, it's Sam's."

"Yes, I know. But if you look more carefully you'll see that it's made out to you and Sam both as joint tenants."

"But Grantwood Manor is *your* home, Mum! I can't accept it and neither will Sam."

"But it's not my home any longer. One has to move on in life, Hubie, as you and I have always done. When I married Jeffrey, he gave me Merrillee Manor, which he called my dower-age. But when I married Martin I had to leave Merrillee Manor behind because we had a new home in Washington. Then I had to leave that too to come live here with Sam's father. And now it's time for me to leave Grantwood Manor. Teddy wants us to have a home without a history—that's just *ours*, his and mine—and I can't deny him. We've bought a wonderful house high on a bluff overlooking the Pacific, perfect for a writer, and I don't know if we'll even give it a grand name. We might just call it 'home.' "

"What can I say, then, but thank you and again that I love you? Now, will you do me the honor of clinging to my arm so that we can go down and get this marriage launched?"

"You go first. I'll come down with Sam in a sec."

*   *   *

She calls through Sam's door. "It's time to go down, Sam. Are you ready?"

"Not yet. There's something I want to ask you first. . . ."

Nora opens the door slowly to see Sam standing at the window with the noonday sun streaming in, turning her hair to burnished copper and lending a golden glow to her wedding gown of palest-pink silk taffeta.

"What do you think?" Sam asks. "*Can* redheads wear pink?"

Nora thinks she mustn't cry. "I think I've never seen a more beautiful bride, at least not a redheaded one," she laughs, which is far better than crying. "Is that what you wanted to ask me?"

"No . . ."

"What is it, then, Sam?" she asks gently.

"Is it too late to change the wedding arrangements?"

"Change how?" Nora asks, puzzled.

"I know I told you I wanted to walk down the aisle alone since my father— But I changed my mind. I . . . Nora . . . would *you* walk down the aisle with me?"

They look into each other's eyes for long seconds before Nora asks hoarsely, "You mean you want *me* to give you away?"

"Well, you *are* my stepmother and some people think a stepmother is as good as a mom any old day," Sam says tremulously, and Nora smiles tremulously, placing the crown fash-

ioned of baby-pink roses on the long red hair, smoothing the
veiling into place. "No, it's not too late to change the arrangements. It's never too late for that. . . ."

Then Sam whispers, "I have a secret. I haven't told Honey
or Babe or even Hubie yet. Can you keep a secret?"

"Oh, yes, I'm the best little secret-keeper you've ever met."

"Oh, Nora, I'm going to have a baby! Isn't it wonderful?"

Nora is too choked up to speak. Finally she says, "That's *too*
wonderful a secret to keep."

"But I don't want anyone to know I was pregnant before I
marched down the aisle. They might think Hubie and I are
getting married because it was a marriage of convenience—you
know, just to give the baby a name. As for Hubie, I want him
to get used to being married first before I tell him he's going to
be a daddy. But he'll be thrilled, won't he?"

"Oh, yes, Hubie's a man with loads of room in his heart for
a child, just like your father." That was *one* secret she'd keep for
sure.

"No, just like *you*, Nora. I hate to think where I'd be today
if I never knew you. . . ."

Nora trys to laugh. "Where? Not marrying my son, that's
for sure. Now, are we ready?"

"Ready." Sam hooks her arm through Nora's. "But you
won't mind if I don't call you Mom?"

"No," she says, though she would have liked it.

"I think I prefer Mum instead. What think you?"

"I think that would be lovely."

"And you *will* keep my secret about the baby?"

One thing Nora knows if she knows nothing else is that there
are all kinds of secrets, some far sweeter than others. But one of
the sweetest has to be a mother/daughter kind of a secret. "Your
secret is my secret, Sam, and that's a deal."

\*   \*   \*

Now the bride and the groom are kissing and the best man is
grinning at the mother of the groom. Then the bride throws her
arms around the mother-in-law who gave her away and kisses

her almost as ardently as she kissed her groom and whispers in her ear, "Thanks, Mum."

Now the mother is kissing her son while the bride kisses her maids of honor, and the best man taps the bridegroom on the shoulder to say, "Cutting in," and he kisses the mother of the groom. And now they're all marching up the aisle, arm in arm, bride and bridegroom followed by the golden-haired bridesmaid interlocking arms with the dark-haired bridesmaid, followed by the best man holding on tightly to the mother of the happy couple.

Now they are dancing as the band plays "Always," and the best man asks the mother of the groom, "What are you thinking?"

"Ah, Teddy, I'm thinking they're playing our song."

"What else are you thinking?"

"I'm thinking that while I have been married many times for all manner of reasons to all manner of men, not *once* have I been married to the right man for the right reason at the right time. And while I've been widowed and divorced and have even had a live-in lover, not once have I been married *forever*! And that's really something I should try before I call it quits altogether! What do you think?"

"Ah, Nora, I think they're playing our song."